EXTRAORDINARY ADVENTURES

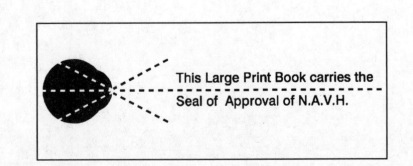

This Large Print Book carries the
Seal of Approval of N.A.V.H.

Extraordinary Adventures

Daniel Wallace

THORNDIKE PRESS
A part of Gale, Cengage Learning

GALE
CENGAGE Learning·

Farmington Hills, Mich • San Francisco • New York • Waterville, Maine
Meriden, Conn • Mason, Ohio • Chicago

GALE
CENGAGE Learning·

Copyright © 2017 by Daniel Wallace.
Thorndike Press, a part of Gale, Cengage Learning.

Thorndike Press® Large Print Core.
The text of this Large Print edition is unabridged.
Other aspects of the book may vary from the original edition.
Set in 16 pt. Plantin.

LIBRARY OF CONGRESS CATALOGING-IN-PUBLICATION DATA

Names: Wallace, Daniel, 1959- author.
Title: Extraordinary adventures / by Daniel Wallace.
Description: Large print edition. | Waterville, Maine : Thorndike Press, a part of Gale, Cengage Learning, 2017. | Series: Thorndike Press large print core
Identifiers: LCCN 2017016975 | ISBN 9781432839482 (hardcover) | ISBN 1432839489 (hardcover)
Subjects: LCSH: Large type books. | BISAC: FICTION / Literary. | FICTION / Humorous.
Classification: LCC PS3573.A4256348 E98 2017b | DDC 813/.54--dc23
LC record available at https://lccn.loc.gov/2017016975

Published in 2017 by arrangement with Macmillan Publishing Group, LLC/St. Martin's Press

Printed in the United States of America
1 2 3 4 5 6 7 21 20 19 18 17

To Roger C. Kellison,
with love and admiration

From a certain point onward, there is no longer any turning back. That is the point that must be reached.

— FRANZ KAFKA

DAY ONE

ONE

The news came just after dinner via a telephone call from a representative of an organization called Extraordinary Adventures. It was early evening, April 8, just as the sun had dipped behind Unit C, when the residual orange softened and dissolved like the yolk of a broken egg.

"I'm calling for an Edsel . . . Bronfman?" a woman said, or asked. "Not sure I have that right." She sounded tired, a little put out, irritated by his very name. "It's Bronfman or . . . Branfmon."

"This is Edsel Bronfman," Edsel Bronfman said, tentatively, as if he actually might *not* be Edsel Bronfman, or was admitting to it under duress. He waited for the woman to respond, and time seemed to move so slowly, as he steeled himself for what was almost certainly bad news. Something had happened to his mother, or he had been fired from his job, or it was possibly his doctor, whom he had seen just last week for a checkup and who had told him he was fine, everything was fine — *fine!* — but who may have just gotten his blood work back and discovered that something was terribly, terribly wrong. "You're thirty-four," the doctor would say. "It was bound to happen. Lucky to have lived as long as you did with a case of what you've got." Bronfman's capacity to anticipate the worst possible scenario in any circumstance was a skill he had been practicing since boyhood. He had become remarkably good at it.

But it was none of those things. In the background, he could hear the muted discordant symphony of other voices, other men and women, chirping and droning, crackling and buzzing. A truck thundered by on the small highway bordering his complex, a bone-rattling sound so explosive that he winced. He'd almost gotten used to it. Or so he told himself.

Finally, she spoke.

"My name is Carla D'Angelo, Mr. Bronfman, Operator 61217, and I'm calling from Extraordinary Adventures. This call may be recorded for quality and training purposes. I hope I'm not disturbing you. Because I have some good news for you, Mr. Bronfman."

This caught him off guard. He couldn't remember if anyone had ever said that to him before.

"*Good* news?"

"Very good. You won!"

The exclamation point was a little forced, but she sold it. Carla had a smoker's voice, scratchy and deep for a woman. It reminded him a little of his mother, whose voice, owing to a pack-a-day habit, had the same qualities. In the interlude between hearing the news that he had won and the time it took for him to absorb it, Edsel Bronfman heard three or four or five other voices echoing the same: *You've won! You've won! You've won!*

"What have I won?" he asked. "How? I'm not sure what you mean."

"Yes," she said, not really responding to his queries or his confusion. She sounded as if she was reading from a script. "You've won a weekend in Destin, Florida, courtesy of Sandscapes Condominiums. Your lodging for the weekend is complimentary, completely free. A continental breakfast is included as well, at no charge to you. All we ask in return is that you attend a short hour-long presentation about Sandscapes and the charms of Destin, Florida. It's the timeshare of your dreams, Mr. Branfman. We

13

want *Destin* to be your *destin*ation, so you can experience firsthand the flawless excellence and luxury that is Sandscapes. It's extraordinary — this I can guarantee, and it will be an extraordinary adventure. That's why we're called Extraordinary Adventures." She took a deep, sad breath.

"I still don't understand," he said. "How did I 'win' this?"

He turned away from the setting sun and wandered into the kitchen. On his little wooden table, pilgrim-simple, the last few strands of spaghetti and red sauce were congealing into a sticky semi-permanence, not unlike the plastic reproductions of food being displayed in front of some restaurants now. A box of Cheerios, a bag of Minute Rice, and the *TV Guide* were on the counter by the stove.

"How?"

"Yes. Exactly how."

Bronfman wasn't so much suspicious as in a state of curious disbelief. He had never won anything before, not in all the thirty-four years he'd been alive. But then he had never really tried to win anything, either.

"Have you ever dropped your business card into one of those jars?" she asked him. For the first time she sounded like a real person. "They have them at restaurants, diners, bars, et cetera."

"I don't know," he said. "I might have."
He really might have. Once. At a deli he
frequented once or twice a month. Dropped
his card in a jar there. That actually might
have happened.

Against all of his better instincts, Bronfman was getting excited.

"So you're saying that out of all the cards
in one of those jars my card was drawn? Out
of all of them."

"Yes, they drew your card," she said.

"Wow," he said. It was finally sinking in:
he had won something, something free,
something he had accomplished just by being alive. "This is amazing."

"I know," she said. "It's like a dream come
true, right?" Did he hear her laugh? No.
Well, maybe. And maybe she should. Because even though he knew very well that
this was one of those prizes anyone could
win, that it really had nothing to do with
him at all, it didn't matter. Another card
could have been chosen. Even in cases like
this you could lose, and he hadn't lost. He
had *won!* Lives were determined in this way:
by random phone calls, bulk mailings, flyers
posted in the break room at work, and garish roadside advertisements. He lived where
he lived now, King's Manor, because of

15

exclamatory signage promising the *First Month Free!* No, King's Manor was not the safest complex in Birmingham: there was a history of nefarious goings-on in the neighborhood. Nor was it the quietest. There was the little freeway right next to it, and about a hundred yards away, hidden behind a tree line, was a dog pound, and those dogs sure knew how to howl, sometimes very late into the night. But still, a free *month*? He was enjoying his first free month now, and a few times a day he'd think of it, especially when the trucks went by: *I am living somewhere entirely free of charge.* Much of his mail was addressed to Current Resident or Occupant, but that was as good as its being addressed to him, because he *was* the current resident, he *was* the occupant, and he took advantage of these flyers as if they were addressed to him personally. He looked forward to getting and going through his mail. Special Offers were everywhere.

"So," Bronfman said. "All I have to do is present myself at Sandscapes Condominiums in Destin, Florida, and other than the one-hour presentation there are absolutely no strings attached?" He felt it was his duty to ask, because there were always strings attached. But Carla D'Angelo assured him: apart from the short presentation, which she had mentioned, there was not a single strand.

"It will be quite a treat," she said.

"It sounds like it."

"Destin is beautiful. You and your companion —"

"Wait," he said. "Wait. My companion?"

"The prize is for two: you and a companion. Your wife, a girlfriend, a . . . boyfriend — you know, anybody like that."

"But I don't have a companion," he said.

Bronfman heard a pause on Carla's end of the line and, in the background, a faraway female voice say, "Congratulations!" Carla said, "It was written on the jar, Mr. Bronfman. The offer is valid for you *and a companion*. You have to have a companion."

"Why? Why a companion? I don't understand."

"I really don't know, either." He was pushing her to the limit with his niggling questions. She just wanted to get this over with, to go home, watch TV, sleep. "I'm just making the telephone calls here. I don't make the rules. It has something to do with sell rates: couples are more likely to buy a time-share condo than singles."

"Well," he said, sighing, "that's a string. That's definitely a string."

"I'm sorry?"

"That's a string attached. You said there weren't any strings."

"It was written on the *jar.* In black and white. Strings are invisible. So, technically, this is not a string."

"And what else? Do I have to be six feet tall with curly blond hair?" Bronfman was five-ten, with straight thin brown hair that he parted on the left and combed over scallop style.

"No," she said, sighing. "But there is —"

"What?"

"One other thing. Winners have to claim the prize by a certain date. In your case, it has to be used by June twenty-sixth. On June twenty-seventh, the offer expires."

"Carla," he said, moderately exasperated, which was about as exasperated as Bronfman ever got. "I'm sorry, but that does sound like yet another string."

"It was *written on the jar,* Mr. Bronfman. I don't know what to tell you. You have to have a companion, and the offer has to be used within — let me do the math — seventy-nine days. That's just the way it is."

He could hear her thinking. When she spoke again, her voice had softened. "Isn't there anyone you could take?"

"Thank you for asking," he said. "But I don't think so." This reality — the harsh and undeniable truth of it — made him wince a little. He would have liked to have a companion, but his desire for one was not commensurate with his effort to get one. He did not put himself *out there,* as his mother might say — wherever out there was. Bronfman's feet were stuck in cement shoes. "Not at this time I don't, anyway. No one I would feel really comfortable with in a condominium at the beach. For an entire weekend. That's some pretty serious stuff."

"Indeed," Carla said. "You wouldn't want to take just anybody. On the other hand, you could think of it as an opportunity to really get to know someone before you took the next big step."

"That's an idea," he said, pretending to mull it over. But there was in fact no one Bronfman had taken even a little step with, not of late or for some time or, strictly speaking, ever. There was not even anyone he could consider and then reject, unless he counted his mother. Tomorrow was her birthday, and this would be the perfect gift. But this was not the sort of companion Extraordinary Adventures was after; even Bronfman knew that. Not the kind he was after, either. They wanted him to take a romantic companion, and that he did not have. Four years ago he had gone out with a woman named Cheryl Jones, twice — dinner the first time and the second to a bluegrass concert in Jefferson Park. During the course of the concert chiggers ate her legs, and that signaled an end to whatever it was they might have had. And three years ago he had gone on a date with the sister of Mike McFee, who worked in receivables. Courtney. Her brown hair was cut the way Bronfman's hair had been cut in the third grade: close to the skull, so close that you could see the bumps there, and ragged. They had been planning on going to dinner and a movie, but she contracted food poisoning from the shrimp-cocktail appetizer and had to go home. They had known each other for only a few hours, but Bronfman counted it as a date. Since then he hadn't been on actual dates but something more like outings with large groups of folk from work in which some of the people were couples but others were individual men and women coalescing into this one large protoplasmic mass.

It's difficult for adults without a strong social network to meet new people; he had read an article about it. And he knew there were apps for that sort of thing, and websites where people actually advertised themselves like automobiles or sofas, most likely based on fictional self-assessments. But he had yet to open himself up to the amorphous digital world; he did not trust it at all. Like a vegetarian living on a pig farm, Bronfman felt misplaced in the twenty-first century. He would have been a happy man with just a few modern conveniences — a car, electricity, warm water. He did not have a smartphone, or even a computer in his home, though he worked with one at the office and was fine with that. But the computer was a tool for him, not a lifestyle. His life was simple: he had his job, his apartment, and his mother. His world was triangulated like this, from point A to point B to point C. His life could be summarized by the first three letters in the alphabet.

Bronfman noted a hint of warm dryer lint in the air. A motorcycle gang whooshed by. And he could hear Carla breathing. She was giving him all the time in the world. But his air pipe felt a bit constricted, as if he were breathing through a sock, and the fingers clutching the phone were shaking just a little.

Carla D'Angelo, Operator 61217, broke the pensive silence. When next she spoke, it was in a whisper. "Couldn't you just fudge a little bit here?"

"Fudge?"

21

"Just say there's someone even if there isn't? Then when the time came you could go to the condo by yourself and say your wife was sick or something like that?"

"Oh, no," he said. "I wouldn't do that. I don't fudge."

"Well, that's a good quality."

"Thank you."

Carla D'Angelo took a very deep breath and exhaled directly into her headset. She was weary. The voices of the others in the room with her were getting louder, rising to a grating crescendo. Clearly, she had other calls she needed to make, other "winners." But she stayed on this call, with him. That was kind. Bronfman didn't mind the attention at all.

"So," she said. "What do you think, Mr. Bronfman? A weekend at the beach sounds pretty good to me."

"What do I think? I think it sounds pretty good as well. In a way. But I don't think I can," he said. "It sounds nice, very nice, even extraordinary, but the requirements you mentioned would seem to exclude me. That's pretty clear."

"Not necessarily," she said.

"No," he said. "Very necessarily."

"Mr. Bronfman? Hello?" The connection had faltered. It crackled and sputtered and sparked. It sounded as if Carla D'Angelo were speaking to him from a tin can on the other side of the world now, or from space. He had to listen closely. Plus she was whispering, which made it all the more difficult.

"What I mean is, you have seventy-nine days, Mr. Bronfman. *Anything* could happen in seventy-nine days. That's almost three full months! You sound like a nice man. Women like nice men. I do. Believe me, most of you aren't nice. Most men fudge, to put it lightly. And who knows? You may not even need that long. Lives are changed in a day, Edsel, they're changed in a moment. You have to open yourself up to life. Face your greatest fears. Discover what it means to be alive in the world." Her words simmered in his soul. "Think about it this way: Maybe these aren't strings we've attached to this amazing offer. Maybe they're lifelines. This is something you need to do."

She paused as if to let that sink in. A moment passed and the connection resolved. The line sputtered like a wet fuse on an old firecracker and then cleared up. He could hear the grating yackety-yak of the other operators again. Odd. Maybe she'd gone outside for a cigarette.

"But," she went on, "if this doesn't sound like something you'd be interested in, or able to do, I understand. The truth is, Edsel —"

No one called him Edsel. Why was she calling him Edsel?

"— and I hate to put it like this, but there are lots of other cards in the jar."

She was eager to end the call now, clearly, so she could tell her operator friends about him. *This guy, this Branfman guy, get a load of this.* And no doubt she was working on commission. Still, what she said to him: *Maybe they're not strings. Maybe they're lifelines.* That sounded like something important. It sounded like valuable information, something Carla D'Angelo probably didn't share with everybody.

She hung with him in the shared silence, connected by this miracle of telephony that Bronfman did not even remotely understand.

He was immersed in this moment — underwater — so quiet. His apartment, small and simple as a moderately priced interstate motel room, all synthetic wood and pale-lime carpet, felt very still, hushed, expectant. The pound dogs ceased their howling. Even his neighbor, who was known to manufacture sound at disturbingly high

24

levels — music, screaming, laughter, phantom breakage — was quiet now. The entire frenetic complex he lived in was uncharacteristically at peace.

"Okay," he said. The word fell out of his mouth like a bad tooth being pulled: it hurt, but it had to happen. He had to say it. He had to say it even though it really made no sense for him to say it. It was a trust exercise with his own life.

"Okay?" She sounded as shocked as he was. "Are you sure?"

She waited for affirmation, and he was about to give it. But then he remembered the day he dropped his card in the jar. It was two months ago, in February, at Goldstein's Delicatessen, his favorite place to eat in Birmingham, and thus his favorite place to eat in the entire world. It was a cold day. He wore an orange woolen scarf his mother had given him many years ago, one a co-worker had told him was a lady's scarf. (Bronfman had said, still felt secure in saying, "Scarves don't have genders.") He remembered that it even snowed a little that day, a flurry, and it so rarely snowed in Birmingham. He remembered that. He had his lunch — Goldstein's Famous Reuben — and it was excellent, as it always was, and he finished up and was heading back to work. The jar was on a table next to the gumball machines, the kind he never saw anymore, where red and blue and yellow gumballs were on display in the transparent globe, the repository for a more colorful universe, and seemed so bygone-era-ish to Bronfman, like LPs and pay-phone booths. And there was this big jar that had once been used to store Goldstein's Famous Ice Tea but now was half-full of business cards, what looked liked hundreds of them, of all shapes and sizes and colors, but most of them, like his, the traditional size and color — white, 3.5 by 2 inches. He remembered removing a card from his wallet. *Edsel Bronfman, Account Executive, Shipping. Martin Imports.* He never used his cards. He didn't know why he had been issued a card at all. He had never been in the company of other junior executive shipping managers, never been at meetings where he might exchange cards for future reference. But he kept them in his wallet just in case, and that day he had seen the jar and written his home number on the back of one and for no real reason dropped it in.

"Mr. Bronfman?" she said.

Maybe this was the reason. Maybe it was for this extraordinary adventure. Maybe this was a sign of some kind, getting this call from Carla D'Angelo. Because this man, Bronfman, was a man who had come home from work that day, as he did every day, and opened his mail (three invitations for low-interest-rate credit cards, a postcard offering him ten percent off his next purchase somewhere he'd never been, his water bill), made dinner (pasta with red sauce, steamed broccoli, a slice of bread), and had only just sat down in the chair facing the television, remote in hand, to watch a show about hoarders when he remembered the sunset, and stood by his window to watch it. He was still in the same clothes he'd put on that morning: gray slacks, pale-blue oxford shirt, red-and-blue striped tie, and black shoes. He had loosened his tie a bit and unbuttoned the top button. Somehow he always forgot how tight his collar was and, unbuttoning it, discovered, as he had the day before and would tomorrow, that for the first time all day he could actually breathe, could feel the oxygen moving to his extremities. Bronfman was thin. His physical angularity suggested faulty construction. Surely the arm wasn't meant to be connected that way, so high on the shoulder. Couldn't an inch or two be taken off the legs without any real loss of functionality? In its current state, the nose appeared to be more ornamental than functional. Could that be smoothed down, or removed entirely and replaced by another? He was an imperfect man. All that being said, he was, for the most part, inoffensive, and not without potential. It didn't really matter what he looked like, though, because he felt so rarely seen. He was a man who was overlooked by everyone, maybe because he had been standing in one place for such a very long time.

But this phone call. This Carla D'Angelo. Destin. *Extraordinary Adventures.* It meant something. Everything meant *something.* He yearned to believe things happened for a reason, and this was a thing. Thanks to Carla D'Angelo, there was a crack in the shell of his life now — an almost imperceptible crack, but one that let in a little bit of light, and one through which he could see a sliver of the world outside himself. The world he saw was a big place, a bright place, full of paralyzing possibility. Plus, it had a beach.

Bronfman wanted to go there, and he wanted to go there with a companion.

"Hello?" said Carla D'Angelo. "Earth to Mr. Bronfman? Are you still there?"

"Still here," Bronfman said. "Still here."

But not, he hoped, for long.

■ ■ ■ ■

DAY TWO

■ ■ ■ ■

ONE

The sunshine snaked through the branches of a pine tree and in through the uncurtained windows, edging beneath his eyelids and blooming in a pool of light on the bedroom floor, waking him. Bronfman thought, That's pretty. Black coffee, a single scrambled egg and a slice of buttered toast, a shower — the same thing he did every day, but this morning all of it was better. "We will be sending you a packet," Carla D'Angelo had told him. "Please look for it in your mail within seven to ten days." He assured her that he would. He did not tell her that he would be looking for it every day for the next six days as well, because the thought of getting mail of this magnitude was all-consuming.

Bronfman walked out into the day and paused on his stoop, taking in the view, scanning for potential hazards. King's Manor was a compound of barracks-like apartment buildings surrounding a vast black swath of cracking asphalt. Parking-lot lines had been hastily painted by hand. Strangers occasionally gathered in the parking lot at night. Bronfman saw them — half-human, half-shadow — laughing, spitting, pushing one another around in a playfully serious way. Beer cans littered what the manager of the complex called "the green space," and that's exactly what it was, a space of green little more than a patch of grass surrounded by a one-foot-tall wrought-iron fence. The dog pound was behind the last unit. All that separated the complex from the pound was a row or two of pine trees. His next-door neighbor was sitting on the stoop in front of his own apartment, in his boxers, his long, ropy arms dangling outside of his sleeveless red T-shirt. He was, of course, smoking. He was always smoking. On this April morning, he looked a little cold.

"Good morning, Tommy," Bronfman said.

His neighbor's name was Thomas Edison, but he insisted on being called Tommy because then there wouldn't be any confusion between him "and the inventor of the fucking lightbulb." Still, Bronfman could not think of him as anything other than Thomas Edison. The day Bronfman moved to King's Manor, Thomas Edison volunteered to help him with the bed, the couch, a few of the boxes. Bronfman was thankful. Thomas turned out to be one of those men who knew how to angle a chest of drawers around a doorframe, how to find a wall stud to hang a picture, fix a persistent and maddening leaky faucet with a washer. Bronfman didn't. Bronfman didn't know how to do anything, really. He could work, eat and clean up after himself, buy new batteries when the old ones wore out, fill up his car with gas. But he didn't have Thomas Edison's vast knowledge of how things worked, and what was wrong with them when they didn't. Bronfman could live successfully in a suburb of an American city; Thomas Edison could live anywhere. Anywhere. Give him a knife, a pack of matches, and a piece of string, drop him in the middle of a rain forest, and he could build a hut, make a fire, kill a boar.

Considering how much his neighbor knew about the world, the real world, it surprised Bronfman when Thomas Edison told him that he didn't have a job. A man who could have done anything, Bronfman thought, and here he was, doing nothing. He was tall, strong, and shaggy. His goatee — as thick as bear's fur — could have been a full beard if he'd wanted it to be. When Bronfman tried to grow a goatee, his chin looked less like it was covered with hair than with metal filings. (Thus the ability to grow facial hair was, to Bronfman, indicative of a manliness he had yet to and might never achieve.) Sometimes Thomas Edison walked outside with his shirt off, beltless in tight-fitting, oil-stained jeans. Chinese tattoos, hard muscles, left arm half-tanned from short-sleeved driving. Again, this amazed Bronfman. He could not imagine going outside half-naked, not under any circumstances.

But Thomas Edison wasn't perfect, not by a long shot. He stayed up late and had friends who came over and laughed and drank and kept Bronfman up sometimes for all hours — literally, for all of the hours. People over there screamed and hooted and bottles broke, and one man would have words with another, threatening to break a bone or his entire face. Then it would all turn eerily silent. Bronfman could have complained, but no one liked a complainer, and who was he to insinuate himself into the good-time-Charlie life his neighbor was living? Bronfman had only been there a few weeks. Maybe Tommy would cut back on this lifestyle when he got a job, once he had a reason to get up in the morning.

Thomas Edison barely lifted his unshaved chin in greeting. Sometimes he was gregarious and talkative, but on other days he was so fatigued that he opened his mouth only wide enough to stick a cigarette in it. That's how he was this morning, which was kind of great, because Bronfman was tempted to tell him what had happened — that he had won this trip to the beach — and he didn't want to tell him. The secret, in a way, was as valuable as the prize itself: both things were entirely his. And though in the sober light of morning he knew there was little chance he would be able to qualify for the offer, the mere fact that he had been chosen was a small good feeling, like finding a piece of chocolate in his pocket.

With a sudden hack, Thomas Edison resurrected something thick and sticky from the bottom of his throat and spat it out, away from Bronfman, and then wiped his spattered lips with the back of his hand.

"Well, I hope you have a good day," Bronfman said, and waved. Still Thomas Edison said nothing. Only by some nearly imperceptible dip of his neighbor's head could Bronfman surmise that the man had heard him speak at all.

TWO

The Cranston Building was Bronfman's home away from home. He felt more at ease there than he did anywhere else. A structure devoted to housing businesses of various types in one centralized location, the Cranston Building succeeded as well as any building possibly could. It may not have been perfect (there were some airflow problems, the floor of the men's room on fifteen was often damp and sticky, and the elevator was slower than molasses in January), but perfect wasn't the point. Constancy — that was the point. So what if it was showing its age here and there. So what if the awning — the one that had been in place since Bronfman's very first day, almost eight years ago — was worn and rain-streaked, torn in places. The way the words

THE CRANSTON BUILDING EST. 1924

had been carved into the concrete façade above the awning suggested that this was a significant building, a historic structure to which attention must be paid: Future archaeologists, take note! You have found the Cranston Building, home of many different businesses and support centers, a well-known plastic surgeon and a West Indian Trading Company, a data-collection center and at least seven legal firms. The marble columns on either side of the automatic doors were august and stately, and had what was perhaps the intended effect on Bronfman: they made him feel special. The columns made him feel that he was important, that his job was important, and that he wouldn't be in this building if these things weren't true. The Cranston Building — even more than his office on the fifteenth floor, even more than his own little cubicle — was his sanctuary, his Notre Dame. This is exactly what he thought he needed. Immutability. Certainty. The very same sameness from one day to the next, forever and ever and ever. How wrong he was.

Work! Work was work, neither more nor less, the perfect distillation of what it was meant to be. He turned on his computer and settled into his cubicle, but his mind immediately wandered to the beach. The beach was a place he had never really liked; now it was the only place he wanted to go. He had been to the beach only once in his life, as a child of ten. He had played at the edge of the surf, never venturing farther than the foamy border, while his mother — with her big hat and her sunglasses — smoked cigarettes under the umbrella. She applied sunscreen to him but in a haphazard fashion, so that he came away burned, scalded in streaks by the sun, tiger stripes in pink. He couldn't sleep that night — the sheets had hurt him, and the edges of his shorts had felt as if they were cutting into his legs. They had never gone back to the beach again, and that had been fine with him.

In the break room, he poured himself a glass of warm water. On the way back to his desk he checked in with all of his work friends, the men and women he felt close to — even intimate with — through the course of the day, but not for a moment afterward. Skip Sorsby occupied the cubicle on the other side of his wall, and Bronfman supposed that, of everyone, he spoke to Skip the most. Not that Bronfman wanted to, it was just that Skip Sorsby was impossible to avoid. Bronfman could hear him humming.

Bronfman could hear him breathing. Bronfman could hear him snickering, and snickering, Bronfman felt, was an unseemly sound for an adult to make. Still, Skip Sorsby was someone Bronfman would "shoot the shit" with, as it were, talking about nothing of any importance at all, which was the tradition at his office, and perhaps at every office — killing time for as long as they possibly could before being compelled by some inner voice to sit down at their desks and actually do something related to what they were being paid to do. But it wasn't the same today. Even when Bronfman said, "Good morning," there was a question in it, a weird combination of joy and anxiety, which anyone who was really listening would have picked up on. But no one really listened. He could have said, "It is a good morning for me — an *especially* good morning for me, yet one that also fills me with a certain dread," but that would have sounded ridiculous.

Keeping the secret, however, became too much for him to bear. He felt as though a geyser inside his heart were on the verge of exploding. He continued to perform his daily functions: He made phone calls, sent emails, filed the light-blue copies, sent the pink ones on to accounts, placed three orders, put out one fire, started another . . . all the while feeling that he had to tell somebody. But whom?

He thought through the possibilities at hand, in cubicles left and right. Gary Kazlow, Garrett Kenan, Jay Miller, maybe those brothers who worked in receiving, Mitchell and Alex Kahn — they seemed friendly enough — or even Skip Sorsby. He imagined telling each of them, one at a time, and gauged their suitability by closing his eyes and feeling the way he thought he might feel after having told them. *Condo at the beach!* But their imagined reactions weren't sufficient to the news he would be sharing with them. Because he would have to tell them the hitch as well — the lifeline, as Carla D'Angelo had put it. The companion. Certainly he would have liked some guidance in how to make it all happen — the steps to take toward finding one, which, of course, entailed a series of actions he was, as far as he knew, incapable of. But someone knew, because it was done all the time. Like the names of constellations, or how electricity worked, or what, really, was inside the inside of a television set: someone knew. All he had to do was ask.

THREE

The elevator descended tentatively. It was full of people standing shoulder to shoulder, backside to front, and as soon as the doors opened to the lobby and they all poured out they were treated to the ebullient welcome of the receptionist, Sheila Mc-Nabb.

"And the lunchtime exodus begins!" she rang out, like a joyous village crier. "Last one to the trough may be eliminated!"

Sheila McNabb was the receptionist — not for him, not even for his floor, but for the building. She was the first person you saw when you entered the Cranston Building, the last when you left. "Welcome to the Cranston Building!" she said as you came through the automatic glass-and-steel door (it wasn't a big building, and her expansive metal desk was only a few feet away from the entrance), and then, as you exited, "Have a nice day!" Between the coming and going of office workers, staff, and visitors — which included salesmen, the mailman, and various delivery services, from packages to pizza — she answered the telephone: "The Cranston Building. How may I direct your call?" And when there were neither phone calls to direct nor people to greet she could be seen with a pen in her hand, furiously scribbling, or sometimes reading a book or a magazine. She had no real power, of course, being just a receptionist, but her position at the desk, so close to the entrance, made her seem sacred, ageless. Bronfman looked at her and felt as if you could trace her position back to Egypt or Greece or wherever, where a priestess may have stood before a temple and muttered blessings as you came and went, maybe splashing you with water, encouraging donations for temple upkeep.

Sheila McNabb was in her late twenties, perhaps, virtually unblemished, with chocolate-brown hair that hung just short of her shoulders, straining for purchase. She had a friendly and unguarded smile, and was objectively pretty, but not the kind of pretty that advertises itself as pretty. (Middle American farm-girl pretty, he would say, an observation that Bronfman could make even though he had been neither on a farm nor to Middle America.)

He had established a relationship with Sheila McNabb, if that's what it was, based on a few hellos and good-byes and a bunch of friendly waves. She knew him, he figured, as well as she knew anybody she didn't know, maybe more so, maybe less. They had never had a real conversation, but he felt as if they could, they might, if only he would stop for a minute and make himself known to her. But he never did, because he was Bronfman.

So around noon that day he exited the elevator and walked quickly past her desk, waving briefly, hurtling toward the doors leading to the outside world and a chili dog.

"Have a nice day!" Sheila called after him.

But then he stopped. And turned. Bronfman recalled what Carla D'Angelo, Operator 61217, had said to him: *You have to open yourself up to life.* He heard it again now as if it were a cosmic echo. Sheila McNabb was life. She was the epicenter of life. He saw that she had already opened up her notebook and was writing something down, but when she realized that Bronfman hadn't disappeared through the automatic doors, as everyone else had, she laughed.

"I thought you were leaving," she said, "and then — well, you didn't." She laughed

43

again. "I shouldn't have said 'Have a nice day' until I was certain you were leaving. I was impetuous. That was an impetuous 'Have a nice day.' I should have nailed that by now." Her head bobbed, not unlike one of those velour dogs people used to set up on the shelf above the backseat of a car, bobbed as if she'd said something she was agreeing with, or that she hoped *he* would agree with, so he smiled and nodded as well.

"Well," he said. "I thought, I thought . . . why not stop and say hello."

He was playing this by ear, improvising. So far, so good.

"You're sweet," she said. "A rare breed. Like a black-eyed tree frog."

"A what?"

"A black-eyed tree frog."

"They're rare?"

"Very."

"Oh," he said. "Okay." He wasn't sure where to go with this, or if there was anywhere *to* go, so he just stood there, silently.

"What's your name?" she asked.

"Bronfman. Edsel Bronfman. Or just Bronfman. People call me . . . Bronfman."

She smiled. Her eyes sparkled through a moist glaze. "Bronfman," she said, as if her tongue were giving it a test drive. "*Bronf-*

man. Why do you think that is?"

"Why what is?"

"Why Bronfman," she said. "Why people call you Bronfman instead of Edsel. Or Ed. Or Eddie. Fast Eddie Bronfman. Something like that."

"I don't know the science behind it," he said. "Some last names just lend themselves to that sort of thing, I guess."

"Like Cher," she said. "Or Bono."

"I've never thought about it like that." He thought about it like that now. *Cher, Bono . . . Bronfman.* It didn't really work. Their names were manufactured, badges of celebrity, and Bronfman was definitely not a celebrity. He was whatever the opposite of a celebrity was.

"I'm Sheila. Sheila McNabb. Same as my nameplate." She pointed at the engraved black plastic nameplate on the front of the top of her desk. Not that he needed to look, because he knew her name, but he read it anyway. *Sheila McNabb.* "I've only been here six weeks and I get a nameplate. Is that amazing or what?" She laughed, shook her head, and sighed. "So. Is there anything I can do for you, Bronfman? I'm here to serve."

On her desk was a debris pile of minutely torn typing paper, pieces of paper that had been made as small as they could possibly be, then torn again, and again. Beside it were a tortoise-shell hair clip and a retractable pencil, and a stenographer's pad that, though upside down to Bronfman, appeared to be a list of cities: Istanbul, Krakow, Salzburg, Beirut.

"My dream list of places I'd like to go," she said, noting his interest. "Someday."

"I'm sorry!" he said. "It's none of my business. I shouldn't have —"

She waved his panic away. "Where do you want to go? One day. If you could go anywhere."

"Me?" *The beach,* he thought. *The ocean. Destin, Florida, is my destination.* It felt as distant and foreign as Salzburg to him, as dangerous as Beirut. He shrugged. "I don't know," he said. "I haven't really thought about it."

"Think about it."

"Paris," he said, without really thinking, and not because he had ever desperately wanted to go there but because Paris was the city he felt one should want to go to if one hadn't been. "Have you been?"

"I lived there as a child," she said. "From the ages of seven to twelve. I was actually fluent by the time we came home, but of

46

course I've forgotten most of it now. *C'est la vie!*"

"That sounded very French to me," he said.

Just then a shorter-than-average man holding an overstuffed leather briefcase rumbled through the lobby.

"Welcome to the Cranston Building!" Sheila called to him. The man nodded, his fleshy neck rolling over his collar, and kept walking. He pressed the up button on the elevator, hard, twice, smashed it as if he were getting it back for something.

Her exchange with the man took only seconds, but when she returned her gaze to Bronfman he could tell that it was unclear to her why she was talking to him at all. He felt as if he should introduce himself to her all over again. She stared beyond him, into space, the way people stare into the night sky waiting for a shooting star.

"That man," she said. "He looked a little bit like a mole, didn't he?"

"What?"

"That man who just came in," she said. "He looked like a *mole.*"

Bronfman glanced toward the elevator, into which the man had disappeared. He really couldn't remember what he looked like. "A mole," was all Bronfman could come up with in reply. "Hmm."

"I'll tell you a little secret," she said in a low, possibly almost flirty tone, so softly that Bronfman had no choice but to move closer to her desk and lean over, like a top-heavy tree. "When someone comes through the lobby, I wonder what kind of animal he or she might be. Everyone is some kind of animal."

"Really?"

"Pretty much. Characteristics, personality traits. The kind of clothes they wear. Their eyes sometimes. Their facial hair. Or lack of it. If they're big or little or — well, you know, various things. Once I had a badger, a zebra, and a marmoset come through here. All on the same day."

"What's a marmoset?"

"It's a little monkey kind of thing with a furry collar. It always has this expression on its face like you just surprised it."

"A marmoset," he said. "That's interesting."

"And in the Cranston Building," she said. "Of all places, right?"

He laughed, she laughed. He caught his reflection in the panes of glass that functioned as walls here, and which turned the lobby into an enclosure for anyone passing on the sidewalk outside to see, as if on display at a zoo. He saw how thin he was, how long was his neck, his hair so lifeless and practical. His tie was too short, and his shirt billowed out of his pants to give him that marsupial look.

"I know what you're thinking," she said.

"You do?"

"I'm totally psychic. You're thinking what kind of animal are *you.*"

"I guess I was."

"I knew it!"

She considered him, starting with his head, his face, his eyes — his eyes, which she settled on for quite some time, longer than any woman had spent there in a long time, probably forever — and moved slowly downward, past his neck, the rib cage–torso, his stick legs and pencil feet. She let the vision marinate.

"Okay. You look like uhhhhhhhhhhhhhhh-hhh — a giraffe!"

He considered this. "A giraffe?" It came as a disappointment to him, for some reason. A giraffe? He wasn't sure that was what he wanted to be. Then again, he didn't know what kind of animal he *would* like to be. But he said, "I guess that's not so bad."

Her mouth dropped. "Not so bad? What do you mean? That's great! Let's look it up."

She swiveled around to face her computer

and typed something quickly. She clicked the mouse a couple of times and then took a deep breath. "Okay," she said, reading now. "The giraffe — *Giraffa camelopardalis* — an African even-toed ungulate mammal, the tallest of all land-living animal species, and the largest ruminant."

She stared at the screen, momentarily hypnotized, and then she turned to him. "Wow," she said. "You're the largest ruminant."

"And an ungulate," he said. "Which sounds like something you'd call somebody you didn't like. Like, 'You're such an ungulate.' "

"Or, 'Don't be such an ungulate!' "

"Or . . . or . . ." But he couldn't think of another ungulate-related joke.

"You're tall," she said. "The tallest of the tall."

"I'm not that tall," he said. "Average, I think. For a person."

"And tiny for a giraffe. Still. That's what Wikipedia says."

They laughed a little more, until all their laughter was exhausted and they had no more. Sheila squinted at him, rebooting herself. "Did you — *need* anything? Here I am going on about ruminants and marmosets and you probably need me for something. This is my job. I have a job." She said it as if she were trying to convince herself that she did, indeed, have a job.

I don't know, he thought. I'm lost in the forest of this conversation. I don't know how I got here or where to go.

"Welcome to the Cranston Building!" she said.

He thought she was on some loop, and that they would relive the entire conversation they just had, and would again and again the longer he stayed. But someone had entered the building, a tall bearded man in a nice blue suit. Bronfman, who knew little about nice suits, thought it was Italian. For Bronfman, all nice suits were Italian, all nice cars German, and all good wine French.

"Good day," the man said as he passed.

"Good day!" Sheila said. "Top of the day to you, sir!" She could really put a spin on a greeting.

She waited for the man to get on the elevator before she looked back to Bronfman. "Well?" she said.

"Well what?"

"What kind of animal?"

The phone rang. She held up a finger. "The Cranston Building. How may I direct your call?" She paused, listening, then pushed a button on her console and hung up.

"Well?"

He swallowed, and thought. The answer to this question seemed more important than it actually was, or more important than it should have been. His heart raced, and he felt a clammy sweat ooze across his palms.

"I don't know," he said.

"Hazard a guess. Trust your instincts. Go for it."

"Okay," he said. "Okay. A groundhog?"

She thought about it, quite seriously, and then she nodded. *"Absolutely,"* she said. "Yes. A groundhog." She seemed more pleased with the answer than he was. They both let that moment happen, and then it was over. There was nowhere else to go with the conversation, nothing else to do. To try to extend it would have been awkward and weird.

"So," she said.

"So, yes." He sighed. "I guess I need to go pretend to work." His stomach growled, reminding him that his original intention had been to go to lunch. But it seemed impossible now. He had committed to returning the way he came.

She forced a laugh, he did, too, then she looked at him, and then away. But she didn't say anything in response. She didn't say anything at all. Space and time seemed balanced on the tip of a needle. Sheila, Bronfman, the lobby, the Cranston Building, the city, the earth, the solar system, the universe.

Of course, this was when everything could have changed for Bronfman. Rather, this was the moment when *he* could have changed everything. Meaning his life. Meaning what remained of his life, the balance of days left to him. A single word from him to her, the smallest possible gesture — that's all the moment called for him in order for him to reinvent his world. This is when he should have said something, like "Would you like to go out sometime? For coffee, lunch, dinner, even a drink? I'm up for anything. Maybe even a weekend trip to the beach a couple of months down the line."

But, just like that, the moment ran its course and was gone, gone because who can do that? Who can change their entire life like that? It was asking too much of him. It would be asking too much of anybody, except maybe some kind of professional swashbuckler. He was not that kind of man, though, and, really, outside of books and movies, who was?

He turned, walked to the elevator, pressed

the up button, and watched the glowing numbers above him as the elevator slowly, slowly, slowly descended per his request. Then it stopped on the twelfth floor and the light hovered there, not moving for a moment before the elevator resumed its course. Then he turned to her, and was surprised to see that her gaze hadn't left him.

"You're different from any receptionist we've had here before," he said.

"That's because I'm not a receptionist," she said. "I'm something else."

Her tone suggested that she was an undercover investigator or maybe a witch, something romantic or potentially dangerous.

"Oh. What are you?"

"I'm . . . a freelance writer," she said. "I guess you could say."

"Ah. A freelance writer." Though it appeared that she was neither spy nor sorceress, Bronfman was intrigued. As a child, he had often dreamed of becoming a freelance something-or-other one day; the word *freelance* excited him. "What do you write?"

She opened her mouth to tell him and it stayed open, but without a single word coming out of it. She looked down at her desk and back at him. Then, "Okay. Like, you know when you buy something and inside it or on the box there are directions on how to use it, put it together, how one part fits with the next?"

"Yes. Sure. Of course."

"That's what I do."

"I'm still not sure what you mean."

"I write directions. Instructions. How-to manuals."

"Step one, step two, step three — that sort of thing?"

"That sort of thing exactly. But sometimes I go A, B, C — it depends." She looked down, spotted her purse, opened it, and produced a generic prescription-pill bottle, plastic, the color of an old orange peel. She read from it: " 'Take two before bed with water.' That's me! I wrote that."

"Wow."

"It's a tough racket, though — very competitive. That's why I'm here now, doing this. Girl's gotta pay the rent, right?"

"Yes," Bronfman said. "She does."

She smiled. When she smiled her cheeks rounded up into grape-size hillocks, and her eyebrows seemed to expand across her forehead, like an accordion. He watched her eyes open, close.

The elevator finally arrived, and the doors groaned open and he felt compelled to get on, even though he didn't want to. He sort

of backed into it, because she was still looking at him, mouth half open, and he was
still looking at her.

"By the way, Bronfman?" she said, half
statement, half question. "The giraffe? It's
one of my favorite animals. Actually, I
would say it is my favorite, for sure."

Then the doors closed, and Bronfman, her
favorite animal, rode the elevator up and up
and up, wondering the whole trip how he,
such a large, ungainly ungulate, meant to
roam the grasslands and the woodlands, the
sun-drenched savanna plains, had ended up
in this tiny metal box, alone. It wasn't until
he arrived at the fifteenth floor that he
manufactured the courage to push the button that would take him back to the lobby
to reclaim his lost opportunity. The elevator
button, formerly a bleak white, glowed a
bright and hopeful orange after he pushed
it, an orange like the sunshine in his apartment that morning. *Going down,* the elevator said to him. But he stepped off just as
the doors were closing, and even when he
remembered that he had forgotten to go to
lunch he took his place in his cubicle and
proceeded to fill orders, order after order,
because, he told himself, there were so
many of them to fill.

FOUR

Skip Sorsby chose this moment to peer over the top of his wall. Maybe he'd heard Bronfman scouring his desk drawer for a candy bar, a piece of gum, anything. That's the sort of office his office was: a hive of drones in unapologetic propinquity, all working toward the same end, which was to keep being drones by successfully completing their tasks. This worked for Bronfman. He felt reassured by the clarity of it all.

Skip was about six feet three, with broad, sloping shoulders and a wild mop of thick brown hair, boyishly unmanageable, bright-blue eyes, and the smile of a door-to-door salesman or a double agent. He was loud, opinionated, and had no social filter at all. He towered over the sitting Bronfman like a god. "Yo, Bronfman," he said. "How goes it, you goofball?"

"It's going okay, Skip," Bronfman said in a way that would have suggested to anyone that it wasn't going well. Sorsby scrutinized him. Nodded. Made a small, almost sympathetic sound, and cleared his throat. This was Sorsby: on the one hand, he knew that something was wrong, and on the other hand he didn't really care.

"I can't find the IKEA invoice," Sorsby said. IKEA purchased a container load of flatware through their distributor every six months or so. It was one of their sexiest accounts. "It's disappeared, erased somehow, seriously vanished. If I had deleted it, it would be in the deleted folder and, lo and behold, it's not. Maybe a virus got to it."

"I'm sorry," Bronfman said, as if it was his fault.

Sorsby looked troubled, shaking his head and biting his lower lip. "You're not a computer whiz, are you, Bronfman?"

"No," Bronfman said, and traveled that line of thought. "I don't think I'm an anything whiz, actually."

Sorsby wasn't listening. "I had another one of those nights last night, Bronfman, the kind I've been telling you about."

Telling him too much about, Bronfman thought.

"Another 'invasion of the body snatchers'?" Bronfman said. This is how Sorsby euphemized it. By that he meant that

58

he was seeing many different women, one night after the other, even in the morning on the way to work for a "quickie." So many that Sorsby couldn't keep them straight. It was *exhausting,* Sorsby said almost every day, and it appeared to be: For the amount of work Sorsby got done, terminal exhaustion was probably his only excuse.

"It's like I've been blessed or cursed, one or the other — sometimes I can't tell." Sorsby laughed, winked, lowered himself into the shell of his cubicle, talking to himself now but loud enough that anyone within a few yards could hear him. "You gotta learn to say no, Skip! You gotta get right with God. But not yet!"

"I don't think it's a curse," Bronfman said, after giving it a little thought. "A challenge, perhaps, yes . . ."

But Sorsby didn't care what Bronfman thought or didn't think. "Gotta check my updates, see what she said about you-know-what. The beast with two backs. *Grrrrrrrrr.*" Sorsby sighed, and then Bronfman heard him swearing at the IKEA invoice. Then he heard him pick up his phone and mumble while he texted and sniggered, and it was clear to Bronfman that Skip was now communicating with one of the body snatchers.

"Skip?" Bronfman said through the cubicle wall.

"Hold on . . ." Text, text, text. Sigh. Sly laughter. Yawn. "What's the what, Bronfman?"

"I'd like to ask you a question," Bronfman said, lowering his voice to a whisper, which, were anyone listening, would only have encouraged them to listen all the more closely. Though Bronfman was merely going to ask a simple question, one man to another, he felt that in doing so he was venturing beyond his safe zone, maybe just by an inch or so. But, once you stepped into the open, there was no difference between an inch and a mile. "It's about women."

The typing stopped. "About *women*? Bronfman, playa, you surprise me." Again he appeared above the wall, jack-in-the-box style. "Consider me Mr. Answer. And if I don't have the answer I will be happy to research it and come back with one tomorrow. Try me."

Nothing about Sorsby seemed authentic or trustworthy, honest or well-meaning, but none of that meant that he couldn't help Bronfman with his problem. Maybe it was just these characteristics that actually contributed to whatever knowledge he did have, since Bronfman, who was exceptionally authentic and trustworthy, honest and well-meaning, knew next to nothing. "Shoot," he said.

"Okay. So. Say you meet someone, a woman, and talk, the two of you talk, engage in a conversation that both of you seem to enjoy, but that conversation comes to an end. If you wanted to continue talking at some other time, possibly even at some other venue, how would you accomplish this?"

Sorsby stared at Bronfman blankly. "Let me stick that into Google Translate."

He disappeared, and Bronfman could hear him pretending to type. It was easy to tell the difference between real typing and sarcastic typing, and what Sorsby was doing now was clearly sarcastic.

Sorsby reappeared. "So I think you mean, how does one ask a lady out on a date."

"Please keep your voice down," Bronfman said. "And no, that's not what I mean." Asking a lady out on a date — or this specific lady — was emotional trigonometry. Bronfman needed to learn the addition and subtraction of simple conversation first. The physics of engaging with the world. Things were happening so fast! Carla D'Angelo said he had seventy-nine days: how was it everything could be happening *now,* on the almost very first of them? He had only a

61

vague notion of what a real date would look like, having been on too few to say for sure. He had a feeling that his experience wasn't really real, though, the same way he thought the food he ate at the Chinese restaurant downtown wasn't what Chinese people ate in China.

"I just want to talk."

"How old are you, Bronfman?"

"Thirty-four," he said.

"You're ten years older than I am."

"What are you saying? Should I be asking someone with more experience?"

"No," he said. "Maybe someone with less experience, actually. The challenge for me here is in understanding how a thirty-four-year-old man doesn't know how to talk to a girl by the time he's twelve. Because some guys are born knowing. There are cases of babies actually asking the nurses who helped deliver them out on a date not long after the cord was cut. Did you know that, Bronfman? True story."

"That's not a true story," Bronfman said.

"No, it's not. I was just highlighting through exaggeration how odd it is that a man your age doesn't know how to have a conversation with a woman."

Bronfman did not like Skip Sorsby, he had never liked Skip Sorsby, and every day something happened to remind him why he felt that way. "Well, thank you for your helpful jokes."

Sorsby winked.

"Look, if I was being a total dick I would say something glib, like *Just ask her,* but both of us know it's more complicated than that. It's *how* you ask. How you look when you make the ask. How nonchalant do you want to be — or do you want to be *non-*nonchalant? And also, you know — not my business — but you might want to think about working out a little, toning up. Presenting a better package." He gave Bronfman the once-over. "I'm not in the greatest shape, either," said Sorsby, who was working on a solid belly, "but for me it's a lifestyle choice. Fatty foods are better for you. With you, it's like you don't give a shit."

This was true. Bronfman tried not to think about how he looked beneath his clothes. He avoided mirrors as he would an oncoming car.

Sorsby chewed on the inside of his lower lip. "That about covers it, I think," he said. He closed his eyes and placed his hands together and slowly lowered himself behind the cubicle wall, perhaps intoning some yogic prayer, where he disappeared, Bronfman hoped forever.

Bronfman didn't move. The sounds of the office enveloped him: the air-conditioning units, the telephone calls and angry typing, laughter, coffee slurping, a dozen whispering fans behind the grated computer towers. Then he removed three silver paperclips from the small plastic box full of paperclips to the right of his mouse, and in deliberate, precise, and yet thoughtless motions he pried and pulled and turned the soft metal until — each clip magically attached to the other — they took on the form of what looked like, what very well could have been, a giraffe. Or something like a giraffe.

Just ask her, said the total dick.

Good advice.

FIVE

He told himself that he had been planning on leaving early anyway, and there was something to that. It was his mother's birthday — she was seventy — and the older she got the earlier she asked him to come over. (Tonight, five-thirty. If she lived to be eighty, they'd be having dinner at breakfast.) But the truth was that he had not been able to stop thinking about Sheila McNabb, not for a single instant throughout the entire day. Even when he was thinking of something else he was thinking of her, or, if not her, then of giraffes, of marmosets, of black-eyed frogs, of what it might be like to live in Paris, France, which was the same as thinking of her, because without her he wouldn't have been thinking of any of these things at all. So he left almost thirty minutes early just so he'd be able to talk to her one more time, one more time on a day in which he had already spoken to her once.

He wondered what might happen.

So, he straightened his desk and put on his jacket and boarded the elevator for his lobby-bound trip. Elevators in other buildings zipped through space with the smooth velocity of those banking vacuum tubes; this elevator creaked and moaned and stopped and jumped and was slower than a two-legged dog. And yet he was glad of the length of time it took today, as he had yet to come up with anything remotely appropriate to say to Sheila McNabb, and, against his better instincts and lifetime of experience with last-minute decisions, he thought something might happen when he got there. Something had happened when they were talking earlier in the day — something wildly different from anything that had ever happened to him before — and he hoped it would happen again. He was hoping for something abnormal. But his mind was still a vast field of nothing at all when the elevator landed, and the doors groaned apart and he took a step into his future, where this woman waited to welcome him.

But Sheila McNabb wasn't there. At her desk was Crawford, maintenance man to the Cranston Building, looking at the telephone console with studied disdain. Crawford was from Texas, and had a cattleman's hard-nosed, no-nonsense approach to broken things: they might try to stay broken, they might want to stay broken, but he was going to fix them — if not today then tomorrow. Bronfman had watched him assemble cubicles, install software, summon electricity from a dead socket. He was as solid as an old fighter and, since quitting smoking six years ago, kept a coffee stirring straw in his mouth that he chewed into a crumpled mass and replaced with a fresh one as soon as he was done with the old. He was a chain-chewer.

Crawford glanced at the puzzled Bronfman. Something was awry.

Her nameplate was gone.

"What can I do you for?" Crawford asked him.

"Sheila," Bronfman said. "Sheila Mc-Nabb. The receptionist. Do you know what happened to her?"

Crawford shrugged. "That is something I do not know. But, from what I gather, she was just here on a temporary basis. I think she's gone."

"Gone?"

"Yep, gone. She's turned into the girl who used to work here now. Like the girl who worked here before her and the girl before that. There are so many girls." Crawford chewed that straw. Bronfman thought he might actually be eating it.

Bronfman nodded. "Ah, I see," he said. "Do you think there would be any way to get in touch with her?"

"I'm sure there is," Crawford said. "Everybody is somewhere. But in my experience that sort of information is closely guarded by the Cranston Gestapo. Why? Did she owe you some money?"

Crawford winked at him. Second wink of the day.

"No," Bronfman said. "I just wanted to tell her something. I was talking to her earlier today —"

"I get it. You were *this close* to getting a little snatch and she left you with a stiffy. I talked to her a couple of times. Nice girl. Had that fresh look, but take the lid off and she was a boiling pot of water. I bet. Spank Bank material, if you know what I'm saying."

Bronfman didn't know what he was saying. He wasn't familiar with that expression. But, judging from the leer on the face of this Crawford, it was either a very good or a very bad thing, possibly both. "I was just hoping to contact her," he said.

Crawford wasn't listening. "A head case,

though, for sure. Happy as a clam at high tide one minute, laughing and all, then sad as a circus elephant the next. I gave up trying to understand women years ago. Not sure there's anything there to understand, actually. Just a bunch of live wires and leaky faucets, if you know what I'm saying."

"I see," Bronfman said, not seeing anything at all. He was unsure how to proceed.

Crawford had lost interest in Bronfman, anyway, and had turned back to the console. "Okay, then," he said. *"Arrivederchi."*

Bronfman turned and walked away from the desk where Sheila McNabb had once sat. He was on autopilot, lost in nameless emotions, confused by the term Spank Bank, probably on the way to his car. His insides felt taut, as if they were being tied into knots, tighter and tighter. He missed her. He actually felt a little lonely without her. But why? He had never even spoken to her before today. The feeling made no sense. Still, there had been a spark in the darkness of his lonesome soul, a spark that could start a fire. But then it died, and Bronfman was Bronfman again, waking as if from a trance, and found that he was in his car driving through the streets of Birmingham on the way to his mother's home.

Six

For her seventieth birthday, Bronfman had ordered his mother a pair of battery-heated socks because she said her feet were always, *always* cold. On the way to her house he stopped at the liquor store and bought her the scotch she loved so much, a scotch so expensive that he couldn't even pronounce its name. Bronfman had to write the word out on a yellow Post-it and hand it to the cashier, as if it were a stickup. He wasn't much of a scotch drinker himself, gravitating toward white wine and the occasional summer sangria. At a stoplight he looked at the bottle, which had directions on how to make a Rob Roy. One part this and another part that. Someone had thought to write these directions. Perhaps it was Sheila. Perhaps this was a sign.

He parked, and gathered his presents. Then he gathered himself. He breathed. Because even though Bronfman loved his mother more than any other person on the planet — even though he had no one else in his life remotely close enough to him to love and it was the same for her — she was challenging, even infuriating at times. In the past few months, though, his visits to her had become tricky at best. She had become erratic — sweet, funny, vicious, forgetful. She'd never not been a free and blatantly outrageous spirit, but it was becoming clear to Bronfman that what was going on now was more than just an extension and exaggeration of who she was. He was afraid she was losing her mind.

The house was so quiet, but it almost always was. Old people, he noticed sometimes, made no sounds at all except when they cleared their throats. Still, he imagined the worst every time he walked into this soundless gloom, one dreadful scenario after another.

"Mom!" he called. "Mother! Muriel!"

Nothing. He called again. He felt his heart race, veins near his ears throb.

The back door was open. Odd. He peered outside and saw that the gate to the backyard — always shut, always — was banging against the fence in a phantom breeze. Bronfman was already rehearsing the words in his head: *And that is where I found her.*

That was where he found her. Not dead but fully alive, with her back to him, on her knees, a tiny shovel in hand, digging in the dirt. She was wearing her yellow Lilly Pulitzer high-waters, a T-shirt commemorating a 5K run for something, and no shoes. Her ankles had a stegosaurian horniness to them, and her feet were deflated, deeply wrinkled, and black with dirt. They looked unsalvageable.

"Mom? What are you doing? It's me, Edsel." She'd called him Frankie a few weeks ago; he wanted to make himself as clear as possible. Still, she didn't turn around. He glanced about. The backyard had never been much of a backyard. Small, scrawny inbred treelike weeds, lunging for light; a cloud of kudzu draping the fence; grassless rocky soil; two sweet-gum trees.

Finally, she turned to him and smiled. Her face, deeply wrinkled and smeared with mud, looked as if it had been made up for some Aboriginal magic party.

"Looking for Barney," she said brightly.

"Barney?"

She turned away and went back to digging, unearthing little treasures that he couldn't see. Barney was the dog he'd had as a boy, from the age of ten to eleven and a half. A quarter of a century ago they had buried Barney together, after finding him on the side of the road without a mark on him — just dead, hit by a car, they gathered. She did all the digging. While Bronfman mostly watched, she set her cigarette down on the edge of a wooden fence, where it could balance and burn in the air. When she finished digging the grave, stuffing the corpse into it, and covering the hole with a dusting of dirt (Bronfman saw part of the plastic shroud that Barney had been wrapped in edging out of the divot), she reclaimed the cigarette, gave it a long, breathy pull, and said, through a lung-rattling cough, "Ashes to ashes, Edsel."

She was so old now. Even her ears looked old, withered, like creatures that had abandoned their shells and crawled from the sea and attached themselves to the side of her head. She'd quit smoking years ago and now chewed Nicorettes obsessively. He kind of missed the cigarettes; the smell of smoke reminded him of home. It was nice. He wanted to encourage the habit, because he couldn't let go of the younger model, the one he'd imprinted on as a child. Even though Muriel was thirty-six when she had him, she seemed younger than all the other mothers of his set — prettier, snappier, smarter, too. A single mother, no husband or father ever even referenced, because there had never been one, except in the strictest biological sense. Bronfman was the product of a one-night stand with a man named Roy something or other. If he was an accident, which he was, then she was an accidental mother. Even when she took part in the functions one expected a mother to take part in (birthday parties, soccer games, neighborhood picnics, school events), she seemed to be attending them ironically. It was as if she were pretending to be a single white middle-class mother — a paralegal, of all things — while in reality she was something else altogether.

True, she leveraged her charm. She was a bit of a vamp. She wore cowboy boots and skirts and blouses unbuttoned one button too far. She chewed gum with the artful ability to pop it whenever she thought she wasn't being attended to. And she had a little mole above her lip, to the right of and just below her nose. She looked exactly like the kind of single mother who would sleep with your husband. He would learn much later, because she told him, that she was the kind who actually did. Bronfman had a lot of "uncles" wandering in and out of his life, their house, brief appearances by men with small roles, few lines. Some of them were lawyers; others were crooks those lawyers were defending. They all seemed pleasant enough, but detached in the way someone renting instead of buying is.

But it had been some time since the last one — Uncle Rajiv. Now Bronfman was the sole man in her life, and he was watching her rob his dog's grave. What was he supposed to do? Pull her away? Call someone? Nothing seemed to be the right thing, but standing there with a bottle of scotch and a pair of electric socks in his arms seemed especially wrong.

And then she stopped digging. She turned and looked at her son with a smile so sunny that it flaked off some of the dried mud on her cheeks.

"I found him," she said.

Bronfman followed his mother down the path back toward the house. She walked so slowly that it wasn't clear to him whether her momentum was enough to carry her forward, as if any second she might just fall backward, or to the left or the right, and if she did he wanted to be ready to catch her. In her arms, she was holding Barney's skull.

But they made it inside without calamity. She regained her balance, some strength, as if the air-conditioning (always kept shock-

ingly cold) had in it some restorative prop-
erties as well — caffeinated air. She took
the skull to the stainless-steel sink and set it
down like a dirty plate and turned on the
water. Bronfman stood behind her, helpless.

The water trickled out. The dirt washed
off the skull in thin brown streams. Dirt he
must have known as a child, dirt he must
have touched. That same dirt had been on
his fingers. That same dirt had been wet
with his tears.

"Look," she said. "Amazing. *That* was
Barney. Barney was inside there. Everything
that made him *him* was in this little package."

Bronfman touched his mother's bony
shoulder. She could feel his concern. "Not
to worry. Just investigating the cycle of life.
I'm next up, after all."

She laughed and focused on the bundles
he still carried in his arms — the socks, the
booze — and she beamed.

"Let's eat," she said. "Then drink."

He should have brought dinner. Why
hadn't he brought dinner? All she had was
one cold chicken leg wrapped in tinfoil, a
box of Triscuits, a package of stale American
cheese, each slice carefully separated from
the one above and the one below it by a

waxy sheet of plastic, and some Dijon mustard.

They ate off the same plate. She pushed the half-gnawed chicken leg toward him. He demurred. If he looked just a little to the left he could see into the kitchen, where Barney's skull was drying, glowing in the fluorescent kitchen light. "Thought you'd bring something to eat," she said, her tone shifting. "But life in a cube is hard."

"I'm sorry?"

"In a cube. Your little cubicle. I'm just happy that you're here."

He was having trouble following her.

"Did you take the subway?" she said.

"There's no subway in Birmingham."

She focused on his words, readjusted, as if tuning in to his frequency. She knew she had said something that wasn't quite right.

"Metaphorically, I mean."

"Then yes," he said. "I guess I did."

They were done with dinner in record time and retired to the living room. She sat in her overstuffed wingback chair with the uplifting floral pattern — yellows and blues and oranges against red — and he sat in the corner of the couch closest to the door. The scotch smelled like a cleaning agent, but she threw it back as if it were mountain water. He did not partake. She opened her socks and tugged them on.

"Toasty," she said. "Inside and out."

"You need to press the button on the side to turn them on."

She did so. "Even better," she said.

She sipped and sniffed at her whiskey, and an expression of such contentment enveloped her that Bronfman thought she might melt.

She smacked her satisfied lips. "So what's the big news?"

"What do you mean?" With the introduction of Barney's skull, her downhill momentum, and a feeling that he was at sea — metaphorically — he had briefly forgotten the game-changing telephone call.

"I can always tell when you have big news," she said. "When you made straight B's that time, I knew before you told me. When you passed your driver's test. It's a fifth sense."

"Sixth."

"I lost my sense of smell, I think, so I'm letting this one take its place."

It was warmish for mid-April, but the gas fire was turned on anyway, along with the AC. The logs were made of stained concrete and carved to look like wood. They had fooled more than one person. The fire itself flickered identically to the fire of thirty years ago, through the same prefabricated knotholes, as if there were some realities that could be repeated over and over without modification forever. In some ways, Bronfman had modeled his life on this fire.

"Okay," he said. "It's nothing, really. But it's still — I don't know."

"What is it?"

"Hardly worth mentioning."

"You're killing me, Edsel."

He took a deep, sustaining breath. "I won something," he said. "A free weekend at the beach, in Destin. At a brand-new condominium unit that sounds, well, very nice. I'm looking forward to it."

"And?"

"And what?"

She closed her eyes and smiled, then shook her head like an old nightclub jazz singer under the spell of a tune. "There is no such thing as a free lunch!" she proclaimed, as if to a large crowd. "There is always an *and,* an *if,* or a *but.* Which is it?"

All three, he thought, strictly speaking. "Nothing really. I just need to bring someone with me. A companion — you know, a girlfriend, something like that. A date, or a wife! Ha-ha! Because — well, I'm not sure why. It's just the rules."

"And do you have someone?"

"I don't," he said. "Not now. Not yet. But I have a couple of months before the offer expires. I think that if I really put my mind to it I might be able to find someone by then. Don't you?"

His mother, Muriel Bronfman, regarded him. Estimated him. Took his measure, and then took a small sip from her tumbler and swished it around a little. Grimaced. "No," she said. "Honestly? I don't. I doubt it. I seriously doubt it." Then, apparently dismayed by his own apparent dismay, she said, "Don't you doubt it as well?"

"Well, I think . . . I think it won't be easy. But —"

She snorted a laugh. "You should run for president."

"Why?"

"The way you talk. In flip-floppy same-isms."

Gibberish. It felt like this with her sometimes lately, that she was in another time-space dimension and they were having two different conversations at the same time, and then, somewhere down the line, they would come together again. Silence settled in for a second, two. Then she aimed her gaze at him.

"So you're not seeing anybody, Edsel?"

"Not presently," he said. "But . . . so? Not everybody in the world is seeing somebody else right now. But maybe —"

"Maybe nothing. You're starting way at the back of the pack. I mean seriously, Edsel. Seriously. Did you ever even date? In high school — if memory serves, and God knows it doesn't anymore, not really — I don't remember you dating. I don't remember you dating *anyone.* You've never brought a single girl/woman/anything into this house to meet me, or gone out to see one, as far as I know. Not one. In all. Of. Your. Life. Do you realize that?"

"Do I realize that? Of course I do. And that's sort of true. But you don't know everything. I have been on dates. A few."

She shook her head. "A few dates . . . good God. A few dates. That's very odd, Edsel. You're thirty-four years old."

Night was falling. Bronfman couldn't look at her. Instead, he looked over her shoulder at a vase full of flowers and weird plants: a big yellow gladiola, a carnation, a pussy willow. None of them, he realized then, were real. The carnation was made of fabric, the pussy willow of what looked like Styrofoam painted brown. This was the home Bronfman had grown up in, where he had lived all his life until he went off to college, and

81

these flowers had been there for as long as he could remember, yet he had never noticed that they weren't real.

"You know I couldn't give a flying fuck, Edsel, but if you're gay you could tell me. No need to be ashamed."

"Mom." He wasn't gay, had nothing against people who were, but the fact that she thought he could be hurt his feelings, as if his failure with women could mean only one thing. Also, "flying fuck"? What was that?

She nodded, lips pursed, as though the fact that he wasn't gay was bad news. She regarded him as a carnivore does her prey in the moment before she eats him. "Edsel," she said, very slowly, very carefully, her eyes narrowed. "Have you ever even —"

He knew where she was going with this and headed her off at the pass. "Really? Mom. *Really?* Please, you have to stop."

She was not going to ask him this. She was not.

She was.

"— *been* with a woman? Had actual sex? Done the deed? Have you . . . Jesus . . . *are* you . . . *are you???* . . . have you never —"

"Yes!" he bellowed, trumpeted, and maybe lied. "Good Lord. Of *course* I have!"

She held up both of her tiny shaky hands, as if they might protect her from his oncoming indignation. But his indignation did not have the horsepower to reach her and stalled halfway across the living-room floor.

Because, of course, there was no *of course* about it.

Bronfman had been in the intimate vicinity of a woman only once in his life, and that was when he was fifteen years old — nineteen years ago. A girl, really, she had been the only one, and that had been it, the only time, the lone instance he had been with a female in that circumstance, both of them mostly naked, sitting on ready. What actually happened that day was debatable, however, and he had debated it with himself for all these years. *Something* had happened, but because whatever happened hadn't happened since, and he had no basis for comparison, he wasn't sure. In short, it was possible that Bronfman, in fact, had technically never had sex with a woman — that he, at thirty-four, was still a virgin.

His mother sighed, and smiled, and shrugged her puny shoulders.

"Methinks thou protesteth too much," she said softly, pleased with herself, nodding, pursing her lips in a pleasant affirmation, throwing back a swallow. "I'm going to use that word more often. Methinks. *Methinks.* Methinks I like it." She lifted her legs and wiggled her toes and smiled to herself, almost seeming happy, but then her old bloodshot eyes filled up with water. "It's my fault, isn't it?" she said. "I coddled you. I should have pushed you out of the nest with more vigor. But I was afraid you couldn't fly."

She shook her head and wiped her cheek, and her eyes looked far away, as if she were watching a montage from the past.

"Not everyone needs to fly," he said.

It wasn't over. Her attention drifted to other things — the persistence of dust, to books she'd never read but wished she had, to the checkout girl at the Piggly Wiggly — until, after her third scotch, she began to sniffle, then cry. Just a few tears, but enough for her cheeks to reflect the light from the lamp beside her. And yet something about them seemed forced, unreal, as if her eyes were merely leaking.

"Mom? What's wrong?"

"Your father's dead," she said. She wiped her nose with the back of her hand. "He died. I'm so sorry to break it to you like this. But I couldn't hold back a minute more."

"My father? What father? How do you — ? I thought . . . you always told me —"

"I spent less time with him than I have with the cashier at the Piggly Wiggly. Wouldn't recognize him now if he bit me. That's true, to some degree. But he came to see me, Edsel."

"He came to see you? Where? Here? Did he *die* here?" Bronfman had a flair for imagining death scenes.

"No, of course not. It was after. It was his *spirit,* or whatever it's called. His essence. Everything that's left after everything else is gone. I don't know. But he was here, right where you're sitting now."

Bronfman suddenly felt uneasy in the chair, as if he might be sitting in an ectoplasmic residue.

"I know what you're thinking," she said. "Why would he come to see me?" That was not what he was thinking. "But it's clear as day to me. These people, when they come back? They come back for a *reason.* With a *message.* When you die that's what happens, I think. You're in with the in-crowd. You are in the know."

"Probably true," he said.

"Probably? I'm certain. That's where the truth is now, Edsel, up there. All we can see down here is a bad mimeograph of it. But dead, dead you know everything." She leaned her head back against the chair's cushion and her watery eyes gleamed. "He was a sight. Nice as could be, too. First time in thirty-five years."

"So now I am wondering," he said. "Why you?" He was appealing to whatever residual rationality she possessed; maybe she'd realize nothing had really happened if he presented things to her logically. And it wasn't logical that this man's ghost would visit her. He probably had a lot of other, more important stops, since out of all the hours in his life he had been with Muriel for only two of them. "You barely knew him. You were in a room with the lights off for most of your relationship. Surely he has better things to do than come see you."

"Not *me*," she said. "He didn't come to see me. It was for you! He had a message for you."

Bronfman settled deeper in his chair (where the ghost of his father had recently been) and took an inventory of the evening: the grave digging, the chicken-leg dinner, the scotch, the smoking, the invasive questions. Now this. What had happened to his mother? Her brain was like a trapped squirrel, frantically trying to find some way out of her head. She would say anything! Until now, his father had never even been spoken of in human terms; he might as well have been an errant sperm flying wildly through the air in a windstorm. And now he had made a special trip to see his accidental son with a message from the beyond.

"But you said you never told him about me."

"I didn't, Edsel," she said. She was losing her patience with him. "But, as I said and will say again, he's dead. He *knows* about you now."

"Okay, sorry."

She held out her glass for a little more scotch. He poured some, and when she didn't drink it or move her hand he poured her some more. Then she drank. She took a second to reflect, or to invent, what happened next.

"He regretted dying before getting a chance to know you. He was glum about it."

"Glum. A glum ghost. They are the worst."

"Now you're having fun with me," she said.

"No, Mom, I'm not," he said. "It's just that if he came back —"

"If?"

"What?"

"You said 'if.' "

"Yes. If he came back."

"But he did come back. I just told you he

did. There is no damn *if* about it."

She waited for him to endorse her. And waited. She was almost crying again.

"Okay. Okay. But if he wanted to tell me something why didn't he just come to me? Tell me himself?"

Her eyes flicked on, shimmered, flashed. "He knew I wouldn't mind seeing him again, I guess. It was a nice gesture."

"Okay," Bronfman said. "I'll bite. What did he say?"

"He said . . . be yourself."

"Be myself?" His disappointment was palpable. "That's the worst advice I've gotten in my life."

"Not that self, Edsel. Listen, Roy had the world wrapped around his little finger. That's your father in a nutshell. The most charming man I ever met, bar none. Sold his soul to the Devil for that smile! And quite the lover. Don't look at me like that. More information than you need, perhaps, but that's the stuff you came from, and you should know it. You need to know it. I was a fool for his bedroom hocus-pocus, mesmerized when he gnawed at my neck. Thrummed when the palms of his hands rubbed my arms, shoulders, hips, thighs. He lived, Edsel — that's the thing. That's all I want you to know and all he wants you to know. He lived life the way it should be lived, to its fullest. Savoring every moment and collecting those moments like rain in a cup. His cup runneth over."

"Mother," he said.

"Bottom line is he wants you to take a page from his book."

"That's what my father came back to say? To be more like him?"

"That's it," she said. "Pretty much."

Bronfman didn't believe her, of course. There was nothing about the story that could even remotely be true outside of the brain of a woman who was losing her mind, or a woman who was making this all up to try and make him feel better. That being said, he was open to believing in the message, the context, the vote in his favor — to having a father cheering in the stands for his son to make the big touchdown. He had never thought that he wanted a father, or to make a touchdown, but now he found himself wanting both, in the same way you swear off dessert until the waiter brings you the menu and you see how good everything looks.

"So he thinks I can do it?" Bronfman asked her. "Get a companion in seventy-eight days?"

She shrugged. "Absolutely," she said. "If

you give it all you've got."

"But you don't think I can."

"I didn't say that."

"Well, actually, you did say that. That's exactly what you said."

She drew back and peered at him. Her chin appeared to disappear into her neck. "Edsel, dear. I'm your mother. I know you better than anyone ever will. It's not a thrilling prospect, but it doesn't really matter, because it's true. You've always been exactly who you are. Hesitant. A second-guesser of second guesses. I was in labor with you for two and a half days because you wouldn't come out. You just wouldn't. You were such a careful child. Quiet, and so easy you were almost intolerable. You cleaned up around your own high chair when you were two years old. You started making the bed when you were five. If there was rain in the forecast, you insisted on taking two umbrellas to school, just in case you lost one of them. Sweetie, I love you. I wouldn't trade you for anything. But you were never . . . *in* the world. Not like I was. Not like Roy."

"Oh, really. And what was that like?"

She turned her good ear toward him. "Come again?"

"What was it like to be 'in the world,' as you put it? Because all I could see, from the safe and quiet spot I watched from, was a woman who was alone for about half of the time, and for half of the other half was introducing me to some new 'uncle,' who was on occasion an ex-con, which was fine, of course, no judgment implied, and the rest of the time realizing what a huge mistake she'd made with this last one and went off in search of another. And Roy — my father — I've learned more about him today than I have in thirty-four years. But that's not surprising, because there's really not much you can tell me, is there? After all, you didn't know him a lot longer than I did. So if I'm a careful person, as you put it, or hesitant, or just plain dull, which I really think is what you're getting at, maybe it's because I've seen the alternative."

He stopped. Realizing it had been some time since he last took a breath, he breathed. His mother was deathly still, but she wasn't dead (was she?). No, she was alive. She was more of a wax sculpture of herself than herself. What had he said? Even now, just seconds after he'd finished, he couldn't exactly remember. He had been hurtful, though. He was sure of that. He could tell by the taste the words left in his mouth: bitter, metallic, covered in rust from years of being unused. And he could tell by his mother, who looked as though she were lifting herself up from the mat just a count or two before the end of the fight.

Her cheeks had reddened; her breath was shallow. Three little veins beneath her eyes — lost tributaries — glowed purple. She leaned back in her chair hard, as if pushed there by an emotional g-force. She closed her eyes, self-composing, and came back a few seconds later all better. Grinning, in fact. Her eyes glistening with what was, unmistakably, love.

"That," she said, "was impressive. There may be hope for you yet."

The air-conditioning hummed on then, and the window curtains billowed, as if a ghost, satisfied with how things had turned out, was making his final departure.

Bronfman decided to stay the night. He could wear to work tomorrow the clothes he wore today. He walked his mother to the door of her bedroom. Before she closed it, he said, "I understand why you'd think I can't do this — find someone at the drop of a hat. But I do have a plan. I'm going to put myself out there. I'm going to make friends, because I think having friends will make me feel like a part of the world. I'm even going to exercise more. Possibly. My overall goal is to face my fears. If I do that, something positive might occur. This is my plan, anyway."

His mother hugged him tighter than he would have thought possible. She let go and looked at him.

"My little boy," she said, "plans never go according to plan. That's what makes them exciting. It's all chance and luck and timing. I never wanted a kid, not ever, and look — I got you. And I'm glad I did. I am unbelievably happy you're my son. But I don't think you understand how life works yet, and maybe that's my fault, but what the hell, my job here is done." She stood on her tiptoes and gave him a kiss on the cheek. "Oh — re-inter Barney for me? The hole's still there. Just drop him in and cover. Thanks, sweetie. Good night."

He went through the house turning off all the lights; she liked to sleep with them on when she was here by herself. At night her house shone like an ocean liner against a velvet sky. In the kitchen, he picked up Barney's skull and took it out back and, by the occasional light of his cell phone, re-interred him. But he held his skull for almost a full minute before setting him down in the hole he came from. He wondered about Barney's last breaths on earth, running free, the whole world spread out before him, nothing but possibility and one meaty bone after another in his future. Then came that car. It seemed impossible that these bones were ever him. Barney, a basset hound, wasn't really lively, but he had a specific personality. Even-tempered, habitually unimpressed, even melancholic, the tips of his ears always a little wet from where they fell into his water dish. He had a theatrical sigh and an air of disappointment that seemed to weigh him down. He was the perfect dog for Bronfman.

Bronfman buried him and, stumbling over rocks and roots, went back inside. He took a swig of the scotch right out of the bottle, and it almost killed him. Doors locked, lights off, he went up the stairs to his old room, the one he had lived in all his life until he left it, where he dreamed his secret dreams and where, when he was fifteen, he almost removed the shirt of Cathy Biggs, vice-president of the honor society, but who at the last minute changed her mind. Chance, timing, luck. He thought about her, and he thought about his mother, and Barney, and he thought of Mary Day McCauley, as he did so often, Mary Day — the girl he may well have had sex with nineteen years ago — and of Sheila McNabb, Sheila whom he would never see again. Luck: bad. Of course (he told himself over and over), he didn't know what might have happened if she had been at her desk this afternoon. It was possible that he wouldn't have been able to speak to her, and if he had and they had continued their conversation later, maybe at a wine bar, with a cheese plate, it was possible they wouldn't have liked each other at all. But he didn't think so. He thought that, had they gone out that evening, one thing would have led to another and they would really have hit it off, clicked, and he would probably have kissed her good night (a fantasy if there ever was one) and, as she was turning to leave, he would have told her about the condominium in Florida. "Something to think about," he might have said. And she would have smiled. Though that may have been rushing things. Regardless, it was possible that she would have liked him.

As he masturbated in the very bed where he had learned how to masturbate, where he had practiced masturbating for so long, he imagined the two of them — Sheila and him — not on the balcony holding hands, watching the waves swell and fade, the sun glow, the breeze blow; and not even in the bedroom, naked beneath those slightly

95

scratchy new-condo sheets. He imagined them sitting side by side at the short presentation, in uncomfortable folding chairs, watching the young/old, short/tall, skinny/ fat man/woman highlight all the wonderful things about Sandscapes — its location, its square footage, its affordable luxury. But they would not be listening. They would be sharing secret silent thoughts with each other — thoughts like *armadillo, cormorant, kookaburra, buffalo.*

SEVEN

Mary Day McCauley. His first, his only, love.

Not his first crush. His first was in third grade; he was eight years old, and her name was Ellen Peters. She had the glossy mane of a golden filly, though at the time Bronfman thought of her hair merely as soft-looking, pretty. He never touched it, but that was all he wanted to do with his life at the time — touch it once, or maybe a million times, and not even with his fingers but with the palm of his hand, his right hand, stroking it gently, as you might the back of a cat. He was an awkward boy, goofy, his pants too short and his shirt too tight, too quiet to be smart or smart enough to stay quiet. It wasn't clear which then, and it never would be clear, not for the rest of his life. Ellen's skin was golden-brown all year round. For show-and-tell once she brought a photo, cut out of the local newspaper, of her on a beach with a manatee. She was in a bathing suit of unknown color, it being newsprint, black and white. The lower half of her body was invisible behind the hulking mass of the gentle giant, and you could imagine, as maybe Bronfman did, that Ellen was a mermaid, a very young one. So she was famous now, which made her both more and less desirable to him, but mostly more.

How did she know how he felt? He never even spoke to her. She sat three rows away, two rows behind; the only time he got a good look at her was when they filed out for lunch or to the playground. She could sense his obsession, his overweening desire, and — wise as she was, even at eight — she did not accept his valentine on Valentine's Day, even though it was the rule that you brought one for every member of the class and everyone brought one for you. He tried to hand her his valentine (sealed in its tiny white envelope), and she turned away. No favoritism here. Quite the opposite: *un*favoritism. It stuck with him, this cold rebuff, like a tattoo. It marked him not as the man he was but as the man he would become.

Unrequited love. That was too big a word — too big an idea — for Bronfman, and it didn't really apply. Unrequited love implies a possibility, however remote, of requital, and there was none with Ellen, not in this or in any world. So it happened then and so it would happen later. Ellen Peters became his heart's motif, the poorly wrapped package that romance came to him in, this girl with the hair of a beautiful animal, friend of the manatee, exotic, famous, forever tanned, perfect and perfectly remote.

And the next? Mary Day McCauley, almost a decade later. This is how it happened with her.

Since ninth grade Mary Day McCauley had been swimming around in Bronfman's brain like one of those dusty floaters he saw when he closed his eyes. So many years had passed and she had remained more than a memory. Memories fade, grayed out by time. Mary Day was destined to stay fresh forever, an indelible persistence in the swampy cortex of his brain.

Back at Baldwin High, he saw her all the time, at a distance, as if he were under a self-imposed restraining order: at school, around town, and on weekends at parties so huge — ragers, they were called — even he was invited. He watched her with her boyfriend, Corey Spaulding. He saw them kissing at least four different times: once in the hallway at school, once outside the school against Corey Spaulding's car, once at the mall where Bronfman was shopping with his mother, and another time in the aisle of a drugstore where Corey Spaulding bought a pack of Trojans.

Corey was a sixteen-year-old skateboarder with wiry blond hair, an icy smile, and pale gray eyes that seemed to be looking at you as if from underwater. He was stoned most of the time, but that was back when most people were stoned most of the time. Mary Day was fifteen. High-school girls always liked the slightly older guys. The older guys didn't seem scared the way Bronfman did. Girls — even the wispy, elfin, shy girls, the girls who had some equalizing deficiency — frightened Bronfman. Corey didn't seem scared of anything, the way he weaved in and out of traffic on his skateboard and smoked a cigarette while doing it. Corey stayed Mary Day's boyfriend for more than two years, off and on (they had a couple of very public, very emotional breakups), and probably would have hung around even longer had he not become addicted to something like cocaine or meth. Nothing worked out for him after that. Eventually, he just disappeared.

Mary Day wasn't wild. She was just fun, open-hearted. She was so beautiful and game — a spitfire, his mother would have called her. One of those rare girls who were genuinely sweet, even though she was so pretty she didn't have to be. Long brown hair, bangs, green eyes, a smile that spanned her face like a silver sliver of the moon. She was full of grace and energy. One summer she helped build a house for an indigent family, and every Christmas she caroled with a traveling choir, singing to the homeless, and leaving them with a hot meal of turkey, mashed potatoes with gravy, and collards. Bronfman didn't have to idealize her, because she was the ideal, a wonder of the world, not unlike the Hanging Gardens of Babylon or the Leaning Tower of Pisa.

It was one of those Saturday-afternoon concerts they used to have in the amphitheater at Caraway Park, where garage bands would play loud and sing unintelligibly, songs that never seemed to end but, rather, petered out, as if the musicians simply got tired of playing. Bronfman knew that most of the people in the park were high on something. He wasn't high, of course; he never felt compelled to part that curtain, then or now. A couple of creepy old men in tattered hats with tangled beards had openly tried to sell him stuff, from pot to other items with mysterious names, but he waved them away. "I'm sorry," he said. "Thank you, but no." He listened to the bands sitting directly on the patchy grass, his knees pulled up to his chest. He sat with a couple of the guys he knew from school — Frank Brower, Marcus Collier. Two boys who, like him, lived uncomplicated, risk-free lives. There was something perfect about that afternoon, a spacey freedom that made his life seem magical. Sun breaking through the branches as if through chinks in heaven, sometimes a breeze, singing, Frisbees, careless laughter. Good times.

That Saturday afternoon in the park the grass was a lush bed of green, the sky as blue and deep as the ocean, the sun a pulsating buttery yellow. Even the shadows felt more real, substantial as the trees that cast them. Bronfman was wearing the blue-jean shorts his mother had bought for him — not even cutoffs but actual shorts! — and a tie-dyed T-shirt manufactured by a corporation, probably overseas. He had taken his shoes off and secreted them behind an oak. Already he had stepped on a rock and bruised a heel, and he was trying not to pay attention to the pain when Mary Day McCauley sat down beside him.

"Hey, Edsel," she said.

Hey, Edsel. He had no words, no voice to respond. Why was she speaking to him? It didn't make sense. The first thing he thought to say–*You know my name?* — he wisely chose not to share with her.

"Hey, Mary Day," he said. It came out weird, stilted and wooden, as if he were in class answering a question that he wasn't sure he knew the answer to. She was wearing a pink spaghetti-strap blouse and cutoff jeans and no bra. Her breasts, which he could see without really trying to look, were actually quite small and simple. Perfect.

She gestured toward the band. "They're good."

"I think so, too," he said, though he had no real opinion about them. Maybe they were good, maybe they weren't, but now he knew: they were good. "The drummer can really play."

"Nicholas Brown," she said. "I've known him since pre-school. He used to pick his nose obsessively and wipe it on the back of his shorts." She laughed and hit her forehead with the palm of her hand. "Oh, my God! That's a terrible thing to say." She fell back onto the grass laughing. "I'm awful."

"No, you're not."

She stopped laughing but stayed down where she was, staring up into the sky. "I like Reese," she said. "You know her? Reese Alexander?"

He shook his head.

"She sings here sometimes," she said. "Pretty. Really long blond hair? She goes to Baldwin."

He shook his head again. He wished he could stop shaking his head. He wished he knew something.

"Look at this," she said.

"What?"

"Get down here."

He lowered himself backward until he was lying on the ground beside her, the rounded edge of her bare shoulder touching his. He didn't breathe, for fear an inhalation would separate them. Already he was in love with her. There was no doubt about it. He'd pledge allegiance to her. He'd have stolen a car and run over a dog if she'd asked him to.

He stared upward.

"See how the branches of that tree are poking into the bottom of that cloud?" she asked him.

"Yes."

"It looks like a marshmallow on a stick, about to be roasted by the sun."

"Yes, that's exactly what it looks like."

He wasn't just saying that, either. This was

exactly how it looked. He never would have
thought of it himself, but, now that she'd
said it he saw it clear as day. A marshmallow on a stick. They were quiet for a minute
— one full, entire minute. Bronfman was a
human chronometer even then. He felt
time, knew it the way other people had
perfect pitch.

Then she spoke.

"Your parents named you after a car," she
said.

"I'm sorry?"

"Edsel. It's an old car, right?"

"It's a family name."

"I see." He glanced at her. She was still
gazing at the sky. "It's a weird family name,"
she said.

"Edsel was the name of Henry Ford's
son," Bronfman said, parroting his mother,
whom he had heard give this rationalization
a hundred times. "My grandfather was Edsel Ford's best friend."

"Then that's not a family name," Mary
Day said. "That's somebody else's family
name."

"Oh, yeah. I guess so," Bronfman said,
and they laughed and laughed.

There was more of her arm against his
arm now, and this was how it went for the
next hour. They talked about nothing —

how dirt felt between your toes, ticklish grass, what clouds might taste like, the best way to prank a sub, and the odious Mrs. Watson, the principal of Baldwin High. It was the longest conversation Bronfman had ever had with a person who was not his mother.

Then she stopped talking, and so did he, and they let the rock-and-roll assault them, until Bronfman felt sure she was staring at him. He let his head loll to one side and, yes, yes, she was staring at him, and her face was close enough to his that he could feel her breath on his nose. Her lips were pink and wet; her cheeks were freckle-scattered. Her eye-lashes were long and thick enough to catch raindrops — eye awnings.

"So," Bronfman said.

She took his hand, found it without having to look for it, breathing in short and shallow breaths. "There's something about you I love," she said.

"What?"

"I said there's something about you I love. Everything about you. Everything. You're a person."

"I don't know what you mean."

"Neither do I! It's just how I feel."

But she didn't laugh. She smiled at him. It was okay that neither of them knew what she meant. It was okay.

He would not say another word. Could not. Their eyes were locked in a never-ending gaze, his drawn into hers as if through a tractor beam. She drew her fingers down his cheek, to the very edge of his lips. It felt as if she was trying to open his mouth with her index finger, but she didn't linger there. She traced the outline of his chin, and then explored the inner regions of his ear, watching her finger as she did it, as if she didn't know what it might do next and she wanted to see. Bronfman watched himself lying on the ground beside her, circling above them both like a falling leaf.

"I took a little ecstasy," she said. "Not much, but, you know. A little."

"Oh," he said. He wasn't sure what that was, and it didn't really matter to him. "Sounds good."

"It is," she said. "Very. I like how it feels."

Then she said she had a friend, or a friend of a friend, or maybe it was her older sister's friend. Anyway, this guy had a place near the park, a room in a house, and she knew where he kept the key. "Come with me there," she said, and she pulled him up from the grass and they walked not talking, just taking the necessary steps, traversing the distance. The key was hidden beneath a foot-worn black rubber WELCOME mat. *Welcome, Bronfman. Welcome to the rest of your life.* They walked inside. *Welcome to the new world, Bronfman,* one so murky after the flashy bright of that July day that he saw nothing at all. Mary Day lit a candle. It was a bare place: a futon with a blue milk crate beside it, on one wall the torn poster of a rock-and-roll celebrity whom Bronfman couldn't name but felt he should be able to. One lonely white sock in a corner.

"Here." She pulled him by his wrist down onto the futon and laced her arms around him. She was pushing against him with her body, breathing in gasps, her warm breath against his neck, sweating. Then, all of a sudden, she held him so tight. As if she were about to fall through the floor and he was the only thing that could save her. He felt her full-on then, all of her. She was made of sturdy stuff.

As he looked back on it now it all seemed so unreal, but it seemed unreal the second it was actually happening to him, too. He remembered wishing he could stop thinking so much about being with her when he actually was with her, but even then, in the present, he couldn't stop thinking about how truly incredible it would seem in the future, how far-fetched, and how being here with Mary Day was something he would remember for the rest of his life, this watching her lift her blouse over her head the way she did, as though she were unveiling a piece of art. It was an experience he would have traded a year of his life to have again. Really. A year.

And then he lost track of time — Bronfman, who never lost track of time. Or no, not lost. He got off the track of time. Somehow she unbuckled his belt and pushed off his pants with her feet. And then, though he had never had instruction of any kind, ever, from anyone (is this something a father would have taught him?), he found himself on top of her. A shaft of sun exploded through a break in the blinds and the air was all tight and still and hot, and there was a fan now — he remembered the sound of a fan, the white plastic fan that did nothing to keep them from pouring sweat — and then the yellow cat that was suddenly there, staring at them with those crazy black eyes. *Where did the cat come from?* Face to face with Mary Day, eye to eye, and she lifted her knees into the air and bent her legs and guided him into her with her right hand while her left rested on the small of his back.

But he knew now that something was

wrong. Even though he had never done this before, he knew that everything was happening too fast for him, and that it was over before it had even started. He came before he was fully inside her. He was inside her, he thought, to some degree. But how far? An inch? Half an inch? Less? Some scientifically measurable amount? And then it was over and she was patting him on the back, so sweetly, and saying, "It's okay, Edsel. It's okay. Let's just lie here."

The next time he saw Mary Day (two days later, more?) she hugged him and gave him that look — that secret look, like *You and I know what happened but nobody else does, or will. Ever. Okay?*

But that was the problem: he didn't know what had happened, not to this day. Only she did. Where was she now? Probably in New York City or Paris or Hollywood. He would never see her again. He would never be able to ask. He would never know. Surely other men had suffered similarly, but other men had been given a chance for a do-over. Not Bronfman. And he never found the shoes he'd secreted by the tree. They had been stolen. "At least you went barefoot," his mother said when she picked him up at dusk. "I bet that felt good."

"Yes," he said. "I think it did."

DAY THREE

ONE

When Edsel came downstairs the morning after his mother's birthday, he found a glass of orange juice on the table in what his mother always called the morning room. It wasn't really a room, just an alcove off the kitchen with a small round table and a couple of small wicker chairs where the sun shone bright and liquid in spring and summer. Today the light was like a flood; he had to squint and look away while his eyes adjusted. The bird feeder on the other side of the window had been hijacked by squirrels.

"Morning!" came his mother's cheerful greeting.

He sat down in one of the chairs. She delivered a cup of coffee — "Cream and sugar, just the way you like it!" — and ruffled the hair on the top of his head, as she had for as long as he could remember.

She sat down. She'd taken a shower; her

113

war paint was gone. She picked up a wasabi pea from a bowl on the table and tossed it at the window. The sudden crack against the pane scared the squirrels away, at least for a minute.

"They drive me insane," she said. "Totally, completely insane."

But she wasn't insane. She was fine — look at her! Where had last night's mother gone? Maybe things weren't as bad as they seemed. Maybe she'd had one of those really minor, almost harmless strokes. He'd heard they were the speed bumps of the brain, nothing to get too concerned about.

"So, honey," she said.

He sipped his orange juice and raised his eyebrows. "Umm," he said.

She had something to say. That's how she introduced a conversation of import.

"So when you moved into your new apartment, I'm guessing you put me down as an emergency contact."

"Yes," he said. "Who else would I have put?"

"That's fine," she said. "Of course. It's just — the manager of your complex, a Mr. . . . I can't remember his name."

"Endicott," he said. "He called you?"

"Just a few minutes ago."

Bronfman waited. His mother stood up

quickly and rescued the bread from the toaster: smoke signals were rising. She placed the toast on a small plate and gave it a swipe of butter.

"Well, apparently," she said, gently setting the plate down in front of him, "you were broken into last night."

"My *apartment?*" he said, as if he had several places that might have been broken into — a summer home, a boat, a storage shed.

"I'm afraid so."

She touched his hand.

"That's terrible," he said. He stood with no real goal in mind. People just don't sit during emergencies. Then he looked at his mother. "I have to go there, now. Right?"

He had always looked to his mother for affirmation, which is why last night had been particularly hard for him: he knew he wouldn't be able to do that anymore. But this morning it seemed that she could help him, one last time.

"You should go, but before you do I have a little story of my own to share. A man broke in here, too, not long ago."

"You never told me that," he said, alarmed. "Why didn't you tell me that?"

"I didn't think you'd want to know. But if you do I'll tell you. He was gorgeous. I was

115

in my bathrobe, and I met him at the door. I'd heard him scraping at the lock. He came in and I opened my bathrobe. That's when I realized he was actually the man who had fixed my car, and I always knew he wanted me. He threw me against the wall and we, um, kissed."

She winked at him.

"Oh, Mother," he said, sighing. "You're not feeling well."

"I'm fine, sweetie," she said. "Now run like the wind! Mr. Eckelberg hasn't called the police yet, leaving that decision in your hands. Take your toast."

He did take it, and drove to King's Manor, taking small bites out of the crunchy toast at stoplights. The world was falling apart around him. Bread crumbs gathered on his lap.

TWO

He parked in the empty space in front of his apartment. Absolutely no one was there — *where was Mr. Endicott?* — and his door was open to the air. He was stunned, almost in shock, detached, watching himself walk in. Maybe it wasn't that bad, he thought. Maybe they'd only taken a couple of things.

Nope. They'd taken everything: the toaster oven, the change jar, the white plastic alarm clock, the wall-mounted telephone, the antique footrest, the tabletop television set ($129 at Target, with a remote control, built-in DVD player, the works, almost new). They took his knives and his forks and his spoons (he had two of each) and the steak knife, *and* the knife he used to quarter apples. They even took his apples. The list was practically endless: a half-used roll of toilet paper, an embattled tube of Crest, the German beer, a towel, his favorite pillow, his cowboy hat — yes, his cowboy hat, they took even that. He'd almost forgotten it was there until he saw that it was gone. Tucked in the corner at the back of his bedroom closet, the cowboy hat (too small now for the head of most adult-size humans) was the only souvenir he had kept from his childhood, and maybe the only souvenir he had from his entire life. Though it probably qualified as an antique by now, based on the number of years that had elapsed since its manufacture, it was worthless, just a straw hat with a silver sheriff's star pinned to the front of it. On the cowboy-hats-for-kids-market, it might fetch a quarter. But they took that, too. The only thing they didn't take was the jar full of monogrammed ballpoint pens he'd been collecting for the past ten years or so. He had almost a hundred. Many of them had come in the mail — Scott's Plumbing had sent one, and so had a local Realtor's office. Others he'd lifted from the display container near the cash register. That's where he got Klondike's Tire Service and Camelot Records. Looked as if they were all there. The burglar must not have seen them. It didn't occur to Bronfman that they'd been seen and left behind.

Bronfman called the police, of course, immediately, and no more than fifteen minutes

118

later a black-and-white patrol car eased into his treeless complex. Then another car came. Two police cars! Kind of amazing, really, that they would send two police cars for this, for him. Bronfman stood on the cement platform in front of the door to his apartment and watched as one of the policemen lifted himself out of his car, so slowly it looked as though he had just awakened from a nap. This was supposed to be a porch Bronfman was on — *a stoop.* When he rented the apartment the manager had placed a small metal chair on it, as if this was where a man might while away an hour or so in the evening, drinking a beer, smoking a cigar, watching the traffic out on the two-lane highway rumble by. But it wasn't a porch. It was no more than a slab of concrete bordered by clumps of clay, tiny anthills, snake-size black holes and grass shoots numbering in the dozens.

The policeman stood, stretched, and as Bronfman watched him uncurl he realized: he wasn't a he at all. He was a she. *A lady policeman,* Bronfman thought, then, correcting himself, *A policewoman.* He had seen one before, of course, on television, and in real life, too, at a distance, but he was pretty sure he had never seen one up close, and certain he'd never had the opportunity to speak with one, as he was just about to do. He couldn't help thinking that this was a sign. That maybe he had been broken into for a reason. Because it was nothing short of miraculous that another woman would be presented to him in such close proximity. Slowly she approached and, as she did, gave the complex a quick once-over, her expression a cocktail of boredom and disgust. Closer still, she acknowledged Bronfman as briefly as she possibly could, took a long, deep, and thoroughly disappointed breath and waved the other car away. Bronfman knew what this meant: before getting to the actual scene of the crime, she knew that, even at its worst, it wouldn't be worth a second cop.

The policewoman made her way up the curb and removed her sunglasses with a laid-back flourish. She had short, sandy-blond hair, high cheekbones, a strong chin, but with no makeup her face took on a tomboyish flavor. She wasn't slight by any means — she appeared to be as solid as an ox — but up close there was no mistaking her for a man. How quickly — and against his will, really — an image of her appeared before his eyes in a semi-sheer off-white sleeveless blouse, and a patterned skirt, and red shoes with a little bit of heel — transforming her, just like that, from a tough and humorless enforcer of laws into a woman, the way it's done in books and plays. Bronfman believed that other people had other selves, even if he didn't think he himself had one. She walked up the battered sidewalk with the slow, steady gait of a sheriff from the Old West, an old coot who had seen it all, was afraid of nothing, trusted no one, was essentially lonely and unloved but for that one sweetheart long ago. She gazed beyond him, or around him, not directly at him. Bronfman shifted his weight from one foot to the other, uncomfortable. Why wouldn't she look at him? Probably just absorbing the crime scene. Entrances, exits, telltale clues. Putting it all together in her sharp-as-a-tack professional mind.

She ambled up, stuck out her hand, and Bronfman took it. He predicted a strong grip, but, even so, she surprised him. She nearly crushed his knuckles. One more pressure point and he'd have been on his knees.

"Officer Stanton," she said.

"Bronfman," he said. She waited. "Edsel Bronfman."

She wrote his name on a little pad.

She pointed to Bronfman's apartment. "This is where the incident occurred?"

"Yes," Bronfman said. "Last night. I

wasn't here." *I was staying with my mother,* he almost said.

She walked past him and, as she did, he noted some fragrance. He had no idea what it was, but it was nice, and he wondered if she got any pushback for it down at the station. *Stanton smells like a flower today. Maybe she's going to arrest some bees who stole some honey.* He kept close to her. Bronfman was an inch or two taller than Officer Stanton, and, who knows, maybe two or three years older. He was of an age where it was impossible to tell how old younger people were. He had yet to accept the idea that someone his junior could possibly be an adult, that such a person might even have children. And now here was another one, and she was a policeman. Wearing a gun and a pair of handcuffs. But no ring on her finger. Bronfman gave himself an imaginary pat on the back for noticing this — a detail that, even a few days ago, he would never have thought to see. He wanted to call Carla D'Angelo and let her know.

She did her slow walk from room to room as Bronfman followed behind. Bronfman never had people over — never — and now that one was here he realized what a shabby place his was, how provisional, the closest thing to a thatched hut America had to offer. She had something going on in her mouth. The little muscles around the edge of her jaw were rippling. Gum? Tobacco? Impossible to say.

"Happened last night?" she asked him.

"Yes," Bronfman said. "At some point. I've been gone since yesterday. I called the police immediately."

"Got it." Officer Stanton peered into the bedroom, and then into the smaller, second bedroom, which was entirely empty. She stood looking at that room for a second. She made a whistling sound. "Wow," she said. "They really cleaned you out."

"Oh, there was never anything in here."

"Nothing?"

He shook his head. "Not even an empty box."

"Computer?"

"I don't have one," Bronfman said.

For the first time since her arrival Officer Stanton stopped, turned, and really looked at him, a man who'd become interesting in a carnival-sideshow sort of way. "You don't have a *computer*?"

Bronfman shook his head.

"Not even an old one? A laptop?"

"I use the computer at work," he said. It was as if he were being cross-examined. He began to sweat. "Email. The Web. The whole Internet. I have it there. I don't know why I'd need one here." But now he felt as if he should have a computer, that he was wrong not to, that by not having one he had given her reason to see him in a diminished light.

Officer Stanton nodded. "Fair enough." Her jaw muscles quivered. "I think computers are taking away our brains, a little at a time. One day we'll wake up and they'll have everything, because we've given it to them of our own free will."

"That's scary," Bronfman said.

She shrugged. "Now it is," she said. "But it won't be. We won't care. We won't have the brains to care."

It took her a single minute to tour the entire apartment, after which she removed the sweat-stained miniature steno pad from her back pocket. She scribbled something. Bronfman tried to see what it was, but she kept one hand over the pad, as if it were a poker hand. Bronfman didn't have to read it, though, to know what she was thinking. She was thinking the same thing he was: *Why had someone perpetrated this ridiculous crime?* Bronfman himself, had he driven past a yard sale full of his own stuff, with a big free sign posted in front, would have passed it by. His stuff was cheap, used, unwanted. Bronfman was where stuff went in the weeks and months before it was taken to the dump. Bronfman was a hospice for things.

"I guess it's not the crime of the century," he said.

She laughed. *He has a sense of humor,* he wondered if she might be thinking. *I like a man with a sense of humor.* "The century is young," she said. "But you're right."

They stood in the narrow hallway, the walls bare except for holes where nails had once been hammered. This is where pictures should go, he often thought. That was a goal of his, pictures.

"I'm guessing this has never happened to you before?"

"No," he said. "Never."

"I'm sorry," she said. "The first time this happened to me I wanted to — well, let's just say I'd never been so angry and so . . . Not sure I can describe it. But then that's life, right? That's why I have a job."

"Why?"

"Because stuff happens. Stuff like this. Imagine a world in which I wasn't necessary."

"You?"

"Police," she said. "Law enforcement. A much different world from the one we've got, right?"

"Absolutely," he said.

"Here," she said. "Here's my card."

"You have a card?"

"I do."

He took it and looked at it. And there in the middle, in big letters, was this: her name. *Serena Stanton.*

"Serena," he said.

"Make a list of everything that was taken, especially possessions you have the serial numbers for, or a receipt, and write it all down. Scan it and attach it to an email and send it to my attention."

"Scan and attach," Bronfman said. He did that all the time on the printer at work. He could scan and attach as well as anyone. "By all means."

She took another look around, and Bronfman noted what he thought was a softening in her hardened gaze. "Honestly, Mr. Bronfman," she said. "I don't know if you'll ever see your belongings again. These are very tough cases to follow up on, and there are so many others out there, other more . . . well, I'll just say it — other more important cases. We don't have the resources."

"Of course," Bronfman said, following her out. "I understand completely. Murder, kidnapping, extortion. They take precedence."

"I mean we may never find out who did this."

"I see." Bronfman sighed. "And if I do?"

"I'm sorry?"

"If I find out who did this. Should I call you, or should I take matters into my own hands?"

Officer Stanton — Serena — took a long look at Bronfman, trying to get a read. She narrowed her eyes. "Do you know who did this, Mr. Bronfman?"

Bronfman shook his head and stubbed the soft black parking-lot asphalt with the toe of his shoe. "No," he lied. "But if I found out —"

"Call," Serena said. "You have my number."

"So it's okay to call you?"

"I just said it was."

"Okay. Great. Thank you. Thank you so much. Oh. One more thing?" She waited, eyebrows arched. "Your pen," he said. He had noticed that her pen was inscribed. *Birmingham Police Department.* Followed by the address, the phone number.

"Yes?"

"Do you think I could have it?"

"My pen?"

"Yes," he said. "I collect them. Pens."

He smiled, blushed: he knew how silly it sounded. But he really wanted her pen.

"No," she said. "You can't have my pen. I'm sorry."

"Understood," he said, crestfallen.

"I would, but it's the only one I have."

"Understood," he said again.

Then she got in her car and drove away, and Bronfman watched her go, waving at her as if she were family — a cousin, maybe — and kept waving until the car swam into the early-evening traffic and disappeared. He had her number. It was on a card — the first time a woman had ever given him one, but the second time his life might be changed by a card in just the past three days.

He walked back inside his sad apartment and looked at the places where things used to be. He knew exactly who had done this. Once he had proof he would call her, and they would meet for coffee, and he would give her the news.

THREE

It was Thomas Edison. Thomas Edison had stolen Bronfman's things. He had no proof yet, but also no doubt about it at all. He knew that if he'd had Officer Stanton go to Thomas Edison's apartment she would have found everything there. His TV, his flatware, his cowboy hat. The apples. Bronfman wanted to handle this on his own, though; it was important to him that he did. It felt as if the universe was testing him, waiting to see how he'd respond, even though he felt like a newborn, three days old. He had called the police to suggest to his neighbor that there were other forces involved in this enterprise — *put the fear of God into him,* as his mother used to say. But when Officer Stanton came by it appeared that Thomas Edison wasn't at home. His apartment was dark, and strangely quiet. He was gone for the rest of the day and into the night, and wasn't even there smoking on his stoop the next morning when Bronfman left for work.

Work was a dull choreographed perfor-
mance, so routine and mechanized that it
was no trouble for Bronfman to go through
the motions — shuffle his papers, shoot off
emails, answer his phone — when in reality
all he could think about was the confronta-
tion that was sure to occur later that evening. He lived through half a dozen imaginary scenarios, one in which fists were
thrown (if that's what one does with fists)
and another in which he made Thomas Edison cry. But here's how it was going to play
out, probably: Bronfman would go straight
to Thomas's apartment after work that
evening, rap on his door, and, in some yet
to be determined way, ferret out proof of
his neighbor's responsibility for the crime.
Boom. Done. Thomas would apologize,
return Bronfman's things, and they'd go on
with their lives. Bronfman would have
passed this test, this labor, and would be
free to move on to the next and the next
after that. This was what happened when
you became a part of the world. The world
gave you things to do.

He left his desk a few minutes early, hoping to get ahead of the traffic, but the elevator took even longer than usual today, and

by the time he got to the first floor he had lost whatever time he'd hoped to gain. In the lobby of the Cranston Building were three maintenance men taking positions around the desk that used to belong to Sheila McNabb. The computer was gone, as was the telephone console, as was everything but the desk itself.

"Hi. So. What's going on?" Bronfman asked the smallest of the maintenance men. Maintenance men intimidated him, large maintenance men especially. So the smaller of the three seemed the safest bet.

He was wrong.

"Do I stand beside you at your job and ask you what's going on?"

"No," Bronfman said. "I'm sorry. I —"

"Don't be a dick, Stuart," said the largest of the three. To Bronfman: "We're removing the desk." To Stuart: "Was that so hard?" To Bronfman: "It's all becoming automated. Everything."

"At least we're not robots," Bronfman said.

"Maybe we are and we just don't know it."

"I don't think so," Bronfman said — which was exactly, he realized, what a robot that's unaware of being a robot would say. But if he were a robot he would have to believe that Sheila McNabb was being deleted from his robotic memory, and that the removal of her desk — which reminded him of her every day — was another step toward total eradication.

But here was Mr. Mangioni, watching the progress while leaning against one of the grand marble columns in the lobby's colonnade. Mr. Mangioni was the manager of the Cranston Building, a dusty middle-aged Italian from Palermo, bald, roly-polyesque, who had nevertheless impressed Bronfman with his accent and his worldly elisions.

Bronfman approached him and let all his words tumble out of him.

"Mr. Mangioni, hi, Edsel Bronfman. Looks like they're taking out the desk — time for a change, I guess. The Cranston Building's coming into the twenty-first century."

"Seems so," Mangioni said. "Seems so."

He held a small Dixie Cup full of coffee, which he sipped delicately as he glanced at Bronfman and back to the maintenance men.

Bronfman formulated his next move.

"So, anyway. It just occurred to me. The woman who was here before," he said. "What happened to her?"

"Ah, Sheila," Mangioni said. "Lovely

Sheila. Crazy Sheila McNabb."

"Wait. What. She's crazy?"

Mangioni shrugged. "Nice lady," he said. "Sweet. But yes, I think so. Up one day, down the next. Sometimes she wouldn't answer the telephone. Said she had enough voices in her head. But, still, maybe not crazy in a bad way."

"What's the good way?"

Mangioni shrugged again. "Mostly, she was interesting," he said. "That's probably what I meant. She was interesting. Very interesting."

This relieved Bronfman. She was definitely interesting, and that was better than crazy, though he could see how one could very well seem to be the other.

"I wonder where she went," Bronfman said, asking a question without having to actually ask the question

"Sheila?" Mangioni said, as if they hadn't been talking about her the whole time. "No idea."

"I guess you don't have a telephone number or anything like that," he said, still not asking for anything, especially the thing he wanted most.

Mangioni really looked at Bronfman, narrowed his eyes. He gave him the evil eye. "Oh, now I see," he said. "Bronfman and

Sheila, sitting in a tree."

"Not so much," Bronfman said. "Not really."

"K-i-s-i-n-g."

"S-s," Bronfman said.

"Huh?"

"Two esses in *kissing.*"

"Thank you. But I can't tell you where she might be. Can't tell. It's the law." He held his hands out in front of him, chained in imaginary manacles. "I tell you and they throw me in the clinker."

"Of course," he said. "I understand."

"What if I tell you and you find her and cut her up into a million pieces, then they come looking for me and say, 'Was it you who told the killer where she lived?' Don't want that."

"I'm not a killer," Bronfman said. "If that matters at all."

"That's good. Still." Mangioni laughed and gave Bronfman a pat on the back, the kind one Italian might give another. "Better, anyway, to let that ship sail."

"Oh? Why do you say that?"

"I don't know," he said. "She may be *too* interesting," and he gave Bronfman a long look, up and down. "For you. If you hear what I'm saying."

Bronfman nodded. "I hear you," he said,

and turned back to look for a moment at the space Sheila had once filled before her perhaps too-interesting ship set sail. There was nothing there anymore. Nothing at all.

FOUR

On the way to his apartment, Bronfman
tried to imagine himself knocking on
Thomas Edison's door. That would be his
first step. But even that small action seemed
unimaginable. He had never done that
before, and he didn't know if under these
circumstances he could bring himself to do
it.

Luckily, he didn't have to knock. Thomas
Edison was sitting on his stoop when Bronfman drove up. He was smoking, whiling
away the time like a man escaping, for a
brief, precious moment, the world's oppres-
sive hurly-burly. At least he was wearing a
shirt, an old faded blue one with a tractor
on the front and the name of the people
who made the tractor on the back. Bronfman had seen it many times.

"Mr. B.!" he called out as Bronfman approached, as if they were the closest of
friends. The truth was, they kind of were.

136

Bronfman had thought of him as a friend before all of this happened, in the way that certain friends were friends because of very specific shared interests or experiences. In the case of Thomas Edison and Bronfman, it was the complex where they lived, King's Manor, the place where they shared their day-to-day lives. This was why it hurt so much, what he did to Bronfman, because now they were friends no more. "Mr. B.," he said again. "On schedule as usual. If I had a watch I could set it to Bronfman time, and it would always be right-on."

Thomas smiled as if even he were surprised at how clever he could be, and he locked eyes with Bronfman until Bronfman felt compelled to laugh as well. Thomas Edison could maintain eye contact longer than anyone Bronfman had ever known; it rattled him. But — *aha!* That casual reference to his schedule. Clearly he was aware of when Bronfman was gone, when he'd return. He knew it well enough to plan the robbery without fear of being caught. Case closed.

"Hey, Tommy," Bronfman said, affecting a breezy tone. "How's it going?"

"It's going how it's going," he said. "It is what it is."

Bronfman nodded, and Thomas took a long, slow, almost scandalous drag on his cigarette, closing his eyes in an evanescent rapture. Then he looked down at his cell phone, resting on the stoop beside his right leg, even though it hadn't made a sound. Then he flicked the rock off his cigarette with his index finger and dropped the still smoking butt into the crabgrass, and sighed. This was a code Bronfman understood: their meeting was over.

But it wasn't. The drumbeat of Bronfman's heart was proof of that.

"I got robbed," Bronfman said.

Thomas Edison jerked his head toward Bronfman in a mechanical, calibrated twist. "What?" he said. "What the fuck!" Oh, he was surprised by this news. Very surprised. *Unbelievably surprised.* Bronfman could have said, "I'm an alien. My true form is much larger, green, and poisonous to the touch," and he would have been greeted with the same expression of shocked confusion. *That such a thing could happen in this great and wonderful world! In King's Manor!* "Oh, man," he said. "That sucks big-time. What all'd they get?"

"A lot of things," Bronfman said. "I didn't have much to get, but what I had they took. Whoever 'they' were. The police came yesterday."

"The police?"

Bronfman nodded, and let that fester. He had Thomas's attention now. Thomas was getting a peek at his future: handcuffed, fingerprinted, jailed, judged, and convicted. That's all it took, and the hardy man who liked to not a wear a shirt when everybody else did withered like the core of a stolen apple in the parking lot right before Bronfman's steely gaze. Bronfman tugged on his tie. He couldn't swallow. The flesh there was damp and soft.

"Officer Stanton?" Thomas asked.

"Yes. But how would you know that?"

"It's a small town," he said. "Sooner or later, you get to know everybody. The checkout girl, the pharmacist. The police."

"I suppose so," Bronfman said.

"She's a cute thing," Thomas Edison said. "You tell her I live here now?"

"No," Bronfman said. "Why would I do that?"

But Thomas didn't answer. He lit another cigarette, his back humped over, as if the weight of the world were on it. He shook his head. "I'm really sorry, Mr. B. I've been robbed, and it sucks. It sucks, like, in a thousand ways. They take your stuff, everything you love and worked so hard to get. But they take something else, too. Something else happens. You know? They take something inside." Thomas touched the place on his chest where the inside was.

Bronfman nodded. A golden ray of sun cut through a web of branches and fell on Thomas Edison's face. Rough-hewn, sculpted out of a hard wood, his cheekbones were high and knobby, and his eyes, a muddy brown, rested on top of them, like marbles, balancing. His cheeks were drawn — from smoking so much, Bronfman thought — and his nose was almost perfect until it turned upward at the end, giving him an elfish look. A dangerous elf.

"I've never been robbed before," Bronfman said. "I know it happens to other people all the time. But I never thought it would happen to me."

"That's how it goes," Thomas said.

"How what goes?"

"No one thinks something bad is going to happen to them. Then it just does. People getting blown away by a tornado aren't flying through the air thinking, I knew this would happen. It just happens. You think my life plan was to end up here without a job or the prospects for one, with no woman in my life, in debt up to my elbows, talking to Mr. B.? No offense intended."

"None taken," Bronfman said, though there was some taken. A little. "I feel the

140

same way. Exactly. Just as I wasn't a part of your life plan, you weren't a part of mine."

The truth was, neither of them had a life plan. Bronfman didn't even know what a life plan was, or how to make one, or why you even would. Life wasn't something that *could* be planned. As Thomas Edison said, life happened in ways you could never imagine. Life was a tornado.

"Tommy," Bronfman said. Clearly, Thomas recognized that tone of voice. *Anybody* would have recognized that tone of voice. *I am about to introduce a topic of some seriousness,* Bronfman was saying. *Listen up!*

He looked at Bronfman, who was still standing over him, like a father lording it over his son. Thomas stared at him with that unfaltering gaze, and this time Bronfman didn't look away. This was Bronfman, facing a fear.

"Tommy," he said again, "did you . . ."

Thomas Edison waited for the end of the sentence, but it never came. "What? Did I what?"

"Did you . . ."

He couldn't say it. He could only say it by not saying it. And Thomas — again, as anybody would have — understood.

"Oh," he said, and laughed — scoffed,

really. Scoffed as if this was just another big pile of shit someone was dumping on his head, and it stank, but he was kind of used to it by now. "You think I did it."

Bronfman would neither confirm nor deny, and thus, in his silence, it was confirmed.

Thomas looked away. Bronfman had never won this staring contest before. It felt good. It felt like a step in the right direction. Thomas rocked back and forth a little, shook his head, sighed. He spit. Then he stood and turned and opened his apartment door. "You coming?" he said.

"What?" Bronfman asked. "Coming where?"

Thomas flourished his right arm. "Inside. I want to show you something."

Bronfman's heart, already beating dangerously fast, picked up speed and began thrumming calamitously. He felt it in his throat. If he threw up now — which was not beyond possibility — it would be his exploding heart that came out.

Slowly he walked into the maw of the beast.

He had never been inside Thomas Edison's apartment before, but he found that it conformed quite closely to what he'd imagined. Exceptionally cluttered: trash cans full to overflowing; beer cans crushed and tottering on the edge of the coffee table; a threadbare tartan couch and an old leather easy chair; ashtrays; bottle tops; plastic cups with half an inch of beer at the bottom — all laden with soggy cigarettes and whatever else he smoked. The disarray seemed permanent. The floor was littered with pieces of paper. Only on close inspection did Bronfman see that they were scratch tickets. In the corner was a miniature Christmas tree, made of some sort of plastic, still draped in tiny lights of many colors and broken candy canes. Happy, joyous, bright, the little tree was in a perpetual battle with the scruffy grimness of this sad abode.

"Yeah, look around," Thomas said.

"Tommy, I —"

"I'm serious. Everywhere. Anywhere. See if there's anything in here that's yours. Look through my closet, the drawers, the kitchen cabinets — hell, look in the *freezer.*"

"But —"

"Please," Tommy said. "For me."

Bronfman looked around. "I don't see anything," he said.

"No? Maybe I hid it in here. Come on in the bedroom. Don't be shy, come on."

The bedroom: farther away from the door, from escape. But Bronfman stepped over a pair of shoes and a pile of clothes — T-shirts, jeans — and followed Thomas into his bedroom. The bed? Just a mattress on the floor, one sheet, a rolled-up towel for a pillow.

"Well?" Thomas Edison asked him. Bronfman shook his head. Thomas opened the closet door. "Here. Look. Really look. Stick your head in."

Bronfman looked. There was nothing at all in the closet. Not even a metal coat hanger.

"I know what you're thinking," Thomas said. "That I've already gotten rid of it all. But why would I have stolen it if I didn't want it for myself? Couldn't sell it. That television? What could I have gotten for that? Five bucks, maybe?"

"How did you know the television was stolen?"

Thomas let that hang there for a beat, thinking his answer through. "Someone breaks into your apartment, they're not going to leave the TV. Crappy though it may be. Am I right?"

Nice save. "I guess so," Bronfman said. "I guess."

"So we're good?" Thomas said.

Bronfman wanted everything to be good. More than anything, he wanted everything to be good. But then he realized that the bathroom door was closed. He hadn't looked in the bathroom. He was already so deep into it there was nothing left to lose.

"What's in there?" Bronfman said.

"Where?"

"The bathroom."

"It's just the bathroom, man," Thomas Edison said. "What do you mean, what's in it? The sink, the shower, the shitter. That's it. And it's disgusting, so . . ."

Bronfman said nothing.

"We're not going in the bathroom, Mr. B.," Thomas said.

Bronfman stood his ground, brave — or, perhaps, numb. He could not look directly into Thomas Edison's eyes now, afraid of what he might see.

"Do you want me to call Serena?" he said.

"Who?"

"Serena, Officer Stanton." He let that sink in. "I have her card," he said.

Thomas Edison visibly weighed his options, executed some complicated math in his mind, and then, with a shrug, he gave in.

"Fuck it, Mr. B.," he said, angry, compliant against his will. "Go ahead. Be my freakin' guest. It's your funeral."

And this is when things got crazy.

He opened the door and the man there — who looked like a boy at first, he was so small, so miniature — leaped up from his seat on the toilet and fumbled for a gun, which was set on the bathtub rim behind him. Bronfman had never seen a gun in person, and it was so big, much bigger than he'd imagined. It was bigger than a small cat. Across the sink was a long plastic cutting board with great pyramids of white powder and smaller piles of white powder, and even smaller piles, and small bags of plastic full of white powder. Bronfman knew what it was, of course, because he had seen something very similar on television. Drugs. The little man was making drugs. He was probably in his mid-twenties, dark-skinned in a white sleeveless undershirt, tattooed ferociously, with pockmarked cheeks.

He had the gun in his hand, but he held it by his side. His hand was trembling. His hand was trembling as if it wanted to shoot Bronfman, but his arm was holding it back.

"Tommy," the man said with a high, sharp voice. "What the fuck!"

"It's nothing," Thomas said. He smiled and laughed, but not even Bronfman bought it. Thomas was scared, too. "Seriously, it's cool. This is my neighbor, Bronfman — Mr. B., I call him, and he's a cool dude.

Aren't you, Mr. B.?"

Bronfman wanted to agree with Thomas — that seemed the best choice among the choices he had. But his brain was flatlining, and the truth was he wasn't that much of a cool dude. The little man raised the gun, then lowered it. His whole body was shaking now. He *really* wanted to shoot Bronfman. He wanted to kill him. This was clear.

The man bit his lip to keep from exploding; that's how it appeared to Bronfman, anyway. "Scared the fuck out of me," he said. "Fuck, Tommy. You think this is a game? It's not a game. It's fucking real life and it's also like a war, a real life war, and in a war there are *casualties.*" He glared at Bronfman. Then at Thomas. "So we going to do this or what? Are we okay? Are we okay? Are we fucking okay?"

"We're okay," Thomas said.

"We're okay," Bronfman said. "Very much so."

The man looked at Bronfman with such malice that he thought he might bite him. Instead, he pressed the nose of the gun into Bronfman's stomach — quite hard, too, so hard it hurt. It cut. Bronfman winced. "And that's not even a bullet," the man said. "This hurts, but a bullet *is* pain. So you know, okay, I'm reserving one of my bullets for you. Gonna put your name on it. Just in case. What's your fucking name again?"

"Bronfman," Bronfman said.

"Bronfman? What kind of fucking name is that?"

Bronfman tried to speak. He thought that he was going to say something, but no words came out. He opened his mouth and one small sound did come out, like a dying dog's final whimper.

"You want to live, Bronfman?"

"Yes," Bronfman said. "I want to, very much."

"Then act like it," the little man said, kicking the door shut and slamming it hard, half an inch away from Bronfman's face.

Thomas took Bronfman by the shoulders, one hand clamped on either side. And then, his lips so close to Bronfman's ear that Bronfman could feel the heat of his breath, he said, "I told you we shouldn't have gone in there." Bronfman knew there was no way he could escape Thomas's grip. Cowboy up! he thought. But there was no sense in that now. He could flail and kick and scream and bite and cowboy the hell out of it, but there was nothing he could do. He had not been blessed with native strength. His muscles were no more than scarves around his bones. Thomas — he was strong. He could break Bronfman. But he wouldn't. Thomas wouldn't kill him. He would just make him wish he were dead. He never should have come in. He knew too much now. Bronfman felt himself crumbling, his knees unable to support his weight. His heart wasn't beating so crazily fast anymore. It had stopped. He couldn't breathe if he wanted to, and he wasn't sure he did want to.

Thomas Edison hugged him.

"I've got your back, Mr. B.," he whispered into Bronfman's ear. "You're my neighbor, dude. You're part of my tribe. You get robbed, I get robbed. If I had been here when that shit went down, believe me, I'd have shot first and asked questions later."

Thomas wouldn't let him out of his sticky hug. "Okay," Bronfman said into his shoulder. "Okay. Thanks, Tommy."

"Want to see it?"

"See what?"

"My gun," he said. "The Glock. It's a lot bigger than his."

"I don't think so," Bronfman said.

"It will take a man's head right off."

"Really?"

Thomas finally let him go. "It would have been nothing for me to wipe that scum off the face of the fucking earth. I just wish I hadn't been out looking for a job when it

149

happened."

"No," Bronfman said. "You definitely should have been looking for a job. You need a job."

"But you get it, right? I'm there for you. And you're there for me. This" — he indicated with his eyes what was going on behind the bathroom door — "this is nothing. It's business. That's all it is. But it's not your business. And it's definitely not the business of Serena fucking Stanton. Your shit's not here. That's what this was all about. You thought I had it and I didn't. You unjustly accused me."

"I'm sorry," Bronfman said. "I —"

Thomas took Bronfman's jaw in his hands — his *jaw* — and closed it. And he held it closed. "You don't need to apologize. Let's forget it ever happened — all of this. Because I get it. Look at me. Look how I live. If I were you, Mr. B., I'd think it was me, too. But I'm not that guy. I'm not. You feel me?"

Thomas let go of his jaw, and Bronfman tried to smile, but all he could manage was a face twitch. "I feel you," he said. He had heard people say that, and he had always wanted to say it himself. That he had the opportunity to do so now made him, in light of what had just happened, inordinately happy. He forgave Thomas Edison completely. "I feel you," he said again.

FIVE

There was no gunplay that evening, no music, no real noise of any kind. But it didn't matter. Bronfman, alone in his apartment, pacing from room to empty room, found it impossible to "take it easy." He couldn't fully breathe. The air could not get all the way to the bottom of his lungs. He was gasping, sweat dripping down both sides of his face, down the shallow canal of his chest. He imagined a bullet with his name on it, and how big a bullet it would have to be in order to accommodate his entire name. None of this was good, not at all.

He had to get out, so he walked to an Italian restaurant a few blocks away. It was called Mario's. It reminded him of a place he'd gone to with his mother when he was a kid, every Sunday night. Mario's didn't serve the best food in the world, but the plastic red-checkered tablecloths, and the waiters with their bow ties and their charming accents, gave the place an authentic Italian feel. Not that Bronfman knew what Italy felt like; he had never been there. Mario himself was a tiny old Sicilian with only three or four teeth left. He always made his customers smile; in fact, he wouldn't leave you alone until you did.

Furtively, Bronfman spied the patrons at the other tables. They weren't eating dinner the way he was eating dinner. Bronfman was eating to live, because without food he would die, and Mario's offered adequate sustenance. For these other people — families, couples, a middle-aged woman out with her grandfather — eating was a kind of celebration, like dancing. Or it was like a very small party. Or it was like a modern reenactment of something our most distant ancestors did, sharing food as an expression of friendship and love. Bronfman was just slopping calories into his mouth.

The spaghetti was very good, though. Eating always made him feel better, no matter what. He read the directions on a jar of chili flakes and thought of Sheila. All it said was "Use sparingly." And when he was done he paid up, and left.

It was cooler on his way back home, now that the night had come. It wasn't windy, but the cars speeding past him made it feel as if it was. It was only when a truck passed and blew his tie into his face that Bronfman realized he had forgotten to take it off. He took it off and stuffed it into his back pocket, where, he knew, it must have looked like a tail. It didn't matter to him now. A patrol car sped by, but it was going too fast for Bronfman to see whether it was Officer Stanton. Bronfman almost waved, but he worried that if he did the officer, whoever it was, might think he was in trouble and stop and then get upset when he discovered that Bronfman was fine and had just waved to say hello.

Should he call Officer Stanton? The wild idea just flew into his head the way an errant bird would fly through an open window. Not to tell her about the drugs his neighbor was selling — he was already detaching from that part of his life, putting distance between himself and a reality that he wanted no part of — but to ask her out on a date, and then another and another and another, and then all of a sudden spring it on her: *Would you like to join me for a weekend at the beach?* No matter how ridiculous, no matter how unrealistic, no matter how inconceivable something was, it appeared the mind could think whatever it wanted anytime it wanted to. Bronfman's mind was like an untrained puppy.

The truth was he should call his mother; she would want to know what happened. And years ago he would have called her. Even a few months ago, he would have called her. But now, the way things were for her, the slippage she was showing, it didn't make sense to. What could she offer him? And she may not even remember that he had been robbed; why upset her all over again? The mother he remembered, the one who had raised him with such courageous flippancy, was gone, and in her place was a fading image, like a Polaroid picture in reverse. This was probably why the table at Mario's felt so big. It wasn't just at dinner that he was alone; he was alone wherever in the world he happened to be. Oh, Bronfman, he thought. Snap out of it! Don't be that guy. Don't be Bronfman!

At night, King's Manor turned a phosphorus yellow. Parking-lot lights — towering above everything on single, impossibly thin, metal legs — illuminated the asphalt like a dozen jaundiced suns. Years ago real gangs used to hang out here, apparently, and shoot one another in the dark. Now that it was bright as noon here, the gangs had found other places to die.

He turned into the complex just as some of Thomas Edison's friends were getting out of a car. He recognized them. There was the fat one, the Hispanic one, the pretty girl. They always came together in the same old car. Bronfman stopped and watched them pour out of the car, laughing. Why did they always come here? Didn't they have anywhere better to go? Apparently not, because who would choose to come to a place like this if there was anywhere else that would have them? Thomas Edison, like Bronfman, was performing a service.

But nothing appeared to bother them now, laughing and laughing as they mounted the stoop to Thomas Edison's place, knocking with outrageous force at Thomas's door. "Police!" the fat one said. "Open up, motherfucker!"

Thomas Edison opened up, and the crowd poured in.

The girl hung back, though. She was lighting a cigarette, and her face glowed in the tiny firelight. He had seen her in passing, her features Japanese, or Korean, or Chinese — he didn't know. She had hair so black that Bronfman thought of it as the black to which all other blacks could be compared, the origin, the source of the color. Bronfman had never been closer than ten feet away and had never spoken to her, but he had a little visual crush on her, the same sort of visual crush he had on a lot of women.

But as the match flamed, momentarily bright as a torch, he could see that she was wearing a hat. She was wearing . . . a cowboy hat. And there was no mistaking it, none. It was Bronfman's hat. She was wearing Bronfman's cowboy hat. The silver star shone like a real one, reflecting the flame as she brought it toward her lips.

Bronfman loved that hat. One of his many "uncles" — Kevin, his name was, or Kev — had taken Bronfman to a fair, and he had won it for him, throwing darts at balloons. *What do you want, my man? The hat or the bunny?* The hat. And Kevin won it. The hat fit so perfectly on his tiny head. It was a perfect fit in every way, and, magically, it turned Bronfman into a kind of cowboy, at least in his own mind. Bronfman was eleven, and he loved the hat so much that it hurt him — it made him ache. He wouldn't take it off. He wore it every single day. He wore it when he went to bed. When he woke up and found it on the floor beside the bed, he picked it up immediately and placed it on his head. When school started in September, he wore it there as well, every single day,

157

until he was told that he couldn't wear a cowboy hat to school. This was arduous, but he endured its absence by thinking about it all day long. The first thing he did when he got home was find the hat and set it, at a jaunty angle, on his head, check himself out in the full-length mirror on the back of his bedroom door. It was as if with the hat he were trying to create a different version of the self he was so clearly becoming.

He was wearing the hat the day he got hit by a car. Eleven and a half years old, Bronfman had wandered into the street, his mind on other things, oblivious of everything, and an old lady in her Buick LeSabre, driving slowly but mindlessly, bumped into him and knocked him about three feet into the sky. He floated in slow motion and landed on his back, on his own grassy lawn, sucking air.

Miraculously, he wasn't hurt — not a scratch on him. Even the hat hadn't budged. It remained on his head throughout his short flight and hard landing as if it were glued there, as if it were a part of him. That was the most remarkable feature of the whole potentially fatal adventure: the hat stayed on. "That's one lucky hat!" Kev said, and his mother, who always tried to believe in bigger things, said that he was blessed.

But that was then, and this was now. The miraculous hat was in the possession of another.

"Hey!" he called out to the girl — bravely, he thought. He ran toward her and the justice he was due. *"Hey!"*

Apparently she heard him, because she dropped the still burning match on the ground and looked up, coolly watching him run toward her, this strange man waving and bellowing "Hey! Hey!" He was out of breath by the time he reached her. Smoke floated like fog around her head.

"Can I help you?" she said.

He took a few more breaths and, when he was able to speak, said, "Where did you get that hat?"

She looked at Bronfman, a puzzled expression, and then shook her head and took another deep pull on the cigarette. "Why?" she said. "You want one like it?"

"No," he said. Then, "Yes. I mean —"

"I've had this hat for a really long time," she said. She never for a second stopped looking at Bronfman. She didn't even blink. "Long as I can remember. It's, like, my favorite thing. Not sure they make them anymore. I could ask my pop."

"Wait. So that's *your* hat?" he said.

159

"Of course it is. Would I be wearing it if it wasn't?"

Bronfman took a long look at it. It was his hat — or, rather, it was the same type of hat his hat was. But his hat was not unique in the world. Who knew how many thousands had been manufactured at the cowboyhat factory way back when. That she would have one and be wearing it the very night his went missing was a coincidence that he found hard to swallow. But he swallowed it. Not swallowing meant that he would have had to take it (whatever *it* was) to the next level (wherever *that* was), and he wasn't ready to go there yet. Or probably ever. He felt the welt rising on his stomach, where the gun had dug a hole.

"I'm Coco," she said, extending her hand.

Her hand was as small as a child's.

"Bronfman," he said. "I'm Tommy's next-door neighbor."

"Well, what do you know," she said. "Howdy, Bronfman."

She offered him the rest of her cigarette and he declined, so she dropped it right there on the sidewalk and crushed it with the heel of her shoe, and, without even saying goodbye, hopped on the stoop and absconded into Thomas Edison's apartment, closing the door behind her, disappearing into the smoky gloom.

■ ■ ■ ■

DAY EIGHT

■ ■ ■ ■

ONE

Almost precisely midway between the seven and ten days Carla D'Angelo had promised, Bronfman received the brochure, the pamphlet, and the necessary paperwork. It was all very glossy, very first-class. Very *real*. And what nice photographs. The condominiums were beyond elegant — sleek and metal, and plush carpets, and overstuffed couches, and gigantic ottomans, and the balcony views of oceanic infinity. And bright. The sunlight seemed to come in a purer form in Destin. It was like butter. Even the bathroom impressed. No one used shower curtains anymore, apparently. Everything was see-through. Everyone showered in glass boxes. There was nothing to hide. And, if the beach shots were any indication, why hide anything indeed? The men and women whose toes played in the snow-white sand were very attractive. They were lightly tanned, taut and smooth, thin, healthy, strong, happy, content. Just living in the now.

He looked at the pamphlet for a long time.

He wanted to be there. He wanted to be them.

He signed and sent in his reply form, indicating his abiding interest and formal acceptance of all stipulations associated with this opportunity.

It was official. He had seventy-one more days.

■ ■ ■ ■

DAY NINETEEN

■ ■ ■ ■

ONE

Bronfman almost moved after the robbery. It wouldn't have been difficult, after all, having so few possessions now to move. But Thomas Edison encouraged him to stay. "My friends will get right suspicious if you move, Mr. B.," he said. "They'll think something's wrong. They will track. You. Down. So just stay put. I'll be your bodyguard. And who knows who'll move in if you go. Some fucking jerk. Someone not half as cool as you, probably."

Bronfman could not imagine anyone so uncool as to be only half as cool as he was, but he appreciated the compliment and stayed. He thought it through like this: He had nothing else to steal. He knew who the bad guys were now. He was, in a completely counterintuitive way, safer at King's Manor than he would be elsewhere. He trusted Thomas Edison not to kill him.

At any rate, he didn't have the wherewithal

to sustain himself through the course of more than one crisis at a time. His mother was the crisis now. Her late-night phone calls were becoming increasingly weird and random. He'd pick up the phone, and it was as if she'd been talking to him for half an hour already but had only just decided to include him in the conversation. ". . . and without fresh pesto it tastes like the bottom of someone's old shoe. You remember the Wilkersons. They moved to Alaska before there even *was* an Alaska. What a sweet family, and so open to new things. I think they bought the first thingamajig — you know what I mean, one of those things, whatever they were. It was the first of its kind I'd ever seen."

He visited her often. She was even-tempered and rational sometimes; at others she seemed untethered, floating far above him and the world, at the mercy of the prevailing winds. After she dug up Barney's skull that day he'd buried it in a deeper hole, out of her reach in case she tried it again. And she had. She called him one night crying, "Where is he? Where is he, Edsel? What have you done with my dog?" The next day he brought her a roast chicken — she could eat off one of those for a week — and found a trail of dirt from the back door to her bedroom.

He took her to see her doctor on Day Nineteen.

His mother had been seeing Dr. Chelminski for only six months or so, having been assigned to him by the practice after her doctor of thirty years retired. "He's not my kind of doctor," she said.

"I'm sure he's fine."

"I despise him," she told Bronfman.

"You've only seen him twice!"

"How many times would you visit someone you despise? For God's sake, Edsel, sometimes I think I raised a rabbit."

But when he got her an appointment she went. They drove together, and sat side by side in the waiting room, just as they used to do when he was a boy, the roles so clearly reversed now that even he couldn't fail to grasp it. She thumbed through the star-laden magazines, pausing at photographs of the actors with the big chins and bedroom eyes. "Yummy," he heard her say. "Yummy, yummy, yummy." After just a little while, they were called back.

Dr. Chelminski was young, possibly even younger than Bronfman, but he was not despicable in any way that Bronfman could surmise. He was tall, with a long, friendly face and balding in a way that made him

171

appear older than he was, even wiser.

"Hello, Mrs. Bronfman," he said. "I've been hoping you could come in."

"Really?"

"We've been sending you all those pesky reminders," he said. He winked at both of them. "They work eventually. They wear you down."

"Well, that's not why I'm here," she said.

"No? Why, then?"

She turned to Bronfman. "Ask my son."

Dr. Chelminski turned to him. "Okay, I will," he said. He smiled, and winked, because it appeared that they were sharing an inside joke, Dr. Chelminski and Bronfman, an inside joke that was his mother. "Why is Mrs. Bronfman here today?"

Bronfman opened his mouth to speak, but his mother interrupted. "He thinks I'm losing my mind," she said.

"I never said that," Bronfman said.

She turned away from him. "You didn't have to," she said. Her eyes wandered around the examination room. In a softer voice, she said, "I suspect you may be onto something."

"A checkup, then," Dr. Chelminski said. "Easy peasy lemon squeezy. Mr. Bronfman, let's leave the room so your mother can change into one of our lovely paper gowns."

They left her with a nurse and took a few steps down the hall, where the doctor placed a reassuring hand on Bronfman's shoulder. "Take a seat in the waiting room," he said. "We'll come and get you when we're done."

He did as he was told. The waiting room was almost full by then, but he found a seat beside a mother and her ten-year-old boy. Mother and son both were focused on screens, the boy on some gaming device, his mother on her phone. She was texting. Bronfman had texted before but not enough to feel at ease with it. He wondered if his detachment from this world — the world of instant everything — meant that there was something wrong with him beyond the ways he already knew things were wrong with him. It wasn't a conscious decision on his part not to have a smartphone, or a computer at home. He wasn't afraid of technology, because if that were the case he would be frightened twenty-four hours a day. And, in fact, technology that came in handy he used handily. Google, for instance. He used Google all the time. The other day he Googled the name Sheila McNabb, and the search engine came back with 5,580 matches, which was unhelpful. Facebook turned up nothing. He would have better luck finding her with a bloodhound than

173

with Google. But the little boy and his mother seemed happy enough. Bronfman wondered what the world would be like when the little boy grew up, his mother got old, and he had to bring her back for a visit with some other doctor to see if she was losing her mind. But perhaps it was more likely, as the maintenance men had it, that we would all be robots by then, if indeed we weren't already.

"Mr. Bronfman?" It was the receptionist, calling to him from her little window. "They're asking for you."

He followed the hallway back to where he remembered his mother's room was, but Dr. Chelminski intercepted him before he opened the door. He brought out the reassuring hand again, and the sympathetic smile of understanding. If he had learned these things in medical school, he must have graduated at the top of his class.

"So, Mr. Bronfman," he said. "Wanted to let you know, your mother is fine."

"Fine? Really? That's great!"

"But I wouldn't necessarily say fine."

"That's exactly what you just did say."

"I mean that, for the condition she's in, she's doing well. She's healthy. Strong heart, good lungs. Blood work, what we've seen of it, looks good."

Bronfman nodded.

"But she has dementia," Dr. Chelminski said. "I think you know that. Not a big surprise, I'm sure. The question is where to go from here, isn't it? It's one of those things that's impossible to predict — how well or how badly she'll do, and for how long. During the checkup, she had moments of perfect clarity and others where she appeared confused, a bit muddled. Occasionally, she seemed to believe I was trying to seduce her." The doctor laughed and then, just as quickly, stopped. "In all seriousness, I can't tell you what to expect, Mr. Bronfman, other than to expect her to get worse. It might be over the course of years or it could happen much more quickly. She might wake up tomorrow and not remember your name. I've seen it happen before, sadly. The bottom line is, she won't be able to live alone much longer. She needs a sitter. A few hours a day, at least, and then more later, probably. Mrs. Bronfman is only seventy, and I realize that seems young for something like this these days. But she could live for a very long time. So just take it a day at a time and count your blessings. Appreciate the good you have. I'm prescribing a couple of things. And bring her back to see me in two months, unless you note something radical happening before that. Sound good?"

"Great," Bronfman said, even though it sounded terrible, in the worst possible terrible way. "It sounds great."

"Okay, then."

And Dr. Chelminski was gone. The nurse opened the door to his mother's room and there she was, dressed, sitting on the edge of the examination table, legs dangling, purse in her lap, no worse for the wear.

"Hey, Mom," he said. He felt oddly afraid of her now — not as if she might hurt him but as if, having only just learned how fragile she was, he might hurt her. He walked toward her, hand extended, in case she needed help getting down from the table.

"I *like* Dr. Chelminski," she said.

"I'm glad," Bronfman said.

"And he liked me, too."

"He said as much to me."

"But," she said, hopping down on her own like a woman half her age, "I told him we should keep our relationship completely and totally one hundred percent professional. Because, you know." And she pointed to her head as if it were a new hat she'd just bought. "He has to take care of my brain." She looked at her son. "Oh, sweetie. Don't

176

cry. There's nothing to cry about."

"I'm not crying," he said.

"Then what is that tear doing running down your cheek?"

Bronfman suddenly embraced her — sudden to him, sudden to her. Before today, every hug in his life had been pre-planned. He hugged her when she gave him a birthday present, for instance, or as he boarded the bus on the first day of school. But this one happened all on its own, and it was almost violent in its love. He wrapped the little woman who was still his mother in his arms, and it didn't appear that he had any intention of letting her go.

■ ■ ■ ■

DAY TWENTY-TWO

■ ■ ■ ■

ONE

He found her name on a sheet of paper on the bulletin board in the break room, advertising her availability and services.

Bettina.

They met at a coffee shop for the interview.

In a world where almost nothing corresponded to Bronfman's preconceptions, Bettina, the sitter he hired to take care of his mother, could not have been more perfect. It was as if she had jumped out of his head. She was old, older than Bronfman ever thought it was possible to become, an age beyond numbers. She was small and thin and black, with a fine blanket of snowy hair on her head and a mouth full of the best teeth he'd ever seen. Bettina meant "God's promise," she told him. She had no license; she didn't work for a company. She had worked as a housekeeper for a co-worker of Bronfman's and had left his family's service when all the children she raised had grown up and left home. Her eyes were tired and rested deep in her face. She looked as if she had learned what the Great Mystery was and was a bit disappointed by it. She mostly said very little. But she could sit with his mother, and she was clearly kind — that was all that was required. He hired her on the spot.

He considered the irony. It had been so easy to find Bettina, this woman who might, in theory, be saving his mother's life, while twenty-two days had passed and he had yet to secure a companion for a weekend at the beach. He'd had that one promising nibble on his line, but now his little boat had sunk and he was treading water, hoping for another woman to float by.

■ ■ ■ ■

DAY TWENTY-EIGHT

■ ■ ■ ■

ONE

Bronfman liked Bettina. He liked to watch her watch TV. She cooked and cleaned and sorted out his mother's meds, led her to the bathroom if she needed to be led. But most of her time was spent in a chair beside his mother's bed, watching her stories, the soaps. Sometimes she'd talk back to the television. "Oh, Lord," he heard her say once. "You're *stupid,* Barbara. He doesn't want anything from you but your money." Bronfman started watching the show with her and discovered that she was right: he didn't want anything from Barbara but money. It would have been obvious to anyone. Why didn't Barbara see that?

His mother pretended to hate Bettina, or hated whatever imaginary thing she had made her out to be.

"She tortures me," Muriel said. "She's like the CIA. Waterboarding would be a vaca-tion for me now. She grabs my arm so hard

— that's why I have these bruises. I met a few like her at the office, the hard-bitten criminals with nothing in their future but the inside of a cell. Mean as a snake. She sits there and stares at me sometimes like the Devil."

"Bettina?"

"Yes, Bettina. She's got you snowed, I can see." She sighed and shook her head, as if her son were no more perceptive than a pine tree. Bettina was right there in the room with them when Muriel said these things, but it was hard to tell if she was listening or if she cared. They were in the living room. His mother was sitting in her big, over-stuffed red chair, all dressed up in an ivory blouse and her old swanky designer jeans, but she wasn't going anywhere. Bettina was watching the portable television they'd set up on the coffee table.

"I wish I had a man here," Muriel said. "That's why people get together, you know, pair up, so that when they're old one can take of the other. Why else? A child is just the backup plan. You're the backup plan, Edsel, methinks."

"Do you want me to move in, Mother? Because I will."

"Kill me first," she said. She nailed him with her stare. "I mean it, Edsel. Life is out there, waiting for you." She pointed toward some indefinite spot behind her, beyond the walls of her home. "Not here. Go thou, son, and fall face-first into the smorgasbord of life. It's not too late, according to your father. All you'll find here is two old ladies getting ready to die."

"Speak for yourself," Bettina said without turning away from the television. So she *was* listening.

"Seriously," Bronfman said. "I'll move in."

"And, as I said, seriously, kill me first."

"*I'll* kill her," Bettina said. "Sure enough I will."

"Oh, Bettina, stop it," Muriel said.

Bettina and his mother laughed. It sounded like an inside joke to Bronfman.

"Are you taking your meds?"

Muriel waved the question away. "Ask Bettina," she said. "She's in charge of everything."

"Where do you live?" Bettina asked Bronfman.

It was the first thing she'd said to him since he hired her. He felt as though he were being called on in class.

"King's Manor," he said. "Over the mountain. It's —"

"Oh, I know King's Manor," she said, nodding. "Um-hum. I know King's Manor."

A commercial came on. Bettina leaned back, nodded at some thought she was having. "Watch yourself," she said. "Lock up. That place is full of dope dealers and layabouts, my nephew tells me."

"Bettina knows all," his mother said. "She's a fount of wisdom."

"You don't have to warn me about King's Manor," Bronfman said. "I've been robbed once already."

"Robbed?" his mother said.

"Yes," Bronfman said. "But they didn't take much. I mean, I didn't have much to take. I've replaced a lot of it."

"Why didn't you tell me this had happened?"

"You told *me*," he said. "Remember?"

She shook her head and waved his words away with her hand, and, just like that, moved on to another subject.

"You should work out, Edsel," she said. "That's something you're interested in, isn't it? I think you mentioned that to me once. Don't you think he should work out, Bettina?"

Bettina shrugged. "I don't think it matters one way or another, in the long run." But she gave Bronfman a long look. "You got a girl?"

"Not yet," he said. "But I'm working on

188

it!" He had spent some time coming up with this, what he thought of as a rejoinder, in case anyone asked. It sounded so much better than "No."

"I think it's clear he does need to work out. Or take steroids. Something. My son's a little puff ball of mush, a marshmallow man." She laughed. "I'm just kidding, Edsel!" — what she always said after saying something particularly wicked. I'm just kidding ha-ha.

"Hush," Bettina said. "The both of you. My story is back on."

Muriel rolled her eyes and laughed and laughed, and Bettina laughed a little, too.

"See?" Muriel said. "See?"

"See what?" Bronfman said. "What?"

"Popsicle, please," Muriel said, her Ping-Pong-ball thoughts bouncing all over the place. "The cherry kind, *per favore*. Miss Bettina, helloooooo?"

The next night, hours after Bettina had left, his mother wandered off into the woods behind their house and took off almost all of her clothes, and hung them on the branch of a tree. Over the next three days, she called the police a dozen times. There were prowlers, apparently, rapists and other characters who were knocking at her bedroom window at all hours of the day and night. The police said the calls had to stop. So later that week Bettina moved into Bronfman's old room, completely took it over and made it her own. It all happened so quickly. One day he was with his mother, celebrating her birthday full of pointless whimsy, and now she was in the round-the-clock care of a sweet old woman. It was as if his mother had jumped on a sled at the tip-top of a tall mountain, and he was watching her whiz by swiftly, gaining speed on her way to the end of her life, while he was just trying, late out of the starting gate, to begin his own.

DAY TWENTY-NINE

ONE

If tomorrow Bronfman was kidnapped and blindfolded and thrown from a plane without a parachute but then somehow landed softly and mostly unharmed in a grain silo full of money, that would still be the second most surprising thing to happen to him after what would happen today.

Today he became a member of the YMCA.

For the first time in his life, he had a gym card and a locker. He had the YMCA pen. It was like having a second home. Almost an entire month had passed since he received the call from Extraordinary Adventures, and though Bronfman could not be said to have a plan — he had never had a plan in his life, and wouldn't know what to do with one if he did — he did at least have a goal, and he was moving in that general direction. Yes, Sheila McNabb had disappeared into the ether, and Serena Stanton was an officer of the law, and Coco — well, she was just Coco, the friend of Thomas Edison, drug dealer. But Bronfman had never had so many conversations with so many women in so short a time in his entire life. That was progress. And so he felt obliged to continue, to get out of his comfort zone, to see what else could happen.

This was the underlying logic that had coerced him into becoming a member of the YMCA.

There were other forces at work, too. The sense of powerlessness he had felt in the home of Thomas Edison, especially when the little man in the bathroom pressed the pistol into his stomach (there was still a small bruise); the advice his mother — and Sorsby — had given him; and the vision he had of himself at the beach, now just a month and a half away, as a man with definition. It's what he was looking for every day of his life, in a larger sense of the word, and what he suspected everyone was looking for: definition, the answer to who you were.

And then, to cap it all off, a flyer came in the mail addressed to Current Resident — to him, in other words. There was a YMCA not far from King's Manor, and the introductory rates were very good, almost too good to be true, and the Y had all the weights and stationary bicycles and medieval-looking torture machines the other, more expensive clubs did.

And so he joined.

He lifted weights. In just ten minutes, he could feel the burn. His arms and legs felt as if they had come to life. Many of the members here were much older than Bronfman, in exceptionally terrible shape, and that made him feel better about who he was and how far he had to go, which was really not that far when he compared himself with an obese eighty-year-old man. Bronfman paced on a treadmill for half an hour or so. He knew it wouldn't make him healthy (he'd eat a box of doughnut holes on the treadmill if they were served there), but just being able to think, *I'm on my way to the gym,* or *I've just gotten back from the gym,* felt so good, so right, that it was worth the time it took to change out of his street clothes into his shorts and T-shirt and tennis shoes, and then, less than an hour later, back into his suit and shoes again and off to work.

He worked up a bit of a sweat, though; parts of him were even sticky. He got why people did this.

But to Bronfman's discomfort — in fact, he could not imagine a discomfort that was greater — for the first time in his life he found himself in the company of penises other than his own. In the beige-tiled and dream-steamy locker room of the YMCA, he had to change back into his street clothes, and here there was absolutely no inhibition. The men stripped down to nothing and made nothing of it, showered with one another and shaved before the mirror without a stitch, and sometimes even engaged in rambling conversations with a friend, both of them utterly naked, and quite old, raisin-withered. Bronfman didn't get it. Usually hidden away from the world, here the penis became just another part of the body, no different from a nose or an elbow. Bronfman stole a quick look at the other penises now and again, as he pretended to check the time, say, or pick up a sock he'd accidentally dropped. He didn't like having to do it, but he had to know what it meant to have the penis he had, and whether it was true, as he feared it was, that the problems he had with women, with men, with life itself, were, in the end, the result of a disappointing penis. Not just its size or shape, really, but something in the spirit of it, its personality — its is-ness. He had wondered the same thing all his life in one way or another since high school, when he had the uncomfortable vision of what Corey Spaulding's penis might look like, or how it might have behaved in a strange dark room with Mary Day.

And this was where he met Dennis Crouton.

Dennis Crouton was a photographer from somewhere else, possibly France. Bronfman knew this long before he met him. Voices carried through the locker room; words seemed to hang in the air, buoyed by the steam. Minutes after they were spoken they could still be heard, floating around in their own particular cloud of sound. He had also seen Crouton — all of him, every bit of him — because, of all the unself-conscious inhabitants of the men's locker room at the downtown YMCA, Crouton was the least self-conscious of all.

In the parking lot, lost, trying to locate his car, Bronfman heard the familiar faintly foreign voice of Dennis Crouton behind him.

"Allo? Excuse me?"

Bronfman turned. "I'm sorry!" he said, having no idea what he might be apologizing for.

"No, no," Crouton said. "This is mine. I just need to get in it."

Crouton indicated that it was the car

whose door Bronfman was standing in front of, a blue Saab of indeterminate age.

Bronfman stepped aside. "I can't find mine," he said. "I thought it was — wait, I see it. There it is." He had purchased the pale-red Toyota Celica thirteen years ago from a first-year college student who had been selling the car that his parents handed down to him in high school. It drove exceptionally well for a vehicle with almost 250,000 miles on it. It leaked oil, though, and Bronfman had to keep a close eye on that (he kept an entire case of WD-40 in his trunk), but otherwise he couldn't complain.

Crouton seemed not to care. He waved away Bronfman's words as if he were shooing away a fly. "Dennis Crouton," he said. "Like the crunchy bread in the salad." Crouton didn't offer his hand and wait for it to be taken, the way most people Bronfman had ever encountered did. Crouton *found* Bronfman's hand, which had been hanging limply against his trousers, and took it in his own, and gave it not a shake but a squeeze.

"Edsel Bronfman," Bronfman said, as he felt his hand disappear into the warm palm of the possible Frenchman.

"So people call you Ed or — ?"

"People call me Bronfman," Bronfman said.

"Well, it's nice to meet you," he said. Crouton found a pair of Ray-Bans in his gym bag and, donning them, immediately became perfectly, totally foreign. "Of course, I have seen you and you have seen me."

"Yes . . ."

"Many times."

"Many," Bronfman painfully admitted. "Many, yes."

"So often we see each other — it is the same with all people sometimes — and we never say hello. It's the way of it now, in the modern world, *non*?"

"No," Bronfman said. Then, understanding what he meant, "Yes, it is. It is the way of the modern world."

"So fast," he said. "So busy."

"Speaking of which," Bronfman said, and pointed to the place where his watch would have been had he remembered to put it on. But, as he hadn't, Crouton watched him point at his naked wrist. "Work."

"Work!" Crouton said. It was odd — Crouton's accent seemed to come and go. "Sorry to keep you from it. What is it you do?"

"Oh, it's . . . hard to explain. It's a business — where I coordinate shipments and billing and . . ."

But he had already lost Crouton, who was fishing around for something in one of his pockets. Bronfman had managed to bore him in one sentence and a half.

"Ah, here it is," and he removed a torn, crumpled, dirty piece of paper. "My card."

Bronfman took it and read, "Dennis Crouton. Photographer."

That was all it said.

"You're a photographer," Bronfman said, pointlessly. "What do you take pictures of?"

"The world," Crouton said solemnly. "All of the world."

"You must be busy."

"Oh," Crouton said. "I am. Very, very busy." He sighed. "And so I will see you in the gym sooner or later, no?"

And with those words Crouton slipped into his handsomely beat-up car and drove away.

Later that same day, thumbing through a local weekly paper called *Happenings*, which billed itself as "the guide to all things local," he saw that the photographer Dennis Crouton had a showing of his most recent work at the Winter Gallery — that very night. Bronfman had to read it twice to believe it. But there it was: "Dennis Crouton at the Winter Gallery — Tonight." The news inspired a series of thoughts. *What a coincidence* was the first thing Bronfman thought. And then, *I know where the Winter Gallery is* (though he had never even considered going inside it), and then, *I have nothing to do tonight; I could very well go.*

But the last thought, the big thought, and the one that hung around in his head the longest, was this: *Why didn't he tell me? He gave me his card, which would have been the perfect time to say, "I have a show tonight. You should come, no?"* But he didn't mention it, which could mean only one of two things. Either he was too shy to invite Bronfman, incapable of tooting his own horn, or he simply didn't want Bronfman — this white, naked, nearly hairless thing he sometimes shared a bench with — to be there. Bronfman opted for the first, because he harbored a secret crazy hope that this man, Dennis Crouton, might actually become his friend.

TWO

The Winter Gallery was bravely situated on a corner in a section of town that had yet to be saved by the ambitiously gentrifying young. It seemed to be waiting for other establishments of similar quality to join it there; so far, apart from a spooky-looking bar down the street, none had. The soft light of the display was overcome by the red-and-green neon of the steel-barred ABC store beside it, one sign flashing OPEN and another blinking NO CREDIT, JUST CASH. There were no bars on the picture windows of the gallery, which meant that either the owners were striking a defiant note of trust in their fellow man or this was an admission that there was nothing inside the gallery that anybody would want to steal. Bronfman watched from across the street as people came and went. Half a block away, a group of slump-shouldered hoodlums checked Bronfman out. He thought about Serena

Stanton. Officer Stanton. He had her card. He could call her right now and say, "Looks like there's some trouble brewing down this way. No, no backup required. I think we can handle this one ourselves." But he hadn't brought his phone. The hoodlums stared him down. All they had to do was nod in his direction to get him to move, and so Bronfman dashed across the street into the cool beige of the gallery, where a young woman handed him a pamphlet, on the cover of which was one word, printed in big black letters:

CROUTON

"I hope you enjoy the show," she said.

She was wearing a nametag: "Alice Gray Stites." Bronfman was inordinately impressed by nametags and intimidated by anyone wearing one, especially someone with three names. Yet he was feeling brave tonight.

"So, you work here . . . Alice?" he ventured.

She drew back. "I'm the curator of the show, actually."

"Ah," he said, not knowing what that was. "I'm looking forward to it."

"As well you should," she said, and turned

away, pamphlets at the ready for the next lover of photography who happened behind him.

The room was packed. "Excuse me, I'm sorry. Thank you, pardon, excuse me." It took a lot of apologies for Bronfman just to get inside. All kinds of people were there, from rich older women festooned with bedazzling jewels, to some young scruffy types in jeans and T-shirts with holes, to a man in black wearing cowboy boots and a blue scarf around his neck. Not a single person from the YMCA was here, though. Only Bronfman.

It did make Bronfman happy to see the gallery full of people; he was pleased for Dennis Crouton in a way that made absolutely no sense. He didn't know anything about the art world, or if this even was the art world. And, of course, he had never heard of Dennis Crouton before that afternoon. But on the way over he had worried that he might be the only person here, which would have been awkward and painful. But apparently this Crouton was somebody, and Bronfman had never known a somebody before. One day, were Crouton's name to come up in conversation, he could tell people that he had once known Dennis

Crouton — that he was, in fact, a kind of friend.

But that day would never happen — who was ever going to mention the name Dennis Crouton? — and it wouldn't matter if it did. Bronfman wouldn't mention it. That really wasn't Bronfman's style. When he was nine years old, Uncle Pat had taken him to a minor-league baseball game. Young Bronfman, for some reason, owned a baseball glove, which he had tucked in the back of his closet along with the ukulele and the cardboard box full of fool's gold — driveway gravel, really — he used to collect. Uncle Pat insisted that he take the glove to the game, because you never knew when a home run might come right at you. "Right *at* me?" Bronfman repeated. He didn't like the sound of that. The chances seemed so slim, though, that of all the people in the entire stadium the ball would happen to travel his way, that he humored his uncle and took the glove along. Of course, that's exactly what happened. Some guy hit the ball so hard that it rose above the confines of the field of play and floated into the stands — *right at Bronfman* — who, closing his eyes and lifting his glove to protect his face, found that the ball had somehow fallen neatly into it. There it was. And the smile on his Uncle Pat's face was monstrously enormous. He often wondered what had happened to Uncle Pat. Where did he go after the months spent with Muriel? He imagined a holding pen where uncles past, present, and future were held. Or did they move on to another woman with another child, another lonely pair who needed an uncle for themselves?

It turned out to be an indescribable feeling, actually, catching the ball. The next day at school Bronfman overheard some seniors talking about it — how some kid at the game yesterday had actually caught a home run and how cool that was, and how much they wished it would happen to them one day . . . and Bronfman had every opportunity to say, "That was me! That was me! I caught that ball, and it was like a dream come true." But he didn't. He had some sort of condition that wouldn't allow him to say anything that might improve his position in the world. He had never told anyone about the miracle catch, as, likewise, he would never tell anyone about Dennis Crouton, even though it was true, he did know him. They might become friends. Bronfman might become Crouton's wingman as together they trolled the bars of Birmingham for women. Stranger things have happened, surely.

He was also happily surprised when it turned out that he actually liked Dennis Crouton's photographs. Crouton wasn't kidding when he said he took pictures of the whole world. There were photos here from all over: California, Tibet, Norway, and little towns in Alabama and Mississippi, towns that appeared to have been abandoned or burned down. Horses. There was a lot of squalor and sadness, and all the photos were in black and white. Bronfman spent some time admiring each of them, and helped himself to some cheese and crackers and grapes, which made him feel somewhat fancy. He went back for seconds and ventured into another room.

That's when he saw Dennis Crouton. Crouton held a glass of wine in one hand and gesticulated with the other, talking and talking, easily stringing one sentence after another together without a second thought. He wore a black jacket with jeans, a pale-yellow button-down shirt — a step up from the T-shirt and shorts he usually wore to the gym. The two women he was talking to — beautiful by any standard, it was ridiculous, really, how pretty they were — nodded and smiled, smiled and nodded. They couldn't get a word in edgewise, because Crouton didn't stop talking. It was as if he'd been stranded on an island by himself for a year and had all these words stored up inside him and had to get them out before he exploded. Bronfman watched as the women exchanged a glance or two with each other, though it was impossible for him to interpret the information they were trying to impart. It was some secret, he would wager, because if he knew one thing about women it was this: they were full of secrets.

Bronfman pretended to admire the photographs in this room, which were strikingly similar to the ones in the other room, and when he was in Crouton's sight line he casually turned around and waved. Crouton wasn't looking his way, of course, but Bronfman didn't stop waving, and eventually Crouton saw him and tilted his head. A series of expressions flashed across Crouton's face, easily interpretable: *Do I know you? Let me pretend to know you while I place you. I can't place you. Wait — I think — really? You?* Then he lifted his hand in a sort of half-wave, and returned to his conversation with the beautiful women who had looked his way as well but with no registration whatsoever. And even though Bronfman circulated through the gallery for another twenty minutes, drifting like flotsam toward Crouton, then away, then toward again, giving his new friend every opportunity, the photographer said not a word to him. Not one word.

About a block away from the gallery was a bar called the Hole-and-Corner, and in the hope that it served hamburgers Bronfman escaped the gallery and made his way down the threatening streets, as fast as he possibly could, and entered. Dingy, loud, full of people who had taken chances with their lives and lost. This was the kind of place Bronfman would have frequented had he been a completely different person. It was like a warehouse. Maybe it *was* a warehouse. Shadowy and cavernous, thrift-store chairs and tables and a long aluminum bar lined with red-topped stools, and behind that — darkness. It was the sort of place where he could imagine running into Coco and Thomas Edison. Bronfman took a seat on one of the stools and waited to be served.

And waited. He felt abandoned, stranded, alone with his thoughts. He didn't understand what had just happened at the gallery. He had been snubbed, yes, that was obvious. But why? He had never expected to be real friends with Crouton. Still, Crouton could have said hello. Just that one word, *hello.*

A young female bartender wearing a boa and a furry blouse materialized before him. Almost the entirety of her was covered in tattoos. Her arms and neck and who knows where else. Bronfman did not understand tattoos.

"Something I can get you?"

"Oh," he said. "A beer, please. And a hamburger, if you have it."

"I'll tell the chef," she said, shooting Bronfman with her stare. After a few seconds, he got it.

"You don't have a chef," Bronfman said.

"No. And when you say 'beer,' which of the thirty-five do you mean?"

"I don't know," he said. He didn't even like beer. He should have just ordered water, but now it was too late. "Something light?"

She sighed. "Sure," she said, and walked away, disappearing into the darkness at the other end of the bar.

As he waited he swiveled on the barstool, back and forth a little, trying it out, then a full 360 degrees. He did it twice. On the third go he slowed, and the rotation stopped him as he faced the door of the bar — at which point who should come in but those girls, the women, the lovely women, the two

Crouton had been talking to. One of them was tall, with shoulder-length brown hair and bangs that fell just a little bit into her eyes, and the other was shorter, with thick curly red hair. They were both wearing little black dresses. He looked at them and then looked away. That would have been enough for him, to have their images lithographically etched into his mind, soon to make an appearance in a 3 A.M. dream. But there was more. Two stools to the right of Bronfman weren't taken, and those were the stools the women chose to sit on. Beside him.

He felt the blood in his heart rush in and out like waves into a cave.

They didn't say anything to him, of course, nor did he expect or want them to. What would he have said if they did? Instead, the women spoke to each other, while Bronfman eavesdropped as best he could. *Crouton,* one said. *Mumble mumble mumble.* Then they laughed — the way only women can laugh with each other (he had overheard them often, standing behind one in a line, or sandwiched between them in an elevator), so full of meaning and unguarded delight. Bronfman thought that anything and everything a woman did had some sort of delightful meaning. He leaned toward them a bit, the better to hear, and was sure that he heard one of them say, "Not my cup of tea," and the other said, "Not my cup of anything." More laughter.

As they turned to look for the bartender, the gaze of the brown-haired woman rested briefly on Bronfman's face, but long enough, apparently, for her to register it. "Oh, hey," she said. "You were . . . weren't you — ?"

"At the show?" he said. "Yes, I was. That was me."

She had seen him.

The women looked at each other and, within that look, had a short silent conversation.

"Okay. So we have to ask you. What did you think?"

He'd been afraid she might ask him this.

"Well," he said. "I thought some of them — the pictures of the barns and the . . . the small children —"

"Not bad. Right. Nothing bad about them, really. I'm Shawn, by the way. This is Lucy." Lucy, the curvy one, offered him her hand. He took it, shook it, and quickly let it go. "It's just that I've seen it all so many times before, you know? John Rosenthal — have you seen his work? It's like Crouton but a thousand times better. It's the real deal."

"No," Bronfman said. He was having trouble reconciling who he had thought these women were — Crouton groupies — with their obvious distaste for his work.

"And what a dog," Lucy said.

"Rosenthal?" Bronfman said.

"Crouton." Lucy laughed. "His eyes were chest level all night long. His mind was even lower."

And then, for a reason he could not fathom, Shawn touched Bronfman on the arm, and leaned in close.

"He asked us to go home with him," she said, sending her and her friend into hysterics. "Not me, not her: *us*. Now, that's a confident man."

"Overly confident."

Shawn practically slapped her mouth with her hand. "Oh, my God. You're not a friend of his, are you?"

Bronfman shook his head. "No," he said. "No, I don't think I am."

He was almost ready to explore this idea with them — this idea of friendship, of what it is, and what it could be — they seemed so nice, they would talk to him, they would listen — when there came the sound of a very familiar voice behind him.

213

"Well, well, well."

Bronfman swiveled, as did the women.

"It is I, Crouton," he said, obviously, pitifully drunk. His smile was lopsided, his eyes were glazed. He spoke to the women, ignoring Bronfman completely. "I thought I might find you two here."

"And we were afraid you might," Lucy said.

The bar was loud. Crouton didn't hear her. Reluctantly, Crouton looked Bronfman's way. "Oh, yes. And thank you, Mr . . . I'm sorry, I can't —"

"Bronfman," Bronfman said.

"Ah." And Crouton was done with him. He turned again to the women, but whatever words were about to lunge from his mouth stopped short. Because the women weren't looking at Crouton. They were looking at Bronfman. It was as if Crouton didn't exist. They were sharing that *look* with Bronfman. He knew what they knew. They shared a secret now, the truth about Crouton — that he was no Rosenthal. That he was not original.

Bronfman felt like one of the women.

Crouton sensed that something was amiss. His instincts for survival were well honed, and he realized that he had found in Bronfman a bit of a rival. Bronfman had never been anybody's rival before — unless you counted Corey Spaulding, which he couldn't. It was intoxicating and not a little frightening. Crouton threw an arm around his shoulder. "Bronfman and I know each other from the gym," he said to Shawn and Lucy. "It's where we get all big and strong. Check these out," he said, sarcastically flexing his meager muscles. "And then, after getting all hot and sweaty, we retire to the locker room, where we walk around naked for a while, swinging our dicks."

Crouton barked out a laugh.

"Oh, my God," Lucy said. "Did you really just say that?"

"Stop," Shawn said. "Please."

Crouton shrugged. "Well, it's true. Back me up here, Bronfman."

The women looked at Bronfman, waiting. He shrugged. "I don't know," he said, "about the swinging part. But there are — you do see a lot of . . . some of the men there, they get dressed . . . slowly."

The women laughed. They seemed to like Bronfman, even though he had only been accidentally funny. "Women aren't shy, either, I guess," Shawn said. "In the locker room. No big deal."

"But it's different with the men," Crouton said. "There's a primal battle going on in there. A competition, no different from what you see in the jungle with those silverback gorillas." Again, his French accent totally disappeared. "We're displaying our prowess. We're staking our claim. Right?"

"Well, I don't know about that," Bronfman said again. "It's not what *I* do, really."

It was then that Crouton stuck out the pinky on his left hand and showed it to Bronfman, and to the women, at whom he winked. "And there is a reason for that." Crouton laughed heartily again, but alone.

"Jesus fucking Christ," Shawn said. "You are appalling."

"The truth is appalling," Crouton said.

"No," Lucy said. "I'm pretty sure it's just you."

"And your photographs are silly and derivative and pretentious," Shawn said.

Crouton manufactured a nonchalance even Bronfman didn't buy. "All I mean to say is," he said, and he slapped Bronfman on the back, "is that this man has a very, very, very, very small penis. Teeny. Teeny-weeny. And it has an odd shape to it. It looks like a harmonica that's been run over by a truck. Just for your information. In case you were thinking about it. Now, if you will excuse me, I will take my much larger and extremely handsome penis to a woman —

or women — more likely to appreciate it."

And he saluted, bowed, and walked away, already waving at a woman sitting at a table against the wall. When she didn't wave back he stopped, still and alone in the middle of the room. He looked lost, stranded.

Bronfman and the two women shared a silence composed of equal parts shock, repulsion, and gloom. Normally, Bronfman would have had the gloom all to himself, but in this instance these two women, whom he had only just met, absorbed a good deal of it. Even so it was unbearable, a nightmare from which he could not wake. In fact, sleep would be the only avenue of rescue from his reality. He cast a furtive glance sideways at the women, but they couldn't even look at him. They were looking at each other, partners in disbelief, sympathetic but helpless.

The bartender reappeared, and Shawn ordered a drink. *Ah!* So the Crouton imbroglio had been just a small speed bump for them; now that it was over, their night could be resumed. Life goes on: Bronfman knew that. It's just that sometimes it went on so fast.

"I . . . should be going," he said, in a voice so small he could almost not hear it himself. He turned to them, and an odd thing happened, something he hadn't expected. Lucy smiled. Something might have been said, a whisper shared between the two women, he wasn't sure, but she smiled, a smile the size of a plantain. Felt good. He had to admit that. To have a beautiful woman smile at you feels good.

He stood.

"Wait," Lucy said. She touched him — his elbow with her hand — and he immediately sat back down. "Have a drink with us."

"I don't know," he said. "I really don't drink except on special occasions," meaning almost never.

The bartender brought six shot glasses full of what appeared to be urine and set them on the bar in front of them. Lucy pushed two toward Bronfman.

"Drink up," she said.

He scrutinized the glasses. "What is it?"

"Tequila. It's really good. You'll love it."

"I've had tequila before," he said, not sure if this was true. It may have been true, but at this point it didn't really matter.

"Great," Lucy said. "Then you know you're supposed to throw it back, right? Like poison. No sipping."

"Like poison," he said. She wasn't selling it, but in for a dime, in for a dollar, as

Muriel said when she was about to make another mistake with a man.

"I'm already a wee bit tipsy," Lucy said.

Shawn laughed. "You have to be tipsy to say 'wee bit.' No one says 'wee bit' unless they're —"

"— a wee bit tipsy!" Lucy said.

And they laughed and lifted a glass, and he lifted a glass, and together they "threw it back," just as Lucy said to do, and Bronfman felt a warm electric pulse pump through his body, felt bubbles blowing in his brain. But it was like taking a hot bath: scalded at first, he soon got used to it, and then it felt very, very good. The bar, so wretched a moment ago, took on the patina of a dream. He identified areas of his brain that he hadn't known were there. It was as if the tequila (which he was now sure he'd never had in his life) knew the secret combination to a locked room, and the creaky door opened, and inside it were treasures beyond measure.

"And now one more," Lucy said. "Okay? Courage!"

"Okay!" he said with gusto. He had possibly never said anything with more gusto in his life. He closed his eyes and down the hatch it went! This one made him feel as if he'd been walloped in the head with a down pillow.

"That's good, right?" Shawn said, or slurred. A wee bit.

Bronfman nodded. Was he drunk? Could he be drunk? How could two small glasses of anything make a man drunk? But he was something not quite himself, something grand. His soul left his body, and rose, and hovered above everyone else in the room. He was high. He could even see himself from where he was, Edsel Bronfman, on a stool in a skuzzy bar, sitting beside two beautiful women. It was a scene from a dream, a fantasy he would never have given himself permission to have.

But it wasn't enough.

"I'm wondering," he said, or this strange person he had become said, "if the two of you could do me a favor."

Lucy and Shawn exchanged another look. The last time he had seen a look like this was at the end of *Butch Cassidy and the Sundance Kid,* when Robert Redford looks at Paul Newman before they jump off that cliff. "Anything," Lucy said.

"We'd need to go back there." He gestured with a nod of his head toward the darkness behind the bar. *Back there.* What an odd way to put it. He was sure they would say no. What woman would agree to accompany a man she had just met into the cavernous darkness of an already dark bar? If he were a woman, that's the last place he would go. But they seemed intrigued.

"Ohhh," Shawn said. "Okay, I'll bite. Why?"

"I'd like your opinion."

Lucy inhaled sharply through her nose, and her eyes widened in a way that suggested both shock and friendly titillation. Somehow they knew exactly what he meant.

"Absolutely," she said, and she took Bronfman's hand and pulled him off the stool. "Let's do this."

The women stood, taking the lead. Happily, gratefully, upright and resolute, he followed them behind the bar, away from everybody and everything, all the noise and light and alien life. Suddenly they were there, in the secret catacombs, alone. Stacks of cardboard boxes created narrow pathways, private spaces — pallet after pallet of unmarked something or other. It was even darker than it looked from the bar. There was no light back here, none of its own, anyway, just the stray and leftover glow from the lamps up front. Temporarily blind, Bronfman's eyes slowly adjusted until he had a sense of where he was, the space they were in. But it was all in a grainy black and white. He couldn't see a single color. At some point, he had let go of Lucy's hand and managed to get a step or two ahead of them. He turned. There they were behind him, mostly shadow now, but still so ethereally beautiful, even as vaporous ghosts.

This had to be done, but he wasn't sure if he could do it.

"Okay," Lucy said. She covered her eyes briefly, and pulled Shawn close to her and almost squealed. Then she looked at Bronfman. "Okay!"

"Okay," he said, but still he stood there, frozen. His Bronfman-mind was surfacing. It was telling him quite clearly not to do what he knew he had to do. He was arguing with himself. He lost the argument, or won it, or both.

Lucy grasped Shawn's arm with a ferociously tight grip. "Okay," she said again. "Let's see it."

His ears were ringing from the barroom's din, though now it sounded miles away.

She took a deep and bracing breath. "Let's see your penis," she said. "You ready, Shawn?"

"Ready," she said, with an encouraging bravado.

Penis. With that magic word it was as if

she'd opened a door and that merely by hearing the word Bronfman had walked through it, fully entering this new, strange world, a place where the people spoke an unknowable language, but with words that sounded much like our own.

"You don't have to," Shawn said. "Really. If you've changed your mind. But you want a fresh perspective, right? We're here for you."

They laughed a little, and then they stopped laughing, and waited. Shawn's phone chirped, but she didn't answer it. The moment seemed to drag on and on for a timeless eternity, but it was probably no more than a second or two. I should just go home, he thought. I cannot do this; the night has been sufficiently horrific already. It was impossible. Nevertheless, he looked at his hands and discovered that they were busy unbuckling his belt — that they had made the decision for him. The belt unbuckled, his trousers slipped all the way past his light-blue boxers before he caught them. He *had* lost a couple of pounds; his pants were almost a size too big. But there was no going back now. He released his trousers and watched them fall, watched as they crumpled on the floor, a wrinkled blanket for his shoes. Never in his life had he done anything more unlike himself than this, which meant that he was not himself, not really. He was someone else now.

Lucy and Shawn waited for the boxers, and in one swift and fearless pull he was, from the waist down, unbelievably, naked.

A cool breeze greeted his penis.

He looked down at it. He really never saw it from any other angle. It was so lonely down there, stranded beneath his stomach and between his legs. Black-and-white and blurry in the shadows, it looked like a character from a silent movie. Not the lead, of course, one of the smaller parts. Not only was it naked; it was the essence of naked, honest and a bit naïve, hopeful, like a poor native of some impoverished island country the Americans had come to save.

Sheepishly, he raised his head and looked at the women, but they weren't looking at him; rather, they were studying his penis with a seriousness and an absorption bordering on the scientific. Lucy nodded, as if agreeing with some secret thought, but the nod could have gone either way, for or against.

Time slowed to a molasses crawl. Seconds stretched to their breaking point, unquestionably the longest of Bronfman's life.

"That," she said, "is very nice."

"It really is," Shawn said. "Very nice."

"I *like* it."

"What's not to like?" Shawn said.

"Nothing, not a thing."

"Shapely. Friendly. And approachable. That's the main thing. A penis you wouldn't mind hanging out with for a while."

"I mean, is it, you know, really big? No. Obviously not."

"Definitely not huge," Lucy said.

"But the truth is, no girl wants a huge one. I've seen a couple, and they scared me."

Lucy shook her head, as if she, too, had seen huge, scary penises in her time. "So, this is good," she said. "And I'm telling you the truth, Bronfman. It's not necessarily going to win an award. It's not the penis-of-all-penises. But it's good. It's good enough. And good enough is great, especially when it comes —"

"— to penises," Bronfman bravely intoned.

"Or to almost anything, actually," Lucy said.

Shawn agreed. "I think you should be proud of it."

Proud. *Proud?* He wasn't sure this was a feeling he had in his repertoire, but there it was, pride, making an entrance, slowly but surely, as all three of them looked on.

"Okay," Bronfman said. "I will."

The two women stood there a bit longer, looking at it, then at him, then at each other.

"Any questions?" Lucy said.

Would you like to go to the beach with me? It would be fun, the three of us. An extraordinary adventure, totally free, the entire weekend, a beautiful condo in Destin, Florida, and a continental breakfast to boot.

"No," he said. "Thank you."

Their job here was done. Lucy took a step backward, and Shawn followed. Lucy may have winked at him, but it was hard to tell in the grainy darkness they were slipping back into.

"You take care, Bronfman, okay?"

"I will," Bronfman said, waving at the departing spirits. "You, too."

Then they were gone.

Bronfman did not move or even breathe, and left his trousers puddled around his ankles. But then the spell was broken, and he pulled them up, belted them, and walked back into the bar, back into the cacophony of other people's lives. Lucy and Shawn were gone, nowhere to be seen. And there was Crouton, at a high table against the sheet-metal wall, talking to a young woman who, Bronfman could see now, was desperate to get away from him. What a jerk.

Bronfman fixed his stare on Crouton like a laser beam until Crouton felt it and looked up, and their eyes met, and with all his cerebral might Bronfman tried to impart to Crouton what had just happened, the magical experience he'd just had. Maybe he did impart it, or maybe he didn't, but at least Crouton stopped talking long enough for the girl to say good-bye, and she left, and then Bronfman left, too, a soldier bravely entering the mysterious night.

What a day. He would never forget it. How could he? He had been wrong about himself forever. He was good enough, and good enough was great. This was Bronfman, becoming defined.

DAY THIRTY-SIX

ONE

It was the first week of May. For the past few mornings it had felt like summer already, the way the dew steamed in the rising sun. A thin wall of heat greeted Bronfman when he opened his door and stepped out into the day, his brand-new penis in tow. He felt the presence of another and glanced to his right. There he saw Thomas Edison's friend Coco, sitting on his next-door neighbor's stoop. He could see now what a small woman she was, and yet one fully grown, wearing old cutoff jeans and a sleeveless yellow blouse with rows of flowered ruffles along the front. It might have been made for a child. Long black hair braided into two identical tributaries, reflecting the light like vinyl, her skin tinted as if in an old photograph, sepia-toned. Bright dark eyes.

She was smoking, of course. No one in Thomas Edison's cluster cared about what smoking did to your heart, lungs, life expectancy, breath. Either they thought they were immune to it or it didn't matter that they weren't. Bronfman wasn't sure which was worse.

"Good morning," he said. "Coco."

She glanced at him, smiled briefly, and lifted one of her hands, approximating a waving gesture, and then went back to whatever it was she was doing — smoking and thumbing through a fashion magazine, turning the pages much too quickly to read. She was just looking at the pictures.

"Are you waiting for Thomas?" he asked her.

"No," she said, without looking up. "He's inside."

Normally, with that he would have moved on, but whoever he was today did not move on. Today he waited for more. The pound dogs were howling lazily, as if they didn't really care about howling; it was just their job as dogs. He scanned the grassy-patched dirt beside the stoop: four cigarette butts, half smoked; a gum wrapper; a chewed piece of gum. How reprobates marked time.

"Coco is an interesting name," Bronfman said.

She turned another glossy page but, when she felt him staring at her, said, "Nickname. Short for Yoshiko. Japanese descent, and, like my parents say, I've been falling ever since."

"Ah. So you're just sitting here?"

She sighed and dropped her half-smoked cigarette into the dirt, where it smoldered. "I'm — you know."

"I don't know," he said.

"I'm on *lookout,*" she said. She gave the word air quotes. "He doesn't want anyone coming in while he's doing whatever he's doing with — whoever he's doing it with. I don't know. I'm not a part of it. He said something happened. With you."

Bronfman nodded. "Something did. A man almost killed me."

"No, he didn't," she said. "Not what I heard, anyway. He just implied that he would, to scare you. That's Jimmy. I shouldn't say he's harmless but — he's harmless."

"So I shouldn't worry." Bronfman smiled.

"Don't worry about a thing."

Bronfman decided to acknowledge the elephant in his brain. "You were wearing my hat," he said. "The other night."

She pretended to think about it. "No," she said. "I don't think so."

Boldly, he pressed on. "That was definitely my hat."

She sighed, as if she had been finished

with this conversation long before he had. "Why would I be wearing your hat? That doesn't make sense. If I was wearing a hat it would be mine, not yours."

"The hat was stolen. Someone stole it. I saw you with it on."

Then there came some angry voices from inside Thomas Edison's apartment. Something shattered, a door slammed. Coco lifted her head, her small face empty of expression, listening. But all was quiet now. She turned her gaze to him.

"Are you saying I stole your shitty fucking hat?"

Bronfman wouldn't say that. He had tried this once before with Thomas Edison, and it had almost gotten him killed.

"No," he said.

"Then what?"

"Nothing."

"Whatever," she said. She turned away.

All the good feeling he'd woken up with was now entirely gone, as it always was after being filtered through reality.

"You have to admit it's a coincidence," he said, "that you would have a hat exactly like the one I had, which was stolen."

"I will admit that," she said. "It's eerie. It's one of those things that happen and you think, I mean, *Wow!* You couldn't make this shit up, you know?"

"I've had that hat all my life. Since I was a boy. It means . . . it means a lot to me."

This moved her. She closed the magazine and, for the first time, really looked at Bronfman. They were connecting. It felt like a connection. Her eyes softened and she almost smiled.

"I had a doll once," she said. "My dad had gone on a business trip somewhere, and he brought it back. It was a Raggedy Ann. My first white doll. 'All the little American girls have this doll,' he said. 'You are American.' It seemed like that was the first time he'd really realized it. That I was born here, that I wasn't really Japanese, like he was."

"And?"

"And what?"

"What happened to the doll?"

She shrugged. "Lost it," she said. "Or maybe it was stolen by some other American girl? I don't know. So I get it, how you feel about the hat. I'm sorry."

"Thanks," he said. He blinked a couple of times and dropped his chin. "I guess I'll survive."

"I hope so," she said. "The hat, it's just a thing. A thing you used to have. Better to look ahead to other things, the things you

235

haven't got yet."

He raised his head and looked at her. She wasn't who he thought she was. She was something more.

"Well," he said, "have a nice day."

He waited for her to say the same — *You, too, Bronfman.* But she went back to her magazine, and lit another cigarette, and brought her knees up to her chest and held them there, and flipped through the magazine until she came to the end of it, at which point she started again from the beginning.

Two

An office has a mood, a personality, a soul. It's a single organism made up of dozens of smaller organisms whose individual experiences contribute to the whole, creating either a buoyant can-do attitude or a beleaguered pessimism that can last the whole day through. Today the office was magnificently bleak. Skip Sorsby had again lost the IKEA invoice in a digital quagmire, and his frustration spread like a virus, affecting everybody. Bronfman, already battling a characteristic despondency, needed a pick-me-up.

That pick-me-up was Goldstein's, of course.

Goldstein's Deli and its Famous Reuben. Never failed to satisfy. Goldstein's made the best Reuben Bronfman had ever known. There was a secret sauce of some kind, one invented by Ira Goldstein, who was at least a hundred years old now and sat behind the cash register like a shrunken effigy of himself, incapable of even a smile. He looked as if he wished he'd died a long time ago. His son Caleb ran the place now. A pleasant, heavy man. A younger version of Ira. He had a spark, an eagerness to please, that Bronfman appreciated. He knew Bronfman well, and always greeted him with excessive enthusiasm. Caleb knew Bronfman's order before he placed it — "One Reuben, the works!" Caleb would call out, sometimes just as Bronfman walked in the door. This made Bronfman unaccountably happy. And when Caleb said, as he so often did, "One day they're going to change the name of this sandwich to the Bronfman. From my mouth to God's ears! Not a Reuben anymore — the Bronfman!" Bronfman soared into thin stratospheric air, where he found it hard to breathe. He had at least half-a-dozen *Goldstein's* pens.

Today was different. Caleb was there, taking orders, same as ever. But there was no spark, no zest. His shoulders slumped into his chest. Bronfman hoped his presence might brighten Caleb up, but even as he approached the counter there was no greeting, no suggestion to God that the name of the Reuben be changed to the Bronfman — nothing. Bronfman wondered, as always, if it was something he had done, or hadn't done. Maybe he should come in more often. Maybe he wasn't being the sort of customer Caleb wanted him to be.

"Hi, Caleb," Bronfman said, a bit sheepishly. "Long time no see. Buried in paperwork, really busy — you know how it is." Caleb nodded, pen in hand, waiting for Bronfman's order. It was so weird. It was as if the real Caleb had been replaced by a fake composite Caleb who was identical to Caleb in every way, a clone who had only one flaw: he didn't know Bronfman; he didn't know Bronfman's sandwich. A minor detail that had been overlooked when this replacement was made!

"So what can I get you?"

"Ha! You know what I want, Caleb," Bronfman said.

He sighed. "Maybe I do, maybe I don't. Why don't you just tell me. Order something. There's a line."

"Caleb." It was important that Caleb knew what Bronfman wanted. It was so important that Bronfman wasn't going to tell him — he couldn't. He was going to make him figure it out. He was going to make him remember. "I want what I get every time I'm here."

Caleb sighed. "Okay, give me a hint," he

said. "Like maybe tell me the name of the fucking sandwich you want."

Bronfman was crushed. Caleb saw that, and softened, and for the first time really focused on the face before him.

"Oh, Bronfman," he said. "Bronfman, I'm sorry. The Reuben, of course." He wrote it down on the little pad and shook his head.

"Are you okay?"

Caleb shrugged, as if considering it. "My father, Ira. He's in the hospital. Pneumonia. At his age, you know . . . you have to worry a little bit."

"Oh, my God." Bronfman sounded surprised, but he wasn't really. Ira had been hanging by a twig from a cliff for a decade. "I'm so sorry."

"Thank you," Caleb said. "Wish I could be with him, but we have a business to run," he said. "Customers. They count on us. Ira never missed a day of work in his life. The day I was born, he was here. I was born on a Wednesday, and he didn't see me until Thursday. Whatareyougonnado? Mama's with him."

"That's good," Bronfman said.

"You know how long they've been to-gether? Sixty-five years. Sixty-five years! And they still love each other. Would that we were all that lucky."

Sixty-five years, Bronfman thought. If he found someone today who loved him like that and stuck with him that long, he would die at ninety-nine.

"You got someone, Bronfman? You got a wife?"

"No," Bronfman said.

"A girlfriend, then."

"No," Bronfman said. "I don't have a companion of any kind."

"Well, get one," Caleb said.

"That's my goal," Bronfman said. "I have forty-three days."

Caleb nodded, though he seemed confused now. "Good to have a goal, I guess. But you don't want to put a timer on it. You never know how long it's going to take."

"But I know exactly how long I have. I won a prize. I won it here, actually. A trip to the beach."

But Caleb had lost interest, was looking over Bronfman's shoulder to the customer behind him. "Whatareyougonnado?" he said. That was his go-to phrase. "Next!"

Sandwich, bag of chips, and sweet iced tea on the brown plastic tray, Bronfman made his way over to a table — a two-top, it was called by professionals in the business. It was against the wall beneath a black-and-white photo of Goldstein's at its original location, about a block from here. It burned down in 1959, so Ira moved it, made it bigger and more "modern," which appeared to mean a truckload of stainless steel and Formica. This is where Bronfman sat to eat his lunch, in solitude, just as he had last week, and the week before that.

What happened next was, like electricity and automobiles, another mystery.

The tables at Goldstein's were set about a foot apart; slipping between them was a challenge. It was easy to knock against a table and create all kinds of havoc, especially for some of the patrons, who were heavy. More than heavy. Some were *big.* Some people were simply enormous. But none of them would ever even have attempted to slip through the narrow corridor of tables. Only the slimmest of people would think such passage was remotely possible and attempt its negotiation.

Such a person did attempt it now. She was slim. Small. Almost petite. She wore a yellow-and-white sundress neatly cinched at the waist, the hem of which stopped an inch or so above her knees, her arms and shoulders so delicately white you could have sifted half a cup of flour on them and no one would have been the wiser. On her tray was some chicken salad — a round mound scooped out and plopped there by an ice-cream scooper — and a wedge of iceberg lettuce and a dill pickle and a corn stick, which was like a corn muffin but instead of being muffin-shaped it was shaped like an ear of corn. The corn stick was something Goldstein's was moderately famous for. Her purse — huge, almost like a backpack, and stuffed with what appeared to be one of every thing there was in the world — swung dangerously from one of her lovely arms.

It was Sheila McNabb.

"Sheila," Bronfman said, not for her to hear but for him. He said it as if it were an incantation. She didn't see him. She tried to slip by, so he pushed his tray toward the opposite edge of the table to give her extra room. But there still wasn't enough room. Her purse knocked against his tray and his entire extra-large glass of sweetened iced tea fell, and was dripping from his lap now, the front of his shirt, seeping into his boxer shorts, and soaked up by the rest of him until he was wet all over. The tea at Gold-stein's was also moderately famous and served in bucket-size red plastic cups.

"Oh, my *God!*" she said, as if she had ac-cidentally severed one of his arms. People turned to see who was dying. "I am *so sorry!*"

"No, no," he said, softly, evenly. "You didn't do anything."

"I knocked your glass over. I'm so sorry. I shouldn't have tried to get through here. I thought — optimist that I am — I thought I could make it through."

Bronfman took a napkin and pointlessly tried to pat himself dry. "My fault," he said. "I moved to one side to give you more room if you needed it, and my arm hit the glass. It was my fault, not yours, Sheila."

She had been examining the damage, the swamp his lap had become, and then, for the first time, she looked at him.

"Oh," she said. "Oh, my goodness. You — you're Edsel. Edsel Bronfman. From the Cranston Building."

Wow. Just wow. She remembered his name. Like a magic trick.

"So I'm going to sit down with you," Sheila said. "May I sit with you?"

"Of course. Please."

She sat, and set her purse down on the floor beside her feet. It was as big as a two-year-old.

"Edsel," she said. She let the sound of his name hang in the air. "Well, that's —. What do you know. How long has it been? Like a month, right?"

"Thirty-four days," Bronfman said, and regretted it immediately. It wasn't as if he had been counting the days since he had last seen her, but obviously, without even knowing it, he had. As if he had a calendar in his heart.

"You look great. You seem, I don't know —"

"More defined?"

"I already defined you. You're a giraffe, remember?"

"You remembered."

"Of course I remembered," she said. "No one forgets an ungulate."

She unwrapped her fork and knife from the tightly wrapped napkin.

"This is where I'm supposed to say I'll pay for your dry cleaning." She paused. Deep breath. "I'll pay for your dry cleaning."

"But it's just tea," Bronfman said. "It's mostly water. It won't stain. I'm just . . . wet."

She shook her head. "I wish I were on crutches so no one could blame me for anything." She laughed, and leaned in toward Bronfman. "I didn't mean that. I'm going to hell."

"No," Bronfman said. "Sometimes I wish

I was on crutches, too. People are nicer to you when you're on crutches."

"Do you love this place? I love this place," she said. "I've been coming here since the Truman administration."

"That's a long time."

"I'm a hundred and five years old," she said. "My secret? Organic vegetables. That's how I keep my looks. And the blood of a virgin, of course. Spoonful a day, and I'm good as new."

"Ha-ha," Bronfman said, thinking that would probably be funny to someone who wasn't Edsel Bronfman.

She removed her salad from the tray and set the tray down at an empty table to her left. Now the food was displayed as if she were at home, or at a restaurant where it was served by a waiter. Bronfman never took his plates off the tray; he never thought about it. It looked like a good idea, though, now that he had seen her do it. Next time.

"It's great to run into you," she said, and laughed. "Stupid pun *completely* accidental. Like almost everything I do."

Bronfman wondered if it *was* an accident, though. As he felt the tea inching toward his neck, he realized that this was one of life's large moments. He was sitting at his favorite restaurant with a woman he hadn't stopped thinking about since the day he last saw her. An immense spotlight from the heavens seemed to be shining on them. This little table at Goldstein's was the center of all creation. His heart was a ball of tangled yarn. It wasn't love — he would not allow for that. But, at the very least, it was a robust and bright-eyed emotion, impossible to ignore.

"How's the Cranston?" she asked him. "I really liked that old building. And just sitting there at my desk, watching all the people go by."

"Turning them into animals," he said.

"Exactly. And you got the feeling lots of the people who worked there over the years were dead now. Brought a kind of gravity to the place."

She took a bite of her salad. He had never thought of that.

"So, how are your instructions going?"

She leaned in, turning an ear toward him. "Sorry, how's my what going?"

"The instruction-writing business."

"The instruction-writing business? Oh . . ." She smiled, recalibrating, momentarily knocked off balance, footing regained. "Yes, that. Well, I've gotten a couple of jobs. Little ones. Let's see. Did something for a stapler company. Getting staples into a stapler — lots of people find that challenging because the directions are so unclear. Re-inking a stamp pad. And batteries — batteries are my bread and butter. Positive-negative, negative-positive. It can be confusing."

"That's so interesting," said Bronfman, who had never learned exactly how to insert staples into a stapler and felt that Sheila was doing something important in the world by clarifying how this happens.

"You remembered that," she said. She seemed pleased that he did. "About directions."

"Of course," he said.

"Sweet. I just sort of — I mean, we only talked about it for a second."

"I'm a giraffe," he said. "Giraffes never forget."

With her fork she aimlessly rearranged the leaves of her salad, impaling a tiny carrot wheel on the tines. She brought it to her mouth and chewed it as thoughtfully as a small piece of carrot can be chewed.

"I want to take back what I said," she said. "About you being an ungulate. It's not right. It doesn't quite fit."

"Okay," he said. He loved this game. "Then what? What am I?"

She thought about it, seriously, studying

him, examining him, investigating the animal before her as he watched her investigate him, and she came up empty-handed. "I don't know what you are, Bronfman," she said. "I'd have to spend more time with you to find out exactly."

"More time," he said. "Of course. That makes sense." He looked at his watch. "Can you do it in ten minutes? Because I have to get back for a meeting."

"No," she said. "It would take more than ten minutes."

"Oh," he said. "Darn."

But Bronfman had been here before. Not here with Sheila at Goldstein's but within this opportunity for possibility. A single word from him to her, the smallest possible gesture — that was all it called for, all he needed to reinvent his world.

He had to breathe. He had to get some air.

"Then maybe," he said, drawing from the well of experience he had discovered just last night: if he could show two strangers his penis, what couldn't he do? "Maybe we should create an opportunity to spend additional time together."

She took a moment to compute his syntax. "Oh. Well. Sure. Yes. I agree," she said, and almost laughed but caught herself. "Let's create that opportunity. When's good?"

Anytime, he thought. Tonight, tomorrow night, the next. But that wasn't how it was done. He had seen enough TV to know that.

"How about next Tuesday?"

"Sure," she said. "This coming Tuesday? Fine. Great. I think — sure. Let's do that. Next Tuesday."

She wrote her address and her phone number on a napkin and slid it across the table the way a mob boss in a crime drama slides an offer to a mark. He took it, and held it. Bronfman had yet to finish his Bronfman, but he got up to leave before she changed her mind.

"Tuesday, then," he said.

"Tuesday. And I'm sorry. About the tea."

Thirty-five days in, and Edsel Bronfman had a date.

On the way out he told Caleb, who said that he was happy for him — truly, truly, so very happy. "Mazel tov," he said.

THREE

On the way home that evening after work, Bronfman stopped by the Harris Teeter, intending to buy some milk, half a dozen eggs, breakfast tea, frozen pizza, an apple, two bananas, instant oatmeal, a roll of paper towels, rotini, half a loaf of wheat bread (he bought halves of everything whenever he could), a pound of free-range skinless, boneless chicken breasts, a bag of frozen peas, a six-pack of Diet Pepsi, baking soda, and a few other items. He walked up and down every aisle, forgetting almost everything, his cart empty save for a lonely bag of frozen peas that lay perspiring at the bottom. It was as though he were wandering through a museum, admiring the careful design, the bright colors, the clever illustrations. Or as if he weren't doing anything at all, just mindlessly pushing his cart down alleyways created specifically for his passage. He might very well have traveled the same aisle twice, possibly three times, without noticing. He was here but not here. Somehow wandering around the Harris Teeter like a zombie, he had no trouble holding on to it, the peculiar grandness of it all, these odd bits of magic floating through his mind like dust in a sunbeam. He had a date, he had a date, he had a date!

He felt new, burnished and bright. The last time he had felt anything like this was when he left home for college. He had applied to only one school — Springmore, a small liberal-arts university an hour and a half outside Birmingham, close enough for visits but far enough to start over, to give himself a second chance to become someone other than the person he clearly was. For starters, he wouldn't have to be *Bronfman* anymore; he could be *Ed.* He had always wanted to be an Ed. Ed was a friendly, common name; there were lots of Eds, and Bronfman had no misgivings about becoming one of them. To Bronfman, it felt as if there was only one Bronfman in the world, and it was him. It was not a good feeling. Like being an endangered species, the last of its lonely kind.

His roommate was from New Jersey, a man-child named Pete Ornstein. He was twice Bronfman's size in every direction.

He had one of those scary New York accents, the sort of accent a cop from the Bronx on a television show might have, and his hair was black and kinky and he left the top two buttons of his shirt open, revealing a carpet of curly turf. He wore a gold chain with the letter *O* attached — that's what everyone called him, he said, O, sometimes Big O — and he had driven a silver Electra 225 all the way from Trenton, even though freshmen weren't supposed to have cars on campus. But Big O didn't care about rules.

The day they met it went like this:

"Pete Ornstein," Pete Ornstein said, crushing Bronfman's hand in his monstrous grip. "But people call me Big O."

"It's nice to meet you, Big O," Bronfman said. "My name — my name is Ed, Ed Bronfman."

Big O sized him up, studied him like a specimen.

"Ed?" he said. "Ed Bronfman?"

"That's right," Ed said. "Ed."

"You know what, Ed?"

"What?"

"I'm going to call you Bronfman. I like that name. Ed's boring. Bronfman's funny, and it looks like you. You look like a Bronfman."

"Call me Ed," Bronfman said. And then,

in a desperate attempt to stave off his first thematic defeat, "Please."

"Bronfman," Big O said and laughed, turning away, unpacking. "Ha! I love it."

So Bronfman gave up being Ed. There was no reason to try to sustain that dream. It was pointless. Big O had friends, and Big O introduced him as Bronfman to everyone who came into the room, and it caught on with everybody across the tiny campus. His very first foray into the hostile and forbidding world of metamorphosis had been thwarted; based on this (albeit small) sample set, his second would be, too, as would his third, and so on. Bronfman knew that he was too easily dissuaded, but he took no for an answer because he had learned that noes traveled in packs, one following another, like street thugs. He saw negative trends where there were none; he created them; he forecast his own story before it was written. If one person didn't call him Ed, that meant no one would call him Ed. What a fragile spirit! His hopes were like a piñata at a birthday party, smashed with a single blow. He went to class, spent time at the library, returned to his room, ate three meals a day at the cafeteria, where he sat at the same table midway toward the back. He sometimes ate with others who were as quiet as he was, but mostly not. The cafeteria was twice as big as it needed to be. Though some students were scattered across it in small bunches of three or four, others, like Bronfman, were alone, had a whole table to themselves, surrounded by a force field of self-protection and freshman fear. You could almost see it. The alone people stayed alone, and grew only more so as the days ground by.

But his room was nice enough. He liked it. He liked how his tiny bed fit snugly in a corner by the window, cocoon-esque. And he and O, while no more like each other than an ostrich is like a telephone, actually got along. They weren't buddies (the entire year they were roommates not a single social event did they attend together), but they coexisted in a chilly peace, just a bit short of actually being friendly.

One day while Bronfman was in his bed, propped up by the bright-blue husband pillow his mother had given him, reading about early American history (what happened with the Indians — tragic, awful, but inevitable, he supposed), there was a *thwack* of something against his window, right by his head. He thought it was a baseball at first, or a rock, or even a bullet, so sudden and sharp and loud it was, a heart-attack-inducing sound.

It was a bird. He saw it out of the corner of his eye, the feathered thing, and, just that quickly, it was gone, falling the two stories to the ground below. Bronfman caught his breath and opened the window and looked. There it was, crumpled, black-and-brown-and-white, resting in the green of a red-berry bush, dead.

Or not. Did it move just then? Did it shiver? Did it shudder? It seemed to.

Bronfman, uncharacteristically hopeful, even prescient, removed from under his bed the cardboard box his mother had sent him, formerly full of fruit and chocolate and three frosty peanut-butter-and-jelly sand-wiches (she must have kept them in a deep freeze for months), and raced down the two flights of stairs, through the heavy steel doors, outside past the ginormous air-conditioning unit — and there it was. The little red-brown beads that were its eyes were so full of fear, its beak opening and closing, as if it were trying to say something to Bronfman. *Help me, please.*

Bronfman gently cupped his hand around the nearly weightless body, lifted it from its precarious bed of leaves and berries, and held it, somewhat stunned himself. This life was in his hands, literally. He could feel its whole body thrumming. The feathers were soft but folded tight around the bird, like an enclosure, and for a fleeting moment Bronfman imagined himself covered in feathers, what that would be like. He set the bird down in the box, pulled up tufts of grass from the surrounding yard, and broke little branches off the berry tree, collected some leaves, and made the little bird a bed, a primitive nest.

Then he took it back up to his room, in the hope that it might get better there. That he, Bronfman, might save its life.

Big O wasn't there, so Bronfman set the cardboard box on his bed and watched the bird lie there. He could see its little chest shuddering. He touched it — so soft.

Bronfman poked holes in all four sides of the box with a pencil and closed the lid, then he put it underneath his bed. He ran to the library (he avoided the computer with the anxiety of a germophobe; the sprawling, seemingly infinite world of information intimidated him) and checked out a book, *Birds of America.* He found the match: black head, white chest, rust-colored wings.

It was called a rufous-sided towhee. Of all the things in the world, to be called *that.* The way Bronfman was called *Bronfman.* Immediately, he established an absurd kinship with the bird, based solely on its name. *Hi, Rufous, my name is Bronfman.* Rufous was another word for "red-brown," and, based on the coloring, it was a boy — or a male, Bronfman supposed is what you would call it.

And then there was this: "The female makes a nest of weeds, leaves, bark, and stems on or near the ground."

On or near the ground. It seemed curious, very curious, that a bird would make its nest on the ground; a bird, it seemed to Bronfman, would take advantage of being a bird and make its nest in a tree, where it's safer, and where it would be, for the most part, anyway, singing, taking in the view, avoiding cats. Although on the other hand, the ground is where the food is. If the early bird gets the worm, the early bird that lives in close proximity *to* the worm would be even more likely to get it.

Bronfman had no worm. He went to the cafeteria and got a piece of sesame-seed bread and scraped the seeds off into the box, and Rufous ate one, then two, then three.

Bronfman watched him eat. He watched the bird as if it were his own two eyes that were bringing him back to life.

Four, five, six.

■ ■ ■ ■

An hour later Big O burst through the door, lumbered into the room like a lost giant.

"What's that?" Big O said, pointing at the box.

Bronfman closed the box flaps one after the other, but slowly, so as not to draw too much attention. "This? Nothing," Bronfman said. "Just stuff my mother sent me."

"Sticks and leaves?" O said. "I know I saw some sticks and leaves. That what your mother sends you, Bronfman?"

"It's nothing."

"I'll be the judge of that."

Big O took three slow steps — all he needed to get from his side of the room to Bronfman's side. He hulked there above Bronfman, waiting. Big O would never have hurt Bronfman — at least, it had never come to that, but had he wanted to open the box on his own Bronfman could not have stopped him. So, fast-forwarding to the inevitable end of the conflict that would never happen, he opened it up.

"See?" Bronfman said. "It's nothing. It's just a bird."

"Holy. Fucking. Crap," O said, his voice a church-pew whisper. "It *is* a bird!"

O stared — epically surprised, semi-stunned. Possibly awestruck. He was on pause, frozen. It pleased Bronfman immeasurably to have affected his roommate in this way. He had never thought it possible. This was what power felt like, control. What it meant to be the puppeteer and not the puppet. He felt as if he was going to implode.

"Can I . . . touch it?"

O checked with Bronfman, *asked permission.* Bronfman considered the request.

"Maybe just the tip of its tail feather," he said. "Along the edge. It flew into the window. I don't know if it can fly. Be careful."

O barely touched the bird, then he drew back his hand. "Ellen has to see this," he said.

"No, please," Bronfman said. "I don't think . . . the bird needs quiet —"

But O was already out the door.

A few minutes later he came back with Ellen, a tall girl with hair the color of butter — Bronfman's idea of an angel. He had seen her half a dozen times but had never said hello, because sure, right, he was going to say hello to her. Ellen had a friend, Deb, who was equally angelic and who wore those blouses that could never quite contain

260

her breasts. Both of them smiled at Bronfman, who was sitting on the bed beside the box, and took little steps toward him.

"Can we see?" Ellen said.

"Sure," Bronfman said. "Of course."

They looked. Ellen's hip brushed Bronfman's shoulder.

"Wow. How did you get him?"

"He flew into the window and was a little knocked out. I brought him up from the bush down there. He's getting better. I think he's going to be okay."

"Charles would love this," Ellen said. "Mind if I get him? He would just love it."

"Sure." Anything she asked he'd do. Anything. "If he'd love it. Sure."

A few minutes later Charles came, and two girls he didn't know and another guy, and so did Jay Bresland, who wanted to put the bird in a film he was making. O — who by virtue of being Bronfman's roommate had taken partial possession of the bird — forbade it. "It's fighting for its fucking life," O said. "And you want to put it in one of your stupid movies?"

Within an hour, their dorm room was jammed with people wanting to see the bird and, by extension, Bronfman himself. Intoxicating, all of this. They asked him questions about the bird — they wanted to know

261

his story, the story of Bronfman and the bird — and he told them, and they were astounded at his ingenuity and bravery, people who had never noticed Bronfman before, even though they lived down the hall from him and had for six months.

Somehow the bird and Bronfman became one thing. That's how it felt. He was light as air. He had grown his own feathers; he could fly. Not necessarily a good thing, though, as a freshman in college, to see yourself or present yourself to others as a thing with feathers. Ellen and Charles and O and those other girls spotlighted Bronfman in their gaze. He had their attention. If there was something he wanted from them, or something he wanted to say to them, or if he'd been waiting for something like this to put a small dent in the status quo, now was clearly the time. But it turned out there wasn't anything he wanted from the moment except for it to be over.

The bird paced back and forth across the bottom of the cardboard box. He hopped. The crowd (how many people behind him now? Eight? Ten?) circus-gasped and applauded. There was affirmation for the bird who hopped, for Rufous. His wings opened, tentatively, they almost spread. Then, just that quickly, they closed again. Stretching.

He was getting the feel of it. An old fighter back in the ring. Rufous took a few more of his scrabbly steps through the sticks and grass and stopped. The little bird froze there. This life. And his head banked skittishly back and forth, settling, finally, on Bronfman. No one had the angle Bronfman had. No one could tell that the bird was looking right at him. But for what? Help? Reassurance? Another sesame seed?

It had gotten quiet in the little room, the stillness that happens before what happens happens.

The bird's tiny eyes, no bigger or deeper than a drop of oil, reflected all the fear and hope there was in the world. Bronfman felt it, too. The crowd behind the two of them receded into an inconsequential blur; it was just Rufous and Bronfman now, connected by the thread of life. And Bronfman wasn't the least bit scared. That was the really interesting thing. He picked the bird up, cupped him in his hands, and held him. He heard someone catch her breath, maybe two someones, and then it was all silence. One of the girls may even have touched him on the shoulder. He didn't know; it didn't matter. Because he was holding a bird in his hands, a bird he had saved a couple of hours ago.

He brought Rufous to the same window he had flown into — open now — and held him on the other side of it, still nestled in the twin palms of his hands, his beak probing for an opening. The sun fell above a pine forest, the dying light fanning across the small campus, and Bronfman didn't know how to do this, so he just did it. He dropped Roufus into the air — and the air was all he seemed to need. A brief adjustment, a moment of awkward flapping, and Roufus righted himself and flew, angling left and right, as if to avoid potential gunfire. Bronfman watched as he became smaller and smaller, disappearing into the dusky gloom.

And that was that. The bird, Rufous, was gone. The brief adventure was over. Some of the kids laughed, some applauded. Bronfman's heart was weirdly heavy, as if what had just happened wasn't an actual happy ending, when it totally was, for sure; it could not have been much happier. But he missed the rufous-sided towhee, immediately and fiercely. He missed him the way he missed his mother from time to time, with a scary hollow ache. He looked back at the others, his brand-new friends, and they were turning away from him already, returning to their wonderful lives. And that was fine. Bronfman himself was fine, at home in his natural environment. *Homo invisibilis.* He wasn't ready to be seen. He knew that without knowing that he knew it. He needed more time, more experience, another fifteen years or so of life on the ground. That was why Carla D'Angelo called him when she did — because he was ready now. Somehow, she knew that. He was ready to be seen for the very first time. By Sheila McNabb. He was ready for the adventure. All he'd needed was a little air.

■ ■ ■ ■

DAY THIRTY-SEVEN

■ ■ ■ ■

ONE

He had no one to share his news about Sheila with but his mother. After work the following day he visited her, a day earlier than he had planned. He couldn't wait.

She was screaming when he walked in, not an uncommon occurrence.

"Stay away from me, Bettina! I know what you're up to!" Then silence, as if whatever Bettina had been up to was done. He closed the front door behind him — accidentally slamming it — and Bettina arrived, investigating, and was not impressed.

"Oh," she said. "It's you."

"How is she?"

This was what he asked Bettina every visit before entering his mother's lair, skittish to walk in there and see for himself. He liked a warning. He wanted to be prepared.

"She is losing her damn mind is what," Bettina said. "Every day a little bit more. Every day it's something. Yelling about something. It's going to be too much for me soon. She's taking too many pills, Mr. Bronfman. They're clouding her up. She didn't know who I was for a little while this morning. Mornings are hardest."

"What were you up to just now?"

"Up to?"

"She said, 'I know what you're up to' when I came in."

"Water," she said. "I was giving her a glass of water."

It was like in a horror movie when the man is going into a room where he heard something but isn't sure what it is, and the camera is right behind him as he slowly opens the creaking door into the frightening shadows where the possibility of evil resides.

"Hi, Mom," Bronfman said.

She was in bed, all propped up, hair brushed back, her face thickly painted with orange pancake.

"What a surprise," she said. "My sweetie sweet come to see me. Come over and give me a kiss! On second thought, don't. You might have something. I might have something. Who knows."

He was fine with that.

She smiled at him. "I just got back from the Kmart in the sky."

"Really?"

"Well, I'm rearranging the house, so —"

"Ah."

"Ah? Ah? What's that sound mean? Methinks I hate it. Hate it, hate it, hate it." She shook her head. "No regrets, Edsel. What's done is done. My time machine is broken anyway. The demons are out of the house now."

"You seem confused, Mom," he said. "There are no demons here." For some reason, he felt this fiction needed to be countered with the facts: there were no demons. And it worked. Just like that, she snapped back. Her eyes cleared up. She knew who he was and, more important, who she was.

"Of course there aren't," she said, her voice so soft now, like a girl's. "I don't know what the hell I'm saying sometimes. What I'm thinking. That's me for you, Edsel. Your mother. This is what I've become." She smiled. "I still have something inside me, though. Something real. It comes and goes. Like one of those little silver Fourth of July sparklers. *Psssshhhhh.* That's the sound they make. Then it goes, all burns off."

He sat on the edge of her bed, next to her feet. She used to paint her nails red. Now they were naked, a little gnarled, browning.

271

"So what's the big news?" she said.

How did she know???

"I have a date," he said.

He blushed, and looked away. Telling her this, it felt like boasting. Worse, it felt like boasting about something no one his age would ever boast about. Like saying, "I crossed the street." Big deal.

"A date? A date! With whom?"

She seemed a little too surprised for his liking.

"A woman named Sheila. I used to work with her. Then she quit, and I saw her again at Goldstein's, and we . . . hit it off. I guess? And . . . so . . . anyway. That's what I wanted to tell you. My big news. I have a date."

And oh, how she beamed at him! She beamed at him the way mothers beam at sons who have broken a world record in something, who have gained fame and fortune via legal means, who have dreamed the impossible dream. She beamed at him exactly like a mother — his mother.

"Oh, Edsel," she said. "That is just great. That's wonderful." Her eyelids fluttered. "And so it begins."

"It?"

"Yes. It."

Hard for him to tell if *it* was a good thing

or a bad thing or just a thing — *the* thing. But she did not elaborate, and he had nothing else to say, but he stayed on a little longer, sitting on the far end of the bed, and she turned on the television and they watched a show together, a nature documentary, something about whales.

■ ■ ■ ■

DAY FORTY-THREE

■ ■ ■ ■

ONE

A million years passed. Each year seemed to drag on for a decade. Every minute felt like an hour, every hour like a day. Bronfman could hear the seconds ticking by, each one accompanied by the sound of the slowly turning teeth of a giant metal wheel. Even at night, alone in his bed, he heard that wheel. *K-choom, k-choom, k-choom.* It was impossible for him to sleep. He felt as if he would never sleep again.

And then, finally, Tuesday came.

He had Sheila's address and telephone number scrawled on the back of the crumpled napkin from Goldstein's. He kept the receipt displayed on the fading white enamel face of his refrigerator, held there by the only magnet he had: a photo-frame magnet in which he had inserted a picture of his mother, taken when Bronfman himself was probably six years old. He had the telephone number of a woman displayed on his refrigerator beneath a magnet in which there was a photo of his young, fetching mother. That wasn't weird.

He looked at the receipt often as the days passed, and thought about it. He memorized her address and telephone number — not on purpose, it just happened from exposure. Her telephone number seemed a more intimate number than her address, for some reason. He worked out the logic of this emotion in his head. The house number belonged to the house, but her phone number — that was hers. It was portable; where she went, it went. He could call her anytime. He could call her right now if he wanted, in the middle of the night, anytime. It was a cell-phone number, so he could call her and wherever she happened to be it would ring. He wouldn't call her, except in the event of an emergency, but he could, and by giving him her number she was tacitly acknowledging this possibility. It was an invitation to be a part of her life.

Sheila lived about two miles away from Bronfman's apartment, in a nicely maintained complex of apartments called Cedar Court. He was familiar with Cedar Court. Vandals often defaced the sign at the entrance, so that it read:

And, no matter how many times the owners repaired it, the vandals would eventually return and deface it, scandalously directing the passing drivers to engage in an act that he was familiar with (somehow) but couldn't imagine participating in. Literally could not imagine: his mind turned off before he reached that mysterious nexus. But, even though he knew exactly where she lived (he had driven past the sign just the other day), on the Saturday before the Tuesday he drove into the complex and viewed her apartment just to make sure he wouldn't make some horrendous mistake on Tuesday and somehow get lost. Her complex was clean, orderly, friendly, neat — the opposite of his. His was littered with beer cans, cigarette butts, and oil-stained rags. At night he saw deer roaming through his complex, snacking, munching on re-tarded shrubs. Something about that was scary. When he came out to shoo them away they would just stared at him, like cows. "The end is coming," they seemed to be saying. "There is nothing any of us can do."

Sheila's complex would survive the apoca-lypse — that was how nice it was. She had a redbrick walkway and two giant azaleas bordering her porch, and windows that were cobweb-free and crystal clear. The door was green, the shutters black. She was way out of his league. He knew that already, of course, but if he hadn't, her modest but manicured lawn would have been sufficient indication. Going there on the Saturday before the Tuesday actually sent him into a minor depression, and he wished he hadn't done it. But it was too late now. *Time machine broken.*

He picked her up at six-thirty exactly. He wore khaki pants, a blue jacket, and an orange IZOD shirt, an outfit so daringly different from anything he had ever worn that he might as well have gone out into the world entirely naked. But he had seen this exact combination on a mannequin in a department store at the mall and he bought it, knowing that he couldn't go wrong. Still, the clothes felt like new body parts that he had to familiarize himself with. He walked stiffly. He didn't know what to do with his arms. He stood on her front porch exactly like the mannequin. Sheila had a dull golden knocker on her front door. Some time passed before he was able to draw from a shallow pool of courage and knock with it, twice. A moment passed, then another.

When a third came, lingered, and disappeared, he wondered if he was at the right door, or had perhaps gotten the date wrong, both of which were impossible. Finally, she opened the door. "Hello," he said. But she said nothing. She shrugged and smiled apologetically and held up her index finger, mouthing the words *I'm sorry,* and mutely invited him in. She was talking to somebody on her cell phone.

"That's not true," she said. "I was always . . . in all the important ways . . . I never told you a —. I'm not — no, *you* listen. I have to go." She gave Bronfman another quick apologetic glance. "Sir," she said. "Please take me off your list. Please take me off your list. Good-bye."

She clicked off. "I'm sorry. Robocalls."

"That was a robot?"

"Might as well have been. Mea culpa."

He was captivated by her apologies. She'd apologized twice in less than a minute. As if she was going for Bronfman's record of seven.

"So hi," he said. "I mean, good evening."

"Forgive me." Three! "Let's start over." She cleared her throat. "So good to see you again, Edsel."

He loved how she used his first name. "Me, too, you."

She switched off the lights before he had a chance to take in much of her place. He had been looking at her the whole time — different parts of her, like her calves and her upper arms, her collarbone. They had never left the foyer. He thought he saw an umbrella stand and a hall table and a framed photo of what he'd swear was either a poodle or a furry black cat, and maybe a bowl of red-striped candies beside it? But in her living room — and he couldn't be sure, because he had only a second to look — were two piles of wood, it looked like, and a tabletop, maybe a hammer. Like a construction zone. As the hallway light dimmed and died, there was that moment of silence, as they prepared to leave, when he heard laughter, applause, a brass band, and children singing, somewhere in the darkness of her apartment.

He stopped to listen.

"It's the television," she said. And, when he still didn't move, she said, "I don't like to come back to the quiet alone."

As they walked to the car, Bronfman said what he'd been meaning to say since he knocked on her door, but the telephone call had thrown him off his game.

"You look nice tonight," he said.

Sheila blushed. Beneath the fluorescent

lights at Goldstein's and in the lobby of the Cranston Building, he hadn't been able to tell just how marble-white her skin was. It almost seemed as if it were powdered, like a geisha's, but on inspection he could tell that she wore no makeup at all. The blush made her cheeks turn a milky pink, the color of grapefruit juice.

They drove in silence, Sheila absorbed in what seemed like a sad thought; Bronfman thought it was the phone call. He had no idea where they might be going. Was he supposed to? Had they even talked about it? No. He was certain they hadn't. He did have some dinner ideas, having done some research on the computer at work. He had made a list of a nice selection of restaurants of every stripe, from American to Italian to Chinese, but he was sure they hadn't discussed it yet, so he just drove, taking the occasional right, the intermittent left.

"It's getting so hot," she said. "But sometimes you can feel a cool undercurrent to the air. It's nice."

"Yes," he said. He hadn't noticed the cool undercurrent. He was just making a sound because it seemed that one was called for. He turned to her at stop signs and red lights, for something, he wasn't sure what, but she had fallen into her thoughts and seemed far, far away. She didn't want to be with him. She was sitting there thinking how to get out of this, her date with him.

Bronfman persevered. He cleared his throat. "Well," he said. "I've been thinking about where we should go to eat. I have some choices, a variety of cuisines. We could talk about them."

She didn't immediately respond.

"I like almost anything," he said, his need to fill the silence overwhelming, painfully so. "As long as it's not too spicy!"

Levity. He smiled and allowed the smile a single laugh to accompany it, because a lot of food was spicy, so it seemed misleading to say that he liked 'anything.' He was about to correct himself when she said, "I'm not really hungry now, Bronfman. Do you mind if we just go on a walk?"

This was unexpected.

"A walk?"

"There's a park at the next block. It's pretty."

He tried to remember the last time he'd gone for a walk on purpose. "Okay," he said. "Sure."

"Unless you're starving."

"No," he said. "A walk would be great. Fresh air, trees . . ." He was unable, off the cuff, to come up with other things that were outside.

"Great," she said.

He parked the car in a lot behind some old concrete tennis courts. Two elderly people were batting a ball back and forth in the dim light, mostly forth, as it only rarely scaled the net. Their skin was whiter than the peculiarly professional-looking tennis uniforms they wore, uniforms that suggested they were about to play the circuit. A path led around the courts to a baseball diamond, which was mostly dirt, empty, forlorn. What's more melancholy than a worn-out old playing field? Almost nothing. Sheila led him to first base, and then left. Before getting to second, she veered off into the woods. Was this a park? It wasn't much of one yet, or, at least, not the kind Bronfman had imagined — it was just a trail, etched into the world by repeated use — but then, as if they had passed through an invisible doorway, the abbreviated forest concluded and before them was a field of wildflowers and grass, waves of hillocks and giant oaks, a swing set where children were being swung so high that Bronfman feared, as he had since he was young, that they would be catapulted into space. There was a seesaw, a merry-go-round, and, his favorite, a hard plastic pony attached to a thick metal spring corkscrewed into the ground, which, when you sat on it and leaned backward and forward on the saddle, rocked and rocked and rocked. No one was on the pony. The trail, bordered by honeysuckle, edged away from the playground and into a glade, where little yellow birds with black crests sang. There were other birds, too, and there was a pond with a log across it where turtles sunned, catching the dying summer light angling through the canopy. But, as Sheila and Bronfman approached, the turtles seemed simply to fall off the log and into the water, as if their genetic coding had warned them that these two approaching animals might use them for soup. Bronfman followed a step behind Sheila, whose icy sadness he could almost feel, like cold radiating from a freezer. This was so not what he expected.

When they came to a long wooden bench Sheila sat on it and Bronfman mimicked her, allowing a good eighteen inches between them, which he felt was friendly without being intimate — not that he had any idea of the protocol in these situations, since he had never been in one even remotely like it. Unless he counted the summer before his senior year in high school, when he showed Maria (what was her last name?) the little bamboo patch in his backyard. She walked into it of her own free will. She kissed him, but he didn't follow up on it and she stopped. He had only wanted to show her the bamboo, which he thought of as foreign and exotic. His priorities had always been misplaced like that.

Sheila caught his eye and, just as quickly, looked away. "This is not how I wanted our 'date' to go," she said. Bronfman heard the quotation marks around *date* but wasn't sure what they were supposed to mean.

"Our date," he said, without the quotes, validating as best he could his deepest secret hope: this was a date. He was dating her. He had a date.

"Sometimes I just . . . plummet. For absolutely no reason at all. The thing is, I'm actually a really happy person! But there's always something else, hovering around. Cloud cover. People are complicated. Relationships. It seems so hard sometimes. God, I know I shouldn't be sharing this with you, on our first . . . whatever it is."

"Date," he said.

"Opportunity to spend additional time together." She almost laughed. "But I don't want you to think that it's you, because it's not. At all."

"Okay," he said. "Thanks. Really. No worries."

She turned to him. "Do you ever feel that way?"

"Which way?"

She paused. It was hard to put a feeling into words, he knew that well enough. "Like there's no way to escape the world."

"Sure, I do," he said. "All the time."

"All the time?"

"Not *all* the time," he said. "But some of the time. Probably a third of the time."

Or more, he thought. Probably more. Outrunning shadows, evading a pervasive sense of loss, suppressing memories and mysteries — that's what she was getting at. His life growing up with uncles who weren't his uncles. Mostly alone. And now his mother, the only person in the world who really knew who he was, was leaving it, and him, behind. This was too sad to even think about for very long. Because now here he was, a thirty-four-year-old man. And who was he? Where was that? Where was he supposed to be? He didn't know. He knew only that where he was, where he found himself — single, alone, a functionary at work — wasn't where he wanted to be. But then not everybody can save the seals, prevent fracking, pick up refuse littering the side of the road.

"Sometimes my mother calls me at three o'clock in the morning," he said. "Usually asking me to do things for her. Clean her sheets, turn off the oven, cut the grass. Right then. She wants me to do it right then."

"That's funny and really weird," Sheila said.

"She has dementia, actually."

"Oh. That's not so funny. Before she died, my grandmother had dementia, too, so I know what that's like. What do you do?"

"I used to try to explain to her that she was being unreasonable, that it was the middle of the night and she should go to bed, but she would insist, so now I tell her I'll be right over, but she forgets, so when I don't come it doesn't matter. Once," he said, in a near-whisper, as if he were telling her a secret that if overheard would put his life and the lives of others in danger, "once I didn't even pick up the phone. I pretended that I wasn't home. I watched it ring and ring and ring. The answering machine picked up, and she said, "Edsel? Edsel? Edsel?" Over and over. And then she hung up and called back and said, "Edsel? Edsel? Edsel?," and then I watched it ring again. She could have been lying there bleeding to death on her bedroom floor. I just thought, I can't do this now. She called back seven times. I didn't sleep the entire night."

Bronfman stopped, unsure of what had just happened. Had he been hypnotized? Given a truth serum? Had he ever said anything remotely like this to another person in his life? He looked at Sheila. "I'm so sorry," he said. "I shouldn't have said that. I don't know why —"

"No," she said. "I want to hear. Couldn't you have unplugged the phone, or —"

"I should have," Bronfman said. "I wish I'd thought of that at the time. She stays in bed most of the time now and yells at her aide, who is the nicest person. My mother goes to the Kmart in the sky."

"The what?"

"The Kmart in the sky. She's not doing well."

Sheila stared at her feet. She was even sadder now. "I know we barely know each other, Edsel," she said. "And we may never see each other again. I hope we will. But if you know me when I'm old and if I'm like that? Crazy and even a little mean? Out of my head, at the Kmart in the sky? Push me off a cliff. Please."

"Will do," he said, and laughed.

"Thanks, Bronfman," she said, but she

didn't laugh at all.

Instead, she placed her hand on top of his, like a piece of bread on a sandwich. Bronfman had small hands, but Sheila's were a little smaller. He could see the tips of his fingers just above hers.

Then she stood. "Walk with me?"

They walked. They walked in silence beneath and between a hundred giant skinny pine trees. Bronfman imagined (why did he imagine these things, especially when things were going so well?) that he and Sheila were fleas on a dog's back, wandering among hairs. He almost told her that this was what he was thinking about, but he didn't. Too soon.

"I'll give you a million dollars," she said, "if you can name just one bird in this place."

"A million?"

"One. Million. Dollars."

She winked at him and laughed, laughed as she had the other day, the day she dumped tea into his lap and made the joke, later retracted, about the benefits of being handicapped. But she was serious now. She wanted him to name a bird. This wasn't really a test — or it didn't feel like one. She wasn't the kind of person who set a person up to fail. But, at the same time, he knew that he had to name a bird. Naming a bird would change something. In a good way. But if he couldn't name a bird he would become the person who couldn't name a bird. For as long as they knew each other, this would become part of the way she'd think of Bronfman, and Bronfman wanted more than that.

So he looked up. They were everywhere all of a sudden, an alphabet of birds; it seemed as if any bird you could ever think of was there, but his mind was a blank — a total blank. The pressure was killing him. Even when he saw a bird that was blue, the name of that bird escaped him. Deeply frustrated, he looked down at his feet and discovered his salvation.

"There," he said. He pointed at a brown-and-black-and-white bird hopping around in a pile of pine straw. She looked at the bird. She looked at Bronfman. "That's a rufous-sided towhee," he said.

She looked at the bird, and sort of scoffed. "You're making that up," she said. "Nothing has that name."

"No," he said. "That's a rufous-sided towhee. It's interesting . . . it's one of those birds that make their nest on the ground."

"*What?* Why would a bird make its nest on the ground? That doesn't make sense. Isn't that the best thing about being a bird, not to have to do that? For God's sake, it has *wings.*"

"It always struck me as odd, too," Bronfman said. "But it's true."

"How do you know that? Are you getting lines fed to you through one of those Bluetooth earpieces I've been seeing on television?" He shook his head. She looked at him skeptically, held her gaze, seemed convinced, nodded. "Well," she said, sighing, "I guess I owe you a million. It might take me a while."

"I'll wait."

They kept walking, lapsing into silence again, until, for some reason he couldn't fathom, she looked up at him and smiled and then pointed ahead. "Look," she said, and as she said it the forest ended and they were standing on a sandstone outcropping, peering down at the city below — far below. The entire city. Wow. This was what he actually thought: *Wow!* The little metropolis they lived in looked even smaller from here, like a city made of scraps of steel and concrete Legos. The sky — blue and white and silver in the distance — surrounded it and everything, even them, completely. He felt as if they were inside a bubble. He had no idea such a place existed, such a view; a brand-new way of seeing the world. He almost told her that, but it was impossible to talk now, impossible to try to put words to something like this. Words — even the perfect words — would spoil it, make it less than what it was. But this much he knew: it was totally romantic. He had never been involved in anything remotely as romantic in his life. She didn't take his hand. She didn't even look at him, and he didn't look at her and they did not fall into a kiss, nothing as radical as that. It was better to do what they were doing, sharing this view, holding in their eyes this same picture of the world. They didn't know each other at all; they were almost strangers. But it was so easy for him to imagine them here fifty years hence, a real couple, outrageously old and a little crazy, coming to that fork in the road of their lives where both forks led to oblivion, just different kinds of oblivion. He would be holding on to the back of her wheelchair, having rolled her — slowly, and not without effort — down the same trail they took today, and, having finally arrived (and pausing, taking it in, this miraculous view), he would lean over, brush a wisp of hair from her face, and kiss her cheek, her lips, and she would kiss his. Then, with whatever strength was left in him, he would push her off the overhang. He'd push her off the way she'd asked him to, and he would follow her, jumping as far from the overhang as his old legs could carry him. Watching her fall this way and then him falling after, imagining the two of them together in the air like this, he had never been happier in his life.

DAY FORTY-EIGHT

ONE

Five days later, they had a second date. They went out to dinner at Red Lotus, probably the best of the pretty-good Chinese restaurants in Birmingham, where you could still get an entrée and an egg roll and a cup of sweet-and-sour soup for $9.95. Bronfman passed on the chopsticks. She appeared to be a chopstick professional, however, deftly removing peppers and bite-size chunks of chicken with ease. Bronfman watched, astonished.

"How do you do that so well?"

"Oh, I was raised in China," she said. "Spent the first fifteen years of my life there. I could snatch a fly out of the air with these things." She clicked the sticks in the air.

"China? Really?"

She hedged, shaking her head as if she had not quite said what she meant to. "Not really. I'm . . . exaggerating."

"About what?"

"Both things," she said. "I've never been to China. I was raised in Indiana. My parents were investors — very Caucasian, in a way that has never been interesting to anybody anywhere. And I don't think I could snatch a fly out of the air with a . . . fly-snatcher."

"That might be more than an exaggeration," he said, delicately hazarding an opinion.

She nodded. "It's like what an exaggeration becomes when it grows up," she said. "A tale. A flight of fancy. A half-truth."

"Not in a bad way at all, though," he said. "I didn't mean that."

He corralled some rice with his fork.

"Of course not. It can be a problem, though. For me, anyway. Becoming so fond of a story that . . . the truth seems irrelevant. Or irksome." Pause. "Love that word."

He nodded, though he wasn't sure that's what he meant or what she meant. No feather-ruffling: Edsel Bronfman's motto from the day he was born.

"What about you?"

"Me?"

"Your life story."

"I was born here," he said, "and I lived here until I went to college, then I came back."

"That sounds very true."

He sensed disappointment. He strained, flexed unused muscles in his brain, gave it a shot. "College in Sweden, of course. Became fluent in Swedish. Got a Swedish dog. Some Swedish fish. And so on."

She nodded, thoughtfully considering his emendation. "Nice," she said, "for a first try."

In this way, they revealed themselves to each other, little by little.

When she excused herself to visit the ladies' room, Bronfman looked around the dining area. There were families here, a few college kids gathered about a circular table, laughing. But everybody else came in twos: men and women, women and women, men and men. All of them to one degree or another together, coupled up, romance in their eyes and in their actions, a mutual gentleness, a bighearted admiration. Fleetingly he thought he saw Serena Stanton, in her streets clothes, with an older, balding man. But on closer examination it was just another sturdy blonde enjoying her kung pao chicken. For a moment, he thought what he'd always thought when he saw these loving unions: How can I get that? How would I even begin? But then he realized that if anyone here had taken a look at him and Sheila they would be thinking what he thought when he looked at them. *Look at them, a man and a woman, together.* He was part of their club.

He had begun. They had begun.

They went for a walk afterward, around the block — a stroll, you might call it, slowly, aimlessly, pausing before shop windows, pointing at funny shoes and mannequins that reminded them of someone they knew, and even though it was only the second walk they'd taken together, it felt as if it was already becoming a thing for them, a thing they did, their thing. Walking. Sheila and him.

Bronfman, it goes without saying, had never had a thing before.

Sometimes she listed against him, as if in a breeze, and he felt the skin of her arm against his.

■ ■ ■ ■

DAYS FIFTY,
FIFTY-FOUR,
FIFTY-FIVE,
FIFTY-SEVEN

■ ■ ■ ■

ONE

It shocked Bronfman, how easy all this was.
There was nothing to it. All he had to do
was answer the phone, be in a certain place
at a certain time, slip into the passenger
seat, and let Sheila drive, both literally and
figuratively. She got carsick when he drove,
he had a heavy braking foot, and her car
was nicer than his by a decade — and it
was all fine with him. Had he known it
would be this easy to be in a relationship
with a woman, he might have tried harder
to make one happen before, but if he had
tried harder it wouldn't have been as easy
as it had been with Sheila.

Five dates.

Dates had themes, like the sections of a
big Sunday newspaper: News, Politics, Arts,
Sports. Apart from Chinese food, they had
Italian and Greek and pizza and cheeseburg-
ers. Did it matter that she liked British
comedies and that he didn't even know

there were such things as that? That she took pictures of everything, or everywhere they went and what they did when they got there. Politically, they appeared to agree on almost everything — they were both Golden Rulers, though Bronfman was a moderate on social reforms. True, there were times when she withdrew. Unaccountably (to him), she would suddenly fall silent, the darkness would descend, her furrowed brow reflecting some inner turmoil that she could not or would not share. But the freedom she felt with him to be able to do that heartened him. He was her secret sharer, her sharer of secrets, even when the secrets remained unspoken.

And, just like that, they were closer to each other than Bronfman had ever been to anyone in his entire life. It felt so sudden, and yet it had taken thirty-four years. It was like evolution: one day you were a fish the way you'd been a fish forever, and then you woke up one morning and you had legs, and you were walking around as if you'd had them since the beginning of time.

■ ■ ■ ■

DAY FIFTY-EIGHT

■ ■ ■ ■

ONE

And then this. This. *This.*

Sunday evening after a long day together. They walked. They ducked into the art museum when it rained and were pleased to see a Rosenthal retrospective on view. They skipped dinner and went straight to dessert, she having heard of a new place that had opened up downtown serving nothing but ice cream and cheesecake, all different kinds of cheesecake, which she said was exactly what she'd imagined heaven to be — full of fat happy people, and this made them feel naughty, eating cheesecake and ice cream, and they laughed so much at themselves and their bravado. They drove back to Cedar Court. He accompanied her to the door of her apartment, where they stood, Bronfman knowing what he should be doing but not doing it, unable to break through the waxy casing of who he was, of who he had always been and feared that he might forever be. "Well, good night, Sheila," he said, and, somewhat reluctantly, she turned to go.

"Wait," he said.

She stopped, turned back, her face a question. He took a half step toward her.

"Not good night," he said.

She smiled. "No?"

"No," he said. "No, 'Good night, Sheila.' This . . . this is where I kiss you. Here, now."

"Is it, now?"

"It is," he said.

"How do you know?" She was playing with him, but sweetly.

"I don't know how I know," he said. "But I think that's the way it is. You don't know, but you know."

She took a deep breath and waited. Suddenly she was very serious.

"I know," she said. "I know exactly the same."

So this is what he did. He went to her. He put his right hand on her left shoulder and brought her toward him. He was taller than she was, so his lips came in an angle. He felt her warm cheek first. Then the corners of her lips. Then full-on, grazing the soft, warm, naked flesh. Her mouth opened, welcoming; his did, too. He felt her wet breath. Their mouths were drawn into each other's like symmetrical vacuums. Gentle at first, the kiss continued with a vigor that surprised him. And when his tongue slipped into her mouth and explored it with an avidity he had never known for anything he had ever done in his life, he almost stopped to think about what he was doing and what she was doing to him. But he didn't. The kiss lasted an entire minute, and he didn't breathe the whole time, and he realized that what sometimes feels like love, crazy love, might be no more than a lack of oxygen getting to the brain. But this was love. He felt his heart becoming that thing that was more than a heart, that was just an idea of a heart, different but performing the same basic function: keeping him alive.

■ ■ ■ ■

DAY SIXTY-ONE

■ ■ ■ ■

ONE

It was already June. The air was getting thick and wet, and the sun was as harsh as a naked lightbulb in a windowless basement. Days were long. It was bright outside long after it seemed natural. He could smell people grilling chicken and steak and burgers. Gnats flew into Bronfman's eyes; mosquitoes gnawed at his ankles. Palmetto bugs and silverfish skittered and slithered across the baseboards of his apartment. So hot, so sweaty. He took a shower in the morning and one at night, and would have taken a shower at lunch if he could. A hazmat suit would have been nice. Daily his mother's condition declined. One day she hired a moving van, and when the two men and the truck arrived she told them that she wanted to go to New York City. "I want to travel in style," she said, "with my sofa and all my hats!" He had to go over and ask the men to take the sofa back into the house.

Bronfman had to cancel all of her credit cards after that.

The hotter it became, the busier things were at Thomas Edison's apartment. Cars were coming and going at all hours of the day and night. Bronfman watched from his window as the refuse of the world came and went. Not just Coco and his core group of friends but a host of people Bronfman had never seen before and never wanted to see again, representatives of a dark place Bronfman had only heard rumors of, a strata of society that operated in the shadows cast by shadows. There was not a single night he slept all the way through: a car horn, a heavy thud against the shared wall, whispers so menacing they woke him. He should have closed his window, but his place got so stuffy when he did. His air-conditioning was pitiful. It would have been worse if the sun hadn't moved beyond the far units. He didn't know where it had gone.

Bronfman couldn't say anything about it to anyone. He was afraid to. He didn't feel quite as if he would be murdered. Even though he knew that people were getting murdered all over the place, he didn't think he was one of those people, which was probably the way many of the people who actually did get murdered felt. But there were worse things than getting killed that might happen to him, lots of them, and for Bronfman they all had to do with losing parts of his body — one part, two parts, more. There was no part of his body that Bronfman wanted to be without, not even the last joint on his little finger, especially now, now that his parts were being seen and (many of them) touched by Sheila. So he shut up and endured the urban hellscape his neighbor had manufactured for him, just to be sure he kept all of his parts.

Thomas Edison seemed to have disappeared. Bronfman rarely saw him anymore — only once, in fact, late one night wandering around the spooky fluorescent parking lot with his shirt off, jeans hanging low. He was talking on the phone to someone he was having an issue with. Bronfman could tell that he was having an issue by the way he was gesticulating, as if he were brushing clouds of gnats away from his face. Bronfman almost went out to say hello, but another man joined Thomas — just drifted out of the darkness. Bronfman had never seen this man before. He was large and solid and wore painter's pants and a wifebeater. He held Thomas by the arms, and talked to him, clearly trying to calm him down. It seemed to work: together the two walked back toward the apartment building. Bronfman tried to move away from the window, but he wasn't quick enough: Thomas Edison caught his eye. For a moment they saw each other, and in that moment both of them froze. But Thomas Edison didn't nod or wave, he didn't smile. He pretended not to have seen Bronfman at all, and walked back into his apartment with the strange man, where Bronfman heard a muffled conversation, the clatter of something metallic on the wood floor.

And then one evening someone knocked on his door. He had come home briefly, just to change from his office clothes into the clothes he'd copied from the mannequin. He and Sheila were going to see a movie. He was almost late. Now this. A knock.

His imagination conjured a crazed and desperate addict on the verge of pillaging his already pillaged apartment. Bronfman held his breath, made not a sound, and waited for him or them to go away, but the knock came yet again. Reluctantly, he went to face his fears.

It was Coco. She was wearing what Bronfman had come to think of as her signature summer wardrobe: stringy cutoffs and a pink tank top with a smiley face ironed on smack in the middle of it. He was pretty sure she'd purchased the tank top at the thrift shop, and that it had once belonged to a nine-year-old. The edges of the smiley face were peeling, and the smile was cracking. But Coco was legitimately pretty. Beneath her tattered exterior was real beauty, just a shower away.

He stood at the door; she stood on the stoop. She wasn't wearing his hat, but he gave her a look — clearly distrustful, plainly dubious — indicating that he knew she had been, or would be again. That she had it.

"Hey, Bronfman," she said. She looked behind her, then to the left, toward Thomas Edison's apartment, then over Bronfman's shoulder. "How goes it, pardner?" *Pardner!* What pluck this girl had.

"Oh, I'm fine, thank you," he said. "And you?" He pinched the side of his thigh. Sheila said he sounded like a robot sometimes, and he was trying to humanize himself, bring a little ease to his interactions. He gave it a shot. "What's up?"

"Yeah," she said, "not that much is up. This is kinda awkward. But can I use your bathroom? Tommy's john — well, it's . . . occupied. Constantly. If you know what I mean." He knew exactly what she meant. It was where he nearly died.

"Sure," he said, stepping aside. She

slipped past him. "It's the first door on the —" But she had disappeared into the bathroom and closed the door before he had a chance to finish his sentence. She knew exactly where it was.

It didn't take her long. He heard the flush, heard her wash her hands and, presumably, dry them on the bath towel hanging from the shower rung before coming back out.

"Thanks much," she said.

"You're welcome," he said. Then, "You bet."

Coco didn't appear to be in a hurry to go. She glanced lazily around the room, sighed, and wandered over to the lonely bookshelf against the wall, where there were no books at all, just the pamphlet from Extraordinary Adventures and his collection of ballpoint pens. She picked up the pamphlet and studied it, page by page, with the same distracted attention he had seen her bring to the fashion magazine.

"Wow," she said. "This is nice. Florida. I went there once, in high school. My 'boyfriend' " — she provided the air quotes — "slipped me a roofie, and after that who knows what happened. But they told me it was a lot of fun. I got a terrible sunburn from passing out on the beach."

"Oh, my God," Bronfman said. "That's awful."

She shook her head. "I'm over it," she said, and showed him a picture she seemed particularly to like, a pair of dolphins leaping through the foaming waves.

"I'm going there," he said. "Sandscapes. In just a couple of weeks or so." Bronfman was hopeful. Hope was something Sheila had given him.

This got her interest. "Fun," she said. "Can I come?"

She laughed. She was making a joke, the kind people make when they know that what they're asking will never happen. She didn't mean it, but it made Bronfman squirm, because he found himself wishing that she *did* mean it. He wished she wanted to go, even though he had no intention of taking her. Contradictory feelings confused Bronfman. He had yet to mention the beach to Sheila, and didn't know when he would. He was waiting for the perfect moment. He was afraid that it would scare her if she knew that he was imagining a serious future with her in it, even if that future was only two and a half weeks away. But there went his brain again: against his will, he was suddenly, pointlessly, playing with the idea of inviting this woman he barely knew. His face flushed red, a primal physical response to this betrayal of Sheila, even this brief betrayal, this passing thought.

"Ha-ha," he said.

"Mind if I smoke?"

"No, please," he said immediately, surprising himself. Almost immediately, he understood why: the smoke would remind him of his mother, the young, faraway mother he so missed. Perhaps that's why he was drawn to this Coco: if his rule-breaking and seductive mother had been young in this day and age, perhaps she would have been someone like Coco.

She lit up and blew a plume of smoke toward the ceiling. It rose like fumes from a dormant volcano. Then she fixed her gaze on him, gave him the once-over twice. "You look different. Have you been doing something? Pumping iron? Working out?"

His soul lit up. "A little," he said. "I mean, you know, not much."

"For the beach?" she said. "Or to protect yourself from the lunatics next door?" She laughed again, but this time it meant something completely different. Laughs were a language all their own. This laugh was serious; this laugh meant there were lunatics next door.

He didn't know what to say, so he said,

"Neither. Just to stay in shape."

She turned away, picked up his jar of pens, selected one, clicked it, drew a line across the palm of her hand. "Hey, mind if I keep this? I need a pen."

"Sure, no, please. I have lots, as you can see."

She read it. "It's from the Sheraton, downtown. Why would you stay at the Sheraton? A secret tryst?" She threw him a wink.

"No! No, no. I didn't really stay there. I was just walking by and went in and got a pen."

"I see," she said, as if that made any real sense. She gave him an estimating glance. "You know, you're a brave man," she said, clicking the pen until it broke. She winced, and stuck it back into the jar. "Not to leave here, I mean, after what happened to you. Tommy felt terrible about it."

"He didn't seem to at the time, but I'm sure that when he reflected —"

"This isn't his thing," she said. "This whole meth adventure. It's very temporary."

"That's good," Bronfman said. "From what I understand, it's a dangerous and unpredictable business."

"So why didn't you?"

"What?"

"Leave. Go. Move far, far away to a place where people weren't sticking their guns into your stomach."

Why didn't he? Because she was right, that would have been the thing to do. He shrugged. "As long as I stay out of his place, I think I'll be okay. And who knows if it's better anywhere else."

"It's probably better everywhere else."

"It sounds like you want me to go." Because it occurred to him then that she had some ulterior motive for the visit. Maybe Thomas Edison wanted to expand his operations and needed this place to do it.

But she shook her head. "You're the king of King's Manor, Bronfman," she said, "IMHO. If you left, I think God would strike us with lightning and send a flood to wash us all away. You remind me of my dad. So upright, direct, honest. A rare commodity these days." And on the way to the door she touched him on the elbow. He felt a static-electrical shock.

"I know why I stayed," he said. He knew now, for certain, a thing he didn't know he knew until the words floated out of him.

She stopped, turned, waited.

"For Thomas," he said. "To protect him. He asked me to stay. He said who knows

324

who would move here if I left. I think that's true. I'll stay here until his 'meth adventure' " — and, yes, for the first time in his life, Bronfman used air quotes — "is over. Until everything is okay."

She looked stunned. Or not stunned, impressed. "Exactly what my dad would do, under entirely different circumstances." He lingered in her faraway gaze a moment longer until she broke herself away from whatever memory she was living in. "Well, see you, Mr. B.," she said. "Thanks for the — you know."

"Yes," he said, watching her go. She had lovely shoulder blades. They were so small, so delicate. "I'll see you, too. Take it easy!" he added with a flourish. But by that time she was already gone, and even though he was certainly going to be late now, he stood there in the cloud of smoke she'd left behind, breathing in his lost, his precious, past.

Two

This was something. He and Sheila had only been "seeing each other" (whatever that meant) for three weeks and four days, but he didn't have to knock anymore when he went to her apartment. She told him just to walk in, so he just walked in. Sometimes they had no plans — nothing "to do." Sometimes she would ask him to come over and said they'd figure something out or watch television or "whatever." *Whatever,* with a woman. A new concept for Bronfman.

Today he walked in and found her on the couch with a magazine. "Hey, you. I was about to order some pizza."

"That sounds great," he said.

"I'll order more than we'll eat, because you can eat pizza for any meal — breakfast, lunch, or dinner. It's the perfect food."

"Totally," he said. The word sounded foreign coming out of his mouth, Tunisian or Greek, but he thought that with practice he would totally get it down.

The two large piles of wood were still in the middle of her living room. He had studied them on earlier visits and quickly realized what they were — furniture in the process of being assembled; the very beginning of the process, the point at which the pieces were dumped out of their boxes and onto the floor. But he hadn't mentioned them yet, and neither had she.

"It looks like," he said — he wanted to tread gently, didn't want to do anything that might hurt her feelings, but he felt more comfortable now, safe — "you're having a little trouble putting those things together."

"Oh, those," she said. She gazed at them. "Yes. Well, the thing is, I've put them together two or three times and taken them apart again."

"That's interesting," he said, though it was much more than that to Bronfman; it was peculiar and a little disconcerting. His own peculiarities he could accept and to some degree appreciate because he understood them, either how pointless or how important they were. But he hid them. He would never show anyone his collection of ballpoint pens. When someone appeared comfortable enough with himself to broadcast his individuality to the world, Bronfman steered clear of him. Now here he was on the couch with such a person.

"Interesting?" she said.

"That you would do that, I mean. Why would you do that?"

Sheila was, with the possible exception of himself, the oddest person he'd ever met. She appeared to survive on tomato soup and buttered toast, slept until ten every morning, and her life goal was to binge-watch every series in the history of American television. She was almost done with *Bonanza:* 14 seasons, 430 episodes, beginning in 1959 and ending in 1973. Favorite character Hoss, of course. She would be ancient by the time she finished watching every episode of every series, but she had done the math and it was possible. It would be nice to be in the *Guinness World Records* for something, she said. It was difficult to ascertain when she actually worked.

They had watched a couple of episodes of *Gilligan's Island* yesterday, and watching, looking back and forth between her and the TV, he realized that Sheila was the perfect amalgam of Ginger and Mary Ann, a girl of wholesome openness with a wanton glimmer in her eyes. He didn't tell her this, because he wasn't sure what she'd think about it, and he was still moving cautiously in this new world where, remarkably, every day for the past four days he had kissed her. Every single day. Nothing calisthenic, but, still, his lips felt raw and tingly. And they were the color of mandarin oranges.

"They're IKEA," she said. "That's a table and that's a chair. The directions are awful, of course. Impenetrable. Unsound. Infuriating and condescending."

"That makes sense. Because they are."

She turned to him. "I'm going to tell you something I've never told anyone."

"Okay."

Her fingers pulled on a loose thread at the hem of her blouse until it snapped. She considered it with a thoughtful seriousness. "It's hard for me to share parts of myself," she said. "My dreams. Or my nightmares."

He nodded. She smiled at him and looked away, embarrassed. Then she returned to Bronfman and studied him, literally, as if he represented some calculus she needed to solve but couldn't, however much she wished she could. She opened her mouth but stopped the next words from coming out. He could see her swallow them, recalibrate, start again.

"Okay. Well, I have a dream, and my dream is to get the gig writing the instructions for IKEA. IKEA is my white whale."

"Really?"

He had expected something different, and maybe she had, too. "White whale" made Bronfman think — not of *Moby-Dick* but of his third-grade un-sweetheart, Ellen, and her manatee. "I don't know what you mean," he said.

"I'm rewriting the directions — the instructions. I'm going to send them to someone at IKEA and see if I can get the job writing the English version. Think about that, Bronfman. Think of the work. I'd have a job for life."

"Who are you going to send them to?"

"That's the rub," she said. "No one is getting back to me. It's probably a very in-house thing, you know, but nothing ventured . . . My grandfather was Swedish, but he never spoke it because of something terrible that happened to him there. I think it was pretty top-secret stuff." But Bronfman wasn't really listening. Already he was nurturing a newborn idea, watching it grow in a fertile and sunlit corner of his brain.

He held her foot, and he held it tight. She seemed to like it when he held her foot. It was a sweet evening. They ordered in from a kind of gourmet-pizza place that had just opened called Maestros! Both of them liked the same things on their pizza — black olives, feta, sausage. Bronfman understood this as further evidence of their compatibility — a sign. *You like feta, too? No way!* And he liked how, when he ordered the pizza, the vaguely Italian guy on the other end called them pies. "What do you want on the pie?" he said. That made the pizza seem extra-authentic. It came; they ate. Half a bottle of red wine later, they fell asleep on her couch flipping between talk shows, and later — somewhere around three in the morning — they wandered in a purposeful stupor to her bedroom, where they fell on top of the covers, fully clothed, and began . . . wriggling, a call-and-response with their bodies, testing, probing. He had even purchased a package of condoms earlier that week, to be prepared in case something like this happened. And now it was happening. "Edsel," she said, as if she were in a trance. "Oh, Edsel . . ." He remembered thinking that this was going to be the night — *the* night. But in the morning they woke clutching each other, still fully clothed.

It took them both a minute to realize what had happened — and what hadn't happened.

"Oh," Sheila said, and tried to smile. "Would you look at us."

"We fell asleep," he said. "Accidentally."

"Red wine does that to me," she said. "I'm really sorry."

"Don't be," he said. He kissed her cheek, and didn't tell her that, regardless of what hadn't happened, this had: for the first time in his life, he woke up with someone beside him. This blew his mind, and his mind remained blown through the rest of the day and into the next morning, when, on waking, he realized that she had to meet his mother.

■ ■ ■ ■

DAY SIXTY-TWO

■ ■ ■ ■

ONE

Skip Sorsby was late that morning, as he had been yesterday morning and the day before. What made it worse was that he didn't even care. He came in whistling. As he'd told Bronfman many times, he ran on "Sorsby time," and on Sorsby time he was never late for anything. "It's all good," he liked to say, as if it were the mangled mantra of an Eastern religion. "It's all good." As much as Bronfman disliked Sorsby, though, he would have to admit that there were times when he wanted to be him. Amoral, self-involved, oblivious of what others thought, and somehow universally attractive to women. If half of the stories Sorsby had told Bronfman were true, he could have sired a small army of little Sorsbys by now.

Bronfman waited until Sorsby was seated at his cubicle and had checked his status updates and texted someone.

"I was wondering if I could ask you

something, Sorsby. A favor."

"A favor," Sorsby said through the wall. "Hmm. You could ask, definitely. No law against asking. I don't know how much I'm interested in doing favors, though."

"Okay. Well. So. I have a friend," Bronfman said. "And she —"

"*She?* Good. Very good. Now I'm interested. Do go on."

"She's a writer, kind of. She writes directions."

"Slow down. Back up. Directions?"

"Instructions. Like those little paper inserts in things that tell you how to put them together."

"I didn't know a real person did that."

"Neither did I. But somebody has to."

"And your lady friend does."

"Yes," he said.

Sorsby sighed. "And now suddenly I find myself not giving a shit, and I don't know why." Sorsby stood so Bronfman could see him hit the button on an invisible remote. "Fast-forward."

"She wants to write instructions for IKEA. And I know you work with IKEA. I wondered if you knew someone, a contact, someone she could get in touch with and —"

"Oh, I get it," Sorsby said. "You want to

be her hero."

Bronfman hadn't thought about it in those terms, exactly, but Sorsby was right. That's exactly what he wanted.

Sorsby eyed him knowingly. "Thereby making access to the vortex that much easier."

"The vortex?"

"We are not so different, you and me," Sorsby said. "Let me think about it."

"Of course."

Sorsby disappeared. A moment passed, maybe less.

"Okay!" he said, and stood. He shook his head. "I don't really know why I would — doing stuff for people other than myself is against my nature — but I will. I will do what I can. I just feel so sorry for you, dude. That's the truth. You seem so forlorn, like a hitchhiker no one will pick up. You bring me down, and I don't even give a shit. So I want you to get a little sumpin sumpin. But you will owe me."

"Of course," Bronfman said, trying to hide his enormous joy. "By all means."

"No, I'm serious," Sorsby said. "If I do this for you, you'll have to do something for me. Whatever it is I ask of you. I can call you day or night. That's the way it works."

"Really?" Bronfman said. "Day or night?"

Sorsby stared at Bronfman until he nodded, and Sorsby disappeared, and began clicking on his keys — beginning the inquiry, perhaps. Bronfman did nothing. He immersed himself in that future where he would be sitting with Sheila on her couch, or somewhere at dinner, or maybe going on one of their trademark walks, his status totally pre-hero, and he would say, "I have something to tell you."

■ ■ ■ ■

DAY SIXTY-FIVE

■ ■ ■ ■

ONE

He drove because that seemed the thing to do when you were taking a woman to meet your mother. Sheila brought flowers, lilacs she'd picked from a neighbor's garden. Bronfman tried to imagine what it would be like to live in an apartment complex where your neighbors grew flowers instead of selling drugs. She held the flowers in her lap as he ground the stick shift into reverse.

"She'll love them," he said.

"Really?" She looked at Bronfman and then away. "I just keep thinking it's too soon. That she'll get the wrong idea."

He idled, still in reverse. "What's the wrong idea?" he said.

"I don't know!" she said. "What's the right one?"

"That we've dated," he said. "That we've been on dates. That we're dating."

"I suppose that's true," she said.

"Suppose?"

She took his hand from the stick shift and held it. "No, it is true. It's very true. I'm just nervous. I've never actually been taken to meet a mother before. I've met mothers, but never on purpose. She's . . . erratic, you said. Anything could happen."

He nodded. In the past few days he had thought of little else but this meeting. And it had been his idea. He didn't know what would happen when he brought this new world home to meet his old one. His mother might bake them a cake or she might throw knives at them, or anything in between.

"It's a chance we have to take," he said. Because he had to bring a girl home with him once before it was too late. And it had to be this girl, Sheila.

"Then let's do this," she said. "Punch it, Chewy."

"What?"

She shook her head and smiled. "It's from a movie, Grandpa," she said. "Maybe we'll watch it together sometime."

"Well," Bronfman said, "we're here."

He slowed and stopped the car at the curb, turning the engine off as it huffed and rumbled and then, exhausted, died. Early June, 5:30 P.M. The windows as dark as they would have been had no one lived here, as if the older you got the less light you were rationed, and when you ran out of light that was it. Your life was over.

Sheila glanced up quickly, and then went back to rifling through her purse. "It's lovely, Edsel," she said. "It really is. I can't find this lipstick I brought. There are so many pockets in this purse!"

There were. Bronfman counted them once. There were six pockets on the outside alone, and inside he knew there were at least that many more. Each of them harbored something, from mascara to her gym card, tissues, keys to an apartment where she used to live a few years ago, a pair of reading glasses and a collection of barrettes and hair ties, three one-dollar bills and some cents, gum, ginger lozenges, her phone, its charging cord, and enough pens and pencils for a class of sixth graders at a public school. This is the bag she was combing through for one small tube of lipstick.

"She won't notice what lipstick you're wearing," he said. "Or she will. I don't know."

Sheila appeared to ignore him. Or maybe she didn't ignore him but listened to him attentively and decided, because what he was saying was inane, not to respond.

"Eureka!"

She pulled down the visor and opened the tiny mirror and applied the coloring.

"Thank you for doing this," he said.

"Nonsense. I just had the jitters. I'm at home with crazy people of all kinds, being one myself. I can handle her."

Sheila was done with the lipstick. She regarded him, and he her, as two soldiers bravely joining forces in battle.

"What did you tell her I do?"

"Nothing," he said. "I mean, she didn't ask."

"I don't think there's any reason to mention it."

"What? Why? I think it's interesting."

"It's not a *thing,* Edsel," she said. "I mean, I want to talk to you about it sometime because it's really . . . the thing is, anyone can say they're a freelance anything."

"Really?"

"Hypothetically," she said. "It's just not that important, that's all I mean."

"Okay," he said. "If you say so."

She took his hand and squeezed it, and then let it go, and they exited the car and made their way up the ancient slate walk, a walk his feet had trod an uncountable number of times. The walk was bordered by monkey grass on both sides.

Bronfman stopped before they came to

the front door and took a few deep breaths. Sheila rubbed her cheek against his shoulder. A move like that, the cheek against the shoulder, to Bronfman, was more intimate than kissing someone's ear. Do I love her? Bronfman asked himself this several times a day. He thought he might love her. But if he had to ask, did that mean he didn't? What was the answer? Do you just know it when it happens? Could it be deduced? There were moments when he couldn't imagine his life without her, and he thought this must be love, but stringing moments like this together over the course of a day or a week or a lifetime seemed to be asking for a lot. They had done everything they were supposed to do: dinner, movies, and walks — lots and lots of walks. They'd even gone to the zoo, where she turned her model on its head, comparing animals to people instead of the other way around. "That goose looks exactly like my grandmother. . . ." They had their walks, their pizza, their *things,* their private vocabulary. It was good. But he didn't know what, taken together, it was supposed to mean. Pop music was his only source of information on the subject, and, according to many of the songs, he might very well be in love, or, at the very least, really close to it. Bottom line, he should be able to see it from here.

Bettina opened the door and stood there, like a sentry or a wooden Indian. Then she saw Sheila and let out a whoop.

"Who do we have here?!? As I live and breathe. Your mother and I have been taking bets on whether she's real. And look here, real as can be."

"You must be Bettina," Sheila said.

"Smart, too."

"Sheila McNabb."

"Lovely lilacs. Mrs. Bronfman's going to love those." She stood there, nodding, smiling. "She's not feeling particular good today," Bettina said. "Still wants to see you, though."

Bettina stepped aside and they entered. The smell hit him immediately. *Old person.* A damp smell, of something not quite spoiled — the forgotten apple, the abandoned peach. Musty and stale. Dust blankets. Darkness. He had never gotten used to it. He never wanted to.

Bettina led them to his mother's bedroom. The door was closed. There was some sort of unit on the wall beside the door, which, on closer examination, Bronfman could see was an alarm system.

"What's this?"

"What's it look like," Bettina said wearily,

punching a code. "No one comes in without her knowing it. So when she leaves and comes back she can know no one is in there, waiting. She's scared a lot these days."

"What's the code?"

"Can't say. She doesn't want anybody to know."

"You know," Bronfman said.

"Nobody else but me," Bettina said.

"How did she pay for it?"

"I don't think you canceled all of her cards."

Bronfman glanced at Sheila, who had a smile engraved on her face. Soldiering on. How paranoid his mother had become, how protective and insulated from life. She didn't trust life not to hurt her anymore, since it had already hurt her so much by making her old.

The door clicked open and the three of them walked in and through the shadowed space until they could see Muriel. He wished she could have met them in the living room. The powdery smell, the underwear drawer open and spilling over with flesh-colored underpants. As familiar as it was to him, he had never really gotten used to it.

The bedside-table lamp cast a half-light on the right side of his mother's face, and left the other side gray, a spectral image. Even Bronfman, who had been watching his mother turn into this rice-paper scary-crazy woman, was hesitant to take another step. But not Sheila.

"Mrs. Bronfman!" she said, passing him on the left. "It's so good to meet you. I've heard so much about you."

"Oh, Edsel?" Muriel said. "Is that you? I must have drifted off there." Bronfman watched her mind come back, roused from sleep's foggy drama. She focused on him, narrowed her eyes. Then she glanced at Sheila. "And you are?" Not knowing, but on the other hand not much surprised to see a stranger there. It must be hard for her to know what was supposed to be right or wrong, acceptable, not. Was this person always there? she was probably thinking. What do I know? What *don't* I know?

To Bronfman: "You brought . . . a girl. Oh, honey, that's wonderful. A real live girl."

"Her name is Sheila," he said. "Remember —"

"Of course I remember. Sheila," she croaked, snapping to. "I'd shake your hand or embrace you, but I've . . . I've just started taking a blood thinner and I'm afraid if you accidentally cut me I might bleed out."

Muriel laughed, her idea of a joke.

"Oh, I know," Sheila said. "When you get old it's all about medication. This one does one thing, this another. Take this one in the morning three times a week and this one in the evening twice a week, and the third might react negatively with the first. Yuck."

"It clouds my mind," Muriel said.

"That, too," Sheila said. "My grandmother — who practically keeps her pharmacist in business — has to be reminded who I am, and then when she places me she'll tell you how she basically *raised* me, and how when I went off to college I wrote her for a while but eventually stopped, and how much I love celery sticks filled with cream cheese, and how I should be married by now and . . . well, anyway, she's a lot older than you, so."

"So I have a lot to look forward to."

"Oh! Not what I meant," Sheila said. "But it's true. We're like leaves, aren't we, desperately hanging on to a little branch, buffeted by the strong winds life blows our way until we wither and fall to the ground."

"You're a piece of work," his mother said.

"I'm just pulling your leg. That was levity."

"Sheila?" Bronfman said.

"Yes?"

"I'm not sure this is where we want to go

with the conversation." He cocked his head, puzzled, remembering something. "And your grandmother is alive?"

He thought she'd told him that her grandmother was dead, along with the rest of her grandparents; her parents, she had said, lived in a retirement community for visual artists in northern Minnesota. He felt momentarily off balance. But it passed.

Sheila glanced at him and winked.

"Bettina broke the remote," Muriel said. "She breaks everything." She pointed the remote toward the television like a weapon and pushed haphazardly at the buttons. "See? Nothing."

She dropped the remote on the bed, and Bronfman picked it up, aimed. Nothing happened for him, either.

"Have you changed the batteries?"

"Have I *changed* the *batteries*?" Muriel laughed the way the Queen of England would laugh if you asked her if she'd changed the batteries. "Edsel, if you think I'm going to spend even a snippet of what's left of my life changing batteries, then you don't know your mother."

He knew his mother. If she had a hundred years left in her life, she would never have changed the batteries. That was his job. Or Bettina's job. Anybody's job but hers. He tried to remove the back cover, but it wouldn't budge. He tore a part of his thumbnail off trying, and winced. He brought the thumb to his mouth: there was a little blood there.

"Are you okay?" Sheila asked.

"I'm fine," he said.

"It's bleeding," Muriel said. "You should get it checked out. Don't go to my doctor, though, because he'll insist that you get the entire thumb removed. End of story."

"I don't think I need to see a doctor. A Band-Aid will probably take care of it."

"Fragile Edsel," Muriel said to Sheila, as if he were the one in bed surrounded by a flotilla of medicine bottles and liquid food.

"Seriously," he said. "I'm fine."

"No one is fine," she said. "I'm older than you, so you have to trust me on this. No one is doing fine, Edsel. Some of us are just doing less poorly than others."

"Someone is fine. Someone must be. Otherwise, how would we know when we're not?"

"You don't understand, and you're giving me a migraine." She closed her eyes and grimaced. "How is my son treating you, Sheila?"

"Perfectly," Sheila said. Muriel opened her eyes. She seemed receptive to hearing about

Bronfman's perfections. "Such a gentle-man." This was true: he was. But even Bronfman knew this. He was a gentleman to the entire world. He would hold the door for a Nazi.

"Why so quiet, Edsel?" Muriel said.

"Oh," he said. Was he supposed to say something? Bronfman couldn't speak. He had never done this before. Introducing a woman to his mother was a strange thing. It felt as if he was saying, "Here is a younger version of you who will take care of me from now on, and thus your services are no longer needed. Feel free to expire."

He looked at his mother with this thought in his head, and she appeared to expire. She closed her eyes and her face melted into the sad and grotesque posture of an old person in repose. How had this happened to her? She wasn't made for this part of life, the old part. As he had grown she had diminished, and so it would continue until he became a something and she became a nothing. Life was a zero-sum game.

Sheila shrugged. They watched Muriel breathe.

"Well," Bronfman said, "I guess we should go."

Her eyes fluttered open, her face set hard — she was someone different now.

"Going?" she said. "Already?"

"I thought you were asleep."

"Go, then. It's what you do. You come and you go, but, mostly, you go."

"I'll check in later," Bronfman said.

"I don't give a shit," she said.

"Mother!"

"Don't *Mother* me. You know what I mean, and if you don't know what I mean I will *try*. To *speak*. *Plainly.*"

He waited. Sheila looked to Bronfman for a clue to what should happen now, but he had nothing for her.

"Giving a shit," Sheila said. "I have never really understood what that means. Wouldn't one want to give a shit to some-body, because giving a shit would illustrate how they felt about it, whatever it was. Because who wants to be given a shit?"

"I agree," Bronfman said. "It's better to give one. It would have substantially more impact."

Muriel seemed to drift deeper into her pil-low, her shrunken head enveloped in its downy folds. Her eyes were empty. It was as if she really were possessed, as if someone or something was speaking through her. "I apologize for making this so hard," she said. "But I suppose that's what mothers are for. I'm sorry."

"That's okay," Sheila said. "I can tell you have a heart of pure gold."

"Really?"

"Fort Knox–grade gold," she said. "I'm surprised you don't have a platoon here guarding it."

Muriel laughed. "That's why I installed the alarm," she said. "In case someone tries to steal my heart."

This brief exchange made Bronfman happy. He felt that he had achieved everything he'd come for.

"Well," Bronfman said, "I guess we should go."

"Probably," his mother said. "I'm drifting away."

"Do you want the television on or off?" He could turn it on the old-fashioned way if she wanted: manually.

"Off," she said. "No — on. The public station. There's a show on about the Great Depression." She shook her head and looked away toward nothing — a wall. An empty wall. "I know about the Great Depression, Sheila. I'm having one now."

"Mrs. Bronfman," Sheila said. She leaned over and kissed Muriel's shriveled cheek and smiled into her old eyes. "It was good to meet you."

"Are those flowers for me?" she said,

bright-eyed, real, human. "You are the sweetest girl in the world. Thank you. Set them down here. Thank you so much."

And she closed her eyes again. "Bye now," she said.

They closed the door behind them. The security system engaged with a beep and a blinking yellow light. Had Bronfman needed to go back in there for any reason, he couldn't. Not even to kiss his mother good-bye. Her own son, and he didn't know the code. Bronfman was overcome with what was perhaps his very first epiphany, face to face with a metaphor for his life: he had yet to learn the code for almost anything at all.

Bettina had disappeared. Sheila and Bronfman walked out of the house and up the walk past the monkey grass to his car, totally silent. Bronfman felt the need to apologize, but he couldn't. He couldn't apologize for his own mother.

They sat in the car, doors locked. Safe. The brief terribleness over. When they were in Florida together, he thought, their shoulders browned by the sun, this would be one of those times they would look back on and laugh. Bronfman took Sheila's hand and held it, affirming their successful visit and subsequent escape.

"Off a cliff," they said, both of them, at

the very same time.

"Jinx," Sheila said. Then she kissed him and he kissed her — again, at the exact same time — jinxing themselves with love.

■ ■ ■ ■

DAY SEVENTY

■ ■ ■ ■

ONE

Bronfman got the call just before lunch. It was Bettina. She didn't have to tell him why she was calling; as soon as he heard her voice, he knew. Bettina had never called him, ever, and there was only one reason that she ever would.

"Hi, Bettina," he said. There was an ocean roar of static. Behind it he thought he could hear Bettina crying a little, or maybe just trying to hold back the tears. Or maybe he was providing the emotional backdrop himself. "She died," he said. "Didn't she?"

"Who?"

"Muriel," he said. The word sounded strange on his lips, especially in these circumstances. "Mom."

Bettina laughed. "I wish. Sometimes. She's so crazy. No, it's worse than that."

"Worse?" He tried to keep his voice down, but the word exploded from his mouth. He felt eyes on him. He smiled and turned

359

away, facing his cubicle wall. But how could it be worse? She could be dying, in the process of dying, on the floor choking or writhing in pain, having a heart attack, bleeding to death, unconscious after falling down the stairs, suicidal — and here was Bettina calling him and not the hospital? He had made a special sheet of important numbers, and the hospital was on it. 911! What was so hard about that? Three buttons!

"I can't do much with her anymore, Mr. Bronfman. She had me get out some clothes and dress her up. She looks real nice. Jewelry, too, and a scarf, even though I told her it was hot out there, she didn't need that scarf. But that's okay. I guess it looks nice, too."

"Bettina." Bronfman was confused. The fact of his mother's death had entered his own life with such force that it was already lodged within him like a bullet. Now that she was still alive, he had to recalibrate. It wasn't easy, but he did it. "What's going on?"

"She's waiting for you, Mr. Bronfman, out front. Waiting on you to come pick her up."

"I'm at work, Bettina. Can't you — I don't know what's going on. What's going on?"

"She wants to take you for a ride somewhere. That's all I know. She's out there just standing in the gutter. She's like a statue. You've got to come, Mr. Bronfman. I don't know what might happen. I can't get her inside. Come on now."

"Okay," he said. "Okay."

He hung up, grabbed his phone and his keys. The *whoosh* of the world blew through his ears and emptied out his head. He was on autopilot now, blank as a fresh sheet of paper.

"Your highness," Sorsby said, rising above the wall. Bronfman stopped. "I continue to investigate the intricacies of this devilishly opaque corporation. I'm moving into some dangerous waters, infested with killer sharks."

"Thank you," Bronfman said.

"I'm bighearted, apparently," Sorsby said, disappearing. "And I kinda hate it."

TWO

She was exactly where Bettina had said she would be. She was wearing worn-out jeans and a paisley shirt, the neck cut in a low V. He didn't know she even had clothes like this anymore. She waved as he pulled up, and smiled, as if something about this was normal. He slowed to a stop and she opened the door, but she didn't get in. She waited for her son to clear the seat, which was crowded with mail and flyers, an empty soda bottle, and a handful of his business cards, which, after the condo win, he'd been taking with him everywhere, just in case another jar found its way into his life. He tossed it all in the backseat.

"Edsel," she said, slipping in and sitting down gingerly, with distaste, as if she were resting her backside on a small turd. "Thank you for coming, Edsel. I know it was on short notice. But there's something I want to do, something I want to show you, and it's a beautiful day and who knows, if I don't do it now, when I can, I might not ever be able to. I've been watching a nature show about the polar ice caps. Have you ever seen film of how the ice is falling away there, piece by piece, dropping into the ocean with a crash and melting? It's called calving. That's how it feels, getting old. I'm calving."

"Don't talk that way."

"Jesus Christ, Edsel. Be real, at least for a moment or two. Even I know Bettina can't take care of me much longer and it's off to the old folks' home for me. They'll probably put me in an ankle bracelet, too — I'll be a flight risk. I'm fucking crazy."

"You don't sound crazy."

"I get these moments," she said. "Clouds parting. Clarity. This is one of them. Let's carpe diem this motherfucker. Turn around. I'll tell you exactly where to go."

He did as she told him. This was the mother he knew, his real mother, a version of whom he kept sequestered in a box in his brain, because he didn't want to lose her. This was a memory he could put in the box. She led him out of the neighborhood and onto the highway, briefly, just for a couple of miles, and then they took the Eighth Avenue exit into Southside. Southside had gentrified in the past few years, sidewalks teeming with the upwardly mobile hip, a few miles and a few years ahead of the neighborhood where Crouton's gallery was. But years ago it had been a skuzzy repository for long-haired layabouts and drugs, lots of drugs. In the middle of the small downtown neighborhood was a concrete fountain, where there was an old man on his knees, clutching a Bible, praying. He had been there for decades, but the story was that he was praying for Southside's young miscreants. The praying didn't work: this was where they gathered to buy and sell, and to find quick and easy company for the night.

"Pull over," she said.

He squeezed into a narrow space in front of a sushi place. Raw fish. Bronfman had never really understood the appeal.

"There, by the fountain," she said. "That's where I met your father."

"There?"

"There. I was desperate for some weed, and this was the place to get it. Back then you could buy an ounce for twenty-five dollars. I was working, living alone, I had a lot of disposable income, so that was nothing to me. Your father walked up and stared at me for what seemed like an eternity, and said something like 'Amazing. I just got a fortune cookie, and it said, "You are about to meet a most beautiful woman." This is the first time one of those fortunes has come true.' It was a line, a bad one, but I appreciated the attention. I scored a lid, and we walked over to the IHOP across the street."

The IHOP was still there, and it seemed that it always would be. It was open twenty-four hours, seven days a week. It served coffee and waffles and sausage and eggs. Bronfman had been there many times, and it hit him hard, like a knee in his chest: he'd eaten in the same place his father had before he was his father. Maybe in the same seat.

"Roy and I hit it off," she said, speaking in a rush of parentheses and vocalized dashes. "I mean, *obviously*. I didn't lie down for just anybody back then — well, for the most part. There was an era when I was . . . the term was . . . 'easy.' (I kind of loved being easy. It was so . . . easy.) But that passed. I wasn't like that back then. Roy. Thick black hair he brushed back with his hand. It was a little greasy, sure, but kind of the way the beatniks wore it decades ago. A strong chin and a smile like the sun. Heavy eyebrows, but they worked on him. Very dreamy. We shared a plate of scrambled eggs

365

and link sausages. White toast with butter dripping off the sides. He put three entire sugar packets in his coffee, four creamers. God. And we just talked and talked. He made me feel like I was the only person in the world, that what we were doing — sitting in a booth at the IHOP — was the most important thing going on anywhere. You know what's that like, Edsel?"

"I do," he said, because he had felt that way with Sheila at least three times in their short romance — short but, compared with his mother's relationship with his father, a relative lifetime. The first was when they were watching *Bonanza* (three episodes from the very end of the series) and she paused the TV to tell him the backstory of every character — not to show off that she knew everything there was to know about them but because she wanted Bronfman to inhabit the same moment in the same way that she was. To share it. The second time, they were crossing the street and he took her hand without thinking about it, and she gripped his with an immediacy that was almost desperate, as if she had been waiting for his loving hand all her life, and to him that moment felt as if all the eyes in the universe were trained on them. The third time, he knocked on the door of her condominium, and when she opened it she was crying. "I don't know why," she said. "Nothing happened. Sometimes . . ." And he brought her close in an inescapable hug, and her face was flush against his shoulder, and he thought it was not impossible that his coat was soaking up every tear she shed, and when she looked up again she was smiling. It felt like a magic coat. He felt like a magic man.

"That's good," she said. She gave him a motherly pat on the knee. "Sheila's a catch. So. We were there for hours — two or three of them, I guess — and we walked over to the Cellar for a drink." She pointed to the Universal Insurance Company. "Gone now. But it was a nice place — the bar was from the forties, and, sitting there drinking, you felt like you were taking part in a hallowed tradition. The manager and I, Edgar, we were friends. He kept a little bottle of Afrin with him, but he dumped the Afrin and put this mixture of cocaine and water in it, and so he was tweaking all night long. He'd give me a bump if I asked him."

"Oh, Mom," Bronfman said. Already he was exhausted, reengineering the concept of who and what his mother was from moment to moment. Information overload. "No. You did — you did not do cocaine."

367

"Occasionally," she said. "It was *free,* Edsel."

"That makes it okay?" he said. "And weren't you a little old for all this? You were older than I am now."

"No one is older than you are now, Edsel." She smiled, touching on one exquisite memory after another. "I had a Manhattan, and then another, and he had the same. He told me he laid cable for the telephone company, but not for long. He was putting money away to go to grad school to be a teacher. A high-school teacher. Somewhere in Wisconsin? Idaho? I can't remember. He loved kids. He was the oldest of five, but he couldn't have one of his own because of some ailment, lazy sperm or some such — motility, that's what it was. They couldn't swim. That's an important detail in this story, Edsel. Obviously. But I believed him, because I think it was true. I think he believed it was true. Though who knows if that would have made any difference." She shrugged. "Drive on up the hill to the Econo Lodge."

The Econo Lodge was a cheap one-story motel that on garishly lit signage used to boast free air-conditioning; now it was free wireless. Bronfman turned into the parking lot. The car idled, sputtering flatulently.

"2D," she said, pointing a shaky finger, the nail shiny with bright-red polish. "Right there. That's where you happened."

"Where I happened," he said, a mindless echo.

"Where Roy and I had sex, where I got pregnant. And where you —"

"No, no," he said, holding up a hand. "You can stop there. I get it."

"Not that we knew that at the time. At the time, it was pure, unmitigated lust. Powerful stuff."

Bronfman felt anesthetized. 2D. Both of them were staring vacantly at the door. But Bronfman had seen and heard enough. From the drug bazaar to the hot dripping butter to Room 2D — enough. There is so much in the world that's not necessary to know to get along. He did not have to know about electricity, or about how cars worked, or whether a chromosome was bigger than a gene, or was it the other way around? This was on that same list. He didn't have to know any of this. And he was just about to put the car into reverse and take his mother home when she placed her hand on his.

"Let's go in," she said.

"No," he said. "I get it. That's where my life began. With someone you'd never seen before and would never see again. I can imagine it all. But I would rather not."

"Please, Edsel."

"We can't go in. Can't. Cannot."

"Why not?"

"Because . . . we can't. It's not our room, for starters."

"Rent the room. It can't be that much." She looked around her — the rusted drain-pipes, the open Dumpster. "It's the same old crappy place it used to be."

"Mom. Seriously."

"Just go do it, Edsel. I will pay you back if that's the problem."

"That's *definitely* not the problem."

She glared at him. "Then what *is* the problem?"

He kept forgetting that she was losing her mind. That she was old, demented. That maybe nothing, none of what she was telling him now, was even remotely true. Weirdly, remembering this reassured him. If none of it had meaning, it didn't matter what he did.

Then the door to 2D opened. A maid came out, wheeling her cart of linens and baby bottles of shampoo. She moved on to 3D, letting the door fall closed behind her. But it didn't close, not all the way. It came to rest before the lock engaged. Both of them saw it.

"It's a sign," Muriel said.

He pulled up into the open parking space directly in front of the room, and almost before the car was in park he had opened the door and was stepping out. He reflexively looked left, right, already forecasting a nasty retribution; they don't mess around at dumps like this. But maybe the presence of his old mother would forestall a thorough beating.

She was fearless, though. She pushed open the door and they walked into the stale, bleak, synthetic darkness of the cheapest motel room in Birmingham. The blinds were drawn. The open door allowed a rush of sun to pour into the room, but somehow the room didn't feel that much brighter. The small double bed, the pressed-wood dresser, the bathroom sink, and, above it, the old cloudy mirror — it felt like such a dismal place to Bronfman, the last stop in a life of many last stops.

For what felt like a very long time, his mother didn't speak or even seem to able to. She touched, very briefly, the drapes, rubbed the material between her fingers, and then walked to the bed and sat down on one side of it, purse still in her lap. She stared straight ahead. She looked as if she had received either the best or the worst news she ever had in her life.

"This, all of this. It's exactly the same," she said. "Everything. I think it's the same brown cover on the bed. And look — Magic Fingers." He had missed it: there was a small black box against the wall: MAGIC FINGERS RELAXATION SERVICE. ONLY 25 CENTS. "Where do you see that anymore? Only a quarter." Pause, memory, smile. "Roy had three."

Bronfman sat down on the edge of the bed beside her, on the bed where he was invented by this woman and a near-stranger's supposedly lazy sperm. Maybe that explained Bronfman's character, to some degree, his record-setting slow-blooming nature. Maybe Bronfman just didn't have what it takes. Maybe it was in his genes.

His mother was silent, watching the show going on in her head, the old movie she starred in thirty-four-plus years ago, eyes open but completely blank and flat. She wasn't smiling, but she wasn't frowning, either. Outside, he could hear the traffic go by, someone in a room nearby shouting.

Finally, she turned to her son with warm, watery eyes. "See, Edsel? I hadn't planned on any of this. Who ever knew that one night with a nice man would end up producing a thousand peanut-butter-and-jelly sandwiches?" A statement that, had anybody overheard her, would have seemed completely insane. Only Bronfman knew that this was the sanest thing she could have said.

THREE

From 1991 through 1995, mid-August, just before school began, Bronfman and his mother would prepare his lunch for the upcoming year. With her son in tow, she drove to the A&P way on the other side of town. The Piggly Wiggly was much closer to home, but she objected to the name, which she felt was vaguely offensive. She cast a deep-blue egalitarian eye on this old southern world, and occasionally that would get her into some trouble, which she loved. "It will be a cold day in hell before I darken the door of the Piggly Wiggly!" she said, as if she had been personally offended by Mr. Wiggly himself and wanted him to know it. Bronfman wondered if it had anything to do with the fact that the Piggly Wiggly was the first supermarket in town to enforce a no-smoking rule. Once (when Bronfman was nine) she was asked to leave the store when she refused to put out her Salem as she waited for the butcher to bring her a pot roast.

No matter. They drove three miles to the A&P, where he would grab one metal cart and she would grab another. Bronfman's job was to fill his cart with loaf after loaf of white bread, the whitest bread there ever was, bread as white as chalk, bread you can't legally buy anymore because its color comes from a bleach known to kill household pests. But Bronfman loved it. The bread was so soft and moist that he could roll an entire slice of it into a ball the size of a marble. He got the bread, while his mother was in charge of the peanut butter and jelly. She bought twenty-five jars of each. It took them half an hour to check out.

At home, the bread was laid out piece by piece across the kitchen counters — slabs of white clones edged with a ribbon of brown. Bronfman thought that meant the bread was baked in an actual oven, but later decided that it was probably just a breadlike substance made to look that way. Sometimes he ate that part first, but not now, not during the manufacturing process. Their kitchen wasn't very large. There was just enough room for fifty slices of bread to be laid out at a time, twenty-five sandwiches

— approximately one month of lunches.

And in this way his lunch was made, *every* lunch was made, one for every day of the week, September to June, sandwich after sandwich, all day long.

As his mother slathered on the jelly and he carefully applied his coating of sludgy brown peanut butter (always smooth, never crunchy), she talked with him about the thing he knew least: himself. Every August there seemed to be a theme. This August, because he was a rising high-school freshman, the theme was girls. It was as uncomfortable to talk about them then as it was now.

"What do you think?" she said.

"Think?"

"Do you see yourself, you know, dating, getting into it all?"

" 'Getting into it all'?"

"Girls," she said. "Not romance, per se. Just those initial exploratory maneuvers kids get into."

"I don't know what you're talking about."

"Come on." She winked. "You're among friends."

He *didn't* know what she was talking about. Was he supposed to? Did not having a father around to tell him these things place him at a disadvantage?

"Exploratory maneuvers," she said. "Like 'Hi, how are you? What's up?' Then boom — you're on your way to first base."

"Mom."

"Second —"

"Mom."

"The crowd is on its feet — he's stealing third!"

"Mom."

She laughed her spritely cackle (she sounded like a fun-loving witch back then) and sipped on her wine — small, delicate sips that didn't appear to subtract a teaspoon from its total volume but then was gone. Pinot Grigio. Bronfman knew that it was Pinot Grigio because every day at around five o'clock she'd sing a little song: "What do you know, what do you know, it's time for my Pinot Grigio!" Then she'd dance to the refrigerator and remove the bottle she'd been drinking from the day before, the mysterious green bottle, corked, standing beside the stodgy carton of skim milk. He liked to watch her sip, the way the thin edge of the wineglass slipped between her lips, the way it fit there, her lower lip bigger, fuller than the upper one; the way her hair (brown, almost comically straight) was cut to fall to her shoulders, and rippled when she laughed. And the beauty mark.

Was seeing his mother in this way — as an object of beauty — normal for a boy? Was there some kind of psychological trauma that came from an idealization of this magnitude?

She moved closer to him, in order to check on his progress. "Get the peanut butter all the way to the edge," she said.

"I *am,*" he said, bristling. "Mostly."

"Hey, they're your sandwiches," she said. "I'm just thinking of your future. The one without enough peanut butter in it. A disappointment waiting to happen." She mussed his hair with her free hand. "One of many, I suppose."

He noted how her jelly — grape, the color of red wine — perfectly covered the open plain. How did she do it? Not even a drop of jelly anywhere but on the bread.

"Maybe I'm rushing this," she said. "Maybe you should just start by talking to them. Don't worry about the other stuff."

"I'm not worried," he said. He wouldn't look at her. "Just —"

"What would you say?"

"To who?"

"A girl."

"Nothing."

"Pretend I'm a girl."

Sigh.

"Hi, Edsel!" she said, pretending to be a girl. Apparently, girls were bright and cheery and happy to see him. "How are you?"

"Please."

"No. Say, 'I'm fine, *insert name here*,' " she said. "That's all. That's it. You're done. Now the ball is rolling."

"Uphill," he said.

"Maybe," she said. "Unless you change that attitude of yours."

"What attitude?"

Bronfman gazed at his mother, and heard only a part of what she said. Sometimes he shut down halfway through one of her stories. It was this view of her, that's what he loved. Just looking. She kicked him in the leg. "You don't have to love me so much," she said. "I mean, it may not be a good thing in the long run. And you're three slices behind," she said. "Get to work."

The production line was active for the next couple of hours. When the components were assembled — a flotilla of peanut butter here, an armada of jelly over there — they were brought together, one on top, one on bottom, like lovers. The product was inserted into a plastic bag, which was carefully sealed, and then they were stacked in the big freezer in the basement, over and over and over, until all 180 sandwiches were finished — 180 being the average number of days in the school year. So now in the morning all she had to do was pop a red bag of mini-pretzels, a Dixie cup for the water fountain, and the sandwich into a bag — it took seconds — and it was done and he was set and she could go back to bed. The peanut butter and jelly and bread would usually defrost by lunch, but in the colder months there were always one or two icy bites.

Oh, he grew up wanting more, better, different. Less of the same. And if it was all going to be prepared at one time and frozen, why *not* do something different: like peanut-butter-and-jelly half the year and bologna the rest. How weird that she did this. How awful! It was so awful that he wouldn't talk about it even with the few friends he had. No one knew, no one. He was ashamed. Was she cruel, lazy, or just overly practical and industrious? One thing for certain: out of all the days, weeks, and years he'd spent with her, he remembered this most vividly, this making of peanut-butter-and-jelly sandwiches.

He did object, once. The summer before his senior year. Said he wanted a different lunch every day. Something new. Something good. Something that he could look forward to.

"Something to look *forward* to?" she said. "Lunch? Edsel," she said. "Listen. If you only learn one thing from me in your whole life, learn this: Lunch is boring. Lunches are boring. Everything about a lunch is middling. It's in the middle of the day, for one thing. It's more of a break than it is a meal, really, isn't it? Just a bunch of kids sitting together at table after table stuffing their mouths with nutrients so they can live until three-thirty. That's all it is. But see? Now it's done; we don't have to think about lunch for the rest of the year. Our minds are free to engage in higher pursuits. We can have bigger ideas, more beautiful thoughts. That's what I want for you, Edsel. I want you to soar. I want you to be happy. Lunch — this is what holds us back, it's what keeps us from being happy. Not just lunch, of course, but things *like* lunch. Believe me, I know what I'm talking about. Good men, happy men — men who are content — they don't worry about lunch. And you're going to be a good man."

She was wrong. Bronfman didn't become a good man; he was more neutral than anything else. It appeared that he had taken the lesson she had tried to teach him and turned it into the exact opposite of what she had intended. *All* he had thought about was lunch — metaphorically, anyway, lunch the way she meant it. All he had wanted was to be held back. Until Carla D'Angelo called him, at any rate. Until he met Sheila.

FOUR

In the quiet of 2D they sat on the bed beside each other, still as wax figures. Then she took his hand and held it, tighter than he thought she could.

"Give me a minute, dear, okay?"

"Of course."

He stood, left, drew the door closed a little more than halfway, and waited on the walkway outside. The sun warmed his cheeks, and his neck, bound so tightly by his too small collar, glistened with sweat. Heat rose in wavy sheets from the parking lot and, through them, mirage-like, he saw a police car approaching, and it parked in the space right beside his. Serena Stanton peered at him through the windshield. She looked mildly amused.

"My, my," she said, leaving the car and approaching him, her left hand resting on her walkie-talkie. "You do get around."

"Hi, Serena," he said. On first names with

a policewoman, something he never imagined happening in the kind of lifetime he'd planned on having. She lifted her two-way and muttered some unintelligible policespeak into it and replaced it on her belt. "We got a call from management," she said. "Said a couple of vagrants had unlawfully taken possession of a room."

"Vagrants?" he said. "I'm clearly not a vagrant. I'm wearing a tie!"

"I'm paraphrasing. What's going on, Bronfman?"

"It's a long story," he said.

"I have all day." She set her feet about eighteen inches apart, hands on her hips, and appeared to be planted there, immovable.

"Okay. So my mother's in the room now," he said. "Almost exactly thirty-five years ago she had . . . intercourse here with a man she'd just met and never saw again. He impregnated her, and the child born through their union was me. She wanted to show me where it happened, and to revisit it herself for old times' sake."

Serena's expression remained flat, unimpressed. But how often could she possibly have heard a tale like this? Many times, it appeared. "Not that long a story," she said, and pushed her hair back and away from

384

her face and let it rest behind her ear. "But sweet. Very sweet." He saw a small hole in her lobe where she could be wearing an earring, and he imagined one there — something long and metallic, jeweled with amethyst — and everything about her changed, like Cinderella. He understood why she couldn't wear it on duty: it would severely compromise her authority. Everybody would want to kiss her. He tried to suppress the guilt he felt at the core of this observation — *Sheila, I'm sorry* — but it wouldn't go away. He imagined himself kissing Serena Stanton.

Had he been his father — clearly the man his mother wanted him to be — he would have brushed Serena's hair back behind her ear himself, and gazed into her eyes and said something catchy, a good line, something that would make her smile and wonder what he was really like. But he wasn't his father, if his father really was the father his mother said he was.

"Here's what's going to happen," Serena said. "I'm going to talk to the manager, and you're going to retrieve your mother and go on your way. No harm, no foul. Understood, Bronfman?"

"You sure you don't want to take me in?" he said. Oh, my God. He did it. He accidentally did it. That was a line. Then he held out his hands, wrists together. "I've never seen the inside of a police car." He felt possessed by his father's spirit.

"Don't tempt me," she said and smiled, smiled as if she *were* just a little bit tempted. "But I should take a look first, just to make sure it's your mother in there and you're not up to any shenanigans."

She gently pushed open the door and peered in and around, and then motioned for Bronfman to take a look himself. His mother was under the covers, breathing softly, bedsheets up to her shoulders, and her eyes were closed, and the bed was magically trembling.

FIVE

Muriel looked as if she could sleep forever. She lay there, still as a mummy, radiating contentment on that overused mattress and those prickly sheets. Serena must have seen it, too, because after the last cycle ended she tiptoed to the side of the bed and inserted another quarter. "Five more minutes," she whispered to Bronfman, "but then I'm calling in the SWAT team."

They waited together on the walkway outside the room. Serena's walkie-talkie and Bronfman's stomach grumbled: it was almost time for lunch. She stood there, hands on her hips, looking out toward the city like a sentry on a parapet, scouting for suspicious movement on the periphery of the kingdom.

"It's going to be a hot one," she said.

"It is," he said, happy to enthusiastically affirm an observation that he might have shared himself, given another moment or two. "And the humidity!"

"I've never gotten used to it," she said. "I love my uniform. I wanted to be a police officer since I was a kid, and when I thought of myself all grown up I was wearing a uniform just like this. But it gets hot under here." Her hands, beginning at her clavicles, drew a line lightly down her torso.

"You sweat a lot," he said.

"I *perspire,*" she said, and smiled.

Bronfman worked to maintain the idleness of the conversation.

"So you're not from here?" he asked.

"Vermont," she said. "The first ten years of my life, anyway. Then my dad was transferred to Atlanta — he was an urban planner — and I came here to school and just . . . stayed. Birmingham's nice. Not too big, not too small. What a town dreams a city would be, you know?"

Bronfman stuck his hands in his pocket and jingled his keys. "What a town dreams a city would be," he said. "That's exactly right."

"Vulcan is a plus. And people are generally friendly. I like that."

"Even the criminal element?" Bronfman said, pleased with the phrase he'd just pulled out of his hat. *Criminal element.* He'd never used those words in that order before, not in his entire life, but somehow he had it at the ready, right when he needed it. It scared him, not knowing what was inside his own head, but today it was a plus.

"I've arrested lots of people who apologize to me all the way to the station. Not for what they did but for making me come out on a rainy night to get them." She laughed.

"*I'm* sorry," Bronfman said.

"For what?"

"For this," gesturing with his head toward the hotel room. "I'm sure you have better things to do."

"I don't," she said. "Actually, this is the fun part of my job."

Serena looked at him with a gentle fondness, a small smile, her eyes softly shining. Bronfman had no words, no sounds at all, to reply with, not even a friendly idle grunt. He couldn't look away from her, but he couldn't respond, either. Now, where was that errant phrase to be rescued from the cobwebby corner of his brain when he really and truly needed one? Why had he wasted it on *criminal element* when what he really wanted now was a series of words that somehow communicated to her that he recognized her partiality to him, what seemed a partiality to him, what he hoped was a partiality to him — that, in words

humans used, she liked him. Because thinking that she liked him, feeling that, felt so
good. Then, finally, something did come to
him, and it was as magic as the fingers on
the bed his mother was sleeping in. He said,
"I bet you say that to all your perps."

She laughed. "Not all," she said. He
watched her chest rise with a breath. "Almost none, in fact."

"Then I'll try to get in trouble more often."

And she laughed yet again. He was making her laugh! Was there any greater power?
If there was, he had yet to discover it.
"Well," she said. "There are other ways to
get in touch with me."

"There are? Oh! You mean your card."

"I mean my card." Her left eyelid fell and
rose in a friendly wink. "You still have it?"

"It's in my wallet."

What was happening? What was he saying? What was she saying?

"Good," she said. "Because you never
know —"

Then slowly, languidly, she removed a pen
from her breast pocket. Just like that,
without a word. She held it out for him to
take, and, hand shaking, he took it. But
there was a moment, not even a moment,
perhaps, but some fraction of a moment,

when their fingers touched. He had never been given a pen by a woman before.

"Well, this is odd."

It was Muriel. She was standing at the half-open door, squinting in the light. She looked at Bronfman, then at Serena, then back to Bronfman. "I hope I'm not interrupting anything."

"What do you mean?" Bronfman said.

"I mean I'm done with the room if you want it."

Bronfman flushed red. "God, Mom," he said. "This is Serena. She's a policewoman."

"I hope so," Muriel said, looking at Serena's uniform. "Otherwise, this would be even odder."

"Hello, Mrs. Bronfman," Serena said. "I got a call from the manager, came down. You're going to have to vacate the premises."

"And vacate I will," she said. "Serena."

Muriel looked at Serena and then at her son as if she was trying to figure out who he was, as if the information she was receiving now contradicted everything she knew about him and it was time to reassess.

"May I use the ladies' room? Or will that get me thrown in the clinker?"

"Of course you may," Serena said.

"You can't wait until we get home?"

391

Bronfman said. Enough laws had been broken, he thought.

"No, I can't wait until we get home. And why should I? I may never get to be in a hotel bathroom again. It's sanitized for my protection. I like that. Breaking the seal on the toilet is like opening a present on Christmas morning. Cool your jets. This will only take a minute. Two at the most."

She turned and reentered the darkness without closing the door behind her. They could see the light come on, hear the paper ribbon tear, some elfish laughter.

"She's a card," Serena said. "I bet she was fun to grow up with."

"Tons," Bronfman said. "It was a regular circus." He stopped. "I'm being sarcastic," he clarified.

"Ten-four," she said.

When Muriel finished several minutes later, Serena led her to the passenger side of the car, opened the door and, after she was settled, closed it firmly, as if to ensure against Muriel's escape. Then she walked around to Bronfman's side and leaned in the open window. Muriel was watching them the way a cat watches a bug.

"Have a good day, Mrs. Bronfman," Serena said.

Muriel turned away and looked down at

her shoes. "I have all my life been in the pursuit of happiness, as is our right as human beings," she said. "Thomas Jefferson said so."

"Can't argue with that," Serena said.

"Boomshakalaka," Muriel said. She stared through the windshield at nothing.

To Bronfman, Serena said, "Get her home safely. And no more B&Es, okay?"

"No more what?" He thought she'd said, "No more bee's knees." That couldn't be right.

"Breaking and Entering."

"Absolutely not. Never again."

Her eyes were as green as a garnet. They were inches away from his. So close they exerted a very real magnetic power, and he felt his face being drawn toward hers in infinitesimal increments. As if realizing the danger she was putting both of them in, she pulled back, put on her sunglasses, and, just like that, reinhabited her professional capacity.

"Be good," she said.

He nodded and tried, unsuccessfully, to see through her glasses. "Is that the motto of the police department? 'Be good'?"

"Nope," she said. She slapped the roof twice with her right hand and stepped away. "Just mine."

Six

Muriel was quiet all the way home. He was tempted to break the silence two or three times — at stoplights, when an old lady pulled in front of them on Montevallo — but it was clear that she had no room for words in her head right now. She sat as if alone in the darkness of a movie theater, watching a movie of her own life. Some of it was probably blurry, and whole chunks of it missing in parts, but there was no doubt more than enough for her to see. If you could remember every moment of your life, every person you ever met, every tear you ever shed, every time you made somebody laugh or cry, would the end of your life be more meaningful? Does more data, collated and filed away, mean greater understanding? Or is it all about feeling? Does it all come together at the end in a great rolling snowball of emotion?

She was still like that, still watching her

movie, when he pulled up to the house. She didn't move, so neither did he. He just idled there at the curb.

"I almost died," she said.

"What? When!?"

"Back there," she said. "In the hotel room."

"No," he said. "You were fine. You were asleep."

"I mean, I almost *chose* to die. You can do that, you know. Kill yourself with a thought, if the thought is powerful enough. You couldn't, you're too young. But you get to a certain age and you've lived a certain life, it's been documented — in rare cases, there's a moment you can choose to die. Have you read *The Denial of Death*?"

"No," he said. "What's that?"

"It's a book."

"And it's in there?"

"Maybe," she said. "I don't know. But I know what I know. Roy invited me to die. He invited me into the light."

She was almost upset with him, so he backtracked. "Okay," he said.

"The thing is, the important thing is, I didn't choose to go. Even though for all practical purposes my life is over."

"It is *not,* Mom," he said. He couldn't bear this, her saying this. "It is not over.

Look at you. We just B and E'd a hotel room. That's a lively thing to do. An alive thing."

She ignored him. "Don't you want to know why I didn't go?"

"Of course. Sure."

"Because I wanted to stay alive a little bit longer. For you."

Finally, she turned to him. She was crying. Not a lot, though, just a couple of leaking tears navigating the wrinkles of her cheeks. She looked into his eyes.

"I fucked up, Edsel," she said. "Big-time."

"Mom," he said. This was excruciating for him. His chest felt explosive. "Muriel. No. You didn't."

"I did! I did, Edsel, and the thing is? I am so glad I did. I fucked up in every way I could think of. Men, drugs, alcohol. I smoked. I made you eat peanut-butter-and-jelly sandwiches for years. But look, everything turned out pretty much okay. Better than okay, actually." She let her old time-splotched hand rest on his knee. "That's why I chose to live. That's why when Roy invited me into the light I said *not yet.* Because it's about you now. Your life. And you haven't fucked up. You've never fucked up. You've never given yourself permission to do something really, really stupid, and I want to live long enough to see that happen. All your life you've been a perfect little boy, and I'm not saying this to be hurtful, sweetie, but it's been a little dull. For me, I mean. Your audience. I'll be fine. Sheila will be fine. But, most of all, you will be fine. I promise. Just go out there and for once in your life fuck things up royally. Put your heart into it. Make a mess of things. I know you can do it. For me."

Bettina appeared at Muriel's window, bent over, and waved. But Bettina could tell something was going on, so she didn't open the door. She took a step back. "You almost fucked up with that policewoman," Muriel said, and laughed. She punched him lightly in the arm. "What was her name?"

"Serena," Bronfman said. "Serena Stanton."

She threw her head back in silent laughter. "You know her *whole name,*" she said. "And she knows yours. That's pretty good right there."

"Mom."

"I'd take her back to 2D if I were you. And bring at least three quarters. It's worth it."

"Mom!" he said. "I'm with Sheila."

She leaned over and kissed him on the cheek, that spot on his cheek that she'd kissed a million times or more. "Of course you are, dear. Of course you are."

Then Bettina opened the door, took his mother by one of her little arms, and led her away. They walked down the driveway, then across the sandstones surrounded by monkey grass, and made it to the front door. It took a while, because these days his mother took teeny-tiny steps. But he watched them the whole way, until they were gone inside and all there was to look at was the house, the house that he used to live in with his mother, where more than a thousand peanut-butter-and-jelly sandwiches had been made.

As he drove away, he had a thought that later he would feel his mother had deftly planted in his subconscious. He made a decision. I'm making love to Sheila, he thought. How that would actually happen was a mystery to him, but he was going to do it. Tonight. Evening was just now falling. Bronfman went straight over, before he changed his mind.

SEVEN

Since Bronfman had been seeing Sheila, his life had expanded geometrically: once a mere triangle, Cedar Court introduced a fourth point, another edge, and now his life looked more like a rhombus, or a parallelogram. It was more complex, more interesting. On the way there, he transferred a condom from the glove department to his pants pocket. He had stopped thinking. He was on a journey, a quest, and since he'd already determined what the end of the quest would be there was no reason to think of it any longer. All that remained was to do it. His body swelled with intent and desire. All he knew was this: he would stride into her condominium, turn off the television, take her by the hand, and pull her into the bedroom. She would not resist. Far from it. Their desire would be as one; they would feel everything the same at the very same time; he could say "Jinx" to their desire.

But that's not what happened.

Sheila came to the door wearing a short black slip with a lacy trim, spaghetti straps, and red stitching. Her breasts seemed bigger than they normally were, bigger than he had ever seen them, fuller. Her hair was down, wavy now (he had never seen it wavy), and her lipstick was so red against her fair white skin that she looked like a lady vampire who'd just finished her dinner. The lights were out and squat little candles were everywhere: on the coffee table, the television set, her bedside table — even on the toilet, he found out later. All Bronfman could think was *fire hazard!* She had a bowl of chocolate-covered strawberries in her hand, and before he could say the first thing she popped one into his mouth, and then went after it herself, her tongue probing the cavities of his cheeks for food, as if a chocolate-covered strawberry was something to be shared like this.

He had the impression (and it would turn out to be the case) she was following directions from a book on how to bring passion into a relationship. Sheila was good at following directions, of course. When she cooked, if the recipe called for one-eighth of a teaspoon of salt she used one-eighth of a teaspoon of salt. Never a pinch. "What's a pinch of salt?" she'd argue to no one. "Everybody's pinch is different!" She had a trust in and an affiliation with other direction writers, he thought, which was admirable. They were a very exclusive club, he imagined, though it was not anything she ever talked about, or wrote in his presence, and he never talked about it, either. But soon he hoped to, when Sorsby came through with his IKEA connection. He promised Bronfman that he would do what he could — "because we're so close," he said. But he was being sarcastic, as they weren't close. So Bronfman wasn't sure he was doing what he could at all.

Bronfman was swept up in the rush of Sheila's plans, and yet, at the same time, completely overwhelmed. He helped her remove his jacket and tie, and then there was the time-consuming and onerous task of unbuttoning his shirt. Once he was half-naked she paused and produced a flute of champagne, which she sipped from and then offered to him. Still, she hadn't said a word. The sex directions must have called for "half a flute of champagne once half-naked." She drank her half a flute in a flash and waited for him to finish his, her smoky eyes glowing with the coals of passion. She licked her lips. He was getting chilly, his arms and stomach a goose-bumped terrain. She took the glass from his hand and, holding him by the wrist, led him into the bedroom, where, thank God, there were no rose petals. But, with her customary foresight, the blankets had been turned down. The bed was passion-ready. She crawled under the blankets, and he did, too, and once there she loosened his belt and unbuttoned his pants and tried to pull them off, but they got stuck on his thighs and he had to help her by undoing the zipper. A team effort. Then she removed her negligee, if that's what it was, and together, under the covers, they could not have been more naked. Her hands were a little cold, and when she touched him his penis — and God, how he hated to remember this, would flinch at the memory for the rest of his life — it totally retracted, turtlelike. It was still there, though. He felt it. It hadn't disappeared completely. There was something there for her to work with: hope. She had a special lotion nearby, and she opened it and rubbed it on her hands and then on him, until there was a sufficient amount of warmth for him to move, and he became bolder, and then — with absolutely no empirical basis to justify the move — he mounted her. He was determined. Something might happen if he was up there. Ninety percent of everything is showing up! That's what they said! And here he was! Bronfman, present!

But even Bronfman, who knew relatively nothing, knew that sex was never just sex. Especially not *this* sex, his sex. This sex tonight with Sheila could be his cure, the cleansing, the erasure of a past in which nothing like this had ever happened — nothing so real and unfiltered and honest — replaced by a future in which it happened all the time. A future in which he was the man he might become. Sex was not just sex: for Bronfman, it was life. It felt facile, even sort of inane, to think so, but the single most important thing in the world right now was this, now, where he was, with this beautiful woman beneath him.

It was almost too much to bear.

Time ground by like fingernails slowly scraping across a blackboard, like a horse dragging a car without wheels up the steep side of a mountain. Interminable.

Nothing at all.

And then Sheila said the first thing she'd said since he arrived.

"It's okay, Edsel," she said. "Really. Let's just lie here."

"I'm a little tired," he said.

403

She brushed the hair off his forehead. "Long day?"

"You wouldn't believe it," he said.

So they just lay there, side by side. His eyes had adjusted to the dark and he could see her now, her eyes so sweet and open, without judgment, without complaint. Then she smiled.

"I have an idea," she said. She was very excited. "Let's share our sordid pasts!"

"Sordid pasts?"

"We skipped that part." *Step 4. Share sordid pasts.* "You tell me about everyone in your past and I'll tell you everyone in mine."

Had he understood her? "*Everyone* in my past?"

She punched him playfully in the shoulder. "It's that long a list, eh?"

"I just don't think I know what you mean."

She kissed his nose. "Everyone you've slept with, silly. And I'll do the same. It's what you do, before . . . you know. It's like an exorcism, full disclosure. Turns the past into the past and the present into the present. I'll go first if you want."

And as if he had assented, which he didn't think he had, she began.

"Okay. My first was Ryan Brouchard. I was eighteen — yes, a bit of a late bloomer

404

— he was twenty-two. Nice guy, scratchy beard. We were together for two years, and then broke up when he moved to Seattle. No, Portland. Then I was brokenhearted and just was very . . . God! Loose, I guess. So embarrassing. Gary Franklin, and, like, a month later, his cousin, who was just abominable. Couple of years — no one. Abstinent. Like a nun. Then, okay . . . just really quickly: Toby Vandeveer, Morgan Freeman (not *the* Morgan Freeman), Ben (I don't think I learned his last name) and, last, Jedidiah Jensen from the bluegrass state of Kentucky." She laughed, and then put her arm around Bronfman's shoulder. "But that was some time ago. I've been on my own for a little while now."

She heaved a huge sigh, as if she'd just finished running a marathon while reciting the alphabet backward. He thought she might be blushing, but it was hard to tell in the flickering light. He was warmer now, under the covers, and so was she, and her nipples kept brushing against his arm, back and forth, as she breathed. It was an odd sensation, as if she was trying to tickle him with a pencil eraser.

It was his turn. She was waiting, expectant; he had probably never seen her eyes more eager. But his mouth wouldn't open.

He was being asked to speak a language he didn't know, one he had never even heard until now, and it made him mute. His head was half swallowed in the pillow, so she could see only one of his eyes, but that was all she needed to understand that there was a problem.

"What, Edsel?" she said. She raised herself up on one elbow. "You don't want to or . . . you're shy about it, I get that. But I did it. That would be really unfair if you —"

"Mary McCauley!" he blurted out, as if he were being cross-examined, beaten down by the opposing council. "Mary Day Mc-Cauley, when I was fifteen years old."

"Fifteen!" she said. She laughed. "That's astounding! I didn't expect that. You surprise me, Edsel Bronfman. Mild-mannered on the outside, a roaring tiger on the inside. So. Okay. Next?"

He turned away from her and stared at the ceiling, where the candles cast eerie spidery shadows. "There is no next," he said.

"No next?"

"No next."

"I don't even know what that means, Edsel."

"It means what I said."

"But, okay, so . . . you were fifteen

when . . . and now you're . . . thirty-four, so it's been" — she did the math — "nineteen years. Nineteen. Years."

He could tell that she wished she hadn't said this, that even though it was true and her math checked out, it brought a harsh light to bear on Bronfman's long hiatus. One of the candles died, the wax a rising tide against the light. Then another. The darkness felt heavy against him. Because he didn't really know, of course, whether he had been experiencing a nineteen-year hiatus at all. He didn't know if his hiatus had ever begun.

"I'm going home," Bronfman said.

"No," Sheila said. "Please. You're already naked. Just stay under the covers and go to sleep."

But without another word he stood, and dressed. He had to get out, as if by leaving her he would somehow be able to leave himself there as well, to escape his skin. But nothing doing. Bronfman accompanied Bronfman all the way home.

EIGHT

When does a door cease to be a door? When it's ajar. This was one of the only jokes Bronfman knew, or could remember knowing, and he trotted it out on occasion, whenever he could. He thought of it now, while driving up to his apartment, and noted, My door is not a door.

It is a jar.

From the car he saw the feeble glow from the lamp on the table beside his living-room chair; it cast barely enough light to leak through the windows, but it did. He wasn't afraid of being robbed, since he had been robbed already and there was nothing left to steal; surely Thomas Edison would have warned his friends away from wasting their time here. So he assumed he had failed to lock it that morning. But he was too tired to think it through, too sad, oppressed with the idea of who he was and the pointless space he took up in the world.

Coco was sitting in his living-room chair, her knees drawn up to her chin, her legs encircled by her arms, barefoot, asleep. She looked like a child: innocent, uncomplicated, dreaming. But she woke on his first step past the threshold. She opened her eyes, blinked, looked around to get her bearings. But she stayed there, wrapped up in her own arms, and yawned.

"Oh," she said. "Hey, Bronfman."

"Hey," he said. He was not pleased. "What's going on? How did you get into my apartment?"

"Really? You're asking me that? I could get into Fort Knox with the right paper clip."

"Okay. Then why are you here?"

She shrugged, as if it was a silly question. "I thought you were gone for the evening. You're usually back by ten or eleven. When it was, like, midnight, I thought — I needed to get out of there." She gestured with her thumb toward Thomas Edison's place. "Some of those dudes . . . it's a different sort of clientele he's getting these days. They're not . . . you know . . . not as human as they used to be." She shivered. "I had this revelation: I don't want to trade blow jobs for drugs. You know what this means? It means I have standards, Bronfman. Who knew." She still hadn't moved from the chair. "So, anyway, I escaped to your place. You being gone and all, I thought it would be okay."

He took a deep breath and slow-blinked. "Well, I'm not gone now, am I?"

This shook her. She unclasped her arms and dropped her legs to the floor. She had never heard Bronfman talk this way. Bronfman knew that, because no one in the world had heard him talk this way.

"So what, you're saying I should go? Back over there?"

Normally, he would have said, "Do you want to stay here? I'll sleep on the couch. You can have the bed." But he wasn't feeling normal. He didn't nod. He didn't shake his head. He just stood there, because he was done with this day. Done.

She got it. "That's cold, Bronfman," she said, and stood. "Really cold. But whatever."

She tried to assemble her callous tough-girl exterior, but it wasn't working. She bit the side of her lower lip and seemed to consider what was waiting for her 'over there.'

"Don't you live somewhere? Can't you go home?"

She smiled faintly. "Home fell through," she said. "For the time being, anyway."

"I'm sorry about that."

"Don't be. It's all good. Everything happens for a reason. God doesn't give us more than whatever that thing is people say."

She clapped her hands together and took a deep breath that rose in her chest. "Okay!" she said with as much faux eagerness as she could muster. "Off I go."

She was almost gone when she stopped and turned.

"Oh. Almost forgot. I got you this."

From her right pocket she dug out a pen. A ballpoint pen. She held it out for Bronfman to take and, finally, he did. "For your collection," she said.

The pen was black-and-gold, and in the dim light it was hard to tell, but the design came together soon enough. It was a leopard-skin print. He had never had a pen with a leopard-skin print on it. He squinted, and was able to read the tiny letters: "The Leopard Skin Lounge. 3001 2nd Ave. North. Birmingham, Alabama." He had actually heard of the Leopard Skin Lounge. It was a strip club. Sorsby had mentioned having an unbelievably wild night there once. Bronfman had never gone, of course, and most likely never would, but he had the pen and that was as good as going, better even. To have this pen made him inordi-

411

nately happy, happier than the circumstances of his life should have allowed. But
he allowed it. And it was the second pen a
woman had given him that day. He looked
up from the pen to thank her — for the pen
and for the short vacation from himself it
had afforded him — but Coco was gone.
He could almost hear her through the walls
now, not laughing.

■ ■ ■ ■

DAY SEVENTY-THREE

■ ■ ■ ■

ONE

Bronfman did wonder how the world was put together, in both the smallest ways and the absolute biggest as well. He wondered if there was a plan, for instance, or a meaning beyond our day-to-day lives, if there was a reason for being, and even if there was a God. And, assuming there was a God, did he actually care about humanity? And say, further, that there was a God who cared about humanity in a very general, inclusive way, could he or she possibly give the slightest damn about anything that one person out of all of it thought, did, planned, experienced, endured? Absolutely not. No way. Impossible.

But what happened next gave him pause. One of those cosmic coincidences keeping him off balance. It was this: the next day, at the very moment Bronfman thought of actually tracking down Mary Day McCauley, of finding her and calling her and asking her if she recalled whether they'd had sex together nineteen years ago — almost at the very second this thought came to him — he learned that she had died.

God! What was that about?

That morning he woke later than usual, at eight, and was tardy for work, but really, did anyone care? No one cared. No one said a thing to him. He had been on time every day for the past seven years. He thought it was important to be on time, but now that he wasn't he saw that it didn't matter. *No one cared.* What was there left to believe in if punctuality meant nothing? He couldn't concentrate. Invoices, bills of lading, inventory adjustments . . . He could not bring the requisite zeal he needed to get through it all. So he set about clearing out his junk folder — the IT people encouraged it — and that's when he got the news, on a listserv from his high school that he didn't even know he was a part of.

Mary Day McCauley was dead.

It made him catch his breath. He read it and read it again.

Melanoma, of all things.

He read it again, because it made no sense to him. She was just a year older than he was. And engaged! Engaged to a man named Jeff Creech.

According to the obituary, she went to Auburn University and then settled down in Martinsville, where she became a chemistry teacher and a softball coach. Not Paris but Martinsville, Alabama, half an hour away. She had lived half an hour away from where he was right this second, and he hadn't known it. This new fact ushered in another tremor, as if knowing that she was so close would have changed anything about his life at all.

But this did: the service, her service, was today.

His heart stopped, then sluggishly resumed beating.

Today. At 11 A.M.

He looked at his watch. This was a sign. He had to go. He had to attend her service. He stood and slipped on his jacket.

"I'm going out for a bit," he said aloud to an invisible Sorsby. Not that he needed to, but he said it anyway, more to convince himself that he was going than anything else. "Probably be back later. I have some . . . personal business."

A beat. "Personal business. Well, that's some big news, Bronfman. Big news. I'm honored you shared it with me. Allow me to applaud you."

Sorsby had an app on his phone that

417

simulated the sound of an audience applauding. He did it all the time for almost any reason, but this time it was for Bronfman leaving work early to go to the funeral of the only woman in the world who had ever allowed him inside her. Bronfman was beyond being bothered by one of Sorsby's apps, though. He walked away without another word.

"Oh, wait," Sorsby said. "I have a name."

Bronfman stopped. "A name? What's that supposed to mean?"

"That IKEA connection you wanted? It took some finagling and skulduggery and software sleight of hand, but I found it." A piece of paper, folded into quarters, sailed over the cubicle wall and landed on the floor beside Bronfman's feet. "I don't know how to put it, honestly — how doing what I've done for you makes me feel. To do something good for another person, something that might actually help them? It's new for me. And I have to tell you, Bronfman, I'm uncomfortable with it. But I've earned a trip to heaven, for sure. I hope I've changed your life — and the lady's, of course."

Bronfman picked up the paper without looking at it and stuffed it into his jacket pocket. It had been such an important goal of his, getting this information for Sheila, becoming a hero, *her* hero, but it didn't mean that much anymore. Mary Day was all he could think about. This was just a slip of paper.

"Don't thank me," Sorsby said. "Whatever you do."

And Bronfman didn't. For the first time in his life, he didn't thank someone who had done something for him. He walked out, stiff, confused, conflicted. He didn't even have to go home to change. The clothes he wore to work every day were perfectly appropriate for a funeral service.

It was a short drive down to Martinsville. He had been on the little highway many times. When he was a kid it was just a long, dense stretch of pine trees, but now it was one garish strip mall after another followed by fallow fields of nothing at all, old brown barns and empty silos. Everything changes for the worse. He shouldn't do what he was doing, he thought. He wondered if he would be making this trip at all had things been different with Sheila, different in *that* way, intimately — had they had intercourse is what he meant, sex, a word that even in his own mind he had to think of aphoristically. Intimacy. They were almost intimate last night; they were *this close*. But then, according to whatever curse he suffered under, they weren't. He wasn't sure if he ever had, and now there was only one way to find out. He had to talk to Jeff Creech. Mary Day had probably mentioned him to her, the way Sheila told Bronfman about her amorous past. Bronfman's name was probably sandwiched between a couple of others. Certainly she would have told him. It was so long ago, and none of that mattered anymore.

Bronfman had worked it out.

Scene: Jeff and Mary, in bed, lingering in the afterglow.

Mary Day: *High school? In high school there was Corey Spaulding. He was my big heartthrob. Then, let's see . . . oh, there was this guy named Bronfman, Edsel Bronfman, one crazy afternoon near the park.*

Jeff Creech: *Wait. His name was Bronfman? Edsel Bronfman?*

Mary Day: *Yes, Edsel Bronfman.*

Jeff: *Ha-ha, ha-ha-ha! What kind of name is that!*

And then they would both have laughed at his name. Which was okay. Because the bottom line was that if anything had happened between Bronfman and Mary Day on that day in the room near the park, she would have mentioned it. She would have mentioned his name to Jeff, and this, today, was his last chance to find out if she had. So Bronfman wasn't attending the service for Mary Day, though he was doing his best to pretend that he was. He was going for himself.

Two

He made it to the service just as it was
about to begin and sat down in the first seat
he could find, which was pretty far back.
He was sweaty, damp beneath his armpits
and nearly feverish where the elastic in his
underwear met his thighs. Around him sat
row after row of silent, somber people. Was
her casket here somewhere? He craned his
neck but couldn't see much, just the backs
of heads and the hair on them, the black
and the gray and the brown and the yellow
and the red, and the other heads that had
nothing on them at all — naked heads,
smooth and pink, creased with neck wrinkles as thick as stomach fat.

Bronfman, adjusting himself on the cush-
ioned pew, cleared his throat as if he were
about to say something. But he didn't say
anything. A few people he knew from high
school were there, from the old days — old
days Bronfman really wasn't a part of but

days he claimed as his nonetheless. There was Susan Ard, right? And Martin Gage, and there — he knew his name, what was it? — Gerald? Kevin? No. Josh Knowles. How could he forget Josh Knowles, who had to carry his wallet in his front pocket because he'd accidentally been shot in the butt by his father on a hunting trip. He could see them looking around, too, same as he was. Eyes passed across his face without pausing even briefly. No one recognized him, and he was okay with that. That's not why he was here. Someone was trying to squeeze past Bronfman's knees — someone who had arrived even later than he had. The space between pews was too narrow for Bronfman to stand, so it was an awkward fit. Thankfully, this guy wasn't big. Skinny. Scary skinny, actually, like a calcified scarecrow. Bronfman could feel the edge of the man's shins on his kneecaps as he slinked past and jammed himself into the empty space, see how his wrist and half his hand disappeared beneath the scuffed cuff of his dirt-brown blazer. A bit rancid, too, the fumes hanging in the air like cartoon clouds after he passed. Perhaps this was a homeless man. Bronfman surreptitiously stole a glance at him, and — of all the people in the world it could be — it was, swear to

God, Corey Spaulding.

Corey Spaulding! Poor Corey Spaulding. He looked as if he'd been put through a meat grinder and then stuffed in a bag and dragged behind a bus for a couple of miles. There was no mistaking him. Same wiry hair, same alien eyes and Mick Jagger lips, the plump kind that turned up at the corners so that he always seemed to be smiling even when he wasn't. It was definitely him. Corey must have felt Bronfman staring at him, because he turned and gave Bronfman a searching look, as if — who knows? — maybe they knew each other. Then Corey smiled, or seemed to smile, and turned away. Bronfman wasn't surprised. Even though Bronfman knew Corey, Corey didn't know Bronfman, the same way Bronfman knew Barack Obama but not the other way around. Bronfman presented Corey with his hand, though, stiffly, as if he was just learning how to initiate this sort of contact. Corey looked at it as if it were a snake, but he took it in his own. "Edsel Bronfman," Bronfman whispered, almost hissed, in the solemn quiet of the chapel. "You were a year ahead of me at Baldwin."

Corey sort of nodded, clearly trying to place Bronfman. He couldn't. Bronfman was unplaceable. "Yeah," he said. "Hey."

The service was just beginning. The priest or the minister or pastor (Bronfman was never sure what to call them, the people who did this sort of thing) welcomed the assembly and then gently launched into a spiritual biography of Mary Day: the work she did with the poor, the hungry, the homeless; she was a rock-solid friend and confidant to many; a great teacher and softball coach, taken from the world too young, a lifetime of such promise we cannot help but mourn. It was tragic and senseless.

"That's the fucking truth," Corey muttered, not to Bronfman or to anybody, unless it was God. "This makes no fucking sense at all."

Bronfman figured that more than half the church was crying now. Even Corey had tears rolling down his battered cheeks, and Bronfman wondered why he wasn't crying, too. He wasn't even close to tears. Then he understood: he wasn't at the service. He was still in the park. He was in that apartment. He was remembering Mary Day alive, with him, and that wasn't distressing at all. That was a happy thought. That was *the* happy thought. He was celebrating her, not mourning her, and he bet she would have wanted it this way.

A number of other people, including her

fiancé, Jeff Creech, stood up to say a few words. Jeff was a bigger man than Bronfman had imagined him to be. He looked like a football player who'd gone to seed, broad-shouldered, tall, but heavy in the stomach. Then it was over, and Bronfman realized that he'd zoned out during Jeff's speech, his mind elsewhere, stuck in that room with Mary Day. Everyone filed out to the church parking lot. Bronfman walked with Corey, even though Corey didn't appear to be walking with him.

It was hot outside. The sun baked the asphalt until it was spongy; it gave a little beneath his feet. In the bright light, it was possible to see the full extent of Corey's disintegration. All his good looks, his charm, that devil-may-carelessness, had all worn themselves out. The rings beneath his eyes looked as if they'd been dug out of dirt with a garden hoe, and his thinning hair — no longer long and golden, it was tarnished now, like old bronze — looked as if it had been cut and styled by a blind man. And his teeth — his teeth, once so wolfish and bright — had yellowed like old ivory.

Bronfman didn't want to think the thought he had then, but he thought it anyway. *O, how the mighty have fallen.* It was an inappropriate thought, for a handful of reasons. First, Corey hadn't really been that mighty. He had just been a kid who had grown up faster than Bronfman had, had more skills, was handsome and strong and alive in the world. He seemed mighty back then, but perspective is skewed when you're young, when you're envious of something so small as where a classmate is going on spring break. Also, here, at Mary Day's service, to have a thought like this was particularly churlish. And, finally, that thing which distinguished Corey more than anything else — his relationship with Mary Day — was something Bronfman shared, if only briefly, that Saturday afternoon near the park. As unremarkable as Bronfman had turned out to be, as invisible to the world as he was, he had somehow ended up in a better place than Corey. That was just a fact. And it was nice not to be the guy at the end of the line, for once.

Corey took out a pair of aviator sunglasses and put them on, probably the sole accessory in his arsenal that could approximate the coolness he had once exuded naturally.

"Well," Bronfman said, not sure of what to say. "Mary Day and I hung out a little bit. You know the park, where the bands played?"

But Corey didn't even look at him. "So

427

fucking tragic," he said. "So many assholes walking around happy as clams at high tide and this happens, a good person dies? I never believed in God, but I wish I did. I'd pee on a cross or something. Just to piss him off."

Bronfman nodded. "Yes," he said. "It is effing tragic." But it didn't sound the same coming out of his mouth. Corey could sell it; Bronfman, not so much. Corey looked at him, surprised: Corey hadn't known he was there; he had been talking to himself.

"So . . . yeah. I'm going to say hello to Jeff," Corey muttered, and backed away from Bronfman slowly, as if from a man with a gun.

"Good idea," Bronfman said, and as Corey walked away he followed him.

Friends and family surrounded Jeff Creech, but when he saw Corey heading toward him he stepped out of the crowd, arms spread wide.

"Corey," Jeff Creech said. They embraced in a real hug, gripping each other as if for dear life, clearly bonded by grief. So, this was interesting. Jeff Creech knew Corey Spaulding. How did that happen? Jeff Creech didn't even go to Baldwin, so . . . somehow they must have — Well, small world, Bronfman thought. Then, Small club.

Bronfman waited until their hug was finished before introducing himself.

"I'm Edsel Bronfman," Bronfman said. "I'm so sorry. For all of us." Bronfman opened his arms and initiated a hug, which Jeff entered into reluctantly. Bronfman pulled back to look into Jeff's eyes, for affirmation of the brotherhood, but there was nothing there. No recognition whatsoever. "Edsel *Bronfman*," he said again. "I knew Mary Day. At Baldwin."

"Oh," Jeff Creech said. "Of course." Still nothing. He was a total blank — and then — then — something. Was that recognition? Or something just short of it? "Thanks so much for coming. So many people from her high school came today. It's just amazing. What a girl. What a woman. She —"

"What a fucking tragedy," Corey said.

Bronfman persevered. He had come here on a mission. "You two know each other?"

And Jeff smiled. The first real smile Bronfman had seen today. Jeff winked at Corey as if they were partners in crime, and then sort of punched him in the arm.

"Do I know Corey," he said. "Do I ever. Mary Day told me a lot about this wingnut. More than I wanted to know! The star of Mary's . . . past. I had to meet him. You been down here half a dozen times, right?

429

And we went on that fishing . . . expedition."

"Fishing expedition?" Corey said. "I didn't catch a fucking thing."

"Okay, for you it was more of a beer expedition."

And they laughed.

But Bronfman had come too far to be put off so summarily. This was too important. "So," he said to Jeff Creech. "Mary never . . . mentioned me?"

Jeff and Corey stopped laughing, returned from their short vacation from grief. Both of them looked at Bronfman as if he had asked them for money.

"Bronfman," Jeff said, turning the name over in his mind, a little disgusted that he had been asked to, that was clear. There was nothing, nothing — but then, something. "Oh, *Bronfman.* Of course. Edsel Bronfman? Well, yes, once — she did mention you, one time." He raised his eyebrows — everything was coming back to him — and almost smiled. And then Jeff looked at Corey, and Corey looked at Jeff, and a story unspooled between them. *Both* of them knew. Bronfman could see it. The day in the park with her, the journey to the apartment, Mary Day naked before him, the beginning of every dream he had ever had on the bed beneath him — and his complete inability to make the dream come true, his failure. Jeff laid a hand on his shoulder. "Hey," he said, "at least you gave it a shot."

Then Jeff turned to Corey in a way that totally excluded Bronfman, and the two of them started talking, engaging in some intimate shorthand. Bronfman stood there for a minute too long, then quietly backed off and away. He looked around for someone else to talk to but didn't see anybody now — no one from Baldwin, anyway. Just about everyone had gone.

For another minute or more he stood there, alone on the blacktop, until the radiating heat warmed the soles of his shoes. He'd gotten what he came for, what he deserved. He knew now who he was. There had been no hiatus at all, just one long life of being singularly himself, pure as the day he was born. He had only to decide whether to tell Sheila the truth or to maintain his pathetic fiction day after day for however long they were together. Telling a lie was like having a baby: you had to take care of it for the rest of your life.

THREE

Bronfman considered taking the rest of the day off, but only briefly. He wanted to be at work. Work asked so little of him. He would sometimes look up to see that a half hour had passed and that he had done nothing at all, and that on his desk there were a dozen paperclips, twisted into indecipherable shapes. This is how the day went by: he worked a little and then took a vacation from himself, but he didn't know where he went, just that he was in the exact same place when he came back as he had been when he left.

The traffic was heavy, though, and he didn't get back to the Cranston Building until almost five. And on his desk was a small red ball.

"What's this?" he said to no one. But someone heard and someone answered.

"That," came Sorsby's voice from beyond his cubicle wall, "is my stress ball."

"You have a stress ball?" Bronfman said. He could not conceive of a world in which Skip Sorsby needed a stress ball. "Why?"

He sat down, but the ball claimed all of his attention. It was on top of some of his paperwork, and it blocked the middle of the lower half of his computer screen. "What's it doing on my desk, Sorsby?"

Sorsby's head rose above Bronfman's enclosure: hair, forehead, eyes. "It's for you, dear friend," he said.

"Why?"

"It's my bon-voyage present. I'm bon-voyaging."

"But what does that *mean*?"

"It means I'm leaving my place of employment. This place. The place where we find ourselves now. I'm moving on, pardner. Skedaddling."

Bronfman put it all together. "You're quitting? Or did you get fired?"

The words just escaped from him. He hadn't meant to say this. But Bronfman had always considered Sorsby to be "fireable," chiefly because of his attitude. The way he loped around the office with his shirttail hanging out, looking for ways to make fun of other people, or to be sarcastic, to draw attention to himself. If Bronfman were in charge and he had to fire someone, it might well be Sorsby, because he didn't seem to care whether he was fired or not.

"Yes, I did get fired," Sorsby said. "But in my heart I had already quit. I quit before I was fired, just to stop my brain fluid from dripping out of my ears. Ever see little wet glistening spots of something on your desk, Bronfman? That's your brain. It's dripping drop by drop, like a leaky faucet, and it will keep dripping until there's nothing left inside your head at all, at which time you'll become the perfect employee."

"You're being sarcastic," Bronfman said.

Sorsby shook his head. "I'm not," he said. He pointed to a small spot on Bronfman's desk. "That's brain juice right there." Then he winked, indicating that he was indeed being sarcastic.

"So . . . do you have another job? Any leads or . . . anything?"

Sorsby disappeared, threw something in a box, and then stood tall again, peering down at Bronfman like a god. "Absolutely not," he said, seeming quite pleased that Bronfman had asked him this follow-up. "I'm just getting Out. Of. Here. Out of the fucking Cranston Building. I'm looking forward to it, honestly. To what comes next." Sorsby paused, as if allowing Bronfman time to laugh unimpeded. But Bronfman didn't

laugh, and Sorsby seemed to take it personally. "It's surprising, isn't it?" Sorsby said.
"Because of the two of us I would have bet
you would be the guy to find his wings first,
make a break for it, the guy who wanted to
build a whole new life for himself — no,
wait. I mean me. I bet it would have been
me. And it is me! So strike that. I guess I'm
not surprised after all."

"But you got fired," Bronfman said. "You
don't get wings when you get fired."

"Then I will fall to my death, I guess.
Either way, I am not here, and that's what
counts."

Bronfman realized why he had never liked
Skip Sorsby that much: he was unlikable.
Even the IKEA connection he had finagled
for him could not overcome that fact.

Sorsby vanished again. The entire contents
of a drawer — all the little things, the paper
clips and pens and pencils and cards and
tape measures — were dumped, and most
of it seemed to find its way into the box.
But not all of it. A marble rolled through a
gap in the cubicle and stopped by Bronfman's left foot. Normally, Bronfman would
have picked it up and handed it to Sorsby,
but not now. He kicked it and watched it
roll across the hallway. Sorsby getting fired
was the best thing that had happened to him

all day. He would not miss him. He looked forward to what would surely be, for a few days at least, a cubicle bereft of life.

"So anyway," Sorsby said. "Bronfman?"

The disembodied voice of Sorsby waited.

"Yes?"

There was a new tone in Sorsby's voice now. It was softer, friendlier, or maybe it was just the sound of defeat. "I usually take the bus home, but I have all this stuff I have to take with me. I'm going to have to call in that favor I was talking about." And there was Sorsby's head, his eyes as sad as a dog's. "I need a ride home."

Skip Sorsby lived in Roebuck. Bronfman had never been to Roebuck before, and though it wasn't that far from the Cranston, it *felt* far away. Nothing was in Roebuck but Roebuck. There was no reason to go there unless you lived there or needed a mural painted on your pickup truck. The last clump of third-rate shopping centers before the mountains took over, Roebuck could fall into a sinkhole and nobody would notice. Toward Roebuck Bronfman was uncharitable, though he didn't know why. Probably something his mother had said.

All in all, though, once he got there he could see that it was a nice enough place.

Sorsby directed him through the mazelike neighborhood streets, but apart from that he was quiet. Bronfman had expected an ongoing commentary on modern life and man — our flaws and our foibles, the sort of thing Sorsby was famous for — but got nothing at all. Bronfman glanced over at Sorsby at stoplights and watched him think, "worrying a thought," as his mother put it. Sorsby was beginning to see the long road ahead, and it was weighing on him. Bronfman pitied him a little when he learned that he'd gotten fired, but by the time they reached the Roebuck city limits he would have given blood for him, and he hadn't said much more than "turn left here, go right." It was just so sad, a sad end to a sad day.

"This is the place," Sorsby said, pointing to an apartment complex not unlike King's Manor. Just one big brick building after the next, with ample parking and free first month's rent. "This is cool. I'll get out here."

Bronfman pulled over to the curb and idled, waiting, but Sorsby didn't get out. The box was on his lap. He was ruminating. He was a ruminant.

"So what happened?" Bronfman asked him.

Sorsby shook his head. "Why did I get

fired, you mean?"

Bronfman nodded.

"Because I'm a shitty employee," Sorsby said. "I'm always late and I do the work of half a man. I've got a terrible attitude. I'm resistant to authority. And I'm also kind of an asshole."

Bronfman said nothing. He knew that he should have objected and said that Sorsby was none of those things. But Sorsby was all of those things.

"The straw that broke the camel's back, though, was the whole IKEA thing."

"What whole IKEA thing?"

"Getting the name for you. I had to do some fancy footwork. Dig into a couple of computer files I didn't strictly have access to."

"Oh, my God," Bronfman said.

"Don't sweat it," Sorsby said. "They were just looking for a reason. Anything would have sufficed."

"I don't know what to say."

"It's not your fault; I don't even know why I did it for you. I just liked the challenge, I think. That job is so fucking dull."

"I can't believe this."

"Seriously, no worries. I'm glad it happened. I hope it helps your friend."

"This can't be okay with you," Bronfman

said. This new Sorsby was odd, hard to understand. He was deeper than Bronfman had thought, or wanted to think.

Sorsby had the look of a lost dog in his eyes now, empty and scared. "Oh, it's more than okay," he said. "I can't say it's not scary, honestly. But I was unhappy there. I was unhappy there, and that's why I was such a sarcastic asshole. Remember that, Bronfman. All assholes are unhappy people. Not all unhappy people are assholes, but the opposite is always true. Be kind to them."

"I'm kind to everybody."

Sorsby smiled. "Yes, you are."

It was still light outside, but dusk was beginning to hint at the tops of the trees, like dusty metal filings.

"The truth is," Sorsby continued, "it's not just that I don't have a job. I don't really have *anything*. No job, not much money, no wife or girlfriend or family. Nothing. I have this apartment where I live, but it's just temporary. It's all good, though. It's Zen. I'll land on my feet. Maybe I'll go to grad school in . . . something. But it's what I want, this situation. Yeah." Sorsby nodded. "It's what I want."

"But no one *wants* that," Bronfman said. "People live that way, I know, but it's not a

439

state of affairs we strive for."

Sorsby appeared to be taking inventory of all the little things in his box. He picked up a rubber band and shot it into the windshield. "How old are you, Bronfman? I know I asked once, but I wasn't paying attention."

"Thirty-four."

"Right. And I'm twenty-four. This is going to sound like such an asshole thing to say, so I'm sorry. But I don't want to be where you are when I'm thirty-four. I don't know where I want to be, but not here, and not there, on the other side of the cubicle wall from you."

"But when you get another job —"

"I don't *want* another job. Not now. I don't want anything, really. Or, to put it in more positive terms, I want nothing. Nothing is like . . . infinite possibility. I have unlimited choices now. Because, face it, Bronfman. We really don't get to make the important choices in our lives. Other people do. They make choices for us. From the second we're born, most of the choices are already made. We're born to one set of parents instead of another, and they give us our genes and teach us their idea of right and wrong, and we live in one town or city instead of another *they* have chosen, and we go to high school. Public? Private? Wherever they want. It's not up to us! And we have this certain group of friends who basically come from the same place and want the same things and go to college — this really good college, not that shitty one, you hope, but whatever — and we learn about what everybody thought and did before we were born, as if that matters, and then they throw us out and we have to do *something,* so we get the first okay job that presents itself to us and slowly but surely we're done, we don't have any choices left. Then we die, also usually not our choice. No free will. We think we have it, but really, when you put it all together — all the shit I just mentioned and more — I mean, they've pretty much made all your choices for you. You're a fucking robot. And by you I don't mean you, though I do, I guess. Mostly, I mean the generalized-everybody-you."

"Noted," Bronfman said.

Sorsby's eyes were full of fire now. He took a very deep breath and exhaled for as long as a person could exhale. It went on and on. It took a long time.

"But I don't want that life," he said. "I want nothing — *nothing* — so I can start over with as close to a clean slate as I can get. I can fly. See?" Sorsby nodded. At least one of them was convinced. "Thanks to you and IKEA, now I can do anything."

Bronfman wished he'd left that last part out; he had sounded so high-minded and philosophical until then. "Sounds good," he said.

Sorsby seemed to have convinced himself of what he wanted to believe; Bronfman could almost smell his self-satisfaction, his complacency. Sorsby turned to look at Bronfman, his old cubicle mate, as if to get an eyeful of him before he was gone forever.

"So what about you, Bronfman?" Sorsby said.

"What about me what?"

"What do you want?"

"What do I want?"

Bronfman was speechless. No one had ever asked him that question before. Why was that? he wondered. Why had no one asked him that before? Why had he never asked himself? Was there a more important question?

In the dark of the car, they sat in a shared silence. A breeze pushed a piece of something down the sidewalk. When the headlights spotlighted it, Bronfman could see that it was a hamburger wrapper. It paused in the light, as if to be admired. Then the wind picked up again and sent it on its way.

Somehow, trapped in this small car with the man he had always loathed, in the last part of town he ever wanted to be, watching a hamburger wrapper blow down the street, he knew the answer to his question.

"I want everything," he said.

FOUR

Bronfman drove to Sheila's house on auto-pilot, turning left and turning right and braking and accelerating without design. Muscle memory and a vague consciousness of place were all he had. The events of the day had paralyzed him. They had desiccated him. Coming to terms with this stranger who was himself had clobbered him flat, like a cartoon pancake. And it was not merely because he had discovered, once and for all, that he had never made love, not to anyone, ever, because he had suspected that, he had feared that. It was that he had used Mary Day's tragic death to wheedle that information out of her grieving fiancé, that he had taken advantage of another person who wasn't even alive, and he had cost a man his job — all this in a single day. He was approaching monster status. If later tonight his DNA were found at a murder scene, he would just have to shrug and turn himself in, since he probably did it. That's the kind of day this was.

For another five minutes he drove mindlessly, and almost missed the complex, but he braked just in time and jerked the wheel to the right, bumping the curb before parking in front of her place. He pulled himself out of his car and walked in, zombie style. The television was on, and Sheila was watching it. She didn't look up at first.

"I'm bingeing on *Green Acres,*" she said. "Eva Gabor is a little irritating, but you have to love the Ziffels." Only then did she look at him. "Oh. Oh, my. What's wrong, Edsel? What happened?"

She stood, hugged him, and then took him by the hand and led him past the unbuilt table and a chair, still in piles, and to the couch. "I'm going to get you a glass of wine," she said, and she did, and then she sat beside him and studied him, as if she could possibly glean from just looking at him what had happened, what was wrong. Bronfman took a sip of the wine, then he took the piece of paper Sorsby had given him that morning and handed it to her. She looked at it suspiciously, opened it, read it.

"Mr. Bogdan Poge?" she said. "What's a Bogdan Poge?"

"That's the contact," he said. "In Sweden."

"What contact?"

"At IKEA," he said, but without the giddy flair he'd imagined bringing to it. Or even the desire to be a hero. "This is the guy who handles the North American division of the IKEA instruction department."

"Okay . . ."

He could see that she didn't know what he was talking about. "You said you wanted a contact at IKEA. Your white whale? So I had a guy at work get it for me. It got him fired. Today. Apparently accessed some file he shouldn't have. I took him home because he doesn't have a car. He doesn't have anything, really. It's my fault, Sheila. And that's not all. I've done some terrible, terrible things."

"Oh, no," she said. "Edsel —"

He interrupted her. That's what it had come to: he was interrupting people now. "It seemed a good idea at the time. I just asked if he knew someone, and he started looking into it and he went a little too far. He's this far from homeless, I think."

She read the slip of paper again. "Because of this?"

"He was a terrible employee in general, but this was the last straw."

She moved closer to him on the little couch and took his hands in hers and then, seeming to think better of it, set them back down. "I was going to tell you, Edsel. Soon. But that was never a thing."

"What was never a thing?"

"IKEA. I never wanted to write for IKEA."

"No," Bronfman said. "You did. You *do.*"

"When we met, that first time, we were talking and having fun and I was just sitting there and it was my last day in the Cranston Building and I didn't think I would ever see you again and I just . . . made all that up."

She could not mean this. Made it up? Out of thin air? Why? How? Sheila was playful and imaginative and he loved that about her. But this. This was a lie, wasn't it? Or more than a lie, really: it was a fiction. *She* was fiction.

"Made it up?"

"But then when we ran into each other again I didn't want to say, 'Hey, by the way, all that stuff about writing instructions, ha-ha, that wasn't true,' because you seemed so pleased with the idea that I did that, so interested in me. I didn't want to scare you away."

"Wait," Bronfman said. He was having

trouble keeping up. As usual. For the first time in his life, he wanted to be mistaken. He wanted to have misunderstood. "So you really *don't* write directions or instructions or how-to manuals, or . . . anything like that?"

She shook her head. "I don't."

"Then what do you do?"

Sheila took two big sips of his wine, and then two big breaths. "Not much," she said. "Honestly. Workwise, I mean. I volunteer at the homeless shelter a couple of times a week. I read a lot and take a lot of walks, of course, mostly with you but also by myself. I have a couple of doctors I see on a regular basis. A little money in the bank from, you know, dead relatives. I watch *a lot* of television. *Fantasy Island,* here I come! Ha-ha. I worked over at the Cranston, but it was only on a temporary basis. Giving it a shot. To see how that would be, if I could actually, you know, hold a job. But it didn't work out. I want so much more from my stupid life. Even that job — I really wanted to like that job. But I was *ill-suited* for it, as they say. The work was just so dull, Edsel! All I liked to do was talk to people like you."

"Not me," he said. "Just people *like* me."

"Edsel," she said. "There is nobody like you."

448

Bronfman thought he may have caught up with her now, and was able to encapsulate it like this: she had lied to him from the very first minute they met, and for every minute following it, and for every single day thereafter, all thirty-eight of them. Nothing she'd said was true. At this point he couldn't be sure her name was Sheila McNabb, even though she had a nameplate saying as much.

"So not only did Sorsby get fired," Bronfman said, "he got fired for nothing. For less than nothing."

"I'm so, so sorry," she said. "How could I have known that something like this would ever happen?"

"So what else?"

"What else what?"

"What else hasn't been true?"

"Oh." She thought back. "A lot, I guess. Not everything but . . . most of everything."

"You don't even want to be in the *Guinness World Records*?"

She shook her head.

"And your list?"

"My list?"

"Of the men," he said. "The men you'd been with. Before me."

She turned away. "I don't know," she said. "Probably? I can't remember what I said."

"You can't remember? You might consider

writing down all the lies you tell, just so you can keep your story straight."

Bronfman couldn't look at her. He thought, *You're a stranger to me now.* A cliché? Sure. But he saw the truth in it. It was as if she'd taken off a mask he never knew she wore. On the wall behind her was a watercolor of the Champs-Élysées that she told him she'd bought from a street artist in Paris. Probably got it at Target. He stared at that until it blurred into a wash of rainbow colors.

"I'm scared, Edsel," she said finally. "I'm scared of everything — even you. Scared that if you knew me — if anyone really knew me — you wouldn't like me very much. So I do this thing. I tell stories. I'm good at that, at least. Telling stories, telling lies."

The light hum of Cedar Court's excellent air-conditioning system purred on. Bronfman felt the cool air slip up the leg of his trousers. "I think you're on to something there," he said. "Because I don't like you very much right now."

"Let me make you a cup of tea."

"No," he said. "I'm going. Home." But he didn't get up.

"So let me come with you. I want to see where you live. I bet it's —"

"You *lied* to me, Sheila," he said, interrupting yet again, raising his voice to an uncomfortably high level. "Not just a little, either. A lot. But it's *more* than that, to me. You're not even real. You made yourself up. I have no idea who you are."

"My feelings are real," she said. "I'm real. That's the important thing, Edsel. I really, really, really like you."

This was not the way he hoped he would hear this. He had waited so long to hear those words — and to hear them now, just as he was leaving her. *Timing!* She had inflated his heart like an overblown balloon and then stuck a pin into it, just to watch it pop. *Only I could get a girlfriend and break up with her at the same time,* he thought. Still, he wanted to hear her say it one more time, not knowing how long it would be before anyone said it again.

"You like me?" he said. "Is that true?"

"You know I do. More than like you. I have never pretended that part. And I know you like me, too."

"I did," he said. "Before."

She waved his objection away. "My point is that we care about each other. As long as that's true, we can figure out the rest. We both have a good baseline to start from."

"You really believe that?"

She didn't even have to think about her

451

answer. She nodded, once, with total certainty. "Of course I do."

He stood up, but didn't appear to know what to do next. He looked at the piles of wood in the middle of the floor — scattered, undefined, a mess. Just as they were. He kicked what looked like a table leg. "I bet you didn't put these together at all," he said. "Not even once."

"That's true," she said. "I didn't. I tried to, but I couldn't follow those idiotic directions."

She smiled a little. He kicked the leg again. "You don't know how to do anything, do you? Nothing. Are you just . . . totally useless?" This was the cruelest thing he had ever said to another human being in his life, so callous that it made him wince. But it didn't appear to hurt her, as he'd intended it to. Even his cruelty fell flat. She just turned a little sad, her smile waning, unplugged.

"No," she said. "I don't. Not much. I really don't know how to do anything yet. I'm no prize. A late bloomer is how I like to think of it. That's why we're perfect for each other. You're the same as me."

"*What?* How can you say that?"

"You don't want anyone to know you, either," she said. "That's why you apologize all the time. That's why you don't have any friends. Just like me. Because you don't know how to do anything either, Edsel."

She wasn't being contrary, or harsh. She said it quite sweetly. It was just an observation, and, apparently, judging by the tone she took, an inarguable one.

"That's ridiculous," he said. "I know how to do stuff. *I* have a job. *I* have a life."

"That's great. But what do you really *do*, Edsel? Think about it. Who are you?"

Against his will and his better instincts, he thought about it: what did he do? He woke up in the morning and dressed himself, cleaned himself up, fed himself, drove to work, engaged in small talk, entered numerals and keywords into a program on the computer, made telephone calls, received telephone calls, ate lunch, read some of the newspaper, occasionally "worked out" at the gym, visited with his mother, went home, watched television, ate dinner, slept. And at the end of the day all he had to show for it was half a dozen paper clips twisted into various positions and shapes. His legacy.

"You and I live in a world that's kind of like a magic trick to us," she said. "We just stumble through it, hoping no one notices. Edsel, please don't take this the wrong way but you're an odd person. Very odd. Of course you don't want anyone to know you. But the good news? *I am, too!* Haven't you noticed that I don't have any friends, either? Not a single one. That's odd, Edsel. You collect free pens; I can't look at someone without turning them into some kind of animal. You never thought that was odd? No, you didn't. That you wouldn't think it odd is odd in itself, because you're so deep into the oddness of who you are that you don't notice when things are odd around you. As long as I've known you, I've had two piles of wood on the living-room floor. That's just crazy, but it didn't bother you that much, which is really wonderful to me. And, you know, there's that other thing."

This, of course, stung him all the way through. "I tried. I wanted to."

"I know! And I'm fine with that. It'll happen when it happens, that's what I think. And when it does it'll be great. My point is, we're different from other people, you and me. We're rufous-sided towhees, Edsel. We make our nests on the ground."

When the air-conditioning turned itself off, the lights surged a little brighter. Then this person who called herself Sheila Mc-Nabb stood before him, blocking his way to the door.

"I have never had a pet in my life," she

said, "unless you count a firefly I trapped in a jar once when I was nine. I'm on all sorts of medication, but nothing illegal or particularly weird. One math credit short of graduating from college. Memorable event from childhood: I was in the car with my grandmother on the way to her church (she made me go) and she ran over a dog and didn't stop because we were late. All true. I don't believe in UFOs, but, on the other hand, I sort of do. My parents had lots and lots of problems, the three biggest being drugs, drinking, and me. They dropped me off at my grandma's place when I was seven years old and never came back. The last I heard, they were somewhere in Central America, but that was a dozen years ago, so I may or may not be an orphan, I'm not really sure. Which may be the only thing worse than being an orphan: not knowing. I've never read anything by Charles Dickens. I have a prehensile tail. Threw that in there just to see if you were listening. I can recite the alphabet backward. Don't go, Edsel. Please. Give me a chance and I'll tell you everything. What about you? Tell me a little something about you. I've never been to France, but I know a little French. Don't go, Edsel, *please*? I had my appendix out when I was twenty-one years old, and my wisdom teeth . . ."

She was still talking when he left. But as the door was closing behind him he thought he heard her say that a peanut-butter-and-jelly sandwich was her favorite sandwich, by far, bar none, but that may just have been wishful thinking. Not that it mattered anymore.

FIVE

By the time he found his way back to King's Manor that evening, a war had broken out in his parking lot, or a circus, or the Fourth of July. It was an electric rainbow of pulsating color, reds and blues and greens; three police cars, an ambulance and a fire truck, all parked almost directly in front of his unit. *What had he done? What law had he broken?* He was guilty, certainly, and he felt that guilt keenly, although bringing this sort of force out for a moral failing seemed over the top. He wouldn't slam the car into reverse, initiating a citywide chase that would only get him into more trouble, because face it: no one can outrun the law forever. No one. He would turn himself in without a fight.

But he was mistaken. The police weren't here for him. He parked his car in front of another unit across the lot, and in his rearview mirror saw two medics leaving the apartment next door to his, the one belonging to Thomas Edison. They were pushing a gurney, and on the gurney was what was most certainly a body, what was obviously a body, and they lifted it into the back of the ambulance and slammed shut the doors and sped away, and the police cars and the fire truck followed. All of a sudden it was just Coco, standing on the stoop in front of the yellow CRIME SCENE — DO NOT ENTER ribbons taped across the front door. He watched her watching the ambulance insinuate its way into the traffic with its blaring red lights and ultraloud sirens with a muted, almost paralyzed expression. She wasn't crying, but he could tell that she had been; her cheeks had a dull-red burnish to them. He had last seen her just a couple of days ago, as he left his apartment on the way to work, and she had been leaving as well. There was a worn-out scruffiness about her then, and she seemed a little sad.

"Good morning," he had said, but it wasn't really clear to him whether it was morning to her or the end of something that had begun the night before.

But today her sadness and grief were so intense that they radiated off her like heat. He almost couldn't bear to look at her as he approached. But at the top of his stoop

Bronfman bravely paused and turned to her.

"Coco," he said. "What happened?"

She turned and looked at him, puzzled, possibly just realizing that he was there. Her eyes were vacant, and far, far away. "Someone . . ." She paused, as if searching for the word. But it wasn't that. She was searching for the ability to understand the word, to process the idea. "Someone killed Tommy," she said, so softly that her voice barely carried from one stoop to the other. Coco brushed some of her hair back behind an ear and let her fingers linger, slowly combing through a tangle.

"What happened was, if you want to know, they rolled him up in a rug. He was trapped in there. He couldn't move. Then they shot him, three times," she said. Now she was talking to Bronfman as if she were recapping a television show he'd missed. No emotion at all. Just the numb, dead facts. "Three times. Twice in the chest and once . . ." He waited to hear where the third bullet went, but then it became clear to him that she wasn't going to say anything about it, because what had happened to Thomas Edison with that third bullet was too awful to put words to.

"Oh. Oh, I'm so sorry," Bronfman said, and as soon as he heard what he'd said he almost punched himself in the eye. Who said that? If he had accidentally bumped into her, that's what he would have said. But when someone was killed in the apartment next door you said something else, though he had no idea what that something else might be. "That's so — I don't know what to say, Coco. It's tragic, incomprehensible, devastating."

"Fucked up," she said. It sounded like something God might say, as if that were the last word on the subject. "Fucked up is what it is. That someone would do this, to him."

"But why? Why would anyone . . . ?"

"Oh, Bronfman," she said, as if he were a child and she was just a little disappointed that he had to ask. "The same reason you almost got yourself killed. Drugs. And money. What it always is." She let that sink in. "The drugs they took are gone by now and the money's probably spent, but he's still dead. And he's always going to be."

She shook her head, not looking at Bronfman now but out into the spirit world where Thomas Edison's soul was being mixed and melded into the ether. She stepped down from the stoop and stood there on the sidewalk forlorn before him until Bronfman, compelled by some emotion he could not name, hugged her. He had not done a lot of hugging in his life, and never with people he barely knew. She hugged him back, like a python, and she shuddered, crying, and that lasted for almost an entire minute, just this intense and powerful hug. Then it ended and, saying nothing further, and without even looking at Bronfman again, she walked down the stoop and got into her rusting and battered little Japanese car and drove away.

He was inside his apartment for less than a minute when his phone rang. He didn't have to look to know who it was. He could hear her talking before the phone made it to his ear.

"I love beets," Sheila said. "In sixth grade I had a friend who had four fingers on her left hand. Favorite Beatle? Pete Best. My grandma —"

"Sheila," he said.

"— ran over me once, backing out of the driveway. Not on purpose."

"*Sheila,*" he said.

They were silent now, both of them.

"*Okay,*" she said, hurt. "I just — I wish you hadn't gone, Edsel. I think we can get past this."

"Someone killed Thomas Edison."

"Thomas Edison?" she said.

And he realized that he hadn't told her about Thomas Edison. And that there was a lot he hadn't told her, including what had happened today in Martinsville. She was right. He hadn't let her know him any more than she had let him know her. But he hadn't lied to her, not directly; there were just things he had failed to mention. That he would be getting to in time.

Now he told her everything, from Thomas's initial friendship to his betrayal to the little he had learned today from Coco. Sheila listened silently, but Bronfman could feel the tremor of her absorption. For the first time he understood what was meant by that phrase *hanging on every word.* She hung. It was possible that he had never said anything in his life that was listened to with this degree of rapt and morbid fascination. The flat line that was his day-to-day life suddenly spiked, all because he lived next door to someone who had lost his.

"Oh, my *God,*" Sheila said when he was done.

"I know," he said.

"Why haven't you told me about this before?"

"I don't know," he said. "I was embarrassed, I think."

"Embarrassed? That someone broke into your apartment?"

"That I lived here at all," he said. "Cedar Court is so ritzy. I probably should have moved then."

"Probably. But now you have to."

"I do?"

"Yes. Someone was murdered in the apartment next door to you," she said. Her vocal italicizations came fast and furious. "Edsel. Seriously. *Murdered.* You could get hurt."

"But don't you think," he said, "that the murdering is done? That everyone to be murdered has been? If it's true, as she said, that it was about drugs —"

"She?"

"Coco."

She sighed. "Of course there's a Coco in the mix. And how do you know that she didn't do it herself?"

"Well, no, I don't think —"

"Or knows who did it. Is part of it. Of course, she is. And she *knows* you. You know her. Say she suspects you know too much. She could have someone wrap you up in a rug and shoot you, too." There was a pause. "Maybe I'm overreacting. Watch too much television. But it's worrisome, Edsel."

"She was really upset. And I don't think

she could hurt anybody. She's a very small person. Her arms are as skinny as spaghetti. She was really upset," he said again.

"I don't doubt it," Sheila said. "Still, who knows what happened?" It was odd, how in such a very short time she had developed such strong feelings about the incident, about Coco, about Thomas Edison, and that she knew exactly what he should do. Bronfman should find another place to live; he should have done that a while ago. But that she was able to tell him what she thought he should do — that felt odd. Especially after what had just happened at her place. He had left her, literally and figuratively. "Based on what you've told me, Edsel, this Thomas Edison — and, seriously, who names their child Thomas Edison? He and Coco — and again, *Coco*? — they were lovers, partners in crime, and she —"

"I don't think they were," he said. "Lovers. I think they were just friends. Good friends."

"*Edsel*," she said, as if to a dog that could not learn even basic commands. "Listen to yourself."

Sheila was angry. He had never heard her angry before.

"I'm listening," he said.

He went quiet. He didn't say anything

464

more about the incident, because he was starting to feel oddly protective, not only of Thomas Edison — who did have some positive qualities, after all (he had more friends than Bronfman, for instance, and more than Sheila, and he could fix cars) — but also of Coco. He felt certain that Sheila was getting the wrong idea of who Thomas and Coco were — even though, as Bronfman would have to allow himself, he didn't really know what the deal was, either.

"All I'm saying," she said, "and I won't say it again, because for some reason it bothers you. But you should consider moving to a different complex where people aren't, even on occasion, being murdered."

"Of course," he said. "You're right. It's something to consider. I don't know where I would, but — there's the whole frying pan–fire conundrum. I suppose —"

"You could move in with me," she said.

"Funny," he said.

An impossible arrangement of words, absurd, a suggestion that in its preposterousness almost bounced off his ears, being too screwy to get any further. He had imagined and fantasized so many moments, so many conversations, so many possibilities and scenarios if and when he ever had a chance to be in a relationship with a woman — so many. But he had never gotten this far. Ever. None of his fantasies had ever asked him to move in with her.

"Until you found a better place, I mean. There's room here."

"You mean temporarily," he said.

"Yes," she said. "Of course. Temporarily. Think about it at least. I have the extra room. I even have a table and a chair. They haven't been put together yet, but —"

She forced a laugh.

"Sheila," he said, because the words he was going for were far, far down inside him, in pieces, at the bottom of his murky heart. "I *can't* move in with you. In no way could that ever happen. Because we're not — we just — what happened just a few minutes ago. We broke up."

"Really?"

"Really."

"You didn't say that."

"In so many words," he said.

"But you didn't *say* it. You didn't jump over the broom three times."

"What?"

"Nothing."

"You lied to me, Sheila."

"I know, Edsel. I know. But that doesn't mean you can just break up with me. It's just not done. It's not even possible."

"What do you mean it's not possible?"

"Because we weren't even together," she said. "We haven't known each other long enough to *be* together. How long has it even been?"

Thirty days, he thought, but seventy-one if you counted the day they had their first conversation.

"I don't know," he said. "Not long."

"No. Not long enough, anyway — yet. You could break up with me in three weeks or so, I think," she said. "Maybe in two. Or I with you, for that matter. But now, a few weeks into it, we're just two people who happen to be hanging out with each other and having a pretty good time. Does that make sense?"

"I don't know," he said. "I think you might be taking advantage of me. You know I don't know how to do this. How to be with someone, much less break *up* with them. You know I'm not . . . experienced."

"No," she said. "You're not. (Parenthetically, I love that about you.) I suppose I could take advantage of you, though, if I were that kind of person."

"Are you that kind of person?"

"See? If that's not a question you can answer, then we definitely haven't been together long enough to break up." She

467

paused to sigh. "And I told myself I'd never date another ungulate," she said. "They can be so dense."

He heard her smiling.

Ashen light filtered through his window curtains. Before Sheila, the dark meant the end of the day, but all that had changed. It brought mysteries with it now, adventures, possibilities — life.

"I think we should go on a trip," Sheila said out of the blue.

"What? A trip?"

What was this? Where did this come from? The presentation of the suggestion was so casual, so off the cuff. But could she know? Could she have known all this time that this was what he wanted, all he had wanted, why he had ever even spoken to her at all? And in giving it to him now, at the eleventh hour, was she just daring him to make good on his threat to leave her? Bronfman was addled.

"Yeah, a trip. I don't know where — the idea just popped into my head. But we could do it. We're adults. We have a little money. Your mother will be fine with Bettina."

He nodded. "Do you . . . like the beach?" he asked her, as if it were something that had just occurred to him, as an example of one of many places where a trip might happen.

"Probably not."

"No? Why?"

"The truth," she said, "is that I've never been. I've never even seen the ocean."

"Never? Seriously? You're not just making that up?"

"I'm not making that up. I grew up in Indiana — again, the truth. So the beach wasn't right around the corner. And then in school we read a lot of books that took place in the ocean — *The Odyssey, Moby-Dick, The Little Mermaid* — and none of them made getting wet seem particularly appealing. It scares the shit out of me, to be honest. But I've decided it's possible to live a good life and be happy without ever going near it. Same as I don't feel like I need to go to China. Why?"

"No reason," he lied.

"There are lots of places we can go that don't have water anywhere near them." She laughed.

Something else was happening now. He cradled the phone against one ear and his shoulder as he pulled back the curtains at his front window. It was a car. He saw its headlights brush along the exterior of the building. He thought at first that it might have been Coco, returning. But it wasn't.

It was Officer Stanton.

Serena.

He watched as she stepped out of the car — slowly, carefully, dismounting really, as if to make sure the asphalt parking lot wasn't actually a thin sheet of black ice in disguise and could support her shapely heft. Were they trained to do it that way in police school, the way they stood up and looked behind, ahead, above — because who knew, there might be a sniper on a nearby rooftop? Her hair looked a little shorter now, the bangs brushed to one side and the sides tucked behind her ears.

"Edsel?" Sheila's tone of voice indicated that she had been talking to him for a little while. Bronfman hadn't heard her. "Hello-o? Earth to Edsel!"

"Sorry."

"What's going on?"

"The police are here," he said.

"The *police!*"

"I should go."

"Why?"

"To talk to them."

"But you don't know anything."

"I don't know if I don't know anything. I might."

"But do you want to get . . . involved?

Seriously, I've watched every *CSI* and all its offshoots, and I can say this with authority: it never turns out well."

"Let me just go see," he said, as if he was asking permission, which, in effect, he was.

Sheila sighed. "I'm coming over," she said.

"No," he said. "Don't. Please."

"I am, Edsel," she said. "I think you need me."

"No!" he said, much more emphatically than he meant to. He took a deep breath and waited for his pulse to slow down. "No, Sheila. The truth is I'm fine. I just . . . don't want you to see where I live. It's not very nice. Actually, it's terrible. It's the kind of place —"

"— where someone might get killed?"

"Yes," he said. "Exactly like that."

"That doesn't matter to me, Edsel," she said. "And how bad could it really be? It's called King's Manor, for God's sake!"

"I think it was overnamed," he said. "They should have just called it Rooms to Live In, or Shelter. That would have been enough."

"I can be over there so quickly," she said. "I mapped it."

"You did?"

His heart swelled. The idea that she mapped it, in preparation for a possible visit, touched him. It's exactly what he would have done, what he in fact did in preparation for their very first date. He strained against his compulsion to forgive her everything, but a part of him wanted to, just for this tiny gesture.

"It's three point two miles." they said at exactly the same time, and then both of them whispered — again, at exactly the same time — "Jinx."

Now neither of them spoke for a moment after that, but Bronfman knew it was his turn, and that she was waiting on the go-ahead from him. But he wouldn't give it. His heart was ossifying. This is what it must be like to be a man, he thought, to have a small and hardened heart. "I'll call when I get back," he said coolly. "After I talk to the police."

"As soon as you get back," she said, and he heard her kiss the phone.

But he didn't kiss his back.

Six

Bronfman opened his door with a suddenness that startled Serena, who twisted toward him with the instincts of a cat.

"Serena," he said. She looked at him blankly, followed by gradual recognition, standing down.

"Bronfman," she said. "I was just about to knock."

"Oh," he said, a little thrilled that she had been about to do that.

"So how's your mother?"

He smiled, remembering 2D.

"She's . . . fine," he said. "Thank you for asking. You know. Things could be better. But thanks so much for asking," he said again.

She peered over his shoulder, into his apartment. "All alone?" she said.

"Yes," he said. "Completely. Completely alone."

She contemplated the situation. "Oh, I

forgot to tell you earlier. Nothing really came of the investigation," she said. "Into the burglary of your place, I mean. I'm sorry."

"Oh, well, actually something did," he said.

"Really? Did we make an arrest?"

"No," he said. "Not from your investigation . . . from mine." And he cut his eyes meaningfully toward the apartment where Thomas Edison formerly lived.

She understood immediately. "Ah," she said. "The deceased."

Bronfman watched her absorb this new information, and her brand-new estimation of him as well. This was not the Bronfman she thought he was, certainly, one who could ferret out a criminal better than the actual police. She took out a notepad and wrote something down, paused to think about what she'd written or what she was about to write, wheels turning. Then she looked directly at Bronfman, right into his eyes.

"Is there anything else you'd like to tell me, Bronfman?"

"Anything else?" You're a very attractive woman, he thought. You have nice eyes. "About what?"

"About Tommy? About the incident?"

"No," he said. "I mean, I would like to, but I don't think I know anything. I just got here." Bronfman always seemed to arrive just as everything that had been happening was coming to an end. "I talked to Coco. I assume you have, too. That's the only reason I know what happened at all."

Officer Stanton consulted her notepad. "Coco," she said. "Yoshiko Hayashi."

"Yes."

"She told you, then," Serena said.

"What?"

"That she discovered the body."

"Oh," Bronfman said. "I didn't know that. She didn't tell me."

"She discovered the body and called it in."

"So she just walked in and there he was? That's awful."

"She'll have that picture in her head forever. For. Ever. Nothing she'll be able to do about that."

He thought about something Sheila had said. "Were they . . . together?"

Which was an odd question, sure. Even Bronfman thought it was odd, and Serena seemed to recognize that it was, too. She gave Bronfman a quick but critical look. "Not according to her," she said. "But who knows."

"I don't think they were," Bronfman said.

"Really? What makes you say so?"

"I don't know," he said, and he didn't know. He didn't know why he said the things he said. Sometimes he felt as if he had a little string in the back of his neck and some invisible man was pulling it.

Serena nodded, took a step toward Edison's apartment, and stopped. "You've been inside before?"

"Of course," he said. "Yes."

"Would you mind coming in with me now? I'd like to take another pass. Maybe there's something you can see, something a little off. On the chance you might provide some direction."

"Direction?"

"To his killer or killers," she said. "Between you and me, Bronfman, we're clutching at straws."

"Oh," he said. Oh, indeed. "Of course. I'd love to, Serena."

I'd love to, Serena. He almost hit himself in the head with the palm of his hand. But she didn't correct him. *Serena* was proffered and *Serena* was accepted. Maybe she didn't notice, or care enough to.

Or maybe she did.

She lifted the yellow crime-scene tape and waited for him to stoop under it.

"Don't touch anything," she said. "Eyes

only, okay? I'm bending the rules now as it is."

He nodded, just a half step behind her now, Serena's two-way radio snapping and crackling, advertising other crimes in other places. She was quiet, too. On display was the Thomas Edison Collection: beer bottles, ashtrays fat with cigarettes (some of which appeared to be homemade), a broken wine bottle, stacks of newspaper inserts, socks and shoes and blue jeans piled in a corner, an oversized yellow blanket on the couch, a wooden African mask with hollowed-out eyes and puckered lips leaning against the coffee table. It had been here before, he remembered, the sole decoration, hanging above the couch like the stolen face of God. And the Christmas tree, still lit.

Then he looked down at his feet. "Serena," he said. "Look."

He pointed to the spot where it appeared that a teeny amount of red wine had spilled. But it wasn't wine; even he knew that. Serena gently encircled the wrist on his right hand and pulled him back. "Thank you," she said softly. "But we saw this and got a sample." Even so, she kneeled to take a closer look, and, as she did, the reality of what had happened hit Bronfman hard. A man had been killed here. Right here. Feet from his own apartment. Shot three times. What if Bronfman had been home when it happened? What if he had left his apartment to investigate? It was highly unlikely that he would have left the relative safety of his own apartment to investigate the source of gunfire — but what if? Sheila was right. He should move.

Bronfman shuddered, dizzy, but not Serena. She had been in places like this a dozen times, he suspected. To her this was nothing, the same way filling out a shipping form at work was nothing to Bronfman. This was a thought he'd have much later; now his mind was an immense blank canvas. He didn't even realize that he was in the early stages of falling apart until Serena placed a hand on his shoulder.

"It's okay," she said.

"What?" he said. "Oh, I know. It's just —"

"I know." She kept her hand on his shoulder for a few more moments, and then a moment more, her hand still there on his shoulder, and still there still — what an amazing gentle strength she had, her hand not moving until his shaking subsided. "I remember my first time. We were in someone's bedroom, and it was so dark, and I barely knew my partner. Didn't know what to expect. It was scary."

Her hand was still on his shoulder. "Have you been working out?" she said.

"A little."

"I can tell." She winked, playfully for a woman at a murder scene. "Keep it up."

She removed her hand and turned down the dials on her walkie-talkie.

"So is there anything, Bronfman? Anything you notice at all?"

"No," he said. "I don't — it was always like this, I think."

"Do you mind coming into the bedroom with me?" She could tell that he was fragile and treated him accordingly. "Just for a minute?"

"Yes," he said. "I mean no."

They walked in together. What a squalid place it was. He remembered the mattress on the floor, the clothes strewn hither and yon, a book about kickboxing, a *People* magazine, more beer cans and wine bottles and cigarettes.

But no rug. The rug was gone.

"Nothing?" she asked.

"I'm so sorry," he said. "I wish I could help."

"It was a long shot," she said. "But everything's a long shot in this business."

She took another long, slow look around

and sighed. "I hate it," she said. "I hate it when it comes to this. I knew him a little bit, you know, took him in a couple of times. He was an okay guy."

"He told me," Bronfman said. "That he knew you."

"He did?" She turned to Bronfman as if he could be of real help, at last, could give her something she needed. "He remembered me?"

"He did," Bronfman said. "He remembered you with a sort of . . . fond respect."

Serena nodded. "That's nice," she said. "That's really nice." She sighed. "But someone was going to kill him sooner or later. You know? He had the mark. Some people are just born to be killed."

And she didn't move. Neither of them did until they heard a pound dog bark, a lone howler, snapping them back into the world. "Do you ever just want to get away from all this?" she said. "The world can be such a seedy place. Sometimes I just want to get in the car and go." She smiled. "Don't tell my sergeant I said that, though."

"Like where?"

"Where what?"

"Where do you want to go?"

She raised her face and stared up and away toward some idea or feeling that only she could see hovering there. "That's an easy one," she said. "The beach. I love the beach. The sound the ocean makes. The wind blowing through the sea oats. The smell of sunblock — I even love that." Then she sort of laughed, moving toward the exit. "We can dream, right?"

"Right," he said. "Because how else can a dream come true?" He had read that on a greeting card, and he believed it. His dream, for instance, had been to go to the beach with a companion. That had been his dream since he first spoke to Carla D'Angelo, Operator 61217. For so long it had seemed that his companion was going to be Sheila, but now that seemed more and more remote. Enter Serena, who loved the beach and who, even Bronfman could tell, liked him, at least a little bit.

This time he lifted the crime-scene tape for her, because it was the gentlemanly thing to do. Then he said, "Let me walk you to your car," and he felt, as he said it, that he could not have come up with a more absurd thing to say. Who walks a policewoman to her car?

But she let him. He even opened the door, though he wondered if he was breaking the law again by doing so. But she seemed pleased by the gesture.

"Thank you, Bronfman," she said. "No one has ever done that for me before."

"Really?"

"Not my police-car door."

"I bet men are opening your regular car door all the time."

She laughed. "Oh, yeah. All the time. Because I go on so many dates."

She waited. His hand was still on the top edge of the door, holding it open, and she placed her hand next to his, preparing to close it. His hand and her hand were touching, and neither of them made a move to change their positions.

"Can I ask you something?"

"Anything," she said.

"Do you think I was born to get killed?"

Not the question she expected, but she recovered quickly. She looked him over, thinking about it. "No," she said. "Absolutely not. You'll live to a ripe old age and die in your sleep, surrounded by people you love."

"Sounds good," he said.

"Doesn't it?"

Then she got into her car and started the engine and rolled away, and waved to him as she was leaving, her arm fully extended out of her window, swaying back and forth like a tree in a hard wind.

SEVEN

Bronfman did not call Sheila the moment he got home, as he had told her he would. It wasn't that he forgot to. It was that he didn't have room for her, or for anything else, in his head right now. There were too many things in there already, too many images, thoughts, ideas, blood-curdling action scenes: Serena's hand on his shoulder, Skip Sorsby lugging his box of stuff to his lousy Roebuck apartment, Mary Day's service that morning, his mother asleep on the bed where he was conceived — it was all floating around in there like chunks of space debris. His mind was a gloppy broth. He couldn't call her. But the idea that he was supposed to call her hovered around the outside of his head like a cartoon fly, buzzing in endless circles. He recognized this fly. It was the same one that buzzed around his head when he knew that he should call his mother, when he would imagine her at the kitchen table with the telephone in her hand, ready to pick up after the third ring — waiting, so as not to appear too needy. He would try to ignore the fly, try swatting it away, but eventually he would give in and call.

Just as he did tonight.

As predicted, the telephone rang three times before she picked up.

"Hello?" Bronfman said. "Mom?"

He called her, on average, every other night, and went to see her between two and three times a week. He had, of course, been raised by her, and had really never been more than a few hours away from her since the day he was born. Still, he didn't know this woman anymore, if he ever did. He didn't know which Muriel Bronfman he would get when he called, who she would show him, which one of the million new selves she had access to now that she'd lost track of who she really was.

Pause. Then a tentative, "Yes? Who is this?"

"This is Edsel, Mom," he said. "Your son."

Beat. "Of course it is," she said, clearly relieved, as if there were other children out there she hadn't wanted to hear from. "The phone rings constantly. Bettina refuses to answer it; I don't know why. Yes, I'm talking about you, Bettina!" she screamed to some distant corner of the house. She came back to the phone with a softer voice. "Thank you so much for calling, and for thinking of your old mother."

"I think of you all the time."

"No," she said. "You don't. And you shouldn't. I'd just be a distraction from your extraordinary adventures."

"My extraordinary adventures?"

Had he told her the name of the company? He couldn't remember. Maybe. But, even if he had, that would have been weeks and weeks ago. How could she have remembered it?

"Yes," she said. He felt her easing back into her pillow, settling in. "Tell me all about them. Tell me a tale."

"Well," he said. "Okay. I'll tell you something. But don't let it frighten you, because I'm fine. I wasn't here when it happened, and it's all over now. But the man who lived in the apartment next to me was murdered today."

"What?? Holy shit! That's fantastic!" she said. "Bettina! Someone was murdered in the apartment next door to my son!"

It was as if he'd won another prize, or been elected to high office.

"What happened? Tell me!"

"Well, I went over there, just now, with the police, because they thought I might be able to help them solve the crime."

"And? Did you, Detective Bronfman?"

"There was blood on the carpet."

"Oh, my God!" she said. "That's horrific. Blood. A lot of it?"

"No," he said. "Just a few drops."

"Even so," she said. "Blood is blood. Methinks I would have fainted dead away. Were they nice — the police? Sometimes they are and sometimes they're not. I'm interested in how they were with you. Did he thank you?"

"It was a policewoman," he said. "You met her, remember? Serena? Serena Stanton."

"Serena fucking Stanton!" She laughed. "Do I remember her? Do I ever. It's a cliché, I know, but good Lord, uniforms are sexy. There's something in our snake brain that just loves a uniform. The Orkin man was here the other day, and I had a thing just watching him walk around the front yard with his tool in his hand. Are you going to see her again?"

"Who?"

"The policewoman," she said. "Stay with the program! Pay attention!"

"I don't know." He shrugged. "Maybe. She'll probably come back."

"I love it that you're out there doing all these things. Solving crimes and breaking hearts."

"That's me," he said.

"I know," she said. "I've always known who you were. Bettina! The show is back on! Parker just got on the plane. Look who he's sitting next to!" She laughed. "I have to go, honey, but, really quick — Tell me how Sheila is."

"Sheila," he said.

"She was sweet on you, if I remember correctly. Cute as a button." She paused. "There is a Sheila, isn't there? I'm not making her up."

"No," he said. "She makes herself up."

His mother said something, but her words were muted. Her voice became small and distant. He could imagine the phone being dropped into the folds of the bed covers, totally forgotten. If he wanted, he could listen to them watch the television all night. But he didn't want to.

Bronfman shut his phone, and everything was quiet and still and he felt a little more settled until a moth crashed into the windowpane. Maybe the moth was the ghost of Thomas Edison. The spirits of the recently departed were known to come back in the form of animals that couldn't talk. On cue, a sliver of ghostly yellow light shot into the room. But there was no mystery about its true source. Bronfman had seen this light many times before, and he knew exactly what it was.

It was Thomas Edison's porch light. Somebody had turned it on.

EIGHT

It was one of those errant June nights, heavy and warm but with a layer of cool beneath it, a night that should have been a name all its own, something like *Echtenburger* or *Morgansturgen,* one of those ridiculously precise German words. Bronfman walked outside and unfastened his shirt a button to let the air filter in through his collar. He could feel the sweat dripping down his chest like raindrops sliding down a windowpane. He could feel his blood thrumming in his ears.

Yes, Edison's porch light was on, and the door was open, and there was someone inside. He couldn't tell who was inside, or how many of them there were. All he saw was an eerie shadow floating across a wall. Like a ghost, really. Like the ghost of Thomas Edison. He knew it wasn't a ghost — because there were no such things as ghosts, something he had to tell himself more often than a grown man should — but certainly it could have passed for one. The crime-scene tape had been ripped away. The shadow loomed large against the living-room wall. A big guy, he surmised, broad, muscular, pitiless. Bronfman froze, watching the man's dark reflection. What was he *doing*? Impossible to say. Looking for more drugs? Money taped to the bottom of the couch? Or simply removing clues he knew had been left behind, because this might very well be the killer returning to the scene. Because returning was what killers did.

These were his choices, then: a thief, a drug addict, or a murderer. Who else could it have been?

It was Coco. She was sitting on the couch, her miniature body engulfed by the cushions, her cowboy-booted feet resting atop the glass living-room table, the overwhelmed ashtray on one side and a half-crushed can of Miller High Life on the other, the can covered in ash and stuffed so full of butts that one of them couldn't even get all the way in. She glanced at Bronfman without expression. She was wearing a green T-shirt with a drawing of a roller coaster and dates and times for the 2005 State Fair — many years ago. Brown corduroys, the boots. And looking at Bronfman as if she had expected him, or — more likely — didn't care that he was there at all.

"Hi," he said. "Coco."

"Bronfman," she said. "Being neighborly, are you?"

She pushed a beer can over with her foot, and the gross liquid spread across the glass. Bronfman could smell it from where he was.

There was only one light on in the entire room, a table lamp to her left. He could see one side of her face, but the other was in shadow. It looked dramatic, even felt dramatic, to Bronfman.

"You're breaking the law," she said. "Being in here. You know that, right?"

"I guess so," he said. "But so are you."

"Yeah, but that's different. Breaking the law is one of my pastimes." For about half a second, she smiled. "Sit."

She pointed at the La-Z-Boy facing her. He sat. Coco almost laughed.

"That was his chair," she said. She looked numb, her eyes flat. "Nobody sat in that chair but him, and if they did he opened up a can of *shit* on them." She bit her lower lip, quivering as if from the cold. "He could be un-pre-dictable."

"Do you want me to get out of the chair?"

"Naw. He's dead," she said, winking. Her eyes were almost black. "I think you're safe."

Bronfman had never met anyone like

Coco. She reminded him of a field mouse, even though he had never seen a field mouse and wasn't entirely sure what one was, or how it might be different from a house mouse. He just thought of this scared little thing lost in a vastness. That was her. He felt the same now, and she saw it.

"You couldn't have saved him, Bronfman," she said.

"I know it," he said. But he didn't know. Had he been here instead of taking Sorsby to Roebuck, he might have been able to do something. He might have heard a scuffle taking place through the paper-thin walls, gotten on the phone with Serena, who would have come immediately, with backup.

She shook her head. "This is the last time you'll see me here," she said, but not, it appeared, to Bronfman. She was talking to the apartment itself — to the walls, the ceiling, the floor, and whatever invisible spirit lived within them now. "Last time you'll see me on this crappy old couch, waiting for whatever comes next, whatever it was Tommy thought up to do." She turned to Bronfman. "He had all these great ideas," she said. "I called him Ben Franklin sometimes, just to fuck with him. For some reason, that really pissed him off."

He watched her glow a little in the sad

memory of that world, gone now, where Benjamin Franklin pissed Thomas Edison off. Bronfman watched her the same way he would be watching TV, on a channel he had accidentally surfed to, curious, about to click — but then gradually becoming absorbed. Really, who was she? What weird subcultural group (hoarder, angry ex-wife, addicted to hairspray or Styrofoam, secretly famous) did she belong to? He was mystified by her very existence.

"Well, he was always nice to me," Bronfman said.

She laughed. "Except for the time he broke into your apartment and stole all your shit."

"No," he said. "He was even nice about that. He said, 'I'm there for you.' I really think he was. Somehow."

"You're adorable," she said, and she seemed to mean it. "But you're right." She pulled the blanket over her lap. "He was a good guy. If anybody besides him had broken into your apartment and tried to steal all your shit, for sure he would have been there for you. He . . . he would have had your back."

Her eyes flooded with tears. She tried to hold them back by blinking, but it was too much. They rolled down her cheeks, her chin, her neck. Her face glistened in the murky light.

"We weren't together," she said. "Together together. I was his friend. His best friend. The others didn't care about him." She kicked another can off the table. "But don't say we were *only* friends. Real friends are never *only*. Friends are who's around when the rest have all gone away, who are here even after you're dead. Who never even think about leaving. That's who I was. That's why I'm here. I guess that's why you're here, too."

He nodded. He guessed it was.

"I have to say good-bye and I had to be in the place without him, knowing he'll never be back and getting that through my fucking head, and then I can move on, I can move on to . . . whatever's next. Don't know what it is just yet. But I got to get away from here, that's for sure."

Coco stared at Bronfman with her lonely dark eyes, and wouldn't stop looking at him, even when he looked away. He felt her stare.

"Take me with you," she said.

"I'm sorry?"

"To the beach," she said. "Destin. You're going down there, right? Take me with you. My car is dead. Just take me down there and then . . . drop me off. Or not. Maybe

we can hang together for a while. I don't
know. But let's leave this shit behind. I
won't be Coco anymore. I'll go back to being Yoshiko. I'll pretend I'm really Japanese.
Forget I can speak English. Start from
scratch. Reinvent. What do you say? We
could have fun." She gave him an open-
faced, playful, moderately sultry expression.

"Maybe," he said. "Sure. I mean, why not?
That might work."

It might. He could take her; she would
fulfill the requirements of the offer. But it
wasn't just about procuring a companion
anymore; it was about procuring the right
companion, a much more difficult requirement to fulfill. He liked Coco, but she
wasn't really who he had in mind. He
wondered if Roy, his father, had felt something like that with Muriel. If he found
himself alone with her in 2D and realized
that he liked her but that, in the end, she
didn't fulfill his requirements.

Bronfman stuttered. He blushed. "It's
something to think about it."

She cracked up.

"You're a piece of work, you know that?"
she said. "You know why I like you so
much? I like you because you're just so . . .
who you are, if that makes any sense. You're
the perfect you. Sweet, thoughtful, very

495

careful, but not really happy, because you think that would be asking too much of your life, so you're happy *not* being happy. Are you even going to go, Bronfman? To Destin? I just wonder if you have it in you."

"I have it in me," he said.

"I hope so. But if you don't, that's okay, too. Not everyone needs to go to Florida."

"I don't need to go," he said. "I want to go."

"Then go! I'd like to go, too, but I get it — why would you take the drug whore? The drug whore always gets the short end of the stick. But I wasn't one. I promise. I swear. I never did it, not once."

"I never said you did."

"You didn't have to."

She covered her face with her hands and rubbed her eyes. She brushed a few strands of hair out of the corner her mouth. He had never seen a sadder woman in all his life.

"I get it, Bronfman. You're good at being you. Tommy was good at being who he was, too. When he had to borrow money to buy a pack of cigarettes, when he drank beer for breakfast, when he'd go out looking for a job and do everything he could not to find it — he was good at all that. He had a kid somewhere, a daughter, but he'd lost track of her a long time ago. He was a total loser, but somebody has to lose, right? Otherwise where would the winners come from? No shame in it. And he was kind. He could have been the best loser there ever was, the King of the Losers, but then he got all ambitious and brought drugs into the mix and that was never him, he wasn't tough like that, or evil. Big mistake. Now he's dead." She lifted her hand, thumb upright, index finger extended, closed one eye for aim, and took a shot at Bronfman. "Bang-bang. Dead. That's what happens when you try to be something you're not. So maybe you shouldn't go to Florida. It could end badly."

"I don't think you can generalize like that," he said. "I'm not selling drugs. I'm just trying to get in shape and find someone I can take to the beach with me. I don't think anyone's going to shoot me for that. I'm going to Destin. I'm not who you think I am."

"Then prove it," she said. Her eyes darkened. She adjusted herself on the sofa, moved closer to the far side, and patted the extra space with her hand. She didn't take her eyes off him. "Prove it," she said again. She laughed. She threw a wet cigarette butt at him, and it hit him in the chest. And she opened her arms, the way his mother did sometimes welcoming him home from school — big, open arms that invited a hug. "Come here, Bronfman," she said.

Come here, Roy.

He felt like another man then: the Un-Bronfman, the parallel-universe Bronfman, the hardscrabble-twin-he-never-knew-he-had-until-today Bronfman. He was himself and he was not. Otherwise, how could he explain what happened next?

He stood. The coffee table had created a barrier between them, a space he could safely be on the other side of, and as he stepped around it he felt the same sense of adventure he might experience were he floating around a bend in the Amazon, or crossing the border to another country, a foreign place with customs he didn't understand, a language strange and subtle and beautiful. He stood over her, shaking a little, and she took his hand and pulled him into her arms. She placed a hand behind his neck and pulled him down and held him against her. Her face was pressed into his chest, and she was crying. He could feel the warm wet tears seep through his shirt and onto his chest. He let his hands rest between her scapula, and she pulled him closer (she was stronger than she looked) until all of him was against all of her. She was crying, and he was comforting her. That's what was happening here, that's all. He closed his eyes. She wrapped a leg around his waist, an arm curled around his shoulder. Her breathing became deeper, more rhythmic. She held him — *clutched* him — like a baby monkey, and as she slowly lifted her head from his chest and her nose grazed his neck and chin she kissed him, and kissed him again. Her lips moved upward until they were right next to his, and in a smart and stealthy maneuver (he couldn't help thinking, dissecting every moment of this as it happened) her lips moved left (his left, her right) and then pressed against his.

She looked at him, and saw whatever it was that was in his eyes now. Fear? Yes, that's what it probably was. That's definitely what it was. "Don't worry," she said. And, pushing him away from her just slightly, she pulled off her T-shirt and dropped it on the floor. Her breasts were so small and lovely, her nipples just a shade darker brown. He stared at them, mesmerized. Coco pulled at his own shirt, untucking it at least partially, working with the buttons until she gave up. She fiddled with his belt, but it was so tight. She sighed, then closed her eyes and laced her fingers around the back of his neck and pulled his face into hers. So he opened his mouth. Her tongue slipped into it and swam around in it. Seconds passed — maybe two of them — before his own tongue did the same in hers. Her hands were on the back of his neck as she pulled his face in closer still, until their faces were pressed together so hard that in any other possible circumstance it would have been considered an accident, and he almost said "I'm sorry" out of habit, because one or both of them were going to come away from this bruised, lips raw, throbbing. *Roy,* she said. *Oh, Roy!* He felt his mind shutting down, going into deep storage, everything inside his head muddled, until he had no idea what was really happening — when, through the strength of a will he didn't know he had or even wanted to have, he snapped out of it, and stopped. He pulled back, and the spell was broken. She waited for him to come back, her lips slightly parted, but he only moved farther away, sitting up straight, smiling a watered-down smile. All in all, about sixty seconds had passed.

"I can feel you against my leg," she said. "You want this."

"Yes but —" He strained to find some more articulate response, but he wasn't able to provide one. "But no. Yes, but no. I do want to fuck up — my mother basically begged me to — but not like this. Not here,

500

in Thomas Edison's apartment."

Coco ran her fingers through his hair, and even brushed the bangs to one side, perfect with the part. She left the palm of her hand on his wet, red cheek.

"Oh, Bronfman," she said, wistfully. "You have no idea what you're missing."

"You're exactly right," he said. "I have no idea."

Through the paper-thin wall separating this apartment from his, he heard his landline ringing. It was certainly Sheila. No one called him anymore except her, now that his mother couldn't remember his number. She was worried about him; Bronfman could almost hear the worry in the essence of the ring itself.

A siren wailed in the distance. His phone kept ringing. And then the phone stopped, and the siren was no longer quite as distant, closer to King's Manor now, and closer still. There could be no doubt now that the police were on their way here. He guessed a neighbor had seen Bronfman and Coco inside, or their shadows, seen the torn crime-scene tape and called it in, which was something Bronfman himself might have done, once upon a time. Coco didn't seem to care, really; she had been on the other end of sirens before, no doubt.

"Oh!" she said. Something had made her almost happy. "I forgot!"

With the blanket still covering her hips and legs, she leaned back and over the side of the couch and rummaged through some things, and in a flourish produced what looked like — what actually was — his cowboy hat, star and all. Poor old beaten thing. It had seen some hard times the past couple of months, not unlike Bronfman himself. It appeared to have been run over and flattened by a car and punched back out with a giant fist, so that it was no longer a hat, really, but something just hat-*like,* a former hat, three star points bent, two broken off entirely. With one hand she held the blanket around her waist, kneeling above him bare-breasted, and with the other she set the hat on her head, and cocked it just a bit to one side.

"You know that's my hat, right?" he said.

"Yeah. But Tommy gave it to me — you know, after he stole it."

"Of course he did," Bronfman said.

She seemed to think about taking it off and handing it back to him, but that moment quickly passed. She struck a pose.

"What do you think?"

"About what?"

"About me in your hat. Can I keep it?"

she said. "Please?"

"Keep? My *hat*?"

"Yeah. I mean, look — it fits me. It's way too small for you now."

And it did fit her, really well. It looked like a hat for nobody's head but hers. But he missed his hat. He missed it the way he missed his mother, his old life, the old world where all he had to worry about was remaining just unobjectionable enough to be invisible. Now that he'd been seen, though — Sheila had seen him — there was no going back.

"That hat saved my life once," he said, "a long time ago."

"Really?" She took it off her head and held it in her hands, turning it back and forth, round and round, looking at it inside and out, studying it, trying to decipher its magic. Then she looked at Bronfman. "Do you think it could save mine?" she asked him. "Because that would be *awesome.*"

The police cars were there now. Two of them, blue and red lights flashing and circling, bouncing off the walls of Thomas Edison's apartment as if it were a discotheque. The sirens brought the pound dogs to life, slowly, as if they'd been sleeping, and they started baying, one by one.

Serena was already getting out of her car

503

when Bronfman walked out of Thomas Edison's apartment. When she saw him, she froze, and seemed either relieved or disappointed; from where he was it was hard to tell. She looked back to the other car, where there was a stern-looking cop with his eyes locked on Bronfman, and waved at him — a signal that he could stay put, she had this under control. He nodded. But he still kept looking at Bronfman as if nothing would give him more pleasure than to lock him up, and, perhaps, throw away the key.

Serena ambled toward him, hands on her hips. "Bronfman, Bronfman, Bronfman," she said. "What have you gotten yourself into now?" She directed his attention to the window where Coco was framed, in the cowboy hat, her bare shoulders and the blanket just covering her breasts.

"That's not what it looks like," he said.

"That's *exactly* what it looks like," she said. But she wasn't upset at all. She actually seemed pleased. "I didn't take you for that kind of guy, but it's kind of sexy. I'm impressed." She winked at him, smiled. "But, on the other hand, you've broken a couple of serious laws here. Criminal trespass is just one of them. You know that, I hope."

He nodded, and with her eyes she gestured

back to the car behind her. "I'd let it go because I like you, but there are other eyes on us." She removed the handcuffs from her utility belt. "Hands, please."

"You like me?" he said as he let her have them. She slipped the cuffs on his wrists, and was locking them in place with a click when Sheila emerged from the shadows, materializing in the crazy manic rainbow of light. She must have pulled in right behind the police cars. He had no idea how much of this she had seen, but, based on her expression, she'd seen enough. She stopped a few feet from the stoop and took it all in: the police cars, Serena, Bronfman in cuffs, his shirttail pulled from his pants, his belt loose and drooping, and Coco, nearly naked, watching it all from the window, a devilish smile on her face. Serena turned and saw Sheila, forlorn and heartbroken, and turned back to Bronfman with an expression composed of a confused mélange of disappointment, amusement, and shock.

"*Seriously?*" she said. "Jesus, Bronfman. You are a dirty dog."

Sheila appeared to have lost some important part of herself, and even Bronfman knew what it was. This is what a broken heart looks like, he thought, desperately sad, hopeless, and alone. And angry, hateful, and just a little bitter.

Her lips were moving soundlessly but he could easily read them. "Never trust an ungulate," she said. She looked Bronfman dead in the eyes, and with them so clearly said the rest of it, good-bye, adios, see you later, I hardly knew you. He knew how it looked, the kind of man he had become in her eyes: he had become Crouton, the photographer. But he wasn't him. That was the last thing he was. She was walking away now — you're too late, Bronfman, too late — but just before she melted into the darkness he called out to her.

"Sheila!" he said. He was looking at her back, the way her hair rested on her collar in the beautiful whirling lights of the law. "I like to watch previews better than the movie. I've never bought a pair of underwear in my life, because that's something my mother liked to do. Midgets scare me. I've never been on a motorcycle and never want to be. I'm not an orphan, but I act like one and I want to stop acting like that. I also have a prehensile tail." He paused. Her head clocked a few degrees to the left. "I threw that in there just to see if you were listening." And she was listening, he could tell. But she still didn't turn, she just stood there, half a step away from disappearing into the night and out of his life, almost certainly forever. "Sheila," he said again.

He turned to Serena. She had her hands on his, holding them beneath the cuffs. He looked over his shoulder at Coco, who was still there with the blanket around her, watching all of this as if it were a movie. She waved at him. The dogs at the pound were going full chorus now, singing their symphonic hearts out. He had never known them to be so eager to be heard. Bronfman could pick out the cry of certain dogs. He had even named them. That's Jawbone, he could say, or Mugwump, or little Jimmy Dean, or Pal. Every night it was like this. Every night was sad, every night was hopeful. Because anyone who really listened could tell what they were doing. They were calling out to someone on the other side of the tree line, someone they used to know or hoped to meet, howling into the dark the way scientists send radio waves into space, looking for unknown companions.

"Sheila," he said, one last time. But softly, so he could be heard.

■ ■ ■ ■

DAY NINETY-FIVE

■ ■ ■ ■

Three weeks after the offer had officially expired, near the end of July, Bronfman called the 800 number on the back of the *Extraordinary Adventures* brochure and asked to speak to someone in a managerial position. He was put on hold for almost four minutes before a woman who identified herself as Beverly Taylor picked up. He was all set to explain to her what had happened, how his goal had been to take advantage of the offer within the proscribed amount of time — but she stopped him before he had completed his first sentence.

"What do you mean?" she said. " 'Proscribed amount of time'?"

"Before the deadline," he said. "You see, I knew the offer expired on June twenty-sixth, but there were some . . . complications, and —"

"There is no deadline," she said, and then, with a weary cheeriness, "There is always time for a time-share. Many units are still available. Come down anytime you like."

"Really?" he said.

"Some operators imply that there might be a deadline — *act now,* you know. That sort of thing. It gives the offer a sense of urgency. Makes it more tempting. But no. Please. Anytime. Let Destin be your destination."

She was a pleasant woman, and didn't seem to be in much of a rush, so he felt compelled to share with her the other prerequisite Carla D'Angelo, Operator 61217, had shared with him.

"She said that?" Beverly Taylor said. She laughed. She chuckled, in fact. "What in the world."

"What?"

"Bringing a companion is not a requirement and never has been. There's not a single requirement, actually, other than attending the presentation. I wonder where that came from."

"So no strings," he said.

"None," she said. "All you have to do is show up, Mr. Branfman —"

"Bronfman," he said.

"I'm sorry. Bronfman. Give me a sec. I want to look something up."

He heard a drawer open, papers being

messed with. She came back on the line. "Are you sure her name was D'Angelo? Because I don't see where a D'Angelo ever worked for us here. She's not in my records, at any rate."

"Very strange," he said.

"Yes," she said. "Very strange indeed."

In the light of this strangeness he waited for her to rescind the offer, but she didn't. The existence or nonexistence of Carla D'Angelo didn't seem to matter to her at all.

"Does this mean I can come?" he said.

"Of course," she said. "Please. Come whenever you like."

"Then I would like to come down now," he said. "Right now, if that's possible."

And she said fine, she would reserve a room in the name of Edsel Branfman — Bronfman — and it was done, and it was as simple as that.

No strings attached at all.

Destin was a five-hour drive from Birmingham, about an hour beyond Bronfman's comfort zone for a trip. Four hours kept him in a moon's orbit of home; five sent him into what felt like deep space. So that last hour was tough. But this was part of a new way of being in the world. He could travel into deep space now. He could put himself "out there." It helped that he did have a companion, of course, to share the driving with. In fact, she drove them all the way there.

They left midmorning on Friday and arrived on a postcard-worthy afternoon, the blood-orange sun suspended above the blue-green sea. Even from the Sandscapes parking lot, it was breathtaking. The pamphlets had misrepresented nothing. It was spectacular. It was even better than the pictures, actually, because no picture could capture the heat of the sun and the sound of the sea and how it felt when the wind blew through your hair. The smell of body lotion.

They did not go to the beach, however, not yet. First, they wanted to see the condo, which was free, he repeated over and over to himself, completely free, with a free continental breakfast to boot, for the next two days.

The condo did not disappoint. It was exceptional. There was a master bedroom and a smaller bedroom for guests — if your mother wanted to come down, say. Table lamps were festooned with scallop shells. There was an island in the kitchen, a long dark marble slab. Bronfman had never even dreamed that he would be a man in a kitchen with an island in it, but for the next two days he would be that man. They did have a minor objection to the thick green shag carpet in the living room (it looked like a neglected lawn to both of them), but after lying down on it for a bit they realized that the floor could actually pass for a bed if necessary, that's how soft it was. He proved it by lying down on it and accidentally falling asleep, and when he woke up, fifteen minutes later, it took him a moment to remember exactly where he was. *I'm in Destin,* he thought. On the carpet beside him was a sheet of stationary embossed with the word *Sandscape.* He picked it up. She had written a note on it:

Come find me.
(Hint: I'm where the ocean meets the shore.)

And beside the note was the official Sandscapes stationary pen. So elegant. They were everywhere. He had already slipped one into his toiletry bag.

He had two bathing suits, brand new, one white with a bunch of blue anchors on it and the other one red with a dozen white palm trees (he had counted). He changed into the red one and slipped on a Hawaiian shirt she had found for him yesterday at a thrift store. It seemed "fun," she said, just like something you'd wear to the place where the ocean meets the shore. Plus, he had sunglasses and a floppy hat. He stopped in front of the hallway mirror on his way out, and he looked kind of perfect, if he did say so himself — a perfect example of who he was, at any rate. The perfect Bronfman.

He took the elevator to the first floor and followed a slatted wooden path through the grassy dunes, and then, without any warning or fanfare whatsoever, there it was: the beach. The sun, the sand. The entire ocean. Stunning. He could see all the way to the horizon, to what appeared to be the very end of the world. For the first time, he understood why sailors used to think there were monsters out there, or why they thought that the world was flat and that eventually you'd just sail right off it, because that's how it looked to him, too. Bronfman was a flat-earther at heart. It was all terra incognita to him.

And people. There were people everywhere — sunning on their backs, splashing in the surf, floating on rafts farther out than seemed quite wise, reading beneath giant umbrellas. Couples, kids, families. All shapes and sizes, colors and kinds. But he didn't see Sheila.

"Edsel!"

He looked left and then right and then straight ahead, and there she was, waving, sitting on a huge blanket a safe distance from the surf. The blanket's corners were flapping in the breeze. He waved back and flip-flopped his way across the hot white sand and sat down beside her. She was wearing a blue one-piece bathing suit, and her shoulders were completely bare, and already turning pink.

This is really happening, he thought. *I'm here on the beach with Sheila McNabb.* Could it have been otherwise? He supposed so. As impossible as it may have seemed months ago, there was a remote chance that he could have been here with any one of three women, because any one of the three would have satisfied the requirements of the time-share as he understood them at the time. He had an authentic fondness for both Coco and Serena, but Sheila was different. She was the only one he would have wanted to remember having gone with. That is, even before coming here with her he was envisaging what it would feel like to have already done so in a past that hadn't happened yet, and it was a feeling that he found himself enjoying many times a day in the days before they left. This was what grown-ups did, wasn't it, how they choreographed their lives, by imagining scenarios? Or was it just what grown-up Bronfmans did? He didn't know, and the truth is he didn't really care. He was happy.

"See that guy?" she said. His eyes followed her finger, going west. "The one with the buzz cut and beady eyes? A hedgehog. His wife, with the long legs and bounce to her step — a wildebeest, maybe. Kids look like rabbits." She shook her head. "Edsel, there's a Noah's Ark of people out here."

But Bronfman only had eyes for her. She was more beautiful than anything he had ever imagined.

They sat there, soaking up the sun and the gentle sound of the surf.

"I'm very happy you're here," Bronfman said.

"And I'm happy you're here, too, and not in jail."

"Thank you," he said, even though he had thanked her several times already. "You didn't have to bail me out," he said, using an expression that he never thought he would have a chance to use regarding himself. "That was kind of you, after everything."

He had been locked up for about forty-five minutes, and it would have been less had Serena and Sheila not gotten into a discussion about Cedar Court, and how Birmingham youths amused themselves vandalizing the sign for it. They had a pretty good laugh over that, Sheila said. Sheila liked Serena. She could even imagine Serena as a friend, she told Bronfman later. He could, too — their first friend as a couple. And this — the story of the night he was arrested, the night she bailed him out — was their first truly thrilling story as a couple. He never tired of hearing it. They could dine out on this story for years.

"A little money changed hands," Sheila said. "Sure. But mainly I just had to promise to keep an eye on you, so you'd stay out of trouble. I would have been crazy to leave you down there, though, with those two women who clearly had a thing for you."

"You were jealous?" He sat up a little straighter. This was the first time anyone had been jealous of him, in any way, ever.

"I wouldn't say *that*," she said. "All I mean is, I had to stake my claim and get you out of there. That Coco was a wild card. Now I feel like I kind of own you. I bought you at the city jail."

The prospect of being owned by Sheila was not unpleasant to Bronfman, so he didn't object, and moved closer to her on the sandy towel. He was getting hot, quickly, so he took off his Hawaiian shirt and boldly bared himself to the world. He was whiter than the underbelly of a fish, but, on the other hand, he was somewhat defined. He was on the road to a definition that he wasn't even sure he needed anymore.

"Look at you," she said. "Where'd you get all those fancy *muscles*?"

He shrugged. "At the gym they have specific machines for specific parts of the body. Biceps, pectorals, et cetera." She nodded, as if he was telling her something she didn't know. He looked down at himself. "I like how I can actually see where my chest ends and my stomach begins."

"That is very cool," she said.

They sat there watching the waves until the silence between them became a thing in and of itself.

"So, Edsel," she said. "Are we — ?"

"What?"

"You know. Are we going to . . ."

He knew. "Do it?" he said.

She glanced at him, smiled, nodded, and looked away. "Because we don't have to if you don't want to."

"I know. But I want to — really."

"Really? No pressure, though, okay? No expectations."

"Right."

Sheila took a deep breath, girding herself. "I think we should do it now, then," she said. "So we don't have it hanging over us. And if we like it we can do it again tomorrow."

"We have time?" he said. "Before the presentation?"

"Sure," she said. "We'll keep it short the first time."

He stood. She raised her arm for him and he took her hand, pulled her up. She stood beside him, and they both gazed at the watery world. The ocean seemed to take the sunlight and explode it; even the foam possessed its own little shine. Then the sun went behind a bank of huge, puffy clouds, clouds that Bronfman knew had their own specific name — currolous, curranbulus, circumculombulus, something like that. He would look it up at some point. He would learn the names of clouds.

They took a few steps toward the edge of the world. A wave rushed in and lapped at his feet, bringing a grainy sock of sand with it.

"Look at all that water," Sheila said. She had stopped moving forward. Even seemed to back up a bit. "Is this really a good idea? I mean, there are *sharks* out there, Edsel."

"True," he said. "Everything is out there, I think."

"But they're not here," she said. "I mean, right here." She indicated the patch of ocean directly in front of them.

"I'm not a shark whiz," he said. "But I don't think so. Other people are farther out than we are anyway. If there is a shark, it would get them, not us."

"That's reassuring," she said. "Thank you."

His eyes went from Sheila to the horizon and back to Sheila again. The wind blew her hair into and out of her face. For some unaccountable reason, he loved that. "But I'm scared, too," he said, and he ducked as a swooping seagull came a little too close for comfort.

Neither of them took a single step forward.

She took his hand and brought it to her lips and kissed it twice, and then a third time.

"Let's think of it this way, Edsel. It's scary doing anything the first time you do it, right? Right," she said, not waiting for what was almost certainly going to be an overly thought-through answer. "But this weekend . . . it's going to be full of first times. What I mean is, we better get used to being scared."

So the sun was shining and the wind was wafting and the waves rose and curled and fell and made a hushing sound as they swept across the shore. It was into all of this that Bronfman and Sheila started walking, from the sand into the surf, step by step until the ocean splashed their ankles, and then was all the way up to their knees, thighs, waist. Stomach. Chest. Shoulders. Spraying into their eyes. They were all in now, lifted by the waves, toes barely touching the sandy bottom, up and down and up again, drifting in the current. Bronfman took all of it in.

"We're floating in the ocean, Sheila," he said. "I like it. A lot."

"I know! Me too," she said. "Look at us. We're like . . . dolphins. Or some other friendly sea creature."

He paddled toward Sheila, the waves swelling around his chin, and met her wet lips with his. "Or just like two people out for a swim," he said.

"Or like that," she said. "Just like that."

ACKNOWLEDGMENTS

This novel wouldn't exist were it not for the following people. I know there are even more I'm forgetting, and others whose contributions were made as part of their jobs and who I may have never even met. Thank you all: Katherine Sandoz, Randall Kenan, Christine Pride, Lillian Bayley Hoover, Abby Brown, Nic Brown, Alan Shapiro, Sally Kim, Joe Regal, Markus Hoffman, Jim Kellison, Dennis and Nancy Quaintance, Lee Smith, and Hal Crowther. The people at St. Martin's Press who ushered this book into the world, including but not limited to Laura Clark, Katie Bassel, Courtney Reed, Maggie Callan, Jeffrey Capshew, Ken Holland, and Elisabeth Dyssegaard. Extraordinary thanks go to Renée Zuckerbrot, my agent, who has been the best possible advocate, and to my editor, the great Brenda Copeland, who loved Bronfman unconditionally. He loved her back the same. Thank you all. And my Laura, of course, especially: past, present, and future.

Portions of this book were written at the MacDowell Colony, the Weymouth Center, and at the O. Henry Hotel, in Greensboro, N.C.

ABOUT THE AUTHOR

Daniel Wallace is the J. Ross MacDonald Distinguished Professor of English at the University of North Carolina at Chapel Hill, where he directs the Creative Writing Program. He is the author of the novels *Big Fish*, *Ray in Reverse*, *The Watermelon King*, *Mr. Sebastian and the Negro Magician*, and *The Kings and Queens of Roam*.